THE
QUIET
GIRLS

Also by Dorothy Koomson

The Cupid Effect
The Chocolate Run
My Best Friend's Girl
Marshmallows for Breakfast
Goodnight, Beautiful
The Ice Cream Girls
The Woman He Loved Before
The Rose Petal Beach
That Day You Left
(*previously published as* The Flavours of Love)
That Girl From Nowhere
When I Was Invisible
The Friend
The Beach Wedding
The Brighton Mermaid
Tell Me Your Secret
All My Lies Are True
I Know What You've Done
My Other Husband
Every Smile You Fake
Give Him To Me

DOROTHY KOOMSON

THE QUIET GIRLS

Copyright © 2026 Dorothy Koomson

The right of Dorothy Koomson to be identified as the Author of the Work has been asserted by her in accordance with the Copyright, Designs and Patents Act 1988.

First published in 2026 by Headline Review
An imprint of Headline Publishing Group Limited

1

Apart from any use permitted under UK copyright law, this publication may only be reproduced, stored, or transmitted, in any form, or by any means, with prior permission in writing of the publishers or, in the case of reprographic production, in accordance with the terms of licences issued by the Copyright Licensing Agency.

All characters in this publication are fictitious and any resemblance to real persons, living or dead, is purely coincidental.

Cataloguing in Publication Data is available from the British Library

Hardback ISBN 978 1 0354 2710 9
Trade Paperback ISBN 978 1 0354 2707 9

Typeset in Times LT Std 10.25/15pt by Six Red Marbles UK, Thetford, Norfolk

Printed and bound in Great Britain by Clays Ltd, Elcograf S.p.A.

Headline's policy is to use papers that are natural, renewable and recyclable products and made from wood grown in well-managed forests and other controlled sources. The logging and manufacturing processes are expected to conform to the environmental regulations of the country of origin.

Headline Publishing Group Limited
An Hachette UK Company
Carmelite House
50 Victoria Embankment
London EC4Y 0DZ

The authorised representative in the EEA is Hachette Ireland,
8 Castlecourt Centre, Dublin 15, D15 XTP3, Ireland (email: info@hbgi.ie)

www.headline.co.uk
www.hachette.co.uk

'No one is better than you. Never forget that.'
Noelle Kingston

This story contains a storyline some may find triggering.

Prologue

Axton Manor, 1991

She stood with her hands folded like an X across her chest, facing away from the open first-storey window of the clock tower. The wind whistled as it blew through, rushing around her like a threat, a warning of what was to come.

She had to do this.

Her mother had done it. Her aunt had done it. Her grandmother had done it.

She had to do it.

Her stomach lurched when she looked again at the group in front of her. *Run*, her mind told her. *Don't do this – just run!*

The eight figures were shrouded in black robes, the hoods pulled up to hide their hair. They all wore shiny, silver-coloured fox masks to obscure their faces. They were giant human–animal hybrids: face of a fox, body of a girl, mind of a killer.

If she went through with this, it could kill her. She was sure it had killed others. It had certainly left others close to death. This was dangerous and deadly. *RUN!* her mind screamed again. *RUN!*

She had no choice: if she wanted the bullying to stop, if she wanted to make her family proud, if she wanted to take her rightful place, she had to do this. She had to prove that she was worthy. That she had everything it took to be one of them. She had to do this.

She closed her eyes.

'For the pure, to the pure,' she said, loud, clear, strong. 'For the pure, to the pure.'

It happened quickly, suddenly. Several hands on her, pushing. It was too quick for her to change her mind. Too sudden to decide she couldn't go through with it.

Too rapid, almost, for her to register that she was falling.

She had to do this. She had to do whatever it took to become one of the Quiet Girls.

Part 1

Kez

March 2026, Brighton

'I believe you,' she says, the gun in her hand pointed directly at me. 'I believe you want to help me.'

I have my hands up, and I am trying to hold my breath, trying to stop this happening. And then I see the flash, I hear the bang, I feel the bullet rip into— I start, rousing myself out of my wide-eyed trance.

I keep slipping into this waking trance where I relive the moment I was shot last year because I am sitting in the large hall of our children's school, attending a parents' conference. Throughout the year there are smaller parent forum meetings for each year's class reps (representatives), and then they hold this larger once-a-year meeting for everyone in the second term. That's when everyone has settled into that year and their gripes are real instead of the product of not knowing how things work in the school or that year group.

It's Jeb who usually gets involved in these things. I tried once – years ago – to do the involved-in-the-school-community mum thing when the school bursar pretty much goaded me into signing up for the parent–teacher association by telling me I wasn't the type of person they wanted on the committee. Talk about red rag to a bull. I called her out in front of everyone and signed myself up . . . only to resign the position after the first meeting. It really was not for me. But Jeb likes to come to these meetings. He finds it interesting and he always gives me such a comprehensive rundown of what happens – sometimes with the voices – that I always feel in the loop. Tonight, though, he absolutely insisted that I come to this meeting because . . . burble, burble, burble . . . I forget why. All I remember is he said it was essential that I attend.

My husband leans in to loudly whisper: 'Are you paying attention?'

'Yes,' I hiss back, outraged by the suggestion that I might have slipped off into a waking trance or something. 'Of course I am.'

'You don't look like you're paying attention,' Jeb replies.

'Well, I am.'

'Are you though?'

'Yes.'

'*Are you though?*'

'Yes.'

'Are—'

'*Shhh*,' comes from behind us, the person clearly irritated that we aren't paying attention but we *are* making it difficult for them to listen. Jeb and I turn at the same time to stare at the shhh-er. Those sitting on either side of her immediately shrink away, not wanting to be caught in the approaching crossfire, and she offers us a weak but brave smile.

'Sorry,' I whisper to her, and we both turn back.

I lean in towards Jeb, ready to restart our argument even though we've just been reprimanded, when he cuts in with, 'This is her.'

'This is who?' I reply.

'The woman I was telling you about.'

I glance at the stage as a tall, slender, honey-blonde woman in dark-blue stonewashed jeans and a chunky roll-neck jumper under a royal-blue blazer strides into the middle of the stage. As she approaches, the headteacher, Mr Greenburg, who is currently behind the microphone stand, introduces her as Penny Pressman (Mrs) then moves aside so she can take his place. Once installed behind the microphone, she uses her left hand to tuck a lock of her hair behind her ear, the move making her seem quite young and extremely vulnerable.

Whoa, I think. *What's going on that has her looking so meek and defenceless? What's been happening at this school that I haven't noticed because I've been so focused on my ridiculous job?*

'The woman who gave me the leaflet,' Jeb murmurs.

'What leaflet?'

'The one— Do you ever listen to a word I say?'

'Yes!' I hiss loudly, remember where I am, turn to the woman behind me, mouth 'sorry' then turn back to my husband. 'I do listen to a word you say. I listen to *every* word you say . . . I just don't remember all of them. Or some of them. Well, most of them. But I do listen.'

Shooting me a sour look, Jeb says, 'This is the woman who came up to me a couple of weeks ago and handed me the leaflet about the book banning.'

'I'm sorry, what?' I have to stop myself screeching. I turn to my mate behind me, raise a placatory hand, mouth 'sorry' again, return my attention to my husband.

'I knew you weren't listening,' Jeb accuses. 'All that "I can do two things at once" stuff you're always spouting and look, you were not l—'

'Listen, Quarshie,' I cut in. 'You need to get me up to speed right now! What book banning?'

'Two weeks ago, she came up to me in the playground, bold as brass, hands me a leaflet and tells me that she knows I'm one of the good ones so she's sure I'll support her "little group" in trying to get certain books removed from school libraries.'

Every single hackle on my body, even the ones that have been slacking off of late, is suddenly at attention and ready to fight.

'One of the good ones?' I reply.

'Yes. One of the good ones. So I ask her, "What does one of the good ones mean?" because I needed her to be specific in front of everyone about what she was saying. And she goes, "I know you're not a radical like some others. I know you'll agree that some of those books in the libraries are inappropriate and damaging, especially to sensitive children. They can make children feel bad about themselves by misrepresenting history, while accusing their ancestors of unspeakable acts. And the lifestyles some of those books depict are shocking. I know you'll agree with our little group – Mummies Making Moves Matter – that some of those books need to be removed. I'll be bringing it up at the next parents' conference."

'I stared at her and she sort of shrank away, acting like she was scared of me or something. So I said, "I don't agree with book banning and disagreeing with book banning is not radical." And she said, "I'm not talking about book banning – I'm talking about protecting children from damage." And then her little mate who's there in the front row said, "It's not on for you to say that when we're just thinking of the children." And then everyone looks at me like I'm some monster because I have not been "thinking of the children".'

I am pretty certain that I am staring at my husband as though he has just told me to do something unpleasant to myself. I am also pretty certain that the fluttering in my chest and the rising adrenalin is because I am in one of *those* moments. One of those moments when my friend Remi, if she was here, would say, 'You could just leave it, you know. Leaving it is an option.' She would say this despite knowing that leaving it is never an option for me.

'That's why I said you had to be here,' Jeb is explaining. 'We need to see who is on her side. We need to see who we need to be careful of and—'

I am on my feet before he can finish his sentence. 'Excuse me,' I say loudly once I am standing. Penny, the honey-blonde on stage, who is speaking passionately about how certain books can ruin children's lives by merely existing in the same building as them, stops talking. She blinks back the tears in her eyes, and stills her trembling hands. (I'm surprised she hasn't brought pearls to clutch.)

'There will be time for questions at the end, Mrs Quarshie,' says Mr Greenburg.

'This isn't a question, it's more of a comment.'

My husband inhales deeply as he folds one arm across his body, rests the opposite elbow on that arm and then covers his eyes with his hand. He's regretting insisting I be here now. He is regretting that so hard because he knows what is coming.

'This isn't the time for comments, either,' Penny says. Annoyance flitters across her face, because, alpha female that she believes herself to be, she does not like to be interrupted. Quickly, though, she pushes her mask back in place, returns to looking delicate and in desperate need of protection.

'All right, well, it's not a comment, then. Maybe think of it more as a promise? Threat? No, promise?'

Jeb quietly clears his throat, telling me if I have to do this, then I need to get on with it. '*Promise*. Let me call it a promise so we can keep this nice and civil.'

'I don't understand,' Penny says.

'Sorry,' I reply with a broad smile. 'I haven't actually told you my promise. My promise is this: if even one book is removed from the school library or prevented from being read on school grounds because of you and your group, I will sue you. I will sue you, I will sue your group and I will sue the school.'

Everyone's eyes jerk wide open, their brains that had been sliding into waking trances of their own are suddenly on high alert and their slumped bodies sit up to pay attention.

'I will sue all of you for blocking access to education for my children,' I continue. 'I will also sue you for creating a hostile learning environment for my children. On top of that, I will sue you for demonising and slandering known protected groups because by attempting to have books banned by those in the groups you are suggesting there is something wrong with them because they are talking about their experiences.'

A tense, expectant silence descends upon the hall and people switch their line of sight between me and the pair on the stage. Mr Greenburg seemed to petrify the moment I mentioned suing the school.

'I'm just . . . I'm just thinking of the children,' Penny says, her wavery voice about to bury itself in tears.

'So am I,' I say gently, regretfully. 'Which is why I have to do this. You do understand that, don't you?'

'But some of those books . . .' Penny allows her words to fade away to emphasise that those books are so awful and threatening that to even talk about them is dangerous.

'Let me be honest with you,' I plough on. 'In court, I might not win. Suing all the aforementioned people will definitely take a long time and cost a lot of money. But, in that time, no books will be allowed to be banned – sorry, what was it you called it? – "removed" from the library until the matter is resolved.'

Penny is outraged. Absolutely livid that I am not arguing with her on her battleground, I am not putting myself in a position where she can manipulate and guide the conversation into either agreeing with her or making myself seem radical and dangerous by not 'thinking of the children'. I am supposed to enter her arena and 'debate' on her terms. But, instead, I am, much to her chagrin, changing the rules of the conflict by not engaging in her narrative, and instead bringing my own. I am about to make her fight on terms for which she hasn't prepared.

'As I said, it'll be costly, but, for me, it will be worth the time and the cash to get to the discovery stage. In case you don't know, that's when you have to hand over all your communications related to this matter. You know, your WhatsApps, texts, emails, voicemails, voice notes, letters, group chats. *Every* single piece of communication will have to be handed over for *me* to look over. And, if I'm suing the school, you'll have to hand over all communications with the school and its members, too. The school will have to hand over all its meeting minutes and anything that could be even vaguely taken as being related to the case.'

I stop talking then. I allow what I've just said to sink in. Not only for Penny and Mr Greenburg, who has paled so much with every second I fear he is going to fall over, but for those words to sink in for everyone in the room. I want the assembled parents to know that this is how you fight these people. This is how you stand up for what is right. You don't have to allow those people to set the agenda, to define the rules of engagement. You can change the rules at any time. You can fight on your own terms. You can fight dirty. You can fight to win.

'You are more than welcome to stop your children reading books you deem "wrong" and "damaging", *Penny*. You can do whatever you like with your children in your house, but you're going to have the fight of your life on your hands if you *ever* presume to impose *your* bans on *my* children.'

With every passing moment, every one of my words, Penny's vulnerability has been peeling away; her fragility is now cracking, any hint of her being a woman in desperate need of coddling and protection is gone. Her hatred is naked and open; her anger is total and all-consuming. She stands on the stage, where our children have performed plays and nativities and music recitals, glaring at me in murderous rage.

I stare right back.

I have stared down psychopaths who want me dead, I have stared down people who have guns pointed at me – Penny from the playground is not going to get me to look away first.

The atmosphere in the room immediately ramps up several notches, everyone on the edge of their seats, waiting for Penny's next move.

Penny's stance suggests she is going to leap off the stage and come running down to where I am and grab a handful of my hair. The look on her face indicates she is trying to erase me from existence through sheer force of will. The tensing in her hands hints that if she was any closer to me she would be squeezing my neck until I stopped moving.

Penny's glare intensifies, her fingers curl into fists and her jaw undulates with the grinding of her teeth. She's going to do it. She's going come charging down and take a swing at me. I stare back, waiting. Ready. Oh so ready.

One beat.

Two beats.

She drops her gaze.

She drops her gaze and everyone in the hall, me included, exhales at the same time.

After Penny drops her gaze, the audience who, moments ago, she had held rapt as she spun her narrative of sensitive young children needing to be protected from big bad books, now watch her with a mix of fascination and pity.

Suddenly Mr Greenburg, still holding his microphone, comes to life and steps in front of the microphone that Penny has now backed away from. 'Erm, well, yes,' he says, and the sound is duplicated then feeds back LOUDLY through the speakers, making everyone jump and cringe.

He immediately steps away again, raises the microphone. 'Erm, well, yes,' he repeats. 'Thank you, erm, yes. I think that concludes the any-other-business part of the evening.' He looks around at the other teachers, all of whom clearly want to be anywhere else but here. 'And, in fact, that concludes the evening. Thank you all for your attendance. Goodnight.'

Adrenalin still spiking in my veins, I plop myself on the seat next to Jeb. He still has his hands over his eyes. And I suspect he's pretending he doesn't know me.

'So,' I ask him, 'how quickly do you think we'd be able to move the kids to a different school?'

Fredi

● **Record Voice Note** ▶ **Recorded: September 2025**

It was one of those days today. When Mum woke me up, I was not ready to leave my bed. I was not ready. [*Groans*]

I kept saying, 'Five more minutes, Mum.' And she kept coming back after five minutes until she finally pulled the duvet off and said she wasn't able to drive me to Everglades today and neither was Dad, so if I didn't get out of bed NOW, I would be late for school. Again.

I've only been late, like, three times this term, but late is late. And four times you get a weekend detention. I did not want a weekend detention. If I got weekend detention that would mean no netball or Mathelion. And if I missed those I wouldn't get to see my friends and the tutors who ran those classes wouldn't pick me for the squads. Which would mean I wouldn't get to go to Leeds for the UK Netball Championship tournament and I wouldn't get to go to Birmingham for the Mathelion Grand Slam. I have been working really, *really* hard for the past year to get onto both those things. This morning, I was not going to let anything get in the way of my mission. Not even myself.

I had literally just stepped into the shower when I heard: 'Fredi! FREDI!'

'Yes, Mum?' I called back when I turned off the water.

'You have exactly seven minutes to get out the shower, get dressed, eat breakfast and leave the house if you want to catch the last bus before you're late.'

What? No! That's when I noticed my phone was flashing because the alarm had timed itself out. Turned out I'd set the alarm, but I didn't turn my ringer up after I turned it off last night, so I didn't hear it. Couldn't believe my phone would do me dirty like that.

'I'll just skip breakfast,' I said to Mum as I went to rush past her.

Her arm came out and connected to the wall next to the bathroom door, halting me in my tracks. 'What did you just say?' she asked in *that* Mum voice.

'I . . . erm . . . said that I was going to get dressed super quick so I can make sure I leave the house with a nutritious breakfast inside me.'

Mum moved her arm and let me run past. She shouted after me: 'That's what I thought you said.'

Breakfast – bagel with cream cheese and smoked salmon, a cup of lemon, ginger and honey – went down quick, quick and I ran out the house for the bus stop. The bus was late so I didn't have to be. It arrived exactly seven minutes later than scheduled, which meant I arrived just when it did. The driver made up time en route, so I arrived at school right on time. I didn't even mind that much that I left my headphones at home. Nor that I forgot my history book. I was just happy that there'd be no detention for me today.

I walked through the gates this morning like nothing could touch me, nothing could go wrong. So, yeah, that's why *everything* started going wrong, isn't it?

■ **End Voice Note** ↓ **Save Recording** ↗ **Send To Private Cloud**

Kez

March 2026, Brighton

Jeb keeps laughing at me. At the look on my face before I stood up, at the way my voice sounded, at my face when I sat down, at the way people waited for Penny to hurriedly leave with her husband and group of friends before they came over to give me a nod, a pat on the back or a smile of approval. My private messages on the group chat have been pinging non-stop with people thanking me for speaking up.

Zoey and Jonah are spending the night at their friends' houses, which is a shame because they're very likely to hear what happened from other people and that could cause problems. *For me.* That could cause very real problems for me. They'll absolutely back me up to other people, but I can just imagine their faces as they walk through the door tomorrow, mortified that I've shown them up in front of everyone. Determined to get assurances that I won't do that to them again.

As Jeb does another impression of me, while unlocking our newly painted yellow front door, I notice the sleek black car parked at the corner of our street. It doesn't look out of place here, but its blacked-out windows do get my attention.

I make a big show of straightening the big black recycling wheelie bin so I can surreptitiously clock the car's number plate and take in more details of its make and shape. I think I've seen the number plate before . . . but it could be just my imagination.

'All right, laughing boy,' I say to Jeb, and close the door behind me, shutting out the car and whoever is watching me. And they *are* watching me. It's obvious from the way the car is positioned and the fact that there is someone inside the car with the engine off, that they are watching our house, observing me. I am not flattering myself; like it or not, this is the type of thing I've been trained to notice. This is the type of thing that my ridiculous job in a government-adjacent organisation makes me constantly aware is happening. I'm glad the children aren't here now that I know I'm being watched, but anxiety dances in my stomach wondering if they are safe where they are. *Is there someone watching them, too? Or watching my other family members?*

As soon as the door shuts behind us, Jeb grabs me and holds me close to him. He stares down at me, amused, but also intense. I sling my arms around him, careful in that way of mine, to not touch him with my hands because I touched the recycling bin and haven't washed my hands yet.

'In all seriousness, though, I am proud of you,' Jeb says. 'It's not often I get to see you in action. And you were – are – magnificent.'

'Yeah, sometimes I wish I could just keep my mouth shut.'

Jeb laughs. 'Never going to happen.'

'Yeah, I know,' I reply. I'm trying not to get distracted. I'm trying to focus on my husband and the fact that we have an empty house and neither of us has any work to do. I'm trying – and failing – not to run that number plate through my head, trying to work out where I've seen it before. I'm trying – and failing – not to panic at the thought of who is outside and what they want.

This is what it's like working for Insight. Although I am technically just a profiler and therapist working with the intelligence services and law enforcement as well as other government bodies, and although I am technically not someone who comes that close to real-life danger or to being targeted, last year, I was shot. I was shot by someone I was trying to help, and it was a reminder that anything I do can become dangerous in the space of minutes or seconds. I mean, I say that like I haven't had people wait for me in car parks, put trackers in my car, stalk me, assault me and other things. I say that like I haven't always walked with an extra layer of danger and it was only last year that I realised it. The year before last, after finding a baby on the back seat of my car, I ended up in a hostage situation that I very nearly didn't survive. My life is ludicrous sometimes, so I shouldn't really be surprised that someone has tracked me down and is waiting outside to . . . what? Kill me? Kidnap me? Teach me how to sew invisible zips? My life is so ridiculous that it could be any of those things, all of those things or none of those things.

My husband kisses me, bending me backwards so he can passionately move his lips against mine, slip his tongue into my mouth, bring me close to his body. I pull away slightly, gasping with how he has literally taken my breath and the thoughts in my head away.

'Wait, wait,' I say to him, when he moves in to kiss me again. 'I have to wash my hands.' I hold my hands up. 'Recycling-bin hands. Why don't you go upstairs, wash your hands and then slip into something sexy while I wash my hands down here.'

'What, you want me to put on your underwear?' he laughs, trying to kiss my nose.

'No, well, not unless you really want to. I was thinking maybe a bath? We haven't had a bath together in an age and since the kids are not here . . .'

'All right,' he says. 'I will go and run us a bath. Lots of magnesium salt to relax the muscles. And I will make a decision on the underwear afterwards.'

I laugh at him again. He drops another kiss on the end of my nose and then heads for the stairs. I go to the bathroom under the stairs to wash my hands. Jeb pauses halfway up the staircase.

'You know, you could have just told me that you were going to check out who is watching us from that black car across the road? I wouldn't have stopped you,' he says.

Gah. I always, *always* forget how well my husband knows me.

'Actually, I would have told you to "call for back-up" before you went out there, but you know what I mean.'

I nod. I know what he means.

'So, since I doubt you will call for back-up or whatever, as I always say, just do whatever you need to do to come home to us.'

'I'm not in danger,' I state to him.

'Course you're not,' he replies. 'Course you're not.'

He forces a smile and then carries on upstairs, probably with dread in his stomach and his heart galloping in his chest. He's getting better at not allowing his overprotectiveness of me to outwardly show, but I'm sure he's going to go straight upstairs to our bedroom window to watch the car, clutching his phone so he can call the number that is to be used strictly in emergencies. That was the deal I made with him after I was shot. I had to give him a number that would mean he could summon help for me the second it looked like I'm in trouble. I'd told him I wasn't in any danger then, too. It might have been a bit more convincing if I hadn't been lying in bed with a gunshot wound, acquired during the course of my work. But it was true then and it is now – I'm not in any imminent danger. Kind of.

While I was lathering my hands, rinsing them off and then drying them on the blue towel in our downstairs toilet, I worked out where I have seen the number plate before. Or one very similar to it. And if I'm right, then I am definitely not in any danger. Not imminently, anyway.

As I approach the car, coming at it diagonally across the road, the driver's side door opens. By the time I arrive in front of the car door, the person has exited the vehicle.

'Hello, MJ,' I say.

Fredi

● **Record Voice Note** ▶ **Recorded: September 2025**

'Why doesn't he know I'm alive?' Bev wailed as we set our trays down on our table in our part of the dining room.

Tuesday was sandwich day. We didn't get hot food, we got pre-packed sandwiches, a tube of yoghurt, an apple or orange and a juice box with cardboard straws. Good food it was not. Mum had brought it up a few times in the parent–teacher conferences, explained that growing children needed more food than that to keep them going. She even said that for some children, lunch at school was the only hot meal they get a day. She always said it in a reasonable tone and smiled and . . . and *still* the catering manager would burst into tears and act like Mum had insulted her and everyone in her bloodline going back generations. More than once, Mum has muttered, 'If this was ancient times we'd be out here duelling with pistols at dawn and if it was the nineties we'd be having a dance-off.'

Either way, nothing ever changed and we had to eat sandwiches that feel like mushed cardboard and taste like a slimy butter-wannabe spread no matter what the filling is meant to be. And Bev constantly crashing out about why Marvin didn't like her didn't add any kind of seasoning to the proceedings.

'Maybe it's because two people with Vs in their names aren't meant to be together,' Carina said, because she was fed up of this. *Either make a move or make a shut up*, she's said more than once to Bev. But Bev ain't budging. Bev was in love and Bev needed to talk it out.

Bev shot daggers at me for smirking at what Carina said.

'It's all right for you,' Bev said to Carina. 'You've got a man.'

'Boy,' I said. 'There's no way that Dexter Robison can be called a man.'

Bev burst out laughing. 'Cold.'

Carina unwrapped her sandwich and arched a perfectly shaped eyebrow at Bev and at me. She was about to bite into her sandwich when Jeanette Reyes, who was walking past, purposely bumped into her, making her sandwich fly out of her hands.

'Oh, sorry, didn't see you there, *Carina*,' she said nastily.

Oh, this was a beef that has been stewing for a long time. Jeanette used to like-like Dexter Robison. And he didn't like her, at all. I don't know why he didn't want to know her, but he didn't and he made it clear. Which she, who always acted as though she was the prettiest girl in the school – the world, actually – took really badly. At every party since Carina got with Dexter, Jeanette has tried it on with Dexter. Carina's mum is really strict so she's not allowed to go to most parties, so she only ever hears about it on Snap and the group chat. And of course Dexter tells her. But Dexter never does anything and that makes Jeanette crash out all the time. And everyone takes vids so she can never even pretend that anything happened because it's right there in 4K that nothing ever happened.

She's been trying to cause trouble with Carina for a long time, but today was the first time she'd done something. Me and Bev were on our feet straight away, standing right behind Carina. My best friend got slowly to her feet and faced down Jeanette.

'What's the matter, Jeanette? Can't walk straight?' Carina said, staring at Jeanette like the nothing she was.

Jeanette's other two friends, Pearl and Marcella, stood behind her like they were ready to fight, too. It was a bit pathetic, really. These girls are going to fight us over a boy. Really? Like isn't there something better for Jeanette to get upset about? Dexter wasn't even that good-looking. He doesn't shape his Afro and his clothes are always creased, but he was nice to Carina so we kind of backed her being with him.

'Pathetic,' Bev coughed into her hand.

And that set it off. Jeanette reached out and tried to grab Carina's hair. Carina ducked back out of the way and Jeanette fell forward, landing flat on her face. Everyone in the place erupted in laughter, and suddenly everyone from around the room was coming over to laugh at her, too. For someone who thought she was so pretty and popular, a lot of people were running up to laugh at her. Thing is, I noticed that she didn't put her hands up to stop herself when she fell so she smashed her face onto the ground. When she sat up, her face was covered in blood.

'Oh wow,' Bev said.

Carina pulled a shocked face and Jeanette's friends didn't do anything but stare. Even though she had literally started it, I felt bad for her because she was crying and bleeding and looking humiliated. So I go to her, try to help her up. And that's when Miss Geraghty arrived. 'What is going on here?' she thundered. Everyone scarpered, leaving just the seven of us there.

'She punched me!' Jeanette says, pointing at me.

'What?' I replied, dropping her right out of my hands because, girl, what? 'I didn't.'

'She did!' Jeanette lied.

'No, she didn't,' said Carina.

'No, she didn't, you liar,' Bev added.

Pearl and Marcella both said, 'Yes, she did!' And Miss Geraghty, who has always hated me, hated Carina, hated Bev, curled her lip up in the way she always did when she looked at the three of us. She didn't like many children, but she seemed to *really* hate me and Carina and Bev.

'Get yourselves to the headmaster's office,' Miss Geraghty said to us.

'But we didn't do anything,' I protested.

'Now!' said Miss Geraghty with her pointy glasses and grey teeth. 'Pearl, take Jeanette to the nurse's office. The rest of you, to the headmaster's office.'

We didn't even get to eat our lunch. We all marched off to the headmaster's office. Bev, Carina and I were furious! Absolutely furious, because we hadn't done anything. But that was how it was at school sometimes. We got into trouble when we hadn't done anything.

■ **End Voice Note** ↓ **Save Recording** ↗ **Send To Private Cloud**

Kez

March 2026, Brighton

'Kez,' MJ replies to my greeting, her voice so frosty you would think it was like our last two encounters when I have shown up uninvited and unwelcome to see her. You wouldn't think that she has brought herself all the way over from the other side of town to my door.

'I'm guessing hell is about to have a cold spell since you're here about to ask me for help,' I say when she doesn't speak. 'Or, will I be needing to go back inside, pack up my life and ship out because someone is coming to get me at dawn?'

The look of pure irritation that passes across her face before she hides it behind an expression of neutral disdain tells me that she *desperately* needs my help. Hell really is about to freeze over, then. The last time I spoke to her, when I was asking for help with a case I was working on, she told me this was 'absolutely the last time' she was helping me out. The implication from that being she didn't want to see me again.

To be fair to me, though, she has been saying similar things to me since we first worked together nearly twenty-five years ago. Along with Brian Kershaw, we were three newbies recruited into The Human Insight Unit run by a man called Dennis Chambers. He bullied Brian by constantly making digs at his masculinity, he made MJ – or Maisie as she was called back then – feel like she was stupid and had nothing but her family connections going for her, and he sexually harassed (and eventually sexually assaulted) me. When everything inevitably imploded and Brian hit Dennis and was forced to leave, MJ shipped out not long after. She'd been telling Brian and me for months that once she left she wouldn't keep in touch with either of us so she could forget all about her time with Dennis. I'd thought that was fair enough. But it didn't work out that way and we have been forced together far too many times in the last few years for MJ's liking. Me? I don't care either way. While there are huge swathes of my past I would like to forget, I'm not bothered if I see people from that past. Except Dennis. I hate having to see him every day because I work for him again now. But I'm starting to build immunity to him, too. In another five to ten years, being in his vicinity might not bother me at all.

'You owe me,' MJ says. 'I helped you out and you owe me. I'm calling in that favour now.'

'All right,' I say neutrally, because I am not used to seeing MJ in need of help. When I knew her, she had all the confidence in the world. She was brought up to believe that everything in the universe was hers for the taking. Even when Dennis was relentlessly bullying her, she eventually got it to stop by asking her father and godfather to have a word with him. And with her family connections, when she left T.H.I.U. it was to become second in command of a government-connected-but-not-run thinktank. In all the time I've known her, there has been absolutely nothing that MJ didn't think she could do. 'What is it?' I ask, because this vulnerable woman in front of me is not someone I know.

She inhales and exhales a few times, won't meet my eye. Suddenly, she becomes breathy and fragile, and I think for a moment she is going to start crying. Whatever has brought her here must be terrible. Really, really awful.

'You're going to have to tell me if you want my help,' I tell her. 'I'm good at profiling people and working things out, but I need a few clues?'

'It's my daughter,' MJ finally explains. 'She's in trouble and I need you to prove that she's innocent.'

Fredi

● **Record Voice Note** ▶ **Recorded: September 2025**

'Carina, I'm very disappointed in you,' Mr Osterman said to me. 'You have such a good track record and now you're standing by while your friends punch other innocent pupils. Miss Geraghty has told me before what a bad influence Winifred is and now you have let yourself get dragged into her mess. Miss Geraghty thinks she might be involved with gangs. Gangs, Carina. I'm sure your mother would be very disappointed to learn that you could become involved with drugs and guns.'

It was very odd, shall we say, listening to Mr Osterman tell me what they really thought of me because he believed he was talking to someone else. But I knew why it was happening. The white teachers were always getting the Black students mixed up. Even though Bev, Carina and I looked NOTHING alike, the teachers were always calling one of us by the other's name. This was the worst time, though.

'Mr Osterman,' I said.

'Yes, Carina?' he replied.

'I'm not Carina,' I said. 'I'm Winifred.'

His face drained of all colour and then it got really red. He looked down at the file in front of him as though it had lied to him and it was that which made him say all those things.

'Winifred, I, erm, why did you tell me you were Carina?'

'I didn't, sir,' I replied.

Mr Osterman was suddenly furious. 'I will be talking to your parents about this.'

'Yes, sir. But I didn't do anything.'

'You will be put into detention and I will have to work out another punishment for your lies.'

'But, sir, I didn't do anything.'

'We will see about that, Miss Kingston, we will see.'

■ **End Voice Note** ↓ **Save Recording** ↗ **Send To Private Cloud**

Fredi

● **Record Voice Note** ▶ **Recorded: September 2025**

'We seem to have a problem here, Mr Osterman,' Mum said.

'A real problem,' Dad said. Both my parents had their arms folded across their chests as they sat on the other side of his desk and stared him down. I stood next to Mum.

Mr Osterman cleared his throat, shuffled paper, looked uncomfortable. I'm not sure what he was expecting. Mr Osterman had met my parents a few times when they've come in for school events and parents' evenings. Of course, they're always super polite and big smiles. My mum likes to garden and my dad likes to play weekend football, they are two of the nicest, most ordinary people you could ever meet. They defo come across as nice and mild, so I reckon that's why Mr Osterman was always treating them like they were meek and weak. He didn't realise that 'nice' doesn't equal 'easy to walk all over'. My parents aren't at all meek.

In my last school, when some kid said something racist to me, Mum tried to talk to his mother about it. Instead of listening, his mother got angry and started shouting. Mum had put the phone down, telling me to stay away from him. When he said it again at school and the teachers didn't really do anything, Mum had written them a letter detailing everything that kid had done wrong over the years (there was a lot) – and then she CC'd in the mother. All hell broke loose, of course. All sorts of threats and recriminations. But it never happened again. Mum said to me, 'Sometimes, you've got to work out who someone is scared of, then you've got to make sure they are more scared of you than they are of them.'

Mr Osterman did not know this about my mother. He thought that just being the headmaster would be enough for my parents to be, what's that word, that long one that means they'd almost kneel in front of him begging for forgiveness. That's it – subservient.

'Apparently, you can't tell my daughter apart from her friend?' Mum said.

'Why is that, Mr Osterman?' Dad asked. 'Why is that?'

My parents were so far from meek and mild, as Mr Osterman was finding out.

'And apparently one of your teachers thinks my daughter, who is a straight double-A-star/straight nines student, who has never been in trouble, is gang affiliated?' Mum said.

'I mean, apart from it being defamatory, can you explain to me why that teacher thinks this?' Dad said.

'What is it about my daughter that makes a teacher – with no proof or reason to believe it – think she might be gang affiliated?' Mum added.

'You . . . I . . . We're very welcoming at this school,' Mr Osterman said. 'We're very tolerant.'

'That's very nice for you,' Dad said. 'I'm not sure why you think it's an achievement to merely tolerate other human beings. And I'm certainly not sure what that has got to do with my daughter being accused of being a gang member and told by you that she is a bad influence on her friends?'

Mr Osterman glared at me. He didn't realise that I had spoken to my parents. I used Dexter's burner phone that he kept in his sock to call my parents and tell them everything so when they showed up they would be prepared.

'Don't look at my daughter like that,' Mum told him, and he quickly redirected his glare to the papers down in front of him.

'Jeanette is a very popular, trustworthy girl. She told Miss Geraghty that Winifred had punched her. Miss Geraghty could only go off the information she was given by another pupil.'

'From what I hear, this Jeanette started the altercation and then tried to hit Carina, missed and then fell, hurting herself,' Mum explained.

'It doesn't sound like she's very trustworthy at all. Have you looked at the CCTV footage?' Dad asked.

'Well, erm, not quite.'

'So, rather than look at the evidence you have on hand, you call my daughter in, mistake her for someone else, bad-mouth her to herself and then call us in to listen to this? Is that a fair summation of what is going on here?' Mum asked.

'Mrs Kingston, your daughter has a reputation for being highly disruptive.'

Mum and Dad looked at each other and I got scared, because even though I hadn't done anything wrong this man was lying on me. And he sounded convincing.

'Right,' Dad said, and got his mobile phone out of his pocket. He started typing into it. 'I'm currently submitting a freedom of information request for my daughter's files. Once I have them, we can all see where we stand. We should have concrete evidence of her alleged disruptive behaviour and we can have a full conversation with that teacher who said the thing about the gangs. And any other teacher my daughter tells me has a beef with her.'

Mr Osterman's face did that white-in-fear to red-in-anger thing again. 'I . . . I don't think there's any need for any of that. I . . . erm . . . I think we should all move on. Put this behind us.'

'What does that look like and mean, exactly?' Dad asked, momentarily lowering his phone.

'Well, obviously, we'll have to make a note—'

Dad kissed his teeth and raised his phone again.

'I'm, I'm sure on this occasion we can simply mention that—'

Dad started typing even faster.

'Winifred can return to class straight away. I will make sure any mention of this incident is removed from her records. It will be as though nothing has happened.'

'And what's going to happen to the girl who started all of this?' Mum asked.

'I don't follow you?' Mr Osterman asked.

'She started an altercation with a pupil. Tried to hit said pupil and when her attack went wrong and she ended up hitting her own face and drawing blood, she lied about the one person who didn't laugh at her and instead tried to help her. What is going to happen to her?'

I could tell Mr Osterman was desperate to scowl at me again for telling my parents everything. He straightened out the files in front of him and bounced slightly in his seat. I wasn't sure if he wanted to run out of the room screaming or to go to the toilet.

I hadn't actually told them everything. Like how much money Jeanette's dad had. And how he regularly donated to the school – every time Jeanette did something bad to someone else, he made a donation and then the thing that Jeanette did didn't get talked about any longer. Every time. I think that was one of the reasons why she was still so focused on Dexter – she usually got what she wanted so couldn't understand someone saying no to her.

'I'm not really at liberty to discuss—'

'Right,' Dad said, interrupting Mr Osterman. Dad must have been really mad because he never interrupted people cos he said it was rude and unnecessary. 'We're going to need assurances that this girl will be punished for her actions. If she is not, we may decide that this place is unsafe for pupils who look like my daughter and then . . . a freedom of information request will be the least of your worries.'

'That sounds like a threat, Mr Kingston,' said Mr Osterman.

'Not a threat at all. I am just reminding you that, for schools, there are far more scary things than me requesting all the information you have on my child.'

Mr Osterman went pale white again. You could see the fear moving across his brain as he worked out what my parents could mean. Did they mean protests, being cancelled . . . or being reported to OFSTED?

'I can assure you that Jeanette will be dealt with.'

'Make sure she is,' Dad said.

'And maybe, just maybe, you should learn what the Black children in your school look like so you don't get them mixed up,' Mum told him.

'And maybe, just maybe, you should train your staff to not accuse a child of being in a gang just because she's Black,' Dad said. 'We take those sort of things very seriously.'

'Very seriously,' Mum finished. Mum and Dad stood up at the exact same time. 'Winifred, let's go.'

In the car, both my parents sighed as though they were exhausted. 'We have got to get her out of this school,' they both said at the same time. 'We just have to.'

■ **End Voice Note** ↓ **Save Recording** ↗ **Send To Private Cloud**

Kez

March 2026, Brighton

If it was anyone other than MJ I was talking to, I would have invited her in, told her to sit down while I made her a cup of tea, then gently asked her to tell me everything. But I know MJ – she will not want to be in my house. Plus, I do not want her in my house. I do not like her; she does not like me. Our association has only ever been one of necessity.

We shut ourselves inside her car; its interior a luxury haven of pale, soft leather and shiny wood veneer. I look around, taking in how the other half lives. Being around MJ has always been a window directly into the world of the seriously wealthy, the true elite – a close-up exploration into how they dress, shop, style their hair, do their make-up, carry themselves, think and talk. MJ has always had the poise and confidence of someone who was born to rule.

'What's this about?' I ask when I tear my gaze away from her car to focus on her.

MJ takes her hand off the steering wheel, runs her fingers through her cheek-length auburn hair, then returns her hands to the steering wheel all while staring fixedly out of the windscreen. 'I wish I knew,' she says in a voice that is unexpectedly soft. Since Brian died, MJ's voice has been cold, slightly harsh; as though his death and everything that has come after sharpened her vocal cords and the sound they make. 'And I wish I didn't know. My daughter goes to Axton Manor. It's the same boarding school I went to. Two weeks ago, a member of staff died under suspicious circumstances.'

'I didn't hear anything about it.'

'No, it's been classified as an accident or misadventure or whatever they call someone taking their own . . . you know. Mostly they've said it was an accident.'

'And you don't believe that?'

She shakes her head, closes her eyes. 'It was not an accident, it was not him deciding to end it. And that isn't all. A pupil has gone missing. On the same day he died, she went missing. They claim she ran away, but she didn't run away. She is Viola's friend. I think . . . I think Viola might have a crush on her. She's taken this girl's disappearance really badly. Coupled with the death of Dr Pemberton, someone she held in high esteem, she's barely holding it together. But it's more than that. The police have concluded their investigation, but the school board and the trustees are talking about secretly putting an undercover private detective in without the headteacher or the administration's knowledge, to see if one of the girls killed Pemberton and who could be behind that girl's disappearance.'

'That seems extreme, especially if the police have concluded their investigation?' I say.

'Yes, but they think Viola and her friends are involved.'

'By "involved" do they mean the girls killed the teacher and did something to the missing girl?'

'Yes. This girl was new to the school. Started late last term. And all of the girls had been seeing Pemberton—'

'Seeing him? As in dating or sleeping with him?'

'No! God, no! He was the school therapist. A lot of the girls have emotional problems and struggle with being away from home for the first time – Axton Manor has a wide range of services to help them settle and thrive. From what I gather, Dr Pemberton was very popular. All of the girls had seen him. Yes, even Viola. She didn't tell me what she talked to him about, although I can guess.'

MJ turns to face me when she reveals: 'My daughter hates me. All that stuff two years ago didn't help.' She's referring to what we uncovered two years ago when I asked her for help with the dangerous situation my oldest son, Moe, was mixed up in. We discovered that MJ's daughter had been involved, too, and was also in danger. I hadn't really known what the fallout from all of that had been for her. I hadn't even thought about it, if I'm honest. Not when the aftermath for me and my family had meant doing whatever it took to keep Moe out of prison, which included starting my ridiculous job at Insight. I had thought that MJ, with her contacts and connections, would walk away relatively unscathed. It didn't even cross my mind that she would face repercussions in her own home.

'It's not just that, though,' MJ continues. 'She's becoming aware of how the world works and her place in it. Our family's place in it. She's testing boundaries.' MJ rubs her fingers over her eyes to cover her upset, I suspect. 'She doesn't want to be at Axton Manor. She's aware of what it means to go there and she doesn't want to be there. We've had some awful . . . She was seeing Dr Pemberton, I think, to try to come to terms with the fact that I want her to stay there. Gerry, Gerald, he's very good at playing the neutral party, but if I pulled her out and sent her to a local Brighton school – even a private one – he'd have something to say about that. His mother went to Axton, too. It's what we do. But she thinks it's all me and she doesn't get that sometimes you have to do things because of your ancestry. It's just the way it is.'

MJ sounds very much like someone trying to convince herself she is doing the right thing even though it feels wrong. I'd imagine most parents – mothers especially – sound like this about something. Possibly not trying to force your child to stay at an elite institution so they can keep their place amongst the ruling classes, but about something.

'What does this have to do with what's going on at the school?' It's not that I'm not sympathetic to what MJ is talking about, I am. But the more she gets off track with this and starts to open up to me, the more she makes herself vulnerable to me, the more it will create problems for both of us later. It will only result in her trying to screw me over to make sure I keep my mouth shut somewhere down the line. She won't be able to help herself. MJ thinks I am like her. She thinks because she would absolutely use any information she amasses about someone against them at some point that everyone else – me included – would do the same. To be fair to her, I think most people would, but only as a last resort. MJ would go there quite early on to make sure she maintains the upper hand in all situations. Which is why I do not need to see the vulnerable side of her – the last thing I need is for someone as powerful as MJ to turn on me.

'I mean, I know he was the therapist, but what does it have to do with your daughter?'

'I'm scared that I pushed her too far. That in forcing her to stay, she got caught up in something that has led to this man's death and this girl's disappearance. What if . . .' MJ sighs, closes her eyes. 'When . . . When I was there, the same thing happened.'

'The same thing?'

'A teacher died; a girl went missing. She was an outsider, too. Came from Cumbria or something. Everyone said she was on a bursary, but I don't think she was. It didn't matter, though, because people treated her like she was. And one of the teachers she was quite close to, she died in an accident. Around the same time, the girl disappeared.'

'Just vanished?'

'The rumour was that she had been chucked out for having an inappropriate relationship with the teacher. That her parents came and got her stuff under cover of darkness because they were so ashamed. But, even back then when I didn't care much about anything beyond my life, that story didn't sound plausible. She'd made some good friends – why wouldn't she keep in touch with them? When all of this blew up, I checked her name and found a few web posts, social-media things that said her parents had died not knowing what happened to her. Her aunt and an uncle were still searching for her.'

'You think something happened to her?'

'She hasn't been seen since 1987.'

'And they didn't show up at the school demanding to know what happened to their daughter?'

'It doesn't work like that, Kez. Back then . . .' She looks off into the distance, obviously trying to find a way to explain things in a way that I will understand and that will make me help rather than judge her. 'Back then, Axton Manor had the means to cover up whatever they wanted. There's no mention of Axton Manor on any of those posts looking for Finnula Hooper. I'd imagine they were threatened to remove all mention of the school in the search for her. All sorts of things happen that never hit the press because Axton has very deep pockets and very powerful allies. Back when Finnula disappeared, all of her friends were implicated. None of us believed she had been thrown out. Or that she had run away. We knew something had happened to her, but we didn't do anything about it. Nothing really was done about it by anyone.'

'What's different this time?'

'The girl's parents. They don't really care about being sued or anything like that. The school board and trustees think they're going to make trouble, that they're not going to stay quiet. They've appeased them for now, saying they'll start an internal investigation to find out what happened, but the board and trustees know that if it gets out that . . . a . . . a . . .'

'A what, MJ?'

'A Black girl has gone missing at a very prestigious school, then it's going to be a huge scandal. Especially since a Black girl went missing last year, too.'

'Excuse me, what?'

'She probably did run away, but no one knows for sure. And that's why the school board and trustees are talking about actually conducting an independent investigation instead of just making the right noises about it. They know they can't cover this one up, they know that a lot of attention could be shone on them, so I'm scared that they may sacrifice Viola and her friends to make it go away.'

'The girl who disappeared when you were at school, was she Black, too?'

'No. She was white. But she was working class.'

'How many girls have disappeared over the years?'

'I don't know.'

'But there have been more?'

'Yes. Several more.'

'And it's never bothered you until you think your daughter might be accused of being involved?' I have to call her out, because *what the actual hell?*

MJ takes a deep breath in, lets it out slowly, expelling the accusation I have levelled at her. 'What's one of the most important things we were taught when we were learning to profile people, Kez?'

'People are far more likely to do something or engage with something if it personally impacts them,' I begrudgingly admit. 'Personal gain or personal loss is the best type of nudge messaging.' I hate that this is true. 'So what do you want from me?'

'You owe me so you have to help me. You have to find this girl and find out who killed Dr Pemberton before they launch this investigation.'

'You think the girl's still alive?'

'I hope so. For Viola, I hope so. The other girl who disappeared last year, she was in Viola's friend group as well.'

My eyes widen in disbelief and my head whips round to stare at the woman asking for my help. 'Are you *serious*?'

'I know. I know how it sounds, but I don't believe Viola had anything to do with it. Honestly, I don't. If I did, I would pull her out of there and send her abroad.'

I can't even respond to that because if I think too deeply about what she has told me, well, I'll have serious doubts about what I'm about to do. Instead, I say, 'I suppose if they need a new school therapist, I could apply for the job. But if I don't get it—'

'You'll get it. In fact, you don't even have to apply – I'll make sure you get it. You realise that you'll have to live there, don't you?'

'I hadn't actually thought about that.' Jeb will not be impressed. Or happy. Or on board with it. Imagine me, living as well as working where a therapist was murdered – as a therapist. I can see his face now.

'How am I going to find out about the girl who went missing?'

'Winifred. Her name is Winifred Kingston. I'll make sure you have access to the therapist's files. Maybe you can go and talk to her parents? I don't know. I just know that I want you to do something before they put someone else on it. Someone that they control and who will be keen to find a scapegoat or five for them.'

'All right. But, MJ?'

'Yes?'

'Look at me. I want it to be very clear when I say this.'

She turns her hazel gaze on me, staring deep into my black-brown eyes. 'I am going to find out the truth. If it does involve something your daughter has done, I will take it to the police. Is that clear?'

MJ's features harden, she grits her teeth and she sharpens her gaze. She knows I'm serious. The last time we were in a life-threatening situation together, I forced her to agree not to lie to cover up what happened. She had been unhappy about that and it had cemented her deep dislike of me. That I'm essentially promising her more of the same if I find out that her daughter is a wrong 'un reminds her why she dislikes me so much.

'That's clear,' she says, knowing that I need her to say it out loud. 'That's crystal clear.'

She breaks eye contact first and I pop open the car door. Before I leave, I say: 'You could have just asked me for my help, you know? You didn't have to come over all "you owe me" mafioso stylee.'

'Really, Kez,' she replies. 'And what would you have said if I had just asked for your help without reminding you that you owe me?'

I put my head to one side. 'I would have said, "Of course I'll help you."'

She double-takes. Today really is the day of new expressions from MJ. *'Really?'*

'Yes. MJ, she's your child and she's in trouble, of course I'd agree to help you in any way that I can – whether I owe you or not.'

Visibly shaken by this revelation that I would help her even if there is nothing in it for me, she nods and then returns to looking out of the window.

Fredi

● **Record Voice Note** ▶ **Recorded: September 2025**

'We have got to get her out of that school,' Mum told her best friend, Auntie Jacinta, after we came back from meeting Mr Osterman.

I could just about hear Auntie Jacinta say, 'I told you, Jacob left money for her schooling. You know how he thought education was the most important thing in life. She's so bright, he wanted Fredi to get out of that school, which has a dreadful reputation. She would get into Axton Manor in a heartbeat. But with the money he left, you could send her anywhere you choose. Anywhere. I know you feel . . . about taking that money, but it's for her. In trust . . . can touch it.'

Mum didn't say anything for a long time. When Mum goes silent, it means she's deep, *deep* thinking about something. 'What about Mariana?' Mum said after a long while. 'She was so unhappy at Axton Manor she ran away and she hasn't been in contact since.'

'It's different with Mariana,' Auntie Jacinta said. 'She . . . over a boy . . . Fredi would never . . . not over a boy.'

'We'd have to think about it some more. But you know how even the most sensible girl can have her head turned by a boy,' Mum said.

'. . . been in touch. I got . . . saying not to worry . . . happy . . . too much pressure . . .'

'Why didn't you tell me she'd been in touch? That's amazing! It must be such a weight off your mind.'

'A postcard isn't having her home. It is a weight off, but I'd rather she was home. But at least . . . It's the best . . . for now.'

'Like I said, we'll have to talk about it. Thanks so much, Jas. Just having that option there makes me feel a whole lot better.'

Two weeks later, when Miss Geraghty decided that me always being the first to put my hand up to answer maths problems meant I was being a wicked show-off, so I should have Saturday detention, Mum called Auntie Jacinta back and said we would take the money her husband, my uncle Jacob, had left for my schooling when he died of a heart attack. I had to change schools and that meant I was going to go to Axton Manor.

■ **End Voice Note** ↓ **Save Recording** ↗ **Send To Private Cloud**

Part 2

Kez

March 2026, Brighton

For long seconds, Dennis frowns at me in silence from the other side of his desk when I explain that I will be taking a few weeks off work.

'That sounds very much like you are telling me what you'll be doing, rather than asking for the time off or, indeed, if you're allowed to do this, Kezuma,' he eventually says.

'Allowed?' I reply.

'I am your employer,' he carefully reminds me, as though I may have forgotten why I enter this hellscape every day and make nice with people who treat me like I'm an idiot. 'It is customary for employees to ask permission before they go off and do whatever it is you're asking if you can do.'

And here we are. Me and Dennis, Dennis and me, about to strap on our fighting gloves and enter that arena where we fight. We haven't had to do this for a while. Mainly because he stays away from me and I stay away from him. The work we do that he passes on to me is mostly low level and innocuous nowadays. As a government-adjacent body specialising in profiling and psychological work with the intelligence services, law enforcement and government departments, we have a broad range of things we do. Some of it is profiling for the police to catch major criminals, like last year, when we were trying to find the person who eventually shot me. Some of it is creating messaging that influences people's habits. Some of it is counselling agents who have been out in the field or have been off work due to trauma and are now ready to return to the field. It isn't that bad. My job isn't that bad. Dare I say, despite all its ridiculousness of regular firearms training and combat lessons, my job can be enjoyable. The worst part of it is this man I am sitting opposite. This terrible human being I had to make a deal with to save my family. I actually thought it would be a lot worse, and, if I thought I had any way out of here, I wouldn't have fixed my perspective to accept my circumstances and so I would be a lot more unhappy. As it is, I am here for ever, I am in this role, and I might as well accept it since the work isn't too onerous. Yes, they are some of the worst people I've ever met, and I could happily scream at the people who are below me on the food chain who all pretty much worship Dennis and treat me like I'm a fool whose job they have designs on (because I'm his second-in-command), but I could get that anywhere. And, so far, only one of my colleagues who is no longer here has stalked me outside of work, which happened more than once when I worked elsewhere. And none of them have punched me in the face (yet) which has happened elsewhere, too.

And because we haven't had any high-profile, high-tension work recently, Dennis and I haven't had to do this. We haven't had to get into an eye-lock battle while we verbally tussle.

'I'm not going to be asking you if I can do this or anything, Dennis,' I state. 'That's just not what I'm about. I am *telling* you that MJ needs my help and I am going to help her. I will not be at work for a while. I don't know how long, but I won't be physically here. Simple as that.'

Dennis's cold grey eyes are drilling into me, his displeasure that I haven't taken the easy route out of this conversation and allowed him to frame it as me asking permission evident in every molecule of his glare. 'Again, you don't seem to understand the dynamic between us, Kezuma. You are my employee; I am your employer, your superior. You need permission from me to take time off work to go and work elsewhere.'

'Don't kid yourself that you're my superior, Dennis. I'm not even sure you're my equal,' I say with a smile. 'Seriously, though, I do not need your permission to do this. If MJ wasn't so paranoid about who might be behind this and how far into the services it goes, this would have been brought to Insight. And I know you would have assigned me to work on it, since no one else has the experience. So what's the big deal about me doing it? All things being equal, I would literally be doing it anyway.'

'The "big deal" as you put it is that I didn't assign it and you have just presented it to me as a fait accompli. You know that's not how things work.'

'Do I?'

'Why are you behaving like this, Kezuma?'

'Like what, Dennis?'

He narrows his eyes slightly, obviously thinking, obviously trying to work out something. 'You still blame me for you getting shot,' he eventually states.

'Of course I blame you. Who else am I going to blame?'

'The person who shot you.'

'That person might as well have been you, since you put me there in the first place.'

'And, because you still blame me, that is why you are deciding to go rogue now?'

'I am not "going rogue",' I reply, suddenly understanding why my children cringe so often about the things I say. Some words and expressions shouldn't ever be in some people's mouths. Like Dennis and 'going rogue'. 'Do you even know what going rogue means? This is the very definition of the *opposite* of going rogue. I am telling you what I'm up to in advance. If I'd gone rogue you would never know what I was doing. I just wouldn't turn up one day and when you sent people to get me back they would have no idea where I was. I am telling you, so you know where I will be.'

He glowers at me.

'Look, Dennis,' I say and glance away, breaking our eye-lock battle and allowing him to win. Whenever I do that, I'm sure Dennis realises he's about to lose a much bigger argument with me. 'I'm doing this. If you want to sack me over it, feel free, but we both know you're not going to do that – I would never be that lucky. And let's not forget, Dennis, I still haven't told MJ how you used her children that time. Even you wouldn't survive her finding that out.'

Dennis's eyes flare as he realises that I would absolutely sell him out to her if he tries to stop what I am going to do.

'So I suggest, boss, you just accept that this is happening and stop fighting it.'

'What exactly will you be doing?' he says, relaxing suddenly. He has done exactly as I suggested and stopped fighting. Except I'm not stupid enough to believe that. He'll find a way to get me back. He won't ever just let me win anything, he will get his revenge and it will be brutal. I can't worry about that right now, though.

'I told you.'

'Tell me again.'

'MJ's daughter and her group of friends are suspected of being involved in a murder and kidnapping. MJ wants me to help prove that her daughter is innocent. As I said to her, I will find out the truth, and if MJ's daughter is guilty, I will absolutely turn her in, but I will find if there are any mitigating circumstances to help her.'

'How will you do this?' Dennis asks. If I didn't know him, I'd say he was almost interested.

'Why do you want to know?'

Dennis folds his arms across his chest and leans back in his seat. 'I hadn't realised how difficult you are, Kezuma.'

'If this is the first time you've noticed that I am difficult, Dennis, then I should be questioning how good you really are at your job. I mean, come on! Three minutes in my company and most people work out I'm "challenging".'

I can see his *'this is why you're my favourite'* smile dancing on his lips. 'All right, Kezuma, let me put it this way. I can help you. And before you ask how I think I can help you, I can give you official cover. Tell MJ to ask the headmaster to call me for a reference. I can tell them that you were one of the best profilers—'

I open my eyes wide in mock shock and point at my chest.

'Yes,' he says sourly, although the amused smile is still there, 'you were one of the best profilers I trained. And that you are exactly the person he needs at this time. I am basically making this an official Insight case, as you call them, but with only you and I in the know about it. I won't even tell Horson. Well, at least not until it is all resolved.

'With a reference from me, you will receive less resistance. I know Humphrey Rhodes, the headmaster. He will do as he is told if the right person is telling him what to do.'

'And the right person is you, I'm guessing?'

'Kezuma, what do you imagine the headmaster of a school like Axton Manor would be like?' he replies. 'Do you think he would in any way listen to a . . . to a person like you?'

'Wow, Dennis, you went right up to the edge of saying that I am too working class, too Black and too female to gain any respect from the headteacher, but you backed away. I'm disappointed in you. I thought you would just come out and say that shizz.'

'I'll miss you, Kezuma, when you're not here.'

'What are you saying that for?' I ask, horrified that he has said something that sounds halfway human and I can feel myself falling for it.

'Because it's true. Why else would I say it?' he replies, seemingly confused. 'I enjoy having you around. You are excellent at your job and you keep me on my toes. I've told you more than once that you're my favourite. That hasn't changed. And I will miss you being here.'

I stare at him, still alarmed by this turn in the conversation. I have been fooled by Dennis many, *many* times before. I've been taken in when he behaves like he can feel emotion, when he acts like he isn't a complete psychopath who will do whatever it takes to get what he wants.

Oh, I get it! 'You're dreading having to deal with that lot out there, aren't you?' I say with a knowing smile. 'That's why you're helping me out. The easier it is to get the info I need and solve this, the sooner I come back and you don't have to speak to them.'

'And that is why you're my favourite.'

I hate being your favourite, I told him once. That's still true, but I don't see the point in saying it again now. I'm sure he knows. And, besides, he is helping me out. He will be able to facilitate my smooth integration into the school.

'Maybe don't tell him I've got profiling experience?' I say.

'You're probably right,' he agrees. 'I'll tell him you're a *therapist.*' He spits the word like it's poison. My boss, the psychopathic behavioural scientist and psychologist, has a really rather healthy disdain for therapy and those who deliver it.

'And I'll need someone to create an online persona for me. Since I started back here, I haven't updated my website. If you could get someone to do that for me and make it look like I still take therapy work and work with corporations and that my work history has always been about that, that would be fantastic.' I am pushing it, but why wouldn't I if I've got him eating out of my hand? Obviously, he's going to bite that hand off at some point, probably quite soon, but I might as well enjoy it while I can.

'Anything else?' he asks, amused rather than annoyed.

'No, no, I think that's it.'

'Well, good luck, Kezuma. I think you're going to need it.'

Fredi

● **Record Voice Note** ▶ **Recorded: September 2025**

Today we went to Little Buxley. What's in Little Buxley, you might be asking? Not much, but *near* Little Buxley is this massive boarding school called Axton Manor.

Axton Manor is one of the premier boarding schools in the country, it says that on its website. And it is *the* boarding school in the world for girls. It says that on the website, too. They've got a whole host of awards – Independent School of The Century, Winner Student Satisfaction Score of 2025, Best Boarding School of 2023, 2024, 2025, amongst others.

The school was founded in 1895 by Miss Valorie Axton as a place for noblemen, royalty and other super-rich merchants and traders to park their daughters until someone with the right pedigree came along to marry them. It doesn't say *that* on the website, but, come on, that's what it means. The girls were initially taught how to run a home with servants, how to embroider, dance, sing and play an instrument. I've done a bit of digging and I found out that while that's what they told everyone, they were actually teaching the girls maths, literature, Latin and science. It's quite cool that they were low-key teaching the girls to be independent even if their folks were just wanting them to look pretty and marry well.

We were in Little Buxley so I can take the entrance exams for Axton Manor.

Mum and Dad said I could choose anywhere to go to school, and I had looked at all the options, not just girls' schools and not just boarding schools. I used to hear Mum and Dad talk about finding the money for private school all the time.

'If she goes to one of those schools, she'll get a chance to be in the rooms where things happen,' I'd hear Mum say. *'She will grow up to believe that she can run the world.'*

'We can show her that,' Dad would say.

'Yes, I know we can. But don't you think the world needs to be run by people who come from ordinary families as well as the super-rich? And when you go to those schools you end up running the world.'

'I suppose so.'

Now we had the money to at least get me to do the entrance exams. I've missed most of the assessment days, where you interact with other kids and that, so they asked me to come for a full day of tests and interviews with a couple of academic staff, as well as to look around. They don't usually take people on mid-term, but my grades from school were 'promising' so they would consider it.

Miss Barkway, the school secretary, picked us up at the station in this big, f-off Land Rover. She was wearing one of those big green wax jackets over a floral-print dress with a white collar and these beige, low-heeled shoes. She had a floral band in her hair and tiny diamond earrings. She was really friendly and chatted all the way to the school about Axton Manor and the area.

I took three exams – all the sciences – then I had an interview with the most beautiful biracial Black woman called Miss Akande. It was kind of a shock seeing a Black woman in these surroundings. She was so nice and as I was leaving she said she had a feeling I would be receiving a very favourable recommendation from at least one of the admissions staff.

I met Mum in the canteen for lunch – and you know what? I don't think they even know what packet sandwiches are. There was so much food and it all tasted so nice. Mum's face. She just couldn't believe how nice it all was.

After lunch, I did the English and Maths assessments, then spoke to the school counsellor called Dr Pemberton. When I heard his name, I was ready for him to be a stuffy old man who smelt of cheese and cigars but he was nothing like that. He was really quite cool. He wore dark black jeans and an open-necked white shirt. He asked me lots of questions and said at the end of it that he would be recommending my admission. *Score!*

After the final exams of History and Geography, Miss Barkway asked a girl called Viola to show me round the school.

'How long have you been here?' Mum asked her.

'Since I was ten,' she replied. 'I'm from Brighton. My mother came to Axton Manor when she was a girl. So did my grandmother.'

'Right, so it's in the family to come here, then?' Mum said.

'It is for a lot of girls. A lot of my friends' mothers came here as well. I think it's almost expected if you're an old girl and you have a daughter that you send her here.'

Viola took us to see one of the unoccupied bedrooms. It was a nice space.

When we were leaving, Viola told me to ask to be put in Lovelace House Dorm to be with her if I wanted. She even hugged me and said: 'I'd be really happy if you came here.' She hugged me again. 'I'm going to wish really hard that you come here. I want to be friends with you.'

So, you know what? I high-key like Axton Manor. I wasn't sure at first. I didn't want to leave Bev and Carina. And I didn't want to leave Mum and Dad, and definitely didn't want to leave Mathelion or Netball Club, but it was such a nice place. Everyone I met was so lovely to me. And it'd be a whole new world of learning. They have six science labs. The library is almost as big as the one near our house. And they've got lots of netball courts, and basketball courts. They've even got a swimming pool.

I think it'd be really fun to go there.

And, of course, there's the other thing I've got to do that I can't do at any other school.

■ **End Voice Note** ↓ **Save Recording** ↗ **Send To Private Cloud**

Kez

March 2026, Brighton

'This isn't even your job, Kez,' Jeb says to me. 'You don't have to do it.'

We are sitting at the kitchen table with the under-cupboard lights on, having a drink and a catch-up on our day. We started doing this about four years ago when our marriage was in a precarious place. We loved each other, sure, but we couldn't seem to talk without arguing, and so in an attempt to remind us both why we were together, I had suggested sitting down every night possible with a drink to have a chat. Not about the children, not about our obligations, but about us as individuals and as a couple. It was a way of connecting on the most basic level.

It had transformed and strengthened our relationship, brought us even closer together. Tonight, Jeb has a large glass of pale amber whiskey from the very expensive limited-edition bottle I had bought him for his last birthday. I have a cup of hibiscus (sorrel) tea, the latest thing I am convinced is going to boost my health. It has a strong bitter taste and I'm reminding myself with every sip that it's good for me; that Three-Months'-Time Kez will appreciate Today Kez taking one for the team. She really will.

I look up from the blood-red depths of my tea mug and at my

handsome husband. *Handsome.* When I first met him at a party and didn't know his name, I had called him Handsome Man in my head. I had called him Handsome Man when I had sex with him in an upstairs bedroom, when we sat in the dark garden talking afterwards and when he took my hand while walking me home. He had been Handsome Man right up until I gave him my number and he promised to call. He hadn't called, of course. He hadn't 'called' for eight years, not until he walked into my therapy room with his first wife, Hella. So much has happened in the time since we met and he was Handsome Man, but the one thing that hasn't changed is Jeb's ability to call me out whenever necessary. Like right now. The call-out is coming from inside the house.

'You don't have to put yourself in danger like this again.'

'Except I do,' I reply. We are keeping our voices down because the children are asleep upstairs. Or, rather, they'll be in their rooms and should be asleep and probably won't be. Either way, I don't want to disturb them because this call-out seems very different from previous call-outs.

I sense the things that Jeb has wanted to say to me for the last three years or so are surfacing, like treasure long-buried in water that just needed the right knock or five to be dislodged to rise to the top. This is an argument that Jeb has been suppressing since before I started back at Insight, and my going off to work and stay at a boarding school in the middle of nowhere is the final knock in a whole series of knocks that has dislodged the treasure of his long-held tongue.

'You don't. You know you don't. It's not your job. When you've previously put yourself in trouble at least you could pretend to both of us that you had to do it as part of your work. But this is something outside of that, something you're doing because you need to play saviour – again.'

'Rude,' I reply.

'No, not rude. Not nearly rude enough, actually. You are being selfish, Kez. You are once again putting yourself in danger and you're not telling me the full story about the things you do, the people you meet—'

'People I meet?' I cut in, and then shake my head. So *that's* what this is about. 'I was honest about him. I didn't have to tell you anything, but I did because I wanted to be honest with you. I wanted us to get our relationship back on track.'

Last year, I met university psychology lecturer and therapist Dr Guy Mackenzie while working on a case. We'd shared a connection that was brief and intense. Nothing happened, but how close I felt to him, how attracted I was to his personality, mind and his looks, had scared me enough to tell Jeb about it.

'You told me because you were scared you were going to end up in bed with him if the chance arose again.'

'That's not how it was, Jeb.'

'However it was, Kez, you doing this, you going to spend goodness knows how long away from us to do this thing when it's not even your job is dangerous. And selfish. Really fucking selfish.'

My husband rarely swears. I used to say he never swears, not even to talk about sex, but in the past three years, I've been averaging doing at least one dangerous or outrageous thing per year that necessitates Jeb using the F-word. It's great to know I have such a positive (!) influence on the man I love.

'I have to do this, Jeb. Do you know how terrified MJ has to be for her to come to me? Pretty fucking terrified, is the answer. Last year she helped me out with the stuff I was working on. The year before that . . .' I stop talking. I don't want to bring up what happened the year before because Jeb will assume I'm blaming him. He always does. He believes that I think all this – my job at Insight, meeting Dr Mackenzie, being shot – is because of him. Because he, non-swearing, fundamentally honest man that he is, didn't tell me the truth about something huge to do with his son, my stepson Moe, the domino effect is all of this.

'Go on, say it,' Jeb goads, contempt daubed on his face and woven into his words. 'You've started so you may as well finish.'

'And the year before that she helped me out with all that stuff I got mixed up in. She didn't want to help me then, either. But the point is—'

'The point is, Kez, even if she hadn't helped you, you would still be doing it. She says something about a teenager or someone needing help and you're there!' He slams his hand on the table, making me jump. 'Right there! On the front line, ready to put yourself in harm's way. Again.'

I lower my gaze because I cannot argue with him about that.

'What would you say to someone you were giving therapy to about that?'

I continue to keep my gaze lowered, my heart sinking because I know where this is heading.

'Oh, wait a minute, weren't you actually having therapy with Dr Mackenzie to deal with this?' He leans closer to me to emphasise his point. 'I mean, you're still doing this stuff, so what was that therapy really about? Getting help so you can stop this, or having an excuse to keep on seeing—'

I stand up, scraping the chair on the kitchen floor as I push it out. 'If you're going to be like this, I'm not going to keep talking to you. Come find me when you're ready to have a serious conversation. I'm going for a shower.'

Leaving the room, I don't look back. I don't need to, to know that

THE QUIET GIRLS

Jeb is boiling mad. It's not often he gets *this* angry with me. It's not often that I walk away in the middle of a row, but I can see where this is heading and it's best to walk away before either of us starts to say more and more messed-up, long-term-damage-causing things.

Fredi

● **Record Voice Note** ▶ **Recorded: October 2025**

'I just know that everyone is going to think I'm on a bursary,' I said to Mum.

'How many times do I have to remind you?' she replied.

I mouthed as she said: 'What other people think of you is none of your business.'

It was easy for Mum to say that. Nothing fazes her. Nothing upsets her. People say all sorts of things about her, to her, in front of her and she just shrugs it off. Or laughs it off. Sometimes she laughs right in their faces, which upsets them even more. But she doesn't seem to understand what other people think *does* matter. It matters a whole lot.

Green upon green upon green was rushing past the car window as Mum drove me through the countryside towards Salisbury, where Axton Manor, the boarding school where I was about to start, was located.

This is going to be totally strange. I'm an only child so when I get in at night, the only people I really get to engage with in real life are Mum and Dad. Now I'm going to be surrounded by multiple people twenty-four–seven. That is going to be wild.

'I know that, Mum, but you don't understand what it's like for us. Once you lose aura, it's impossible to get it back.'

Mum, taking her eyes off the road for a second to glance at me, replied: 'I know I say all this because I am older than you and I learnt this the hard way, but I want you to learn all this now. I wish I'd learnt it when I was your age. I wish I'd realised that what people think can only hurt me if I let it. I mean, yes, I'm being simplistic, and it's not that simple or easy. But if you get even halfway to the point where you don't allow someone's snide remark to destroy your entire day, then you'll be so much happier.'

'Hmmm . . .' I replied, because Mum, as cool as she is, as nice as she is, doesn't get it sometimes. She really doesn't.

'I'm not talking about when it comes to bullying. Bullying is a whole different thing. I'm talking about someone saying they don't like your hair or saying you used the wrong word for something or saying you got in on a bursary or a diversity programme. It doesn't matter what they say – you know the truth. You know how hard you worked to pass the exams. You know how much you deserve to be there. You know . . .' You know that the money to pay for this comes from your mother's best friend's husband dying and him leaving you this money in his will.

'You know that Uncle Jacob would be so proud of you passing those entrance exams. Not only passing them, smashing those grade boundaries. Crashing out on them.'

'That's not what crashing out means, Mum.'

'OK. But you know what I mean. You did that. And it doesn't matter what anyone there thinks of you when you know how hard you worked. I remember reading once someone saying that sometimes you have to accept the fact that often people will never know your side of the story. So what if they think you're a bursary kid? You can tell them you're not. And you can tell them there'd be nothing wrong if you *were* a bursary kid. Scholarship or bursary doesn't mean you're less important than them.'

Mum really doesn't get it sometimes. She really doesn't. She doesn't know how things work and how some people are just better than you. No matter how much you might not want to admit it, they are better at looking good, dressing good, doing their hair good, walking, talking, *being*. Some people are just better.

'They're not, you know?' Mum said.

'Who is not what?' I asked, screwing up my face.

'No one is better than you. Just because you'd like to be able to do your hair like them or wear clothes like them or have jewellery like them, doesn't mean they're better. No one is better than you. Never forget that.'

Yeah, it's high-key freaky how Mum can know what I'm thinking and then make me see that what I'm thinking may not be the complete picture.

'Say it,' Mum said.

'Say what?'

'Say that no one is better than you.'

'Mum—' I started to protest.

'Just say it. No one is better than you.'

'No one is better than me,' I mumbled.

'Louder, for the people at the back.'

'No one is better than me,' I said a bit louder.

'Louder, for the people back in London.'

'No one is better than me,' I said louder, getting into it now.

'LOUDER, for the people we're driving towards.'

'NO ONE IS BETTER THAN ME!' I shouted.

'And again!'

'NO ONE IS BETTER THAN ME!!' I screamed.

'And don't you ever forget it!' Mum said.

We turned the corner of the motorway and suddenly the world

opened up. In front of us was a vista so green and luscious that we both took a sharp intake of breath. We didn't see this the last time we came because of getting the train to Little Buxley.

'I wish Dad could have come with us,' I said to Mum as we navigated off the motorway towards Axton Manor, through more luscious greenery, until we hit a small village called Axton Vale, with a large supermarket and a few boutiques, a deli, a greengrocer and butcher and fishmonger. There was even a small bookshop and some kind of herbal potion shop. Miss Barkway didn't drive us this way when we came on the train, so it was good to see it. She'd said there was a village about a thirty-minute walk away and made that sound really close.

'He would have loved to have come, too, but he just couldn't get out of the work he was doing in the States. As soon as he's back, he's going to come here and take you to one of the five tearooms in this village. Can you believe it? It's this tiny little village and yet it has five tearooms. Five.'

Mum may have read up on Axton Vale a bit. A big bit. Out the other side of the village, you head down a few more streets with stone cottages and large, redbrick houses with massive drives and then you find yourself on a narrow road with lots of fields, all leading you up and up towards Axton Manor.

It is *cold*. Stone *cold*. There's no other way to describe it. There are gates at the bottom of the driveway up, and a little security hut where a man in a high-vis jacket sits. You have to tell him who you're going to see before he'll open the barrier to let you in. Mum smiled at him and he grinned back, probably remembering her from last time. Mum always takes the time to speak to people and they seem to appreciate it. She sees them and, as Mum often says, people like to be seen.

Up the gentle slope towards the massive redbrick buildings, you're surrounded by lots more fields. So many fields. There's even more round the back where they used to keep the horses and the chickens. At one point, they had lambs, too. Also round the back, there are separate blocks for the sports buildings, one of which holds an Olympic-size swimming pool, netball courts and an indoor tennis court. There's an outside swimming pool as well as outside tennis courts and a running track with seating for sports days and athletics meets.

All the bedrooms in the house dorms are around the back of the main building, with their own separate but connected blocks. The main entrance that you come up to has a fountain in the middle of the beautifully landscaped lawn at the front.

The gravel sounded really loud when Mum drove over it and I cringed. The entrance is a massive archway. It's redbrick like the rest of the buildings and on the side there is a huge clock tower that has turrets at the top. Miss Barkway was standing under the archway as we pulled up and I suddenly felt sick. *Like, nah. I'm not doing this. Nah. I need to not do this.*

'You'll be OK,' Mum said because I must have looked properly scared.

Miss Barkway waved at us with both hands and had this huge smile.

Mum reached over to me, clasped her hands around mine. 'You'll be OK, I promise,' she said.

My mum is one of the cleverest people ever. She knows so much. And she's right about almost everything. Almost everything. I hope she's right about this. Because I really do need to be all right if I want to find out what happened to Mariana.

■ **End Voice Note** ⬇ **Save Recording** ↗ **Send To Private Cloud**

Kez

March 2026, Brighton

I have stormed upstairs to our en suite shower and toilet that we had installed in the box room next to our bedroom about four months ago. It wasn't necessary, but it was the kind of luxury that I preferred over expensive cars or lavish holidays. It took longer to complete than expected, it cost more money than originally quoted, but I love it in here. I love the teal tiles inside the shower and the white and chrome everywhere else. I love standing under the mahoosive shower head and having the water cascade down on me. But, most of all, I adore the final thirty seconds of my shower where I let the hot water pelt my body while I relax every muscle and breathe deeply. I just stand and relax. Empty my mind and let go.

When I step out of the shower, Jeb is holding the fluffy white towel I was about to wrap myself up in. His face tells me that his mood hasn't changed: he is still angry, furious. Most of the time he accepts the things I do as part of who I am. He says the things I do and the way I do them are 'terrifying' but he usually also says, 'I know you're going to do it anyway' and leaves it at that. This feels like the first time that he is actively pushing me to not do something. It probably isn't, but I can't remember a time when he has been this dogged about me not doing something.

Jeb isn't wearing any clothes. He obviously got into bed – he sleeps naked – then decided that finishing our argument was far more important than trying to sleep. He holds up the towel for me to walk into, a gesture of friendship, a peace offering, a suggestion that we can maybe talk calmly about this, despite his fury.

I reach out to lower the towel so I can slowly, carefully, look at his body. My eyes linger on every part of him, drinking in his dark brown skin, his sleek, defined muscles, his strong stature. I don't often get to see him like this. Unadorned. Bare.

Occasionally, when he goes to the toilet first thing in the morning or in the middle of the night, I might catch a glimpse of him, but, despite our healthy sex life, I rarely, very rarely, get to see my husband uncovered. To appreciate him without a stitch on.

Jeb is startled by me openly scrutinising his body. His gaze sweeps over me, taking in all the parts of me that are glistening with droplets of shower water.

He comes closer to me, moving slowly while I continue to assess him. He is becoming ever so slightly flabby on his strong, solid frame. And it's gorgeous. Delicious to me because I've seen his body change over time. I've watched him age and that is a privilege I don't often acknowledge. I love everything about Jeb and getting to see the different aspects of what time does to him is wondrous. Truly.

Once he is close enough, Jeb drops the towel and encircles me with one arm, pulling me close to his body. Desire floods me in that way it always does with him. Even after all these years, Jeb sometimes makes me weak with longing just by being near me. He stares down at me, the anger from earlier still there, gliding gracefully on the edges of his expression. I stare up at him, the same unwillingness to back down probably still on my face.

Without warning, Jeb jerks me around, turns me to face the large mirror over the sink.

'Open your legs,' he orders.

And a familiar thrill at the forcefulness of his demand ricochets through me.

'I said, open your legs, *now*,' he says, lowering his voice.

I do as I'm told and without hesitation, he's inside me, making me gasp at the suddenness, the slight brutalness of it. No ceremony, no foreplay, he is just inside me. He pushes me forwards, so I have to put my hands on either side of the sink, and then he places his hand on my shoulder, gripping me tight as he starts to hammer into me to release his anger.

We haven't had angry sex in an age. Haven't needed to. Our sex life has always been a bit close to the bone, often tiptoeing along that line between pleasure and pain, sometimes tipping over into that realm of pain, but rarely has it been like this. Enraged, heated, almost violent.

I grip the sink even tighter as he pummels me, and I stare at him in the mirror. I can see the frustration, the worry, the very real fear he has about losing me in his eyes. Staring into my eyes, he can see the refusal to do anything different, be anyone different because this is who I've always been. He knows who I am, has always known pretty much everything about me. And I know it makes him scared, I know it makes him angry sometimes, but I'm not going to change.

Yes, it makes me selfish.

But I wouldn't ever want him to change, I wouldn't ask him to, so he can't expect me to, either. I am who I am.

He knows this. And that's why he's fucking me like this. And that's why I am enjoying every painful pleasure-glazed thrust. We both need this release.

While his hand holding my shoulder tightens its grip, his free hand circles my clitoris, then presses in that place beside my clitoris he knows always causes me to moan loudly. I can't do that with the children just down the corridor, so I swallow my groan and he smiles, knowing how much self-control that took.

'You like that,' he whispers, moving even harder. 'You like that?'

I can't respond because of what he is doing to me. How he is teasing me as he fucks me. If I open my mouth, I'll scream the answer and he knows I can't do that. He knows I can't be as vocal as I want to be, so he eases off, gives me a chance to think he's just going to fuck me without playing with me, and just as my body is slowing into this being about him driving himself into me, he starts again, circling then pressing, pressing then circling.

I reach behind me, grab the base of his erection. He convulses, the shock of it making him stop for a moment. Our eyes lock in the mirror as I move my hand up and down, gripping him so tight I'm sure it's almost painful. He wants to cry out, but can't. And I grin at him, because now he's where I am. He starts to thrust again, each second that perfect blend of pain and pleasure for both of us, each moment filled with the argument we are now having physically.

Fredi

● **Record Voice Note** ▶ **Recorded: October 2025**

'It's a shame your husband couldn't join us today, Mrs Kingston,' Headmaster Rhodes said.

We had been taking my stuff to my room when Miss Barkway said that it was customary for the headmaster to speak to parents on the first day of term, so, even though I had missed a few weeks, he would still like to speak to us.

His office is really posh, you know? He loves his dark brown wood – it is everywhere. Desk, wall, floor. If it was me, I'd throw in a bit of light wood or white to mix it up a bit, but not this fella. We were sitting in the very soft green leather chairs opposite him at his desk.

He and Mr Osterman could not be more different. Mr Rhodes was wearing a formal tweed suit with an orange tie that had the school crest on it. His hair was thinning but still dark on top, and the sides and back were a light grey. He looked at us like he thought we should be grateful to be there.

'My husband and I are aligned on pretty much everything, so he doesn't need to be here,' Mum replied, making it clear that she wasn't grateful for anything, that she knew we deserved to be there just as much as anyone else.

'I always find it's the "pretty much" that causes the most problems,' he replied.

Rude, I thought, but Mum just smiled and said, 'We'll have to find out, won't we?'

'Winifred's entrance exam scores were some of the highest I've ever seen,' he said, opening the file in front of him. 'Over ninety in every subject. Over ninety-five in Latin, Chemistry and Biology. She is clearly a very intelligent girl.' Then he looked up and said, 'But here at Axton Manor, intelligence will only get you so far. We have a very strict code of conduct. We expect a lot of the girls. And we expect them to contribute more than they get out of the school. That ensures the school continues to be a welcoming, open place for all.'

'Sounds . . . sensible,' Mum said.

'I am confident Winifred can be very happy here,' he said. 'As long as she learns to fit in and follow the rules and commits herself to being a contributing, valuable member of the Axton family. Our girls go on to achieve great things. I hope Winifred becomes one of them.'

'So do I,' Mum replied. I could tell she was a little freaked out – at my old school nobody really cared that much. As long as you showed up, things were fine. Mostly. Here, it looked like they kept close tabs on you and they ditched you if you messed up.

That thought was more than a little scary to me right then. It was actually a little bit terrifying because it hit me for the first time, what I'd actually signed up to do.

■ **End Voice Note** ↓ **Save Recording** ↗ **Send To Private Cloud**

Kez

March 2026, Brighton

'I just need you to stop putting yourself in danger,' Jeb says to me. After the angry sex, we've had a shower together, both of us more chilled, all of our rage spent on each other's bodies. We can talk calmly now.

I pause in dabbing water off his back, sigh. 'I know you do. And I'm not knowingly putting myself in danger. I just need to do this.'

'You don't need to do this. You want to do this.'

'All right, yes, I want to do this as well as needing to do this. I went to therapy to help me deal with what I did all those years ago. But that doesn't mean I don't still feel guilty about it. Therapy can't erase what I did, nor my need to atone for it.'

'You can't atone for it by constantly putting yourself in danger.'

'I'm not constantly putting myself in danger.' I stop drying him off and come to stand in front of him. 'Why are you being like this?' I ask. 'Why won't you let this go? You usually argue with me and then accept what I'm going to do. Why is this time different?'

'Oh, I don't know, maybe it's because you were shot last year.' He lightly touches the scar on my shoulder. 'Maybe it's because it feels like every year what you do gets more extreme, more dangerous. Maybe it's because none of this is normal. And I know it's my fault. I know you wouldn't constantly be in danger if I hadn't kept all that stuff from you.' He takes the towel out of my hands. 'Maybe I can't let this go because I feel guilty every time you leave the house to go to that place because this might be the time when I lose you. When Zoey and Jonah lose you. It'll be all my fault if that happens.'

I put my arms around Jeb, gaze up at him. 'It's not your fault. It's not anyone's fault really. This is just the way things are now. I mean, Insight is full of some of the worst people in the world, but it's all right. I've made my peace with being there. It's not so bad now, you know. And, look, we got this en suite out of it. We've got financial security for the next little while. And I can basically do what I want. You don't have to feel guilty, because it's fine. It's honestly fine.'

'That's just it, Kez. The more "fine" it gets, the more like them you become. And *that*, that's not fine.'

Fredi

● **Record Voice Note** ▶ **Recorded: October 2025**

'Your room is right down the corridor from mine,' Viola told me after the meeting with Headmaster Rhodes.

We were on our way to my room, Mum carrying two of my bags and pulling one of the suitcases, while I pulled the other suitcase and carried two bags. Viola was carrying my laptop bag and my dress/suit-holder.

'You have a lot of things,' Viola commented.

'I wasn't sure what to pack,' I replied. 'I know I got the list and everything, but I wasn't sure what else I would need. I haven't stayed away from home very much, and I wasn't sure how much I can get while I'm here.'

'I know what you mean,' she said in understanding. 'Sometimes, when we summer in the south of France, it's miles to the nearest charcuterie. And forget it with clothes boutiques!'

That wasn't quite what I meant, and I didn't think she was being mean or anything, just trying to put me at ease by relaying something that she thought was relatable. I like Viola, I just think she's a bit clueless and doesn't realise that not all of us are in a position to use the word 'summer' as a verb, nor spend weeks in the south of France. I bet they have a villa or something there. I bet it's beautiful, with its own pool and immaculate bedrooms. I knew Mum would have picked up on her using 'summer' as a verb, too, and was probably imagining the same type of villa set-up.

We walked down long corridors of orange and purple carpets with the school's crest woven into them. On and on we went until we finally arrived outside number 301. My room.

'I'm in 305, just down there,' Viola said. 'I have my own room now. My mother said I need to concentrate on my GCSEs. Like I can't concentrate with other people around or something.'

I opened the brown envelope that I was given at reception. It contained the welcome booklet, conduct information, general information and school–pupil contracts as well as my keys. The room was quite big compared to some of the ones I saw on the website and the one I looked at when I came last time. It has a wardrobe, desk and chair, shelves, bed with storage underneath and large windows. There's a large mirror on the wall and behind the door are hooks, I presume, for my dressing gown and towel. By the door is a small stand for shoes.

I had a decent amount of floor space but my luggage took up more than half of it. Mum would have to take some stuff back with her.

'There's a luggage room down in the basement,' Viola said, obviously seeing my despair. 'One of the porters will come and get anything you want stored. Just email them.'

'Are there any other girls starting around now?' Mum asked Viola.

She shook her head. 'It's quite rare to join at this age.'

My anxiety ignited again like a pilot light being given a huge injection of gas – it burst up, jumping as though trying to touch the sky.

'But rare isn't never,' Viola added, as though realising exactly what I was thinking. 'And it doesn't matter when you join, they always make sure they assign you some people to show you around. And you'll have me. I am just down the hall, as I said.'

'Well, thank you, you've been so kind,' Mum said to Viola to get her to leave.

'Of course, Mrs Kingston. I hope I see you again soon. I'll see you at supper, Fredi. I'll come and knock on your door when it's time.'

'Thank you, thank you so much,' I said.

Once we were alone, Mum encircled me in a hug, rested her cheek on mine. 'I suddenly wish I could scoop you up and whisk you away back home.'

'I'll be fine,' I said to her. 'You said it yourself – I'll be fine. Nothing is going to happen to me.'

'I know, I know. I'm just being silly, that's all. But if you want to come home, just text me.'

'Mum—'

'I'm your mum so I need to say this. If you want to come home, message me and I will be here in a flash. Yes?'

'Yes.'

'Right, let's get you unpacked.'

It took us no time to recreate my bedroom in this room and when we were finished, I felt a million times better. Mum cried when she left, taking one of my suitcases with her.

I shed a couple of tears, but I stopped myself before I lost control. Instead, I sat on my bed and took out my mobile phone. I looked up at the door, checked it was definitely locked, then I called up *her* number on my phone.

I was going to find out what happened to her no matter what. No matter what.

■ **End Voice Note** ↓ **Save Recording** ↗ **Send To Private Cloud**

Part 3

Initial police report into death of Dr Angus Pemberton at Axton Manor School

On Wednesday 11 March at approximately 8 a.m., we were called to Axton Manor School for Girls to investigate the death of a 52-year-old white male who was later identified as Dr Angus Pemberton of 41 Maiden Lane, Little Buxley, Greater Salisbury.

Dr Pemberton, who was the guidance counsellor and therapist at Axton Manor, was found at the base of the school's clock tower at around 7 a.m. by a group of pupils going to co-curricular yoga classes that were taking place near that part of the school grounds.

The pupils who found the body were: Isolde 'Issy' Grenville, Astrid Barron, Paris Montgomery, Viola Hudson and Haniya Vyas. All five girls say they discovered Dr Pemberton at the same time, with Miss Hudson running to raise the alarm with the school authorities when they realised he was dead and not lying on the lawns in a drunken or drugged stupor.

All the girls were highly distressed when initially questioned, having said that Dr Pemberton was a very popular member of the school staff.

Subsequent questioning revealed more information, although all the girls remained distressed every time they were questioned.

The body was secured and that area of the school cordoned off while waiting for a forensics team. After forensics had processed the scene, an investigation commenced, which showed evidence that Dr Pemberton had likely fallen from the top of the clock tower some time before his body was discovered at 7 a.m.

The top of the clock tower was processed by the forensics team and several cigarette ends were discovered there. On questioning, most of the school body confirmed that both adults and pupils were known to use that area to smoke nicotine and sometimes cannabis. A couple of the cannabis cigarette ends retrieved that were processed had Dr Pemberton's fingerprints on them.

Without any other evidence to suggest otherwise, it was concluded that Dr Pemberton had climbed the clock tower to smoke cannabis sometime between the last time he was seen at 9 p.m. the previous evening, he lost his footing and was not discovered until early the next morning.

However, a further investigation into Dr Pemberton has been opened in relation to a missing pupil called Winifred Kingston. Miss Kingston was reported missing by the school to officers attending the death of Dr Pemberton.

Initial impressions are that Miss Kingston, unable to handle the pressure of the Axton Manor regime, ran away. She left a note, and her mother and father have confirmed that some of her favourite clothes and possessions are missing, with the bulk of her belongings remaining in her room at Axton Manor.

Her parents – a Mrs Noelle Kingston and a Mr Harry Kingston of 76 Beach Road, Wandsworth, South London – are adamant that she did not run away. Their insistence has led us to accessing her text messages. Her mobile phone has not been used since her disappearance. On checking her text messages, a whole cache of explicit messages were discovered (detailed in Appendix 1). These messages matched the ones that we discovered on Dr Pemberton's phone.

Despite her parents' insistence that their daughter was not sexually active, the sheer number of messages, going back to not long after Winifred joined the school in late October last year, suggests otherwise.

Although we investigated whether Miss Kingston might have seen Dr Pemberton before his death, this was discounted since there is evidence of Miss Kingston's phone being active in Salisbury while Dr Pemberton was still alive.

All the authorities at Axton Manor have been very helpful and the headmaster, Mr Humphrey Rhodes, was highly distressed to discover that Dr Pemberton was conducting an inappropriate relationship with one of his pupils.

He was also distressed to discover that the CCTV covering the front of the building and clock tower was not in operation in the days before Dr Pemberton's death. He has launched an investigation into why, as well as going to his school board to secure funds to upgrade and overhaul the system.

Dr Pemberton's death has been ruled an accident and the investigation has been closed. We are keen to talk to Miss Kingston and a missing-person's report has been filed.

Signed: *J Shanks*

Surname: Shanks **First name(s):** Justine

Rank: Detective Inspector

Date: Friday 13 March 2026

Fredi

● **Record Voice Note** ▶ **Recorded: October 2025**

'Miss Winifred Kingston, please come to the front.'

This was my first class on my first official day and I was being called to the front. The teacher, Mrs Lazloe, was standing impatiently by her desk. She's a tall woman, broad with a severe haircut and a face that looks like it never learnt how to smile.

I couldn't think what I'd done wrong, seeing as I just literally walked in and sat down at the only free desk in the room. I'd never been pulled to the front to be told off before – usually they let me sit in my seat while they tore strips off me.

I knew everyone was watching me as I stood up. My chair scraped on the floor and it was so loud I jumped at it. Then my legs were trembling while I moved. Mrs Lazloe's face grew angrier, her cheeks becoming flaming red the closer I got to her. I was pretty sure when I was close enough she was going to actually hit me. And I didn't even know what I'd done wrong.

'Yes, miss?' I said. She didn't hit me, but she did grab my shoulder and then spin me to face the other girls in the room. She kept her hand on my shoulder – maybe to stop me running away. There were twenty-four pairs of eyes on me and I wanted to shrink into nothingness.

'Apart from the obvious, what is wrong with this . . . *child*,' she said to the whole room. They all sat upright in their seats, staring at her and me. I wasn't sure what was happening right then, but I knew it was not good.

One of the girls who sat near the back, near where I was sitting, put up her hand.

'Yes, Miss Bayliss?' the teacher asked.

This girl with her hair pulled back into a neat bun, this 'Miss Bayliss', got to her feet and stated very loudly and clearly: 'She has her top button undone.'

My eyes flew around the room, and all of them, *every single one* of them, had their top button done up.

'Thank you, Miss Bayliss,' the teacher said.

Another hand went up. 'Yes, Miss Shanks?'

She stood up and with a small smile on her lips said, 'Her tie isn't knotted correctly and she has a chain on.' My tie was tied exactly like hers. So why was she trying to get me in trouble? And the thin gold chain was what my parents gave me for my thirteenth birthday. You can barely see it under my shirt.

'Thank you, Miss Shanks.'

Another hand went up.

'Yes, Miss Wilkerson?'

'Her hair isn't tied back.' My hair was in two afro puffs. It was not technically tied back, but it *was* neatly secured, just to the sides.

'Thank you, Miss Wilkerson.'

Another hand: 'She's wearing hoop earrings.' They were tiny little hoops that were barely there, not the huge dinnerplate-size ones I normally wore.

Another hand: 'She's wearing a ring.' It was a tiny, slim thing on my little finger.

Another hand: 'She has a bracelet on.' *Oh, come on!* You could barely see it under my sleeve.

Another hand: 'She hasn't handed in her mobile phone.' I hadn't known we had to. They just said we had to hand it in at night, I hadn't known you had to hand it in during the day, too. Who was I supposed to hand it in to? When? I read the handbook – it didn't say these specific things. They said you had to have neat uniform. You had to have neat hair. You had to have sensible shoes. You could wear demure jewellery at your teachers' discretion. And you had to hand your phone in before lights-out. I had stuck to that. I had stuck to it, but, still, instead of learning about Geography, my classmates were highlighting every little thing I had done wrong on my first day at school. Anyone would think I'd been here years and was still flouting the rules. The rules that only this lot knew about!

Traitors.

I was going to give them the side-eye every time I saw them from now on.

I had to stand a bit longer and listen to my classmates point out the crease in my jumper, the swipe of nail polish I hadn't completely removed, the wrong shade of black tights I was wearing.

At least, I thought, as they slowed down in finding my imperfections, *I've found out what they're like now. At least I won't think they'll back me up or take my side at a crucial time.* When they finished and Mrs Lazloe seemed satisfied that I'd been properly eviscerated by my classmates, I moved to return to my seat.

'Where do you think you're going?' she snapped.

'Back to my seat?' I said, hopefully.

'Get down on your knees,' she ordered.

No way. No way did this lady say what I think she said. 'Pardon me?' I asked.

'Kneel down.'

'Why?'

'Axton girls do not ask why, Miss Kingston – they do. Get down on your knees.'

No one in here was going to help me. Or tell her to stop. My whole body burning with shame, I bent my knees, lowered myself down until my kneecaps hit the ground.

'Now, girls, as you know, Miss Kingston's skirt will be the appropriate length if it touches the ground. Does it?'

They looked at me like I was the latest meme on the clock app. Peering, probing with their eyes at my hemline, at where it touched the ground. Barely.

'I don't think it does all over, does it, class?'

This woman was *SUCH* an Opp. How was she saying my skirt didn't touch the ground all over? Who said it had to touch all over? Touching the ground is touching the ground. She was just changing the rules to suit herself. I was used to that. I was used to people – teachers, especially – changing the rules to suit themselves. I didn't think it would happen here. And if it did happen, then it wouldn't happen so soon.

'What do you think, Miss Kingston? Does your skirt touch the ground?'

'Yes, miss,' I said, but didn't dare look up at her.

'Very well. I will have to give you the benefit of the doubt, this time. Do not enter my classroom again looking slovenly.'

'Yes, miss.'

'I will *not* tolerate this. Next time, Saturday detention.'

'Yes, miss.' I had to sound beaten. To be honest, I was beaten.

'Get back to your seat.'

I was still gathering myself up when Mrs Lazloe switched on the electric whiteboard and started the lesson. She didn't even wait for me to get up, let alone sit in my seat, before she started her lecture on population. She just began the lesson and expected me to hurry to my seat like nothing had happened.

I was shell-shocked. Shell-shocked. I also prayed there weren't any other teachers like that.

■ **End Voice Note** ↓ **Save Recording** ↗ **Send To Private Cloud**

● **Record Voice Note** ▶ **Recorded: October 2025**

Had to stop recording earlier to go to supper.

Anyway, where was I? Oh yeah. 'You're lucky,' Astrid, one of Viola's friends, said. We were having afternoon tea and I'd told them – with Viola's encouragement – what had happened to me. Afternoon tea is a snack served between the end of school and dinner, before you go do your co-curriculars in the common room in our house dorm. Laid out in front of us was a tea of crustless cucumber sandwiches, tiny-bite cakes and a blue ceramic pot of tea.

'How am I lucky?' I asked.

Astrid continued as she finished the morsel of sandwich in her mouth: 'Last year, she made a girl called Mariana undress in front of the whole class and then get dressed, "properly".'

'No!' I gasped.

'Erm, yes!' they all chorused.

'We thought that was the end of Lazloe. Turns out the school decided it was Mariana's fault. She was wearing the right uniform, but not in the correct way or something.'

'I am telling you, she has stuff on them. That's the only reason why she can keep doing up Miss Trunchbull and nothing happens to her,' Issy explained.

Viola's friends are nice. I met them at supper last night and they all seemed really cool. Paris, who has dark-red hair and navy-blue eyes, doesn't talk much. Astrid, with her big bouncy brown hair and pale, pale skin, is always talking too much and telling everyone what to do. Haniya has the widest smile and shiny black hair, while Issy, who has a platinum-blonde bob, always comes up with something funny to say.

They're all in Franklin house except for Viola and me. Lovelace and Franklin are next to each other and connected by an outside walkway. I was about to take a bite from the sandwich in my hand when Viola said, 'Right, put that sandwich down. We're going to sort you out.'

'But I'm hungry . . .' I protested.

'You can be fed or you can have the right uniform for school tomorrow,' Viola said.

Sighing, I put down the sandwich. Stupid Lazloe teacher. Stupid uniform.

Bad temperedly, I stood up and followed them out of the room. In Viola's room, she gave me two new pairs of tights, the right shade of black. Personally, I couldn't tell the difference, but I was not arguing. In Astrid's room, I practised tying my tie over and over and over until I could do it in under a minute perfectly. In Issy's room, we got a timetable and worked out which teachers weren't as evil, sorry, *strict* as Lazloe so I knew which days my discreet jewellery wouldn't get me in trouble. It all took longer than I expected, but by lights-out, I was completely sorted.

I sat in the dark with only my computer for light and I used my fingers to make partings in my hair. They were going to be a little crooked, but they would do for now. After I'd made the four partings in my hair, I started at the base of each section, gripping it tightly and then started to plait my hair. I worked slowly and methodically until I had carefully canerowed my hair off my face. There, Mrs Lazloe, hair off my face.

I can't believe that I've been here less than thirty-six hours and already have an enemy. But I seem to have some friends at least.

And, most importantly, they'd mentioned Mariana like they knew her. I haven't told Auntie Jacinta yet, because it doesn't seem like much. But to me it's really significant.

■ **End Voice Note** ↓ **Save Recording** ↗ **Send To Private Cloud**

Fredi

● **Record Voice Note** ▶ **Recorded: October 2025**

The past couple of weeks have flown by.

It's OK here, and I'm doing all right. Mrs Lazloe is always on my case about something and a couple of the other teachers seem to have it in for me as well, but overall things are good. It's a whole new world, though. There is so much to learn, to understand. Ritual. There is so much ritual. And you have to learn it all.

Every Sunday evening, we have a formal dinner when the weekly boarders return and Headmaster Rhodes delivers a speech to us about personal responsibility, virtue, keeping ourselves pure, remembering our future is dependent upon our eligibility. His wife always sits beside him and smiles as though she wants to chop his head off.

And his sons, who are identical twins called Garwin and Duncan, sit and stare straight ahead, clearly not wanting to be there. They live with their parents in their house right at the back of the school grounds. And there are some really sick rumours about the Rhodes boys. Apparently, every term, one of them picks a pupil and decides she's his girlfriend. He then sneaks into her room with a copied master key. I don't know what happens, but he always drops that girl the next term and finds another one the following term.

Really creepy. Viola says she's sure his parents know and just look the other way because none of the girls have complained. When I looked at her like she was out of her mind, she shrugged and said, 'I know.' Then she added: 'I asked my mum about it and she said that I didn't have to worry because they'll come nowhere near me. That I would be safe. I told her that wasn't the point, that it was still happening to other girls, but she said it was the best she could do, and that, until one of the girls came forward, nothing could be done.' Viola came closer to me and whispered, 'I told her that I'd get proof because it shouldn't be happening.'

'And what did she say to that?' I asked.

'She said I should leave it alone. She didn't want me to be hurt so I should leave it alone. She tried to make me promise to leave it alone.'

'You're not going to leave it alone?'

'I'm not going to let other girls get hurt and not try to do something. You can help me if you want.'

'OK,' I said quietly, because I couldn't say no. But I had to be careful of her. I had to be careful of everyone. If I'm going to find out what happened to Mariana, then I have to be friends with everyone but not trust anyone, fly under the radar as Uncle Jacob used to say.

'How are you going to get proof?'

'I don't know yet. I've been trying to be friendly to some of the girls, see if I can get them to talk. And I've been trying to build up a profile of which ones the Brothers Grim target. I call them that because . . . grim behaviour.'

The other tradition that could do with being ended is the clear-up for Sunday night dinner. The tradition is that the newest girls have to clear away the plates after everyone has eaten. Clear plates! After my food, I have to get up and walk to the front with six other girls. If they aren't newbies like me, they were the last to check in at the beginning of term. It's apparently to teach discipline, to remind the girls that not doing what you're supposed to do when you're supposed to do it has consequences. But I've noticed that all of us who do the clearing don't come from super-rich families, nor do we have mothers who were old girls. In other words, I don't see them making any of Viola's friends do it, even though Issy told me she didn't check in until gone midnight last term because they were late flying back from holiday.

Everyone knows that the tradition of who clears the plates away is for bursary or poor children. Of course, this makes the rumours about me being a bursary kid all the more real to some of the girls. Some of them look at me like I don't belong. Some of them whisper about me in the PE shower rooms. Some of them cough 'Betty Bursary' into their hands when I walk into a room.

I'm trying not to let it get to me. I'm trying to pretend that I don't care what they think of me, like Mum said, but it's hard. Really hard.

One of those girls who was all up telling Mrs Lazloe what was wrong with my school uniform on my first day and who calls me Betty Bursary, is called Lavinia Shanks. She is head of year in our year and everything she does has to be perfect. You're not allowed to do anything that makes her look bad, apparently.

Earlier today, during hockey, I had the ball and a clear line to score. I ran towards the goal, dribbling the ball, almost there and then I heard Lavinia shout, 'To me!'

She seriously wanted me to give her an assist. She was nowhere near the goal or in a good position. I carried on, dribbling, got around one girl, then another and I got to the goal mouth and she shouted again, 'To me!'

I seriously thought she was messing, so I took the shot. Whacked it!

It went straight in! Everyone cheered and all the girls on my team came running over to pat me on the back. All except Lavinia and her two friends. They looked really angry, but I didn't care. What sort of person cares about their glory over the team?

Viola told me later to be careful because Lavinia can be really vicious, but there's not a lot I can do about that. I'll just have to see what happens next on that score.

Despite all those things, I like it here. I miss Mum and Dad more than I thought I would. I speak to them every other night before I hand my phone in. I miss Bev and Carina, of course. Especially since Marvin has made it official and asked Bev out. The four of them – Bev and Marvin, Carina and Dexter – go out together all the time. It's kind of weird that life is going on without me back home. But good, too, because I don't want anyone to be unhappy without me there.

I forget, sometimes, that I'm here for two purposes. I get into the groove of life here and then I forget I'm supposed to be finding out about Mariana, too. Then I feel bad that I'm having a good time here when she's gone. But, anyway, that's what it's like here. Overall, I like it. I like it a lot.

■ **End Voice Note** ↓ **Save Recording** ↗ **Send To Private Cloud**

Part 4

MISSING

Winifred 'Fredi' Kingston

Have you seen this girl?

Police are appealing for help in the search for missing teenager Winifred Kingston.

Winifred (15), 'Fredi' to her friends, was last seen at Axton Manor school in Axton Vale on the morning of Tuesday 10 March, and has not been in contact with her friends or family since.

Fredi is described as being Black, 5ft 4in, of slim build with braided black hair. She was last seen in her orange and purple school uniform, but could be wearing something different by now.

Officers are concerned for her wellbeing and welfare. Anyone with any information on her whereabouts or if you have spotted her please contact Salisbury area police on the number below.

Kez

April 2026, Brighton

It's only just hit me that I won't be seeing my children for at least two weeks, most likely longer. I'm about to leave to drive up to Axton Vale, a place not far from Salisbury. I've never been near there in my life although I did once kiss a guy from Salisbury when I was in college. Which has nothing to do with anything. Yup, this is why people look at me strange.

It's only now that I am packed up to go, with the children in their school uniforms, that I realise I won't see them for months, possibly. During the summer months, Zoey and Jonah go to stay with my parents for two weeks and then Jeb's parents for two weeks so that we can finish up at work. Then we spend the rest of the holidays together. Technically, I don't see them for four weeks. But that is different to this. This time, they will be carrying on with normal life while I am not here. Jeb will be making breakfast and dinner, filling water bottles, doing backpack book checks, timetable wrangling, taking them to extra-curricular classes, doing the laundry, checking homework, etc., etc., etc. They will be essentially living the life they would have had if I hadn't survived either of the life-threatening situations I've been in. That thought makes me grab them both for another hug while I watch them eat breakfast. And I grab them again for a hug while they put on coats and do one last bag check.

That's one hug too far, apparently, because Jonah asks testily: 'Are you going to get shot again, Mum? Is that why you're being like this?'

I look to Jeb, who, rather than back me up, raises his eyebrows and fixes his face as though he'd quite like to know the answer to that, too. I look to Zoey who is all ears, as well.

'I am not going to get shot again,' I state very clearly. 'I am not going to put myself in danger. This is just a job that I have to do working away from home. Isn't that right, Jeb?'

'I don't know, is it?' he replies, the treacherous toad. He's got a lot to say for a man who claims to enjoy having sex with me. I plan on telling him that when the children have gone to school.

'Mum, you know how proud we are of you, don't you?' Zoey says, seeming to take control of a fast-deteriorating situation in the way that Zoey does. I look at my tall daughter and think of MJ, navigating a reality where her daughter hates her. I don't know how I would cope if Zoey hated me. I mean, I know she has her moments when she absolutely dislikes me or disagrees with me or feels decidedly disgruntled, but I don't think she's ever truly hated me. Or that those moments last very long. Maybe because we haven't come up against anything that could cause deep, lasting conflict? She goes to parties, but keeps in touch and comes home well before her 11.30 curfew. She's hung out with boys, but sees all of them as friends not potential partners. She's expressed no interest in girls as sexual partners and she's already written up her own GCSE revision timetable – for next year. I have no real tension with my daughter, although I know that could change.

'As people who are proud of you, we do need to mention that things don't always go to plan and you can find yourself in, shall we say, less than ideal situations,' Zoey says. 'Ergo, please don't get hurt and please try not to get into situations where people might be compelled to try to hurt you.'

'What she means is, try not to – what does Auntie Remi call it? – "read people for filth and then smile",' Jonah rather helpfully clarifies. 'Don't get me wrong – we're not saying don't be you.'

'We're just saying don't be too much of you,' Zoey concludes.

I turn to Jeb. 'You got anything to add?' I ask.

'No, no, I think they've pretty much covered it,' my husband says.

'Well, thank you all for that,' I say. 'I will keep it in mind. Although it's not going to be a problem because I'm a really nice person and no one will want to hurt me.'

It's almost choreographed, the way they fall about howling with laughter and clutching each other.

'Fine,' I say to them sourly. 'Message received and understood. No filth-reading, no smiling afterwards if any filth-reading does take place.'

Zoey stops laughing first and comes to me, engulfs me in a hug. 'I'll miss you, Mama. Love you.'

Jonah is next. He comes to me, engulfs me in an even bigger hug since he is now as tall as Zoey and much taller than me. He's also been going to the gym with his friends so his muscles are developing. 'I'll miss you, too, Mama,' he says. 'Especially your chefing because Dad's skills are mid at best.'

'I heard that,' Jeb says.

'You were meant to,' Jonah replies.

My eyes well up. I'm going to miss this. This banal, everyday ribbing of each other we do. This being normal and being ordinary is the foundation of our lives. How will I be if I don't have this to come home to every night? If I'm not reset for the extraordinariness of my working life by walking through that door every night to be Jonah and Zoey's mother, Jeb's wife?

'Oh man, the tears are starting,' Jonah says.

'Don't acknowledge it, don't look directly at them and they may go away,' Zoey replies.

'I love you, too,' I say to them. 'And I know you're all going to be crying your eyes out tonight when I'm not here. It'll be Noah's flood in everyone's rooms tonight, I know it.'

'Let her have this one,' Zoey says, generously.

'Yeah, allow it,' Jonah agrees.

I love that my children know how to read me for filth because I know it's their way of telling me they love me.

Fredi

● **Record Voice Note** ▶ **Recorded: November 2025**

I think I heard them before I was actually aware of what was happening.

It was the sound of the key in the lock from the other side, the handle turning and the door being carefully pushed open, accompanied by the soft steps of several pairs of feet coming into my room. And then their hands were on me, grabbing me, pulling me, dragging me out of bed.

I wasn't going down like that, so, almost automatically, I hit out. My fist connected with something solid and the owner of the solid thing loudly exclaimed, 'OW!'

I was about to hit out again when two people grabbed my arms and hauled me out of bed. As I came out of the covers, I kicked out, and my foot caught something soft this time, followed by another 'OW!'

'Stop it,' someone hissed. 'We're not going to hurt you.'

'Don't tell her that,' someone else hissed.

'Especially not now,' the first 'OW!' voice said.

'Just stop it. We're not going to hurt you.'

Even though I wanted to keep fighting, I figured it would be over quicker if I stopped and found out what they wanted. So I did. I stopped, allowed the voices and dark shapes to put my feet on the ground, wrap a blindfold around my eyes and lead me out of my room.

I was scared. Deep, deep scared. I'm not going to pretend I wasn't. They said they weren't going to hurt me, but they would say that, wouldn't they?

We went left out of my room, them holding on to my shoulders, pushing me forwards. We walked through the door at the end of the corridor, and down the stairs to the ground floor. I waited for them to open the front door to the dorm, but instead they pushed me to go right towards where the door marked 'private' was. That's the door to the basement. I heard them unlock that door, and suddenly I was hit with a smell of damp. Cold. Definitely the basement.

I felt my way down the stairs, them guiding me until we hit the stone floor at the bottom of the staircase. The place felt huge, cavernous. And suddenly I was really, really scared. If they did something to me or left me down here, no one would find me for ages.

They pushed me forwards and then let me go.

'Get down on your knees,' one of them said. All their voices were muffled, so I didn't recognise who it was. I could understand what she was saying, but I couldn't make out anything identifying in her voice.

'I'm low-key not going to do that,' I replied. I was scared, but they didn't need to know that.

'We said we wouldn't hurt you, but only if you do as we say.'

'I'm not going to do that,' I said again. 'And, not being funny, but this doesn't scare me – I grew up in South London, this is how we say hello.'

It went really quiet all of a sudden. I don't think they knew what to do. I don't think anyone knew how to respond when someone wouldn't just do as they were told.

'Stay standing,' someone else eventually said. 'It doesn't matter.'

Another pair of hands took the blindfold off, and in the low light of the basement I could see eight figures, all of them in dark robes with their hoods up. They all had shiny silver fox masks that totally covered their faces.

'We are Platinum,' they all said at the same time. 'We are total. We are one. We are everything.'

The way they were speaking at the same time was proper creepy, and made me quiver inside.

'What do you want with me?' I demanded, hiding my fear.

One of them stepped forwards. 'We are Platinum. We decide who does what. Who is top and who is not. You are not. You must learn your place.'

'Learn my place? What place is that?'

Another one stepped forwards and the other stepped back. 'We are Platinum. You didn't pass to someone when told to today. Don't do that again.'

'All this because of a pass that didn't happen? Are you serious?'

Another one stepped forward while the other stepped back. 'We are Platinum. We decide who scores. Who wins. Who has to stay in their place.'

Even though they were creeping me the hell out, I said: 'I'm not going to stop being me because you have told me to. Who even are you? I know you are Platinum and all that, but that doesn't mean shit to me. It might mean something to everyone else around here, but, like I said, I'm from South London! I don't know about your weird rituals and that. So you can take it in turns to talk in one sentence all you like, but it ain't going to make a difference to me.' I sounded so brave and convincing.

The one in front stepped back and they all said: 'We are Platinum.

There are consequences for those who go against us. We are Platinum. We do not accept dissent. We punish those who do not comply.' They all stepped forwards. 'We hurt those who do not comply.'

Of course then I started thinking about Mariana. Is this what happened to her? I couldn't see her complying. I couldn't see her not just laughing in their stupid masked faces. Did they hurt her?

'Did you hurt Mariana?' I asked. They looked at each other, shocked, surprised that I was asking about her. At that moment, I knew for sure that they had done something to her. 'Did you?' I asked again.

'We are Platinum,' they said. 'We hurt those who do not comply.'

I was really scared then. Scared for Mariana.

'Do you understand?' they said.

I nodded. I did understand. They were dangerous. They'd harmed Mariana. They were going to harm me if I didn't do what they said.

Now that I know she definitely didn't just run away because she was upset over a boy, I'm scared about what all of this means for Mariana. What if she ran away because they hurt or they threatened to hurt her. *Threatened to kill her?* What if she didn't run away at all and instead they did something to her?

This is my first proper clue, even though I've kind of shown my hand now. They now know I know Mariana, so they'll be guarded and gathering more clues will be much more difficult. I am going to have to lie low until I can find out what they did. What they are capable of. To gather more clues, I have to pretend I am going to comply for a while and then defy them to get them to come for me again at some point.

The problem is, I think the next time they do come for me, it'll be much more dangerous than this.

■ **End Voice Note** ↓ **Save Recording** ↗ **Send To Private Cloud**

Kez

April 2026, Axton Manor

The drive here was pleasant enough. I'm not good at driving long distances, so Jeb generally does it when we travel far away from home. If I go away on my own, I generally get the train. But for this, I need to be able to make a quick getaway and the distance from the school to the nearest train station is too far to rely on local taxis or lifts.

I had been open mouthed when I approached Axton Manor, the sheer vastness of it taking my breath away. The grounds seem to go on for ever and the redbrick building at the centre of the land is a huge, stately-home-type structure that instantly tells me two things: the place is most likely haunted and the people inside are probably hiding many, *many* secrets.

I had looked at pictures of the place during my research, but the website didn't do the scale of it any justice. I feel like I am arriving on the movie location set of a quirky British rom-com about upper-class people with pockets of cash but messed-up love lives.

Axton Manor boasts tennis courts, indoor and outdoor swimming pools, netball and basketball courts, a cricket pitch or two, hockey and football fields. It also has an athletics race track, as well as stables that are no longer used. Behind their property is an area of thick woodland vegetation that leads down to the village. Add in a few shops and you would never have to leave this place. Which is kind of comforting and kind of terrifying at the same time.

'Please take a seat, Miss Lanyon,' the headteacher, Mr Humphrey Rhodes, says to me, indicating to one of the chairs on the opposite side of the desk to his seat.

I am getting strong 'will hand you a detention and call your parents for the smallest infarction' vibes from him and I have to remind myself that I am an adult. That even if he *did* set me detention, I wouldn't actually have to show up for it. Although of course I would show up. And on time, too, because that's how I was brainwashed from a young age. I have never had a school detention. I was a total swot – one of the quiet girls whose only detention came from class punishment. But I could always imagine what it felt like, especially since my friends, Janey and Jane (yes, there was a lot of confusion) were always in trouble. Mostly through no fault of their own – they had teachers who seemed determined to make sure they didn't pass their GCSEs.

I take the chair he gestures to, placing my bag and laptop bag on the other seat.

'I am so . . . unhappy and disappointed to be meeting you under these circumstances, Miss Lanyon,' he says. I cringe inside at him calling me 'Miss' again. From kids I'd understand, but from a grown-ass man who has just hired me? Who read my CV, who called Dennis to get a reference and signed off all the paperwork for me to work here? Not so understandable. And yet, if I correct him, especially when he's alluding to the circumstances that have brought me here in the first place, I'll seem petty and heartless. It seems a small thing, but it is significant. I don't care in an abstract sense what anyone calls me, but in this situation, when I am trying to establish myself as a worthy replacement for Dr Pemberton, I do not need a man who clearly looks down on women to be classifying me for others. Especially when I suspect this is a test.

'I'm sorry to interrupt, Mr Rhodes, but I go by the title "Doctor". There is nothing wrong with the title "Miss", to be clear, it's just my name is Dr Lanyon.'

'Of course, of course,' he says. 'Dr Lanyon.' He smiles warmly at me, confirming that it was, in fact, a test, a way of scoping me out, trying to work out who I am by pushing my boundaries, seeing how strong they are. Great. Not. This means he will be trying to interfere and insert himself into whatever I do at every turn.

'I wish we had met under better circumstances,' he says. 'These are unprecedented times. And the children and staff are navigating it as best they can. Your presence will be just what they and I need to help them.'

'Yes, it must be very difficult for everyone. This will be the first experience with death a lot of them will have. It will take a while, but I think I can help get people on the road to recovery until you can find a permanent school therapist.'

'Yes, my thoughts exactly. Now, how would you like this to work?'

'I was thinking of allowing my door to be open to anyone who needs to talk, holding group therapy sessions and scheduling individual sessions with those who were seeing Dr Pemberton when he died.'

'Sounds very sensible and workable. Will you be debriefing me nightly or every other evening?'

Excuse me, what? I want to say but don't. 'I'm not sure I understand the question?' I reply instead.

'Dr Lanyon, this school, the pupils, the staff are my life. Everything I do, I do for them. I need to know what they're feeling, thinking, in order to work out how best to care for them.'

'I do understand what you are saying, but I won't be able to tell you anything said to me in confidence, Mr Rhodes. Surely you know that? I am a registered psychotherapist. People talk to me because they believe everything they tell me will stay confidential. The only time I would be forced to share what is talked about is in a situation when someone is in immediate or imminent danger to themselves or others. Then, I am obliged to inform the relevant emergency authorities. Not you, I'm afraid.'

This causes him to frown at me, but also gives me an insight into how things work here. If he is expecting this, then it might be the case that my predecessor, the man who was killed, was doing it. It might be one of the reasons why he was killed. People really will go to extremes to keep their secrets, and to hurt those who betray those secrets.

'I'm afraid I'm going to have to insist,' he says.

I blink in surprise. *Insist?* I don't think anyone has ever said that to me. Not as a child, definitely not as an adult. This is what the boundary testing before was about: he knew what my name was, he was just trying to work out how to get what he wants from me. Dennis is the master at this, expert at very quickly assessing how to get what he wants from someone, but I don't think even Dennis would so overtly and immediately assert authority over someone he doesn't know.

The phone on his desk rings, cutting into the moment like an axe hacking apart a tree trunk. His face relaxes into a charming smile, all hint of the man insisting I do as he wishes gone. He raises the receiver.

'Oh, yes, yes,' he says, visibly brightening and delighting at what the person on the other end of the phone says. 'Send him in. Thank you.'

What's this now? I wonder as Mr Rhodes stands.

'Your supervisor is here,' he says gleefully.

My what? I don't get up from my seat when the door opens and Mr Rhodes goes to meet the person as they enter the room.

'Hello!' Mr Rhodes proclaims with such happiness you'd think his best friend had just walked in. I suppose he will be his best friend if he will help Rhodes pressurise me to do what Rhodes wants me to. 'I was just explaining to Miss Lanyon that she has been sent a supervisor, which I think will make things a lot smoother in these circumstances.'

I get to my feet, ready to fight. It's going to be difficult enough doing this, but having to answer to someone who thinks they are in charge of me will add a new, unnecessary and unwelcome layer of stress. I turn with a 'don't mess with me' look on my face then nearly fall over when Mr Rhodes says, 'Miss Lanyon, meet your supervisor, Dr Guy Mackenzie.'

Fredi

● **Record Voice Note** ▶ **Recorded: November 2025**

I asked to talk to Viola in her room earlier.

She looked really alarmed. 'What's the matter?' she asked when I came in. She sat on her bed and pointed for me to sit on her desk chair.

I was taking a big risk here, but I wanted to know what was going on and I figured she was the one most likely to tell me. 'Can I trust you?' I asked.

'Yes, of course. You're my best friend, of course you can trust me.'

I was a bit . . . confused? 'I'm your best friend?'

'Yes. You're my favourite person here. I love the others, but you're my most favourite. I really wanted to be your friend when you came to look around. And I was so excited when you came here.'

I was not expecting that at all. But it made me trust her because I didn't think she would lie to me if she liked me.

'A couple of weeks ago, I had a visit from The Platinum.'

No cap, Viola went straight up white as anything. Proper white, like someone had scared her or something. 'Did they hurt you?' she asked quietly.

'No, but they said they would if I didn't do what they wanted. Who are they?'

'They're like the secret police of Axton,' she said. 'If you step out of line, they make sure that you step back into line. It's not that bad, they don't do that much stuff to you if you upset them. It's the Quiet Girls you have to be really scared of.'

'The Quiet Girls?'

'They're like a secret society who are in charge and they make all the decisions about everything that happens here. Like who is popular and who isn't. They decide things like Lavinia Shanks getting to be head girl of our year and stuff like that. I mean, it's a vote and it all looks above board, but if they decide something you have to go along with it. The Platinum makes sure that everyone does what the Quiet Girls decide.'

'And everyone just goes along with it?'

'You kind of have to. They're in control and they will send The Platinum after you if you don't go along with them. That's why I said to be careful of Lavinia. She's one of their favourites. I don't know if she's a Quiet Girl or just part of The Platinum, but she always gets what she wants, so I guess she's part of something.'

'Why are they called the Quiet Girls?'

'Because it's a secret society? I don't know. But I do know that if they decide they hate you, they make your life really miserable until you leave or try to harm yourself.'

'How do you become a Quiet Girl?'

'I think your mother had to be one? I think my mother was one. But I'm not sure. The Platinum came to me one night and took me to see them.'

'What? Really? What had you done?'

'Nothing. They just took me and said that I was being recruited into being a Quiet Girl.'

My heart stopped dead in my chest. I was talking to one of them? How could I be so stupid? Of course she was going to be one of them – her mother and grandmother went here. That's a bloodline thing that would mean of course she was going to be part of the shadow people who ran the place.

'I didn't do it,' Viola said quickly. 'I wanted nothing to do with it. You have to do all these crazy things to prove your loyalty. I told them no thank you. They said I didn't get to say no to them. And I said yes I did. I said I didn't want to be a Quiet Girl. And if they kept pushing me I would tell my mother to have a word because I was pretty sure she was one of the original Quiet Girls and they didn't want to cross her. Probably the only time I've used my mother's name and reputation like that.'

'And they just left you alone?'

She shrugged. 'Mostly. I mean, sometimes someone will have a go at me on the netball court or in hockey, and I think it's because of that.'

'Do you have any idea who is and isn't a Quiet Girl?'

'I have my suspicions. But I don't think or talk about it, because if it's one of my friends I don't want to stop being friends with them.'

That made me realise that I had to be careful of the other girls. That was Viola straight up telling me that one or more of her friends were Quiet Girls. Maybe that's why she thought of me as her best friend? Because she knew for sure I wasn't one of them?

'You have to be careful, though, Fredi,' Viola said, all serious. 'You can't go around asking questions about them. Don't talk about them at all. And you have to do what they say. If The Platinum tell you to do something, then do it. Please. I've seen what they're capable of. I don't want anything to happen to you.'

The way she said that gave me goosebumps all over my body. I knew she was serious. And I knew that this was all tied up with what happened to Mariana. It definitely was. But if Auntie Jacinta knew about The Platinum and the Quiet Girls, then why didn't she tell me? Why?

■ **End Voice Note** ↓ **Save Recording** ↗ **Send To Private Cloud**

Kez

April 2026, Axton Manor

'Do you two know each other?' Mr Rhodes asks when Mac settles himself in the chair next to mine after I have removed my belongings from it. He is asking this because, instead of saying hello just now, we'd both simply stared at each other, then we had come to life at the exact same time, both stuck out our hands and shook while saying, 'Oh. Hi. How are you?'

To this question from Mr Rhodes, we both hesitate, unsure what to say, what to admit. I mean, I can't exactly say: 'This is the man who I confessed to my husband I had feelings for a while back', can I? And he can't exactly say: 'This is the woman who I had to stop working with because I told her I'd fallen for her', can he?

'How well can you ever really know anyone?' Mac and I both say at the same time. The exact same time. I cringe. I haven't seen or spoken to him in nearly six months and yet we're still like this; the bullshit between us, the connection where I see myself in him and he sees himself in me, hasn't stopped. Mr Rhodes looks from Mac to me, then back to Mac, trying to work out what is going on.

'Years ago, when Dr Lanyon worked in London, I used to refer patients I felt I couldn't adequately help to her. She is very experienced and capable.'

Mr Rhodes can tell there is more to it than that. It would be obvious to someone without an ounce of empathy in their body that there is more to our association than that, let alone to someone like this man, who actively seeks out information on people so he can work out quite quickly which buttons to press.

'We also came across each other recently in Brighton. Professionally speaking,' I add.

'Well, that's going to be very helpful,' Mr Rhodes states, even though he is a little less happy now that I and 'the supervisor' already have an outside connection. It's harder to play two people against each other if they're likely to talk to each other away from you. 'As I was just explaining to Miss Lanyon—'

'Dr Lanyon,' Mac interrupts. 'She's Dr Lanyon.'

Mac's boundary checked and confirmed. 'Apologies, as I was just explaining to Dr Lanyon, I will need her to keep me apprised of what is talked about in the meetings she has with pupils and staff. I have a duty of care to each and every one of them, and Dr Pemberton, who, unfortunately, passed away, understood that. He welcomed the help I could give him in treating and counselling the pupils with their problems. You do not maintain a position like mine without knowing a thing or two about children. Girls, in particular. I have two children of my own. I have significant insight into the workings of young minds. Dr Pemberton welcomed that input, especially since he was a fatherless bachelor.'

The number of red flags Mr Rhodes has just hoisted with what he said are almost too many to count. 'And what did Dr Lanyon say when you told her this?' Mac asks. His voice has an edge to it that I know is because he wants to scream at this man, while finding a way to retrospectively have Pemberton struck off.

'We were in the middle of discussing the matter when you arrived. I feel it important that Dr Lanyon keeps me apprised on pupils' progress and the matters that concern them. Don't you agree, Dr Mackenzie?'

'I think you misunderstand what therapy is in these circumstances,' Mac says, reasonably. 'Dr Lanyon is here to pour oil on troubled waters. She is here to offer assistance and insight into what will be a devastating event for all concerned. She has to have those she talks to trust her. And, in order to secure that trust, everyone has to know what they say is confidential. She won't even be able to tell me the details of what they say. She can only give me a broad outline and ask for my advice if she doesn't know what to do.'

'You're her supervisor, surely—'

'I'm not her supervisor in the sense of telling her what to do. Nor ordering her to tell me what she's been talking about, I'm more of a back-up? A sounding board. I have to be here because these are intense times, so Dr Lanyon will need more regular support – ordinarily, I would see someone I am supervising once a week.'

Mr Rhodes is heartbroken, truly devastated that Mac isn't the ally he thought he would be. That he hasn't joined his little gang and won't be giving him access to his pupils' minds like the previous fella did. But I can see this isn't over. He isn't giving up that easy, people like him never do.

He stands. 'It's been a pleasure,' he says, clearly dismissing us. Probably so he can rage in private at being scuppered at this stage, before he composes himself and finds another way in. 'My assistant, Miss Barkway, will show you to your rooms. We decided against housing you in one of the apartments because we want you to be seen as members of our family. I'm sure you'll understand.'

Understand? Understand me being nearly fifty and having to shower with teen girls and eat in a dining hall? *Understand?*

'Your rooms are en suites,' he adds, obviously seeing my distress, 'with limited kitchen facilities.'

'Wow, thank goodness,' Mac says with a laugh.

'Yeah, thank goodness,' I add. Now I just have to deal with what this guy is doing here.

There's a knock at the door and without waiting for an invitation to enter, the door opens and in bustles a woman who is clearly Mrs Rhodes. She wears a skirt suit in the same tweed as the headmaster, but her long blonde-brown hair, streaked stylishly with grey is rolled away from her face into a chignon at the nape of her neck. She wears sensible lace-up brown shoes and long orange and purple socks that, I guess, are Axton Manor sports socks. In her hands she carries a large platter of cake slices that smell like freshly baked banana bread.

Rhodes's face changes from imperious to highly irritated, he just about stops himself rolling his eyes.

'Only me!' his wife trills, with Miss Barkway standing behind her, looking as irritated as Rhodes. 'I thought I would drop by and bring you some banana bread.' She turns to Mac and me. 'He became quite partial to it during the first part of 2020, when everyone was making it online.' She grins at us and I have a feeling she isn't here by accident. She wanted to get a look at us, but needed an excuse, because – from the look on his face – her husband forbade her from coming anywhere near here. 'Oh, hello. How rude of me to talk about banana bread before I have even introduced myself.' She deftly transfers the plate to her left hand and then holds out her right hand to Mac first. 'Victoria Rhodes, headmaster's wife, for my sins,' she says with a huge grin. She clearly takes pride in her role.

'Guy Mackenzie,' Mac says, shaking her hand and giving her an unexpectedly flirtatious smile. Rhodes notices and his face draws in, obviously marking this down as something to use against Mac at a later date.

She then offers her hand to me. 'Victoria Rhodes.'

'Kez Lanyon.'

'Pleased to meet you.'

Rhodes, through gritted teeth, says: 'If you're quite finished, *Victoria*, Dr Mackenzie and Miss Lanyon need to be settling into their rooms.'

Mrs Rhodes looks sheepish, as though she was about to launch into a big conversation. I wonder what it's like being a headmaster's wife in a school like this. Your husband never really leaves his job because he lives at work. Does she have a job? Or does she make banana bread and find excuses to come and meet the new people who show up?

I don't really have time to work that out right now – I have to deal with this man who has popped up to, it seems, cause me trouble.

'What the hell are you doing here?' I say to Mac when we arrive at my car, parked next to his car, as it turns out. I have waited until we are away from other people to turn on him so there is less chance of being overheard.

'And hello to you, too.'

'Don't start. What are you doing here?'

'Didn't you hear me? I'm here to provide you with back-up.'

'What? How did you even know . . .' My words are swallowed up by a giant globule of realisation that has just dropped on me from a great height.

'Dennis Chambers sent me,' Mac says, confirming what I've just worked out. 'He said you were in a potentially dangerous situation and would most likely need back-up.'

I knew Dennis was going to get back at me for telling him rather than asking him to do this, but I had no idea his revenge would be so immediate and so devious.

'And you just couldn't say no, huh?' I replied.

'Say no to spending an unspecified amount of time in close proximity to the woman with whom I've had the most intense emotional, physical and mental attraction I've ever experienced? Not even I'm that much of a martyr.'

Outlining the flippancy of Mac's words are the very real streaks of his pain. Last year, I went to see him so he could become my therapist. I thought it was the best way to stop the emotional connection that was developing between us in its tracks. Professionalise our relationship so nothing could possibly happen. And I needed help. I needed to face up to my past, finally own my stuff. And because of what had happened with Brian, there were very few people with whom I could talk openly and honestly. Mac was one of those people. And he helped me. The ghosts that haunted me stopped shouting at me as much, they would often sit in a corner of my mind, *there* but unobtrusive, *there* but quiet. *Quiet.* And I could, for the most part, deal with quiet. When the voices of my past were quiet, I could function.

Six months ago, after one of our sessions, Mac told me that he couldn't be my therapist any more because he couldn't be around me any more. His supervising therapist had confirmed what he already knew – he had to take a break from seeing me for his own wellbeing. Jeb called me fucking selfish the other day and I had been extremely selfish with Mac. Unfair and selfish. I didn't mean to be, I didn't intend to cause him anguish, but I had. And I regret doing that because I cared about him. *Care* about him. He's one of the nicest people I've ever met and the fact I caused him pain still makes me ashamed. I went to see him to put us both in a better place and instead it had made him feel worse.

'I can't let you do this,' I state, firmly and decisively. 'Ethically, as a therapist, I can't let you do this. Emotionally, as your sort of friend, I can't let you do this.'

'Chillax, as the youths say,' he says with a massive grin. He puts his hand on my shoulder, gently squeezes. 'I'm seeing someone, it is all good.' He takes his hand away, slowly, his fingers lingering on my body a fraction too long for that touch to be purely platonic.

'Seeing someone as in . . . ?' I ask.

'As in dating someone. Sorry, should have realised you might think I need therapy to get over you. I didn't – and in fact, don't – need therapy for that. Other things, yes, but not that. I mean I am seeing someone as in I am dating someone.'

I stare at him and he stares back unabashed. I don't believe him. Simple as that. I don't believe him. When I was seeing him for therapy, I remember realising that he was dating someone. I could just tell. He started to dress a little better, used more expensive aftershave, glowed. Around the time he stopped dating that person, he decided he couldn't see me any longer. He has none of that glow-up right now. He seems ordinary and normal, not like a man who is in love or in the first throes of a relationship. But how can I dispute it?

'Are you really seeing someone?' I ask, because I know he'll tell me the truth if I ask directly.

'Do you really want me to answer that?' he replies.

Of course I don't. I would love to have him here as back-up. I would love to have him here, full stop. I like being around Mac. I love being around him, actually. I hate myself for admitting that, but I do. He makes me laugh, he makes me feel good, in a completely different way to Jeb. Of course I don't want him to admit he isn't seeing someone because that will mean I have to send him away. 'Yes,' I say decisively. 'Yes, I want you to answer that question honestly.'

He crosses his arms across his body, fixes me with his steady blue gaze behind his glasses. 'Well then, yes, I am seeing someone,' he eventually admits. 'You do not have to worry about me.'

'All right,' I say. 'I guess you're staying, then.'

'It wouldn't make any difference even if I wasn't dating someone, Kez, you do realise that, don't you?' he says. 'I've accepted this job, I have to go where I am sent, do as I am told.'

'You mean . . . ?'

He nods.

He means that by taking this job he is essentially working back in the intelligence services, something he walked away from many, many years ago.

'But why?'

'Why do you think?' he replies, reaching into his trouser pockets for his car keys and opening the boot of his car. 'Why do you think?'

Kez

April 2026, Axton Manor

My school lunches were never like this. Some of the restaurants I go to don't serve food this good. And the surroundings . . . I could never have conceived of something like this when I was at school. This is a real reminder that MJ and I are from completely different worlds.

We are in the main dining hall, called the Major Dining Room, with long tables – where up to twenty children can sit on either side – set out in long rows across the honey-wood parquet floors. The ceilings are high, vaulted with dark wood beams, and in between the beams beautiful intricate mosaic tiling of blue and red and cream tiles display a design that is repeated along the ceiling and comes down to about the top third of the wall. Wood panelling rises from the bottom third of the wall to meet redbrick masonry. The full length of this giant hall there are framed pictures of, I guess, founders and alumni, since some of the pictures are photographs rather than paintings. Giant, curved-topped stained-glass windows allow light to come in, while wall lights cast more illumination across the room. At the midway point, there is a lectern, where, I guess, the headteacher sometimes makes speeches. At one end of the Major Dining Room is a large, wooden buffet bar, groaning with every choice possible for different salad and cold meal and drink choices that children could want for lunch. At the opposite end, set at the bottom of the tables for the pupils, are several smaller square tables for about eight people, where the staff and teachers sit.

When I walked in I stopped and stared – I couldn't help myself. I don't think I've ever been in a place this grand that is inhabited. Museums, stately homes and the like, yes, but nothing like this. Children come here and think that living like this is normal. As I say, MJ and I could not have had more different upbringings if we tried. I understand a little more now where her sense of entitlement comes from. If you grow up with this, why wouldn't you expect this sort of thing to continue your whole life? Why wouldn't you just not understand people who tried to tell you that all of this isn't real life for the vast majority of those who make up the rest of the population? I knew this was how people like MJ thought in an abstract sense, but this is all putting it into context. This is all showing me that you have to be someone pretty incredible to not be swayed and influenced by living like this. And what of the working-class children? What of the poor children who came to live like this for forty weeks of the year and then had to go back to their real life? To their house the size of the house I grew up in, which was a three-bed terrace in South London, which was pretty darn large compared to most of the houses my friends grew up in. Even then, I don't know how I would have squared that circle in my head, the difference in lifestyles that were both essential parts of my life.

Mac and I have been issued staff lanyards that we wear around our necks. This allows us to eat meals and access most areas. Some areas are for resident teaching staff only. We do not have access to those areas even though, technically, we are resident and Mac is officially a psychology teacher. We take our trays to the teachers' area of the dining hall, me still in wonderment at the place.

'This is like nowhere I've ever eaten,' I tell him as we settle down and I stare at the food mounded on my plate in front of me. I'd seen the range of things on offer and panicked! I'd never had so much choice in my life and I just . . . took everything I liked the look of. As it turned out, I liked the look of a lot of things. I glance at Mac's plate. He's done the same.

'You'd think I'd be used to this, having gone to Cambridge and being in surroundings like this for four years and everything. But, in these situations, it's really hard for my working-class roots not to panic and think I don't belong. Or panic because I remember the nights we went to bed hungry when I was a child, so I want to grab as much as I can now. It's ludicrous.'

'Not ludicrous. I had the same feelings, the same experiences growing up. It's just who we are and where we come from, I think.'

'How are you planning on going about this, then?' he asks.

I am holding my fork, poised, trying to work out where to begin with all this food. 'To be perfectly honest, I don't know. I thought one-to-one sessions with each of the accused girls would be good. But I need to see the group dynamics. There's something about this that says to me there is more than one person behind this. Is it a child? I'm not sure. Is it an adult and a child working together? Is it a group of adults? A group of children? Again, I'm not sure. So, in conclusion, I know nothing and I'm not sure what I'm going to do.'

Mac laughs. I suspect he wants to say something, give me advice, but is holding back.

'What would you do?' I ask to prompt him. I need all the help I can get here. I mean, I said I was doing this and I acted like it was simple and I had it all worked out in my head, but I have no clue. Not really. The real police should be doing this, not profiler and therapist me. I wonder, sometimes, why I don't admit I don't know something and just let other people do it? I mean, I know why. I just question why I can't. 'I'm genuinely at a loss here, so any insights or thoughts you might have I will receive gratefully.'

'If I was doing this, I'd ask to go and speak to each of the different houses. Gather them into a meeting-type session, say to them what's on offer is counselling, helping them to make sense of what has happened, say they can talk about anything they like, anything that is bothering them. And watch the crowd's reaction. Spot who is particularly anxious or who turns away, notice which ones look around at the others as though warning them not to even think about approaching you. They're the ones to put in requests to speak to. I will come with you, if you want, to watch the crowd, point out who you need to talk to.'

'Thank you,' I say. 'That's actually really helpful. I was going to speak to the missing girl's friends, as well as the people who didn't like her. But this group questioning will work, too. You're really quite useful, aren't you?'

'Bet.'

'I'm sorry, what?'

'Bet.'

I shake my head at him. 'That sounds like something my child says. And, bro, I'm pretty sure he doesn't say that any more.'

'Talk about loss of aura.' Mac shakes his head as though wounded and shamed. Then he pushes his glasses back in place, puts his head to one side and laughs, his face creasing in several cute places.

I can't help laughing, too. It's easy to laugh with him. He's this entity that is a walking ego boost – he makes me feel good about myself all the time. Even when I feel guilty about hurting him, I still feel buoyed because I'm with him.

Jeb.

A voice at the back of my head breathes my husband's name, reminds me that Jeb is still heartsick over my previous attraction to this man. I immediately stop laughing and instead fill my mouth with food. I don't taste it. I'm sure it's delicious, but it tastes of nothing in my mouth because I have to tell Jeb about Mac being here. And I am not looking forward to that conversation at all.

'Right,' I say brusquely. 'Once we've finished lunch, let's go get those meetings set up.'

'Today?'

'No time like the present. The sooner we start the sooner—'

'You get to stop being around me?' he says with an amused hitch of his eyebrow. Mac really can't help flirting with me and it's nigh on impossible for me not to flirt back.

'The sooner we find the answers we need,' I say.

'Of course,' he replies.

I really need to get on with solving this so I can get back home to my real life, to my family, to Jeb. I really, really need to.

Kez

April 2026, Axton Manor

'Hang about, run that by me again,' Jeb says.

I'm speaking to him later in the day than planned because it took a bit longer than expected to go around all the houses and explain to the pupils who I am, what I offer, and let them know that I will be requesting to speak to some of them, even if they don't sign up for counselling sessions.

Now I am back in my room, changed for bed, so I have called my family. After speaking to Zoey and Jonah, I asked to talk to Jeb privately. And I've just explained everything to him via video call because I needed him to see my face when I told him. I don't want him to have any doubts about what my face is doing, to wonder if I'm covering anything up.

'I'm serious, Kez, run that whole mess by me again, because I think I've hallucinated everything you've just said to me. I mean, I must have done. Tell me again.'

He's taking this worse than I thought he would. And I thought he would take it pretty fucking badly. 'All right. Dr Guy Mackenzie, the man I told you about who was helping me on the last case with Robyn Managa, and who was my therapist for a time, is here at Axton Manor. He's here to help me with this case.'

'And this is the bit where I ask, "You said you hadn't spoken to him in six months, how the hell did he know you were there?" And you say . . . Go on, you say . . .'

'I *haven't* spoken to him in six months. Dennis sent him here. Dennis is messing with me because that's what Dennis does. And he's pissed off with me because I took this job on without asking his permission, so he's getting back at me by sending Dr Mackenzie here.'

'And then I ask, "How the hell would he know that Dr Mackenzie would be a source of trouble? I'm presuming you didn't tell him how damaging your feelings for this man were to our marriage," and you say . . .'

I hesitate, not willing to do this all over again. It was pretty awful the first time – this time it is objectively worse.

'Go on, you say . . .'

'No, I didn't tell him. He . . . he guessed when he saw us together. He guessed that at one point, one very brief point, I had a stupid, silly, meaningless crush on him.'

'And I say, "But you said it wasn't a crush, Kez. You were at pains to emphasise that it wasn't a stupid, meaningless crush because if it was you wouldn't have told me. You said your feelings for him scared you, which is why you told me about him. And now you're telling me that how you two felt about each other was so obvious, so plain for everyone to see, that Dennis has decided to use it against you."'

I can say nothing that will make any of this any better. Nothing.

'What the *fuck*, Kez?'

And now, I have caused my husband to swear again. Twice in less than a month. 'I know it sounds bad, but it really isn't—'

'Do not say it isn't that bad. It *is* bad, Kez. If you were me right now, wouldn't you think it was pretty fucking bad?'

I wish he would stop swearing. It makes me physically cringe and adds an extra layer of awfulness to all of this. I don't think I could feel any worse if I tried. 'Yes, I would think it was pretty bad, but . . . I would trust you.'

'Really? What did you say to me that time we split up? Oh yes: "I can't trust you, Jeb." So you really gonna try to style it out that you would trust me? Knowing how we met?'

'But I didn't know what your situation was.'

'If you had known, would you have stopped? Would you have walked away instead of fucking me upstairs?' More swearing. I'm cringing even more.

He's never asked me that. In all the years we've been together and been married, he's never asked me if I would have walked away from him if I'd known he had a fiancée when I first met him. I stare at my husband's handsome face on the screen, and he watches me back. Why do I forget how well my husband knows me? Why do I think I can sometimes downplay things to him? He knows the answer to his question. The way I immediately fell for him? The way I had unprotected sex with him without even knowing his name? We both know nothing could have stopped me that night. Nothing and no one. So who do I think I am fooling by even pretending to consider if I would have done the decent thing and walked away.

'And here we are,' Jeb says quietly.

'No, not "here we are". You're talking like it's inevitable. It's not. I'm not going to do anything with him. I don't even feel like that about him any more. As I explained to you at the time, it was mostly to do with how me and you weren't getting on, not to do with him specifically.'

'Mostly to do with how we weren't getting on. *Mostly.*'

'I will come home if you want me to,' I offer.

'Yeah, right.'

'I will. I will pack up right now and drive home tonight.'

'If I want you to?'

'Yes.'

'No, I don't want you to. Stay, Kez. Let's test our marriage again. Let's see what else we can throw at it to prove that we're meant to stay together. Falling out over what colour carpet to have in our bedroom is a bit too mundane for us, let's try to weather another life-threatening situation and now add the threat of you going off with the man you have feelings for into the mix. Really get in there into the danger zone of breaking us.'

'I'm sorry,' I say.

'I know. Look, I'll call you tomorrow. Love you. Bye.'

And then he's gone. Disappeared in a fug of hurt and deep disappointment.

The only thing I can do to make this better is to finish here as soon as possible. Stay professional with Mac and find the killer and/or the lost girl and get the flock out of here as soon as humanly possible.

Part 5

Jeb

April 2026, Brighton

'Is everything OK at home, Mr Kuarzie?' Penny from the meeting the other week asks, approaching him in the playground while he waits for his children to appear. He's not sure why this woman seems determined to interfere in his life, but it is irritating, to say the least.

'It's Quarshie,' Jeb replies. Had it been anyone else, he would have told her to call him Jeb. But not this woman. She was never going to get that invitation from him.

Penny flips her veil of honey-blonde hair over her shoulder, her little mate standing just behind her like the minion that she is. 'Oh, my apologies. Quarshie. Is everything OK at home, Mr Quarshie.'

Jeb is aware – acutely – that all eyes are on him in this moment. Everyone has heard about what happened at the parents' conference. They would be waiting to see how he deals with this. 'Why wouldn't it be, Penny? It is Penny, isn't it?'

'Yes, it's Penny.' She smiles as though flattered that he knows her name. She does that thing of tucking her hair behind her ear while looking supremely vulnerable. 'I'm just concerned because it seems no one has seen your wife in a while.'

Jeb frowns. *What?* he thinks. *What?* 'Were you meant to see her?' he replies. 'She does virtually none of the school drop-offs and pick-ups. Why would anyone see her?'

'Oh, well, it's not just drop-offs and pick-ups, though? No one has seen her at the supermarket or even just walking around Brighton. People regularly saw her. *I* regularly saw her, even if I didn't interact with her. But not recently. She seems to have just disappeared?'

Penny pitches her voice so those standing near him will hear what sounds like the start of a mystery and wonder what is going on.

Jeb takes a deep breath, and stares down at Penny, his face trying not to frown. Trying not to step into the angry, aggressive Black man persona he knows most people see when they look at him. Instead he relaxes his face, looks at Penny with pity. 'I see what's happening. You think because I'm not a radical, like some of the others, that I was quite rightfully horrified after what my wife did at the meeting the other week,' he states. 'How she spoke to you, when all you were doing was thinking of the children, probably made you think my wife *is* a radical, while you think I am not.'

'This isn't about me, Mr Quarshie, I was just wondering if your wife was OK. If you need any additional help at home. Mummies Making Moves Matter don't just campaign for the emotional and mental safety of children, we also can help provide additional support at home when the need arises. Gratis, of course. I was just wondering if you need that type of support.' Penny actually has the audacity to rest her hand on his forearm, briefly, letting him know that she is there for him. 'You only have to say the word.'

'Thank you for the offer, but I know how to cook, clean and make sure my children do their homework, even if my wife isn't around.'

'So she isn't around?' Penny says, gleefully.

Jeb sighs. 'Penny, are you thinking that my wife getting up in front of a group of people to challenge you has disgusted me so much that I've made her leave? Is that what you think is happening here?'

Penny returns her hand to his forearm, rubs carefully and patronisingly. He stares at the hand, tempted to shake it off, but again doesn't want to come over as aggressive.

'I'm just trying to make sure you and your children are all OK,' she says gently – and loudly. 'A break-up is so hard on the children, even if the circumstances are understan—'

'Let me stop you there,' Jeb says, notching up his voice so everyone who heard Penny can hear him, too. 'Kez and I are fine. More than fine. As I said to you previously, being against book banning is not radical – it is the normal setting for most people. And for the avoidance of doubt: I am extremely proud of the way Kez, my beautiful wife, stood up to you in front of everyone.'

Penny snatches her hand away, furious suddenly.

'And, actually, I'm glad I've seen you because Kez was just asking after you. She's working away, if you must know, that's why you haven't seen her. She was asking if I'd seen you because she wanted to know how the scorch marks she left on you after the absolute roasting she gave you are healing. What was the song she sang? Oh yes: "Penny roasted on an open mic . . ." She's hilarious, my wife,' Jeb says, noting the smirks and amusement from those all around him. 'She makes me laugh pretty much every day. I really am lucky to have her.'

He smiles at Penny. Grins at her. She shoots him a look of utter disgust in return, spins on her Ugg boot heels and marches away, her friend rushing to keep up. It takes him a few seconds to realise what he's just done: read someone for filth . . . then smiled. He's done what Kez did.

He hadn't realised how very easy that was to do. How necessary it is sometimes.

God, he misses her. She's only been gone a few days, but he really, really misses her.

Kez

April 2026, Axton Manor

Group therapy session held with Dr Kez Lanyon with friends of Winifred 'Fredi' Kingston

Number of clients: 5

In attendance (all names to be anonymised later): Astrid Barron, Isolde Grenville, Viola Hudson, Paris Montgomery, Haniya Vyas.

Most important moments from session:

KL: Thank you all for coming here today.

AB: Didn't actually have much choice.

KL: That is true. I did ask to speak to you all specifically so an element of your choice in this has been taken away from you. And, while you have been told to attend, you do not have to interact. In fact, if you want – if any of you want – you can sit here in complete silence for an hour.

THE QUIET GIRLS

I hope you don't do that because it'd be boring, but, more importantly, I am here for you. You five in particular have been through two very traumatic events in a short period of time. I am here to help support you through that by giving you the space to talk about what you might be feeling.

This is a safe space, nothing said will leave this room. You can speak confidentially to me and I will listen and try to help in any way that I can. There are a few ground rules: no shouting, no violence, no gaslighting, no dismissing, no interrupting, no looking to me to settle any disagreements.

If you have anything to discuss privately, let me know via email after the session and we will move forward from there.

AB: So, if we all decided to sit here in complete silence, to not speak for the whole hour, you won't write us up? Snitch to the teachers?

KL: This is your hour, you can use it as you feel fit.

AB: Right, well, I think you are going to find the next hour is very, very quiet.

[AB adopts a very aggressive stance of arms folded across her chest, one foot resting on her opposite knee. She has made a declaration, indicating to the rest of the group that they are not to speak.]

KL: Like I say, this is all up to you.

[*Seven minutes pass in complete silence.*]

PM: What are we supposed to talk about? Dr Pemberton or Fredi? [*She constantly plays with a keyring in the shape of a gold bullion bar, rubbing it between her thumb and forefinger in a clear sign of anxiety.*]

KL: Either or both. Or something completely different. As I said, this is your hour.

PM: It does feel weird, knowing that we're never going to speak to Dr Pemberton again. And that he was a perv.

KL: What makes you think he was a perv?

PM: All those messages between Fredi and Dr Pemberton. She's too young for him.

VH: I don't think Fredi would do that. I don't believe those rumours about the messages between them are true.

AB: That's because Fredi can't do anything wrong in Viola's eyes.

KL: No snideness, please. How did Fredi fit into your group? You all seem to have been here a long time, have a very established group, how did an outsider fit in?

VH: She wasn't an outsider to me. Don't @ me, AB. She was really cool and she fitted right in.

PM: She was actually really nice. Didn't think she was better than anyone else. If you wanted to talk to someone, she was always there. [*Her rubbing at the keyring intensifies.*]

IG: She was fun, too. She made me laugh all the time.

HV: And me. She had a funny way about her.

VH: Have you lot heard yourselves? You make it sound like all she was there to do was entertain you. Or listen to you. Or make you feel better. She's just Fredi and she's really cool. And she's not dead. You're all talking about her like she's never coming back.

KL: You believe she's going to come back from wherever she's run away to?

VH: Yes.

KL: It's unusual for children who have run away to return to where they were before.

HV: It's happened before. When we were younger, that girl, Rachel. She disappeared for weeks and she came back. I don't remember how long she was gone because she was in the years above us. But she came back.

KL: Did anyone ever find out where she had been?

IG: She was older than us so we only heard the rumours. They said she was living in the woods at the back of the school.

HV: It's a forest not a wood. But that's where they said she was. Her parents came and took her back to America.

PM: No, you've all got it wrong. Rachel's parents did take her back to America, but that was because they think she was chased through the woods by someone. It was *Audrey* who was found living in the countryside beyond the woods. She was really messed up and is in an institution now.

AB: Mariana didn't come back, though, did she? [*Her tone is quite nasty.*]

[*Silence from the group.*]

AB: Well, she didn't, did she?

KL: Did she also run away?

AB: Yes.

KL: Recently?

AB: Suppose.

KL: And no one has heard from her?

VH: I got a postcard from her.

AB: Of course you did. Out of everyone in the whole school, you were always bound to be the one who got a postcard from the girl who ran away.

VH: What's that supposed to mean?

AB: It means you're always talking to the natives. That's what my mum says.

KL: That doesn't sound very kind.

AB: But it's true. She's the one who always brings people like that into our group. And then they run away.

KL: Again, that doesn't sound very kind and is against the rules of this room and the need to make this a safe space.

PM: We're meant to be talking about Fredi, not anyone else. I really like her and hope she comes home soon.

IG: Me, too.

HV: Me, too.

VH: What AB just said was low-key racist. She says stuff like that all the time. Fredi called her out on it. So did Mariana. Even if HV, who is a person of colour, is standing right there, AB says that sort of stuff all the time. She doesn't care who she upsets. She thinks she's better than everyone else so can say whatever racist or messed-up things she likes.

KL: I can hear the upset in your voice. What would you like to say to AB about what she just said to you?

VH: Nothing. There's no point. You can say all the words in the world to her and she will still do what she wants to do. Say stuff like that. She doesn't care how it makes everyone else feel. Fredi told her she was out of order all the time. So did Mariana.

KL: How did you all feel about Fredi, who was a recent addition to your group, calling out a more established member?

PM: We're all equal. Friends challenge each other all the time. They're the ones who can do that safely. It didn't cause any tension if that's what you're asking. Everyone can speak freely. [*Her playing with the keyring intensifies, showing more of her stress and anxiety.*]

KL: Do you know of any reason why Fredi would run away? Was there anyone who she was upset with or who bullied her? Anything like that?

IG: Mrs Lazloe.

HV: Mrs Lazloe.

VH: Mrs Lazloe.

PM: Mrs Lazloe.

AB: Mrs Lazloe.

KL: What does she teach?

VH: Geography. On Fredi's first day she humiliated her about her uniform. She didn't really stop.

KL: You think her actions could have driven Fredi to run away?

ALL: Definitely.

KL: How do you feel about Mrs Lazloe and how she treated Fredi?

PM: It's part of being here? We've all known Mrs Lazloe since we arrived. She has always been like that. If you're not used to being treated like that, it can drive you to do desperate things.

KL: Like run away?

PM: Like run away. [*The playing with the keyring intensifies again.*]

KL: So you believe that she ran away?

PM: We do.

KL: And, given what happened to Dr Pemberton, you don't think something might have happened to her, too?

PM: Like what? [*She stops playing with the keyring.*]

KL: You tell me.

PM: But what could have happened to her except her running away?

KL: I was wondering if any of you had an idea about that? Seeing as you all knew her and what her day-to-day life was about, I thought you might have an idea of what would make her run? Or even make her a target?

PM: We think she was happy. She had us. We think she was happy in her everyday life.

KL: Is it your experience that happy people run away?

PM: No. But the thought of something happening to her is too horrible. We couldn't stand to think something happened. I know she was new, but she was one of us. It's better to think she was unhappy and had a moment where she couldn't cope than someone doing something to her. If she ran away, we might see her again.

VH: We are going to see her again. We are.

IG: Yes, we are. I know it. I just know it.

[*Note that AB does not say anything about seeing Fredi again. Significant?*]

HV: We're all praying for her. Praying that she comes home. We just know we're going to see her again.

KL: Thank you, ladies. I think we should leave it there for today. If anyone would like to talk to me individually, my door is always open. Before I finish a multi-person session, I always like people to say something positive about the other person. In this instance, I'd like you all to say something positive about Fredi. Remind yourselves why you like her. Who would like to go first?

VH: I will. She's funny. And sweet. And pretty. And I knew we were going to be friends from when I showed her around.

IG: She knew a lot about movies. And she cared about all of us. Even the ones who weren't that nice to her.

HV: We had some really fun times, especially when we would sneak into each other's house dorms. I miss her.

AB: She was nice.

PM: She was a really bright spark. A real credit to Axton Manor. We're going to keep a light on for her and keep wishing for her to come home.

POST-SESSION GROUP OBSERVATIONS: The group are cohesive. AB is very vocal and positions herself as the leader of the group. There are tensions through the group: AB's manner is jarring to other members of the friendship group. Although she positions herself as leader, the one in true control is PM. When AB decreed no one would speak in the session, PM spoke and opened the meeting up for others to interact. PM regularly speaks for the group and is never contradicted. PM showed some irritation when challenged by KL about whether a happy person would run away. Although there is some disconnect – PM showed some stress and anxiety at several moments during the session, using her gold bullion keyring as an outward expression of her anxiety. Based on today's session, need to investigate the relationships between AB and Fredi as well as PM and Fredi. Likely that something took place between them that the rest of the group do not know about. VH is only member of the group who does not speak about Fredi in the past tense. Could indicate she is the only one who does not know what happened to Fredi. Investigation into dynamics of the group will continue.

Fredi

● **Record Voice Note** ▶ **Recorded: January 2026**

We do this thing where, after lights-out, we wait until the teachers are settled in their rooms and we grab our duvets, put on our slippers and then go down to the ground floor. You have to make sure no one sees you. You get out of the house, then you run as fast as you can across to the other house dorm and then you put in the key code on the door. We're not supposed to share keycodes between house dorms, but everyone does it.

You have to run up the stairs when you get into the other house dorm because if you get caught – it is the end. Not just for you, but for everyone. They'll change the keycodes, they'll put in patrols and they'll definitely do proper searches for phones.

And if you're the person who gets caught and ruins it for everyone else then you're dead meat.

At 10 p.m., they turn off the Wi-Fi in the house dorms, so you have to get creative. One way is to make sure your parents give you lots of data. So when you hand in your phone at 9 p.m. (10 p.m. for us older ones) you hand in a fake phone. Well, one that you don't really use. You just turn it off and hand it in. Your real phone, you use as a personal hotspot so you can watch things on your laptop. Which is why you need your folks to hit you up with as much data as possible.

Paris, Astrid, Haniya and Issy are in Franklin house dorm, while me and Viola are in Lovelace, I don't know if I've said that before? So if we plan to get together we have to go over to see them. It's better if just the two of us go because three are much more likely to get caught than two. And besides, there's no way that Paris would ever go to see anyone. She's way too important to do that.

Last night, Viola went over to Franklin ahead of me because I had stuff to do. All right, I had to attend to some truly gross pimples that have been developing on my chin. Mum says they're hormonal, but, whatever they are, they're disgusting. I had to do some serious deep cleansing and ointmenting to get rid of them.

After that, I went running over. It'd started to lightly rain so I hooked my duvet over my head to protect my hair before I pushed open the door. And just before I stepped out onto the redbrick path that links the house dorms, I noticed movement. Busted!

I quickly stepped back in and stood to the side, out of sight. My heart was pounding, you know? I was so scared I thought I was going to throw up. Because getting caught, spoiling all these things for everyone when I've just got here and not many people like me? That would be the end of everything.

But, guess what? It wasn't a teacher – it was one of Headmaster Rhodes's creepy sons. I said before about how Viola told me they choose a girl and decide she's their girlfriend no matter what she says about it, right? Well, clearly he was visiting his 'girlfriend'.

It made me sick to think about it. Really sick. Like Viola, I wanted to do something. But what can we do? Everyone obviously knows it happens, but, like Viola said her mum had said, unless someone makes a formal complaint, there's not much anyone else can do.

I know I should have hung back, maybe gone back to my room and waited until the coast was clear, but I wanted to know who it was. Who had he picked and who was he doing horrible things to? I left the hallway of Lovelace house dorm and dashed across the slick redbrick path and typed in the code to get into Franklin house dorm. I held the door so when it slowly swung closed, it would be quiet. I could hear heavy footsteps on the staircase above me, and assumed it was him. I needed to be quieter as I came up behind him on the stairs so he wouldn't know I was there. He didn't go onto the first two floors – he just kept walking with that slow, heavy, methodical tread. It was pretty creepy, actually.

I kept up with him until he got to the third floor – the floor I was going to. He pushed in the code for that floor and opened the door and went in. My heart kind of dropped, you know? Cos I know everyone on that floor and it meant one of them was getting goosed by this guy. I hated that for them.

I hung back at the door, and kept kind of ducking my head to look through the slim glass panel in the door. He had the hood up on his green wax jacket, which was speckled with droplets of the light rain. He had heavy boots on his feet and he walked slightly hunched over, like he was trying to minimise his height. He walked halfway up the corridor and then stopped. And my heart stopped.

Paris's room.

He was going to be with Paris. My mouth kind of dropped open and I quickly stepped through the door, just to be sure. I didn't even care at that point if he saw me. He used a key to open the door and I simply stood there, watching him. He didn't even bother to glance either way before he entered the room, he just went in. I heard muffled sounds and then, instead of the door closing, Paris's head popped out, her dark-red hair swinging as she moved.

Our eyes locked.

Even from that distance I could see her face grow bright red with the horror of being caught.

I wasn't meant to be out here, was I? I was meant to be in Issy's room three doors down, eating popcorn while we watched a movie on her desktop computer. But my chin spots had caught her out. I knew her secret.

Without saying anything, she pulled her head back in and then slammed and locked her door.

I suddenly remembered that if I got caught, I'd be in big trouble. I ran down the corridor, past her room, trying to ignore what I'd seen, and knocked on Issy's door.

'Where've you been?' they all chorused in complaint. 'No one wanted to start the movie without you.'

'Sorry, sorry,' I apologised, and stepped over Viola and Haniya and Issy who were snuggled under their floral duvets to get to the space by the bed that they'd left for me.

'Where's Paris?' I asked as I pulled my duvet up to my chin.

'Northern France,' Issy quipped. 'Although I hear there's one in Texas, too.'

'Let her catch you saying that,' Viola laughed, cuffing Issy around the head. 'Just let her catch you.'

'You must never tell her,' Issy said in mock horror. 'And, if you do, I'll tell her all the times all of you have done it.'

'She'd never believe it of me,' Haniya replied. 'I'm too nice.'

'She's studying,' Astrid interjected. She dropped down next to me and slid a bowl of popcorn – salt and sweet – onto my lap. 'I told her she'd be fine, but she insisted on studying for next week's biology exam. So, more popcorn for us, I guess.'

I looked around at everyone, wondering if they knew. If they knew what she was really doing when she said she was studying. I don't think Viola knows. She is so angry about what the Rhodes sons are doing to other girls, I don't think she'd keep it to herself.

But Astrid would. Issy would. Haniya would. They're all a bit scared of Paris so if she told them that she was sleeping with an older man they would totally keep her secret.

I'm back in my room now, but I can't sleep. I'm not sure what to do. Do I tell someone? Tell Viola? Do I tell a teacher? But which one? Miss Akande? She seems nice and even though she's posh, she doesn't seem at all like the other teachers. She seems to genuinely like and care about us girls. Or what about Dr Pemberton? If I speak to him, it'll be confidential and maybe he can tell me what I should do.

I can't talk to Paris because she is properly scary. I like her, but when she's cross with you, she'll get this look on her face. Sometimes she'll be smiling and you can tell that she's furious with you as well. I don't know what she'll do if I confront her outright, although if it was Bev or Carina I would absolutely call them out.

Maybe that's a sign that this lot aren't my real friends? I can't just be myself with them?

But Mum says all the time that during your life you will have different types of friends – some are acquaintances, some are for a certain period of time and some are for life. But you often don't find out which is which straight away. You have to give it time. Maybe that's what I need to do with these friends. Give it time.

And I'll just have to sit on this thing with the headmaster's son and Paris. Not a lot else I can do right now.

■ **End Voice Note** ⬇ **Save Recording** ↗ **Send To Private Cloud**

Fredi

● **Record Voice Note** ▶ **Recorded: January 2026**

I didn't have to speak to Paris about what I saw. She came to me. Actually, she came *at* me – in the showers after Games.

Everyone who was there with us for Games seemed to know to get changed quickly and then get out, because when I came out of the shower wrapped in a towel the whole place was empty. Usually, it's full of girls drying their hair, taking their time to towel themselves off, reapplying make-up, but today I came out of the showers and they were all gone. Except for Paris, who was dressed in her uniform, with the top button open but without her tie done up. Her hair was ninety per cent dry and her make-up was in place.

'Who have you told?' she demanded. Her voice was quiet, but I could still hear her from across the room.

I shook my head because she had that look in her eye. She was high-key going to do something to me. I've seen her face change a few times, when Astrid or Issy or Haniya has upset her. Then her face goes tight and her eyes grow hard and her voice is like an ice pick.

'Who have you told?' she asked again.

'No one.'

'You've told Viola, haven't you?'

I shook my head. 'No. I haven't told anyone.'

'You better not. If you tell anyone – anyone – I will make you so sorry. So sorry. You won't get to see your family again. I know people. I know people who can make you disappear, like that!' She snapped her fingers.

She came right up to me. 'I've done it before. That girl you asked about, Mariana? She crossed me, and she disappeared. If you don't want the same thing to happen to you, then you better keep your mouth shut about what you saw.' She pulled her lips right back, until she looked like one of those vicious hunting dogs that's about to attack you. 'Do you understand me?'

I nodded with quickness.

Her face changed all of a sudden and she was all smiles. Like you wouldn't think that she was threatening me literally seconds ago. You wouldn't think that she told me that she'd possibly murdered someone.

'You better hurry up and get changed if you don't want to be late for Mrs Lazloe's lesson. You know how she gets if you're late.' Then she picked up her backpack and walked out of the locker room whistling 'Anxiety'.

I'm glad I didn't talk to anyone about it, because, even though she didn't say it, I'm pretty sure that she would hurt them, too.

But this seems to be another lead about Mariana. Did Paris really do something to her? Paris must be part of The Platinum. I haven't asked anyone else about Mariana. The other girls have mentioned her a couple of times, but only rarely. They mostly pretend like she didn't exist. And I never ask about her when they bring her up. The only time I asked about her was that time The Platinum took me to the basement. So Paris is definitely part of them. I think she might be one of the

Quiet Girls as well. Is that possible? Either way, whether part of The Platinum or the Quiet Girls, was Paris one of the people who disappeared Mariana? Will she think about disappearing me, too?

■ **End Voice Note** ↓ **Save Recording** ↗ **Send To Private Cloud**

Part 6

Kez

April 2026, Axton Manor

'What did you find out from talking to the staff?' I ask Mac. It is lunchtime on our first Saturday here at Axton Manor and he has just sat down beside me with his tray of food. I shift a little away to give him space. We haven't really seen each other since that first day when he came with me to all the different houses, letting everyone know about me being available for them to talk to. Afterwards, we compared notes and I made a list of girls I needed to speak to. Surprisingly, the only people who it was clear I needed to approach were the five girls who were Fredi Kingston's friends. No one else showed much of a reaction, really. More surprising is how busy I have been: a lot of girls have made appointments and have come to talk about their normal problems, not simply about the death on their doorstep or a contemporary going missing.

Mac assesses me for a brief moment before he picks up the freshly baked bread roll on his plate and breaks it in two. 'I take it from the unsubtle shift away from me just then, the avoiding me for five days and the straight-to-business talk, that your husband took me being here worse than you did?' he says conversationally before fixing me with a stare so penetrating I can't look away.

Guy Mackenzie is expert at holding my gaze, making it impossible for me to look away. Making me feel like we are about to be intimate in many, many different ways. Eventually, he drops his gaze to unwrap a small gold rectangle of organic butter and start to slowly spread it on the soft, fluffy innards of the roll.

'I'm curious . . . Why did you tell your husband about me?' he asks. 'I mean, I should be flattered, I suppose, that you mentioned me to him, but it seems an odd thing to do given how nothing is ever going to happen between us.'

He ensnares me with his gaze again, keeping me skewered to the spot while he slowly opens his mouth and carefully slips the edge of the roll in between his lips. Heat flushes through me at the sheer eroticism of what he is doing – how he is eating that roll while staring deep into my eyes and talking about what could happen between us. He sinks his teeth into the bread roll, pulls it out from between his lips and then raises an eyebrow as he waits for an answer to his question.

Mac once said he didn't think I would torture him with my presence. I didn't think he'd torture me with this conversation, especially while reminding me how damn attractive I find him, so we're quits, I guess.

'Hello, Dr Mackenzie, how are you?' I say after swallowing. 'I haven't seen you in a few days. I hope you're getting on OK? How is the teaching going?' I want to pick up my bread roll but daren't since the way he is eating his is so erotic I fear I may send the wrong signal by doing the same. Instead, I pick up my fork to shove some salad into my mouth. 'Better?'

'Much.'

'What have you found out from the staff?' I ask again.

'Not as much as you'd think. They are understandably guarded. It's going to take a bit more talking to them to get them to open up. I sense, though, that they aren't exactly cut up about the demise of Dr Pemberton.

Nothing to do with him per se, it's more what has been uncovered since his death. There've been hints that he had an inappropriate relationship with the missing girl, Winifred?'

'Yes, that's what I've found. He was one of the last people to see Fredi alive before she went missing. According to Dennis, the phone records show that he was in pretty intense phone contact with Fredi recently. She started going to him for counselling not long after she arrived. Apparently, she was homesick a lot. From his limited files, he talked about her having an attachment disorder. But then, outside of the therapy room, contact increased recently. Emails, texts, all saying stuff that isn't outright dodgy but points to being inappropriate. The police report says as much. However . . . I don't buy it. It's too much of a coincidence that this relationship was going on but none of her friends seemed to know about it, and now there's a load of evidence? Could *all* of the teachers really have been fooled by him? All of them? The maths ain't mathsing, as my daughter says.'

'I know what you mean. For a lot of them it seems this came from left field.'

'And the phone and other records only show recent activity like that. Not anything more before that. It feels very much like all of it was planted to feed a certain narrative that will stop people looking very hard for Fredi and not feel too cut up about Pemberton's death.'

'I think you're right.' Mac picks up his fork, having finished his bread roll. Before he puts a cube of butternut squash in his mouth, he asks: 'How did Dennis get hold of the phone and other records? As well as the police report?'

'How does Dennis get hold of anything?' I reply with a shrug. 'He's Dennis; he does whatever the hell he likes. It's good at times like this because, well, because.'

Mac chews slowly while he cautiously studies me, his gaze steady and wary.

'What?' I ask.

'Nothing,' he replies before he puts another cube of food in his mouth.

'Can we not with the back and forth? Just tell me what the matter is.'

'As you know, I am no longer your therapist so I am not saying this in a professional capacity, but you seem very accepting of Dennis and what he does, all of a sudden. Before, you were very resistant to becoming embroiled in his world. Now . . . you seem not only resigned to it but almost . . . part of it.'

I redirect my line of sight to the plate of food in front of me. I've managed to curb my panic at the amount of food on offer in this place and my plates are no longer huge heaping mounds that I have to force myself to finish.

'Your husband said the same, didn't he?' Mac comments.

'Not exactly. He said I'm becoming fine with it and that wasn't fine.'

'And how do you feel about hearing that twice now?'

'You're not my therapist, Mac.'

'I am your friend, Kez. Or colleague. Or whatever. I don't know what I am to you, but I care about you, Kez. And I care enough to not be easily distracted. It's a problem that you're becoming acclimatised to that world. But it's a bigger problem that you can't see that it is a problem.'

When Jeb said it, it'd bothered me. Made me look at myself and I did not like what I saw. So I avoided thinking about it. In the same way I used to avoid looking in the mirror because I would often see Brian's deathly face staring back, which would remind me that I once upon a time killed someone and I could never make up for it.

I didn't want to face what Jeb said because I knew he was right. And I wasn't sure what to do about it. That was the main issue.

In a way, I had known that I was becoming a proper part of Insight, but when Jeb voiced it I realised that the fight had gone out of me. In the everyday of every day, I had, little by little, stopped keeping myself separate, stopped battling to not become one of them. It's exhausting, fighting all the time, keeping your defences up, not allowing even the smallest crack to show in your armour because that's how they get in.

And, in the main, if you overlooked how they sometimes treated me and the underlying psychopathic tendencies you generally needed to be able to do that kind of work, they weren't all bad. They were all right, actually. And if I didn't deep it, as Zoey would say, I could almost forget the reality of my situation.

It's been a long time since I've had to deal with needing a gun in an interview room or someone trying to kill me. Life at Insight isn't always life and death in the same half an hour, so it's easy to relax a little. And being comfortable, being slightly bored, feels so much better than constantly being on edge. The high alert of having post-traumatic stress is something that I lived with for over twenty years. But, when I came to Insight, I was constantly having to reframe every conversation, interaction, piece of communication – whether instant message, call, email or meeting – to remind myself that I didn't belong there. And that, well, that wears you down, burns you out. Over the last little while, I've got comfortable with not feeling uncomfortable all the time. And it's led to me becoming a proper part of Insight. When I first met Mac, I asked him why he had left the intelligence services and he said to me: *'I saw what they wanted and I wasn't prepared to give it. Much like you, I guess.'*

I hadn't told Mac that it hadn't been my choice the first time I'd left

The Human Insight Unit (as Insight began life), where I'd been working with Dennis – what had happened with my friend Brian meant no one could stick around. Dennis hadn't wanted me to leave, but he had no choice in the matter. So when I returned to his life asking for help, he took advantage of that. And this time around I knew I couldn't leave again, not without putting my family in danger, so I just got on with it. I got on with it so much that here I am with two people I trust telling me I have a huge problem because I got comfortable with not being uncomfortable.

'I'm not saying you have to deal with it right now,' Mac assures. 'You're not in a place where you can do that, but we can talk after all of this.'

'You're not my therapist, Dr Mackenzie,' I state.

'You sure about that, Dr Lanyon?' he replies.

We both give each other side-eyes and the affection I suddenly feel is mirrored on his face.

Stop it, Kez, I tell myself. *Just stop it.* I push a forkful of food into my mouth to stop me saying something that could be misconstrued as flirting and suddenly in front of us is a tall Black woman dressed in an orange tracksuit with white trim. She has headphones around her neck and her shiny black hair is folded into two neat cornrows that begin at her forehead and go down onto her shoulders.

'Guy?' she says, her voice dancing with delight. 'It is you!'

'Portia!' he exclaims, getting to his feet. He has the same delight in his tone. 'I thought you said you didn't work here any longer.'

'I didn't. I left. Ages ago, but they kept asking me to come back to cover classes or maternity cover. Even before what happened recently, they asked me to come back for a year.'

'Why didn't you tell me?'

'*Me?* What about you? Why didn't you tell me you were going to be here? I've heard all this chatter about this new fit bod around and then it turns out to be you!' She opens her arms. 'Am I getting a hug, then?' Her voice is very posh, very someone who belongs in this world.

'Oh, sorry,' he says and gathers her into a close, warm hug. They cling to each other in a way that is almost indecent, and it's clear these two know each other in the naked sense of knowing someone. Once released from their hug, they both hold on to each other's forearms, obviously unwilling to let each other go. Then Portia seems to remember she is surrounded by pupils who will rip her to pieces over this, so she takes her arms away and steps back.

'Aren't you going to introduce us?' she asks, gesturing to me with a slight tip of her head.

'Oh, yes,' he says, pushing his hands into his trouser pockets. 'This is Dr Kez Lanyon. Kez is the new school counsellor and therapist. I'm here teaching A-level psychology and acting as Kez's supervisor while the school is still on high alert.'

'Pleased to meet you,' I say, when it's clear that is all the introduction I'm going to get.

'You, too,' she says. 'Since he's decided to stop the introductions there, my name is Portia Akande. I'm a business studies teacher here and a superannuated Axton old girl. Guy and I met in college, many, many years ago.'

'That's really cool,' I say, and notice them exchange *Do I tell her or will you?* looks.

'We met in college and dated for a while,' Mac says reluctantly. 'A long while. We, erm, we were actually engaged.'

Ohhhh, plot twist, as Zoey would say. *Plot. Twist.*

Fredi

● Record Voice Note ▶ Recorded: January 2026

Total mind melt today. Total. One of the worst days ever. No cap.

So, Mrs Lazloe stood in for Games today. It was cold, which made her happy because she could make us take off anything that wasn't exact regulation uniform. Even the sports jackets. Most of us were wearing uniform sports jackets. The green body, orange sleeves one is for spring and summer, the orange body, green sleeves one is for autumn and winter. But it's cold so most of us were wearing both of them. And Mrs Uniform Policer made us all take off the spring and summer jackets as well as any base layers or jumpers.

We were freezing and she didn't even care.

Anyhow, during drills, when I missed the ball because my hands were too cold, she made me run back and forth across the field to warm up. Then she told me to go and get the spare balls from the equipment shed right on the other side of the school. I wonder sometimes if she's related to Miss Geraghty from my old school the way she hates on me for no reason.

I go off to do as I'm told and I come around the corner past the outbuildings where they used to keep horses, and by the last outbuilding before you get to the equipment shed I see Miss Akande and Dr Pemberton kissing. Full-on kissing.

I couldn't move. I just stood there staring at them.

And then, next thing I know, no word of a lie, he puts his hand up her skirt and roughly pulls down her knickers. Just like that. Then he puts his hand back up her skirt, moving it back and forth and she starts whimpering while they stare in each other's eyes. And then she's undoing his belt, unbuttoning his trousers and pulling them down over his hips. Next, he pushes her back against the wall and grabs her leg and then he's, you know, doing it with her.

I was just standing there, probably with my mouth open like a fish while they did it. I mean . . . Just like that! In broad daylight where anyone could see? Well, any me *did* see!

I must have made a sound or something because Miss Akande, who had her eyes closed and was quietly moaning along with Dr Pemberton and what he was doing to her, turned her head and opened her eyes and saw me. She sort of shrieked like this [*softly shrieks*] and then pushed Dr Pemberton away, which was terrible because then I could see his thing and that was not good for me at all.

I turned around and ran back the way I'd come.

I wasn't cold any more, strangely enough. But I did get in trouble with Mrs Lazloe for not getting the balls and now I have detention. I don't know what's worse, seeing two teachers I like having sex, seeing Dr Pemberton's thing or getting detention because of it.

Just kidding, seeing Dr Pemberton's thing is the worst thing among all those worst things.

■ **End Voice Note** ↓ **Save Recording** ↗ **Send To Private Cloud**

Kez

April 2026, Axton Vale

I have left Mac and Portia talking so I can wander down to Axton Vale, the village that forms a crescent shape around the school grounds.

'The quickest way is through the forest at the back of the school,' Portia explained when I told them my plan. I had looked at her like she had grown another nose right in front of me. What sort of person who has seen more than one horror movie willingly goes off alone into the woods? 'Fair enough,' she said, seeing my face. 'Go right out of the school gates and follow the road back on yourself. You could drive, but there isn't much parking on the high street.'

Axton Vale is one of those quaint villages that has everything you need, including a supermarket, but still seems untouched by time. I wander along the street until I arrive at a store with tinted windows and a variety of displays of pots and potions. Dr Jewel's Herbal Emporium. A more incongruous place in a village like this you could not get. Unless she was someone who held all the mystical secrets of the village and who ran a secret society that ended up sacrificing unsuspecting arrivals to the town. Which would absolutely be the sort of thing that would happen to me . . . Obviously, I have to go in. Find out who Dr Jewel is and just how much quirk she has.

The bell behind the door announces my arrival and from the curtain-covered doorway behind the large glass counter, an extremely tall Black woman with waist-length dreadlocks emerges. She is wearing a long emerald-green velvet dress that complements every curve of her broad, solid frame, and she seems to glow because of the brightly coloured metal hair jewellery she wears. Her nose is pierced and her skin is flawless. She grins at me.

'Hello. A new face in the village. Holiday or work?'

'Work,' I reply.

'Well then, you'll be needing one of my de-stress mixtures.' She comes around from behind the counter, and heads towards a display of small brown glass bottles. She holds it out to me and I notice that every single finger has a ring, some of them two rings.

'Yes, sure, why not?' I reply, and take the bottle from her.

'Well, that was easy. How are you for bridges? I've got a couple I can sell you if you're that easy to sell to.'

I laugh and so does she. 'How long have you had your shop?' I ask as I examine the shelves. I'm looking for an eczema cream, one that will help my older son, Moe. His mother, Hella, Jeb's first wife, and I have been battling it since he was a child and in recent times it's out of control again.

'About five years?'

'Where were you before?'

'I've always been here,' she replies. 'I grew up around here. And, yes, we were the only Black family in the village. Fun times as you can imagine. I went away to university and medical school and then returned to fight the good fight.'

'So you're a medical doctor?'

'I am indeed. I was a GP for several years. I made these creams and lotions on the side, but I'm fully embedded in the medical world. I had my son in a hospital with an epidural and we're both fully vaccinated against everything. All of this grew from a need to treat things that modern medicine couldn't.'

'Do you know anybody from Axton Manor since you've been here for ever?' I ask.

She visibly cools towards me. 'I do,' she replies. 'Quite a few of their pupils come in here. Often looking for love potions.'

Love potions? What if . . . ? I take my phone out of my bag, call up a picture of Fredi. 'Did she come in at all?'

Dr Jewel takes the phone from me and holds it delicately between two hands as she looks at it. Several micro-expressions cross her face that tell me not only did Fredi come in here, she talked to her. More than once. They had some kind of connection.

'I might have seen her,' she says, and gives me back my phone.

'Just seen her?'

'Yes, she might have come in a couple of times.'

'Are you sure it wasn't more than that?'

'Who are you? The police? A private detective? Why are you asking so many questions?'

'I'm working up at the school. I'm their new therapist. I'm Kez Lanyon.' I hold out my hand. She looks at it but doesn't take it. 'I'm also trying to find out what happened to Winifred. A lot of her friends are distraught at her disappearance and I'm trying to piece together what happened, what went wrong in her life that would cause her to run away.'

'Bold that you think she ran away,' she says.

'You don't think she ran away?'

'People who run away and don't show up again generally don't have anything to run back to, I find. Did Winifredi have somewhere she could have run back to? Did she have parents who loved her and would take care of her no matter what she's done?'

'I don't know. I know her parents haven't just accepted that she ran away. And it sounds like you're saying the same?'

'I'm saying maybe you should find out who Winifredi was from people other than those who live on that compound.'

'Compound?'

'I said what I said.'

This woman profiles as caring and empathetic; she comes across as someone who would give their last penny or last minute to help someone. Did Fredi go to her for help? Does she know why Fredi ran away or does she know what happened to her? Or does she suspect something has happened to Fredi but can't say because she lives in the shadow of Axton Manor?

'Is there anything else you would like?' Dr Jewel has cooled so much towards me that I feel a physical chill. It's a shame, because she seemed quite nice and this place is cosy as well as quirky.

'No, no, just this de-stress oil will be fine.'

She returns to the other side of her counter, and rings up the bottle of oil. I tap my card while she pops it into a small brown paper bag. 'Bring both the bag and the bottle back for a refill and you'll get a ten per cent discount,' she says.

'Thank you,' I say and leave.

It's not until hours later that I realise what she said. She called Fredi Winifredi. Not the type of mistake you make, more of an affectionate nickname.

Jewel knew Fredi. She knew her well – I'm certain of it.

Jeb

April 2026, Brighton

'What you wearing?' Kez asks him.

His eyes immediately go to the bedroom door, to check it's fully closed and that he'll have some warning if Zoey or Jonah decide to come to their bedroom. 'Nothing,' he replies and watches her face find a seductive smile.

She hasn't been gone that long, but he can see how difficult this is for her. She hates being away from them and the strain of what she is doing is already showing on her face. If you don't know her, you wouldn't guess, but he is aware how deeply she feels everything, and this is weighing heavily on her. And she's only there because of him. Because of what he did and didn't do three years ago.

'What you wearing?' he asks, then relaxes as they fall into the now familiar rhythm of phone sex with his second wife . . .

Afterwards, after he's said goodnight and reminded her to come home to them no matter what it takes, the guilt returns, but this time like a fist slammed into his solar plexus. She'd asked him several times during their conversation before the phone sex if there was anything wrong. She'd seen his latent worry and had asked him to tell her if there was something or someone bothering him. And he'd told her it was nothing, that he was tired from work, that he was missing her more than he expected, that he hadn't appreciated how difficult it was to do everything to keep their lives running on your own. That was all true, every word.

But . . . there was more. There was something else. It was bothering him. But it could be nothing. He didn't want to worry her when she was away. And it probably was nothing. It probably was just his paranoia at being so far away from Kez and worrying about her in case she was hurt again. It was probably, most likely, nothing.

Which is why he didn't want to tell her. To put her on high alert and possibly make her come home early, which would probably mean she would need to leave again to go back and finish what she'd started. No, she needed to stay and sort this out and then come back to them for good.

And this feeling he has that they're being watched? This worry that someone is following them, observing their every move? It really is probably nothing.

Kez

April 2026, Axton Manor

Every time Mac knocks and then enters my office, I have to remind myself that he is here for work. *Not* to see me.

I need to remind myself of that because I am weak? Stupid? A horrible person who is going to hell for having impure thoughts? All or none of the above? I don't even know. I don't want anything to happen with him – I don't even consider it. Not even in the abstract. I don't think of him when I'm alone, I don't fantasise about him. It's just sometimes, like now, my stomach dips when I see him. And he notices. Which makes his face do that thing where I know his stomach has just dipped, because, well, it has.

Whenever this happens, I curse Dennis in my head, because he has done this. He has put Mac here to mess with my mind to try to mess with my marriage.

'How can I help you, Dr Guy?' I say to him as he takes up a seat on the other side of my desk.

'Are you seriously going to pretend that I'm not wearing a school-teacher's tracksuit and have a whistle round my neck, Dr Kez?' he replies.

I curl my lips into my mouth to stop myself laughing. 'I didn't like to say anything.'

'Can you believe this?' he says. 'I tried to convince them that the last thing they wanted was to have me teaching PE, but apparently all teachers have to do this. Portia thinks it's hilarious. She knows how good I am at exercise.'

'You could have just said no.'

'Did you not hear me? I did say no. I even said "no means no" and they told me that all the teachers have to cover Games and PE. There's a difference, apparently.'

'I have children, so I know there's a difference.'

'Well, aren't you the biggest swot in all of Axton Manor,' he grumbles.

'I am indeed.'

'It doesn't seem fair to me that I have to do this and you don't.'

'Me with my lungs and dodgy joints? No chance.'

'I'll see your dodgy joints and raise you one dislocated knee that still causes me pain in the cold.'

'How does that even compare? Lungs and joints – *multiple*.'

Mac points to his left knee. 'Knee, one. Dislocated.'

'You really don't know how to play the one-upwomanship game, do you?'

'Whatevs, as the kids say.'

'What is it with you and the sayings? Did ya steal the phone of a teenager or something?'

Mac grins at me and I have to look away in case I get that look on my face that causes that look on his face. 'My students at the university were Gen Zeds mostly, so I asked them for phrases so I could talk to this lot. Well, understand this lot. It has proved to be very fruitful.'

'Something like that,' I say with a smirk.

'How are you?' he asks, the smile suddenly gone and a serious look in place.

Normally I would brush him off with a 'fine'. But he isn't my friend, he is my support system, so I can't do that. I shrug, not sure what to say.

'You look strained,' he says gently. 'No one else can tell, well, maybe your husband, but I can see this is difficult for you. How can I help?'

'I don't think you can,' I say.

He sits in silence until I meet his eye. 'How can I help?' he repeats, gripping on to my attention like he is clinging on for dear life.

'You can come over before every PE or Games lesson wearing your kit and sporting your busted knee and let me laugh at you,' I reply.

He grins at me. 'I'm here if you need to talk,' he says.

'I know,' I reply. 'And thank you.'

There's a knock at my door causing Mac to jump to his feet and head out. He nods to my next appointment on the way out.

'Come in, Viola,' I say. 'Take a seat.'

She is the image of MJ, but with lighter hair and less of a sternness about her. That is where the similarities end. Viola is very much about people. She is open and friendly, cares what happens to others. She has been talking to me a lot about Fredi, and I think MJ is right, she does/did (?) have a crush on her. I'm not sure if she is gay or if she is pansexual in that she doesn't go for a particular gender – she is just attracted to certain people regardless of their gender. She adored Fredi and feels her loss acutely. She mentions Mariana sometimes in passing, but doesn't go into it at all.

Her main issue is, as MJ said, her mother.

Her hurt, her very real hurt at being sent away, as she sees it, and having to stay despite how much she hates it, causes her anxiety and stress. She feels powerless and abandoned. Her friends who have been here for years do not understand. She felt a connection with Fredi, felt less alone with her around, so her disappearance has hit her hard.

Viola Luna Hudson has become very good at hiding her distress. She knows that the world – *her* world – does not want to see her pain. They do not want to know about the dread she lives with that something has happened to her best friend, that something may happen to her. They believe in stiff upper lip, in keeping on despite the circumstances. Viola Luna Hudson has become a very good actress and it's breaking her down from the inside out. And it's her pain, her distress, the anguish of all the girls I speak to, that is breaking me down from the outside in.

Kez

April 2026, South London

Fredi Kingston's family live in a familiar-looking street in South London.

The terraced houses are redbrick with thick, sand-yellow grouting. The front gardens are edged with redbrick walls and many of them have elaborate hedges and plants that decorate and brighten up the street. My parents live ten minutes up the road, this is where I grew up, and at any other time I would drop by to see them, but I can't step out of the headspace and legend (undercover persona) I am in.

Yes, I am essentially playing myself, but it is a version of myself that my parents don't know. The second I walk through their front door I will become Schrödinger's Kez Lanyon – someone who delights and disappoints her parents at exactly the same time. To go to see them, I would have to step out of being the person who can stay away from her children for possibly weeks, the person who is about to walk into the house of a mother who is grieving the loss of her daughter. Even though Mrs Kingston is probably clinging to the belief she will see her daughter again, she will still be grieving. She will be lamenting the relationship she *thought* she had with her daughter, the missed opportunities to see that her daughter might run away, the moments that she didn't realise she could have said something that would have stopped her child from disappearing.

I am here because Jewel was right: I do need to talk to someone outside of Axton Manor. She clearly doesn't believe Fredi ran away, I don't believe Fredi ran away either. I'm not just saying that because of what MJ told me, but from the very limited knowledge I have of her from talking to her friends; she doesn't profile as a runner. Obviously, profiling is not infallible, I'm far from infallible and the more information you have on a person or a situation the better, but the reported battles she had with Mrs Lazloe and calling out Astrid when she was rude and racist, suggests someone who will always stay and fight. Someone, like me, who would always stand her ground. Who, like me, would stare her enemy in the eye rather than flee.

Maybe I see too much of myself in Fredi? Maybe I am thinking of her as the version of me who was plucked out of her life to go live this other life among a group of people – adults – who made it very clear they didn't want her in their world. Maybe with the growing up in the same area, the personality that won't run away from trouble, the thought of how I might have turned out if I had all these pressures as well as people telling me I wasn't good enough, is distracting me from my purpose. I am not here to put younger Kez in place of Fredi. I'm here to get more background on Fredi and to find out if there is anything any of us has missed that might actually tell us where she is.

The woman who answers the door is a wreck. She has a black and yellow scarf tied around her head, covering her hair, her face is drawn in, her eyes are dull and disengaged. Among Fredi's belongings that I have had a chance to look at is a picture of her with her parents. She is in the middle of the two adults, all of them are beaming for the camera. It's hard to think that the woman in front of me is the same woman from the photograph. It's hard to think the woman in front of me knows what smiling is, let alone indulged in it at some point in the past.

'Hello, my name is Dr Kez Lanyon,' I say as gently as I can. This woman is in an unimaginable amount of pain, I do not want to do anything that will add to that. 'I called yesterday about coming to see you about . . . about your daughter?'

The word 'daughter' jerks like an electric shock through every muscle in her body. I used it instead of 'Fredi' or 'Winifred' because I thought it might cause less pain. Not the case.

'I'm so sorry to come to see you at a time like this. I can go away and come back another time if it would be easier for you?'

'You said you want to help find her?' she replies, her words as fragile as freshly blown glass.

'Yes. I wanted to talk to you to see if there was anything you might know that you didn't know you knew that might help.'

'Come in,' she says. 'Come in. I'll do anything to find her. Anything.'

Mr Kingston is at work, she explains. 'Life goes on,' she says with a note of resentment. I'm not sure how I would feel about Jeb if he went back to work if Zoey went missing. They are practically the same age, and the pictures of the three of them adorning the walls could very easily be replaced with the photos we have of just Jeb, Zoey and me. I don't think I would cope very well at all if Jeb went back to work after something like this happened. Yes, I would know that he would need to keep working to make sure we didn't fall behind in mortgage payments, etc., but a part of me would still hate him for being able to.

After what happened when I . . . when I killed my friend Brian, I fell apart. I couldn't function, I couldn't even contemplate life returning to 'normal', which means I know I would probably cease to exist if something happened to one of my children.

I have to pull myself back, keep myself in check right now. Me feeling too much, relating too much, will not help this broken woman or her missing daughter.

In the living room is her friend. She has straight black hair to her shoulders, her trouser suit is stylish enough to have come from a high-fashion runway and her skin, as dark as mine, is absolutely flawless. She is immaculate in every way. She also has a demeanour that carries the weight of all the planets on her shoulders. She stands when I enter the room. She moves as though ready to come and shake my hand, but then quickly decides against it. I'm not sure why. Mrs Kingston – Noelle – introduces her as Jacinta Sanford, an old friend.

Mrs Kingston gestures to the squishy-looking brown leather chair beside me, telling me to sit. We all sit at the same time and I immediately sink into the chair's depths, feeling as though I am being wrapped up in a hug. My whole body relaxes in a way it didn't know it needed to until my bottom hit the material. These people love comfort. They value cosiness as much as aesthetics. This seat is so soothing I know I'm going to struggle to leave it. I resist the urge to look around at their home, to see what else will add to my profile of them and their lives. I resist, because the last thing Mrs Kingston needs is to suspect she's let in someone who is merely here to rubberneck and snoop.

'My Fredi didn't run away,' Mrs Kingston says. Her voice is stronger, more substantial when she says this. 'She is not the type of girl to run away.'

'That's why I am here,' I reply. 'A couple of her friends don't believe she ran away, either. Despite what they're being told, they don't think

Fredi ran away. And I'd much rather believe them over the school. But, I don't want to get your hopes up. I can't promise you I'll be successful, but I will do everything I can to find her.'

Noelle's expression hardens slightly. The sorrow in her eyes is replaced with mistrust. 'I think you're here to spy on me for that school,' she says quietly. 'That school thinks they can do anything they want because a few members of royalty and prime ministers' daughters were taught there. They think they can send in someone who looks like me to shut me up.'

'I can assure you that's not the case,' I say calmly. 'That's nowhere near the case. The headmaster tried to dissuade me from coming here. He would like nothing better than for me to accept that Fredi ran away. From what I've found out about her – her essays I've read, her friends I've spoken to – she doesn't come across as someone who would run away.' I open my hands, try to soften my seated stance so she begins to trust me on a subliminal level as well as listening to my words. I want to tell her everything, why I'm here, but I can't. I don't know if I can trust her not to go marching up to the school and to throw it in their faces that there is an investigation going on because her daughter did not run away. That would be a disaster. 'I was brought in to temporarily replace Dr Pemberton and, speaking to the girls, it's clear they have all been deeply upset by Fredi's disappearance. They desperately want to find her. Even if she has run away, they want to find her. I want to find her, too.

'I have a teenage daughter, pretty much the same age as Fredi. If this happened to her, not only would I not believe she would run away, I would want all the help I could get to find her, whether I am wrong or right about her running away. I am that help. And I can speak to the police, try to find out what they are and aren't doing.'

'Well, I can help you with that one. They are doing nothing.' Her face is suddenly daubed in agony, and she shuts her tear-filled eyes for a moment to steady herself. 'They told me all these things about my daughter.' She shakes her head, every line in her prematurely aging face is emphasised, entrenched. 'They said she was sleeping with him. That they found messages between them that proved she was sleeping with him. Fredi wouldn't do that. I would know.'

She probably wouldn't know. Very few parents, even the coolest, most open ones, have the relationship they think they have with their children. Very few actually know who their children are and what their children are capable of. You can tell yourself they would share things with you, their triumphs and their falls, but they never do completely. Zoey was called names every day for months before another parent rang me to tell me what was happening; Jonah was smacked around the head by other children for weeks before he broke down and told me. Brandee, my sort of foster child, had a baby without even telling me she was pregnant. And, of course, Moe got mixed up with some terrible people and ended up pulling a gun on me. I've always prided myself on having a great relationship with my children, and still these things happened that I had no knowledge of at all.

I used to kid myself that my children would tell me everything about their lives. That if they were in a bad situation I would be the first port of call, but that is exactly what I'm doing – kidding myself. Just like this woman is kidding herself. No matter how close she was to her daughter, she does not want to face the reality that her daughter won't have shared everything with her.

'Apart from the text and email messages, I can't find any evidence that Dr Pemberton would have had a relationship with a pupil,' I state. 'Did your daughter have any boyfriends past or present?'

'Now you sound like them!' she snaps. 'My daughter isn't fast. She wasn't interested in boys in that way. She didn't want a boyfriend and she didn't spend all her time preening herself to try to get a boyfriend. She found the whole thing weird. She was too young, it just wasn't in her head. That's why I know all those messages and emails are fake. They're all fake. My daughter isn't like that.'

I know all about people faking things. How easy it is to plant disinformation. Deep fakes don't just relate to the overwhelm of videos of celebs and influencers doing things they claim not to have done – it can relate to things like this. To information – evidence – that is manipulated and sometimes outright manufactured to create a certain narrative. In this instance, a young Black girl groomed by an older white man in a position of trust; a young Black girl who seduces, controls and eventually murders a decent older white man who is simply trying to help her. Those messages could be read in either way.

'I was asking in case she had anybody from her past who she might run to, who might have heard from her?'

Noelle shakes her head. 'No, I thought of that. I called everyone I could think of. All of her friends from her old school. Even a few from her nursery days. Nothing.'

While Noelle has been talking, cracks have been appearing in Jacinta Sanford's polished exterior; the burden she is carrying is suddenly unbearable and she needs to put it down.

'Mrs Sanford, are you all right?' I ask. 'You seem distressed. Is there something wrong?'

She glances first at Noelle, then at me, then at Noelle. She begins to wring her hands, her manicured nails gleaming as they go over and over each other.

'Jacinta feels responsible for Fredi going missing,' Noelle explains.

'Her husband passed and left money in his will for Fredi's schooling. He wanted her to go to the best schools possible.' Her voice cracks. 'We gave Fredi the choice to go anywhere she wanted. Anywhere in the country. She chose Axton Manor, probably because Jacinta's daughter went there.'

'You have a daughter at Axton Manor?'

Mrs Sanford puts her hands up over her face and starts to sob. Her sobs are deep, loud; they move her whole body. Noelle doesn't comfort her friend. She instead shows deep contempt for the woman beside her. She clearly blames Jacinta Sanford.

Tears teeter on the edge of Noelle's eyes, but she is a person who cries in private, alone. She does not want anyone to see her true grief. 'Mariana went missing last year,' Noelle explains.

Mariana. The girl Viola Hudson's friends were talking about. The girl that MJ must have been talking about when she said someone else went missing. But I'm obviously not meant to know about that, so I say, 'At school?'

Jacinta's sobs grow louder and Noelle nods, before explaining: 'She had an accident. Fell from one of the windows of the clock tower. She broke her wrist. A couple of weeks later, she ran away. Disappeared without a trace. Jacinta thinks she had the accident while running from bullies. But no one will admit to the school having a bullying problem. And I don't know, Mariana was popular there. Fredi said Mariana always said she loved being there in her letters. Her running away made no sense.'

Noelle doesn't profile as someone who is reckless enough to just send her daughter into a place where someone she knew had disappeared. *So why would you choose to send your daughter there?*

'I didn't,' she says, seeming to read my mind. 'I didn't choose to send her there. I told Fredi I didn't want her going there. I didn't want her anywhere near that place. It has always seemed like bad vibes. But we said she could choose. And she kept saying she wanted to go there. The letters Mariana sent before . . . the letters she sent made it seem like the perfect place to go. I said no. *I said no.* But her dad. But Jacinta . . . They both said it would be all right. Especially since Jacinta said she'd got a postcard from Mariana. The postcard said she was fine and she was happy. Jacinta said it would be all—' Noelle jumps up and runs out of the room, leaving me with a sobbing Jacinta Sanford.

This is not what I was expecting, at all. I was expecting to get some background on Fredi, to maybe see her room, to try to connect with her mother. Now I'm in the middle of a maelstrom. And I suspect . . . I suspect all is not as it seems.

'Do you want to tell me what's really going on?' I ask Jacinta once her sobbing has finally subsided. There is something going on, because why would you encourage your friend to send her daughter to somewhere from which your daughter had disappeared? Why would you do that? Unless . . . 'Were you an old girl of Axton Manor?' I have found this streak of loyalty among the ex-Axton Manor pupils that seems to trump everything that would stop most people doing stupid stuff.

She takes her hands away from her face, the rivulets of tears have streaked the heavy make-up on her cheeks. But, for the amount of sobbing she was doing, her make-up should be down her neck, not just a bit streaked. Crocodile tears? What the hell is going on here?

'I thought she would be OK,' she eventually says. 'I never dreamed . . .'

I notice she has avoided answering my question about being an old girl.

'When was the last time you spoke to her?'

Dramatically, she closes her eyes, shakes her head, affects a tortured face. And it is affected, it is not what she is truly feeling. 'My husband, Jacob and I, we really only wanted what was best for Fredi. Education is so important, being around the right people from an early age is so important.' *Definitely an old girl.* And, again, not answering the question asked. 'Jacob knew how bright Fredi was. He always said she was wasted at her school, that she deserved the best, to go to the best schools to give her the best chance in life. After what happened to Mariana, he was determined to make sure Fredi was looked after; she was like another daughter to him. And then he died so suddenly. Heart attack. I think his heart broke because he was so close to Mariana. That's why he wanted to do everything he could for Fredi. He set up an educational trust in Fredi's name. She had money to see her through until after university. I thought . . . I truly believed she would be all right. That she would thrive.'

'When was the last time you spoke to her?' I try again.

'She was perfect for Axton Manor. I never thought this would happen to her. That she would end up like Mariana.'

'When was the last time you spoke to her?'

'Noelle is never going to forgive me. Neither is Harry.'

'When was the last time you spoke to her?' I keep asking because there is so obviously more to this than this woman wants to share. And the more I ask, and she ignores the question, the more I am forming an idea in my head about what is really going on. About how Fredi really ended up in Axton Manor. This woman. She is the reason.

'I just can't believe—'

'The more you avoid answering my questions, Mrs Sanford, the more I think the worst of you and the more it looks like you manipulated your friend to put her daughter in harm's way.'

Her perfectly lipsticked mouth opens to speak and suddenly Noelle is flying into the room, grabbing her friend and dragging her to her feet. 'What is she talking about?' Noelle demands, her face wild.

Oh Lordy, that was not meant to happen.

'*What is she talking about?*' Noelle screams.

'It wasn't how she was saying. I didn't deliberately put Fredi in harm's way. It wasn't meant to go like that.'

'Did you really get a postcard from your daughter?' I ask.

Jacinta hesitates and then shakes her head. Noelle gasps in horror.

I hate being right about things like this. Because it means that there are more terrible human beings out there, and that they don't just work at Insight – they can be ordinary humans that we live with. Not all psychopaths are serial killers. Not all psychopaths run government-adjacent units. Some of them live ordinary lives and think nothing of using those closest to them to get what they want. I'll have to get someone to look into her husband's death because it seems a bit convenient that he died leaving all this money so Fredi could go to Axton Manor and investigate her daughter's disappearance. Because that is clearly what has gone on here. I mean, I'm sure she didn't think this would happen, that Fredi would disappear, too, but she did put Fredi there.

Noelle is about to do Jacinta real harm, and it takes real effort to separate them, and to hold Noelle back so she doesn't keep going for Jacinta.

'You need to tell us the truth,' I say to Jacinta. 'The whole truth this time, so we can find out what really happened to Fredi.'

'I swear to you, I didn't put her in harm's way on purpose. I promise you.'

'Tell me what you did to my daughter!' Noelle snaps.

'I had to find out what happened to Mariana. It wasn't my idea. It was hers. When I offered you and her the money, it really was for her to go wherever she wanted. She came to me. She came to me and said she wanted to go to Axton Manor to find out what had happened to Mariana. You know how much she loved Mariana. I couldn't stop her. I kept telling her no. I kept saying I didn't want anything to happen to her, but she begged me.'

A girl begged her and she said yes? Really. I don't blame Noelle for trying to punch her lights out. I want to punch her lights out and it's not even my daughter.

'You could have said no,' I reply. 'You could have stopped it in its tracks by telling Noelle. You didn't have to go along with it because a teenager said you should.'

'I know you won't understand, but I had to find out what happened to Mariana. I'm sorry, Noelle. I'm so sorry. I never thought—' She stops talking when Noelle slaps her across her face; the sound of her palm on Jacinta's face makes my stomach turn.

Now she starts to cry. Really cry. 'I'm so sorry. I'm so sorry,' she sobs.

'I need you to sit down and tell me everything you know about Fredi and Axton Manor, if I'm going to find out what really happened to her. And then you need to tell me everything about Mariana and her disappearance, because it's obvious that the two things are connected.'

Jacinta Sanford nods her head and takes a seat. Noelle moves as far away from her as she can in their living room. 'I'm not supposed to tell you this. I'm not supposed to tell you anything, but especially not about this. There is a code of silence that has been in place for over a hundred years. I think it's why Mariana disappeared. I think it's why

Fredi disappeared.' She begins to talk and talk. By the time I leave I am boiling mad.

MJ. *MJ.*

Of course she sent me in without all the information. Of course she didn't let me know a vital piece of this mystery. Of course she didn't tell me about The Platinum.

Fredi

● **Record Voice Note** ▶ **Recorded: January 2026**

Had the most awkward conversation ever today. Dr Pemberton sent a message to my Biology class asking me to come see him in his office. I was dreading going there after seeing his thing, but when I got there Miss Akande was there, too.

'First of all,' Miss Akande said, 'if you would like another teacher here, I am more than happy with that. We can call in anyone who would make you feel more comfortable.'

'I'm fine,' I said to her. I mean, I was as fine as I could be sitting in a room with two people I saw doing it and one whose *thing* I saw.

'I want to apologise for what you saw,' Miss Akande began. 'It was very inappropriate and I can imagine that you have questions . . .?'

In my head, lots of images of them doing it flashed up. But I had zero questions about it. 'I really do not have any questions,' I told her.

'We will understand if you want to tell the headmaster,' Dr Pemberton said. 'Nothing will happen to you. What we did was completely inappropriate and I am sorry for the impact it might have had on you mentally or emotionally.'

I was like, I don't know, [*sounds of shrugging*] sitting there staring at the ground, not knowing what to say. What was I supposed to say? I wasn't going to tell the headmaster. Or anyone. Miss Akande and Dr Pemberton are two of my favourite adults at Axton Manor.

I am not snitching on them. Even if it was like seeing your parents having sex. And they're older than Mum and Dad. I mean, kudos for still doing it at their age and not needing a bed to do it. But they should have been more careful about it. If they had been caught by Astrid, she would have told everyone before the end of Games.

But it was over now. Done with. I never wanted to think about it again. It was like something written in the sand on the beach. As soon as the tide comes in, it washes the words clean away, leaving the sand as good as new. That's what I was thinking of this as. The image of him taking off her knickers, putting his fingers up her skirt, her pushing down his trousers, him pressing her against the wall and then doing that, and the image of his thing when she pushed him away, all of it is on the beach. And here comes a big, strong wave, washing it all away, erasing every single bit of it so it looks like it was never there.

There, the beach is criss, completely clear and pristine. It's like it was never, ever there.

'Would you rather we forget all about it and never bring it up again?' Miss Akande said, reading my mind like Mum does.

I nodded very fast.

'We'll do the same,' Miss Akande confirmed. 'Thank you for your time, Fredi. You can return to class.'

I left the door slightly open when I left because I wanted to hear what they said.

'Do you think she'll tell anyone?' Dr Pemberton asked.

'I don't know. She hasn't so far, so maybe not.'

'What will we do if she does?'

'Whatever we have to, I suppose,' Miss Akande said. 'Whatever we have to.'

I really like her, so I'm sure she didn't mean that to sound as threatening as it did. I'm sure she didn't.

■ **End Voice Note** ↓ **Save Recording** ↗ **Send To Private Cloud**

Kez

April 2026, Axton Manor

'You told me that you didn't want to know too much before you arrived so it wouldn't taint how you conducted this investigation,' MJ says when I ring her from my car to ask about The Platinum.

'Don't give me that,' I say to her. 'You know full well what I was talking about. I didn't want to be tainted or swayed by your impressions of people. Not something as huge as this.'

She is silent on the phone for several seconds, hoping, I'll wager, that I will just move on. I will not be 'just moving on'. Not even a little.

'This is how Dennis got me shot last year,' I tell her. 'He kept huge amounts of information from me and I ended up in hospital for a week as a result.'

'Kez, do you think I would have come to you if it was as simple as just telling you everything?'

'So you're keeping even more stuff from me?'

'I . . .' Her words fade away and I sense she is struggling with herself. Struggling with her natural instinct to tell me to do one and to be completely honest with me. Except her version of 'do one' would involve nicer words, explaining there were things I couldn't know.

I can see in my mind's eye her closing her eyes, trying to calm herself as the battle rages inside. 'It may not seem it to you, Kez, but everything I do, I do for my children. Even though she hates me, I am doing this for Viola. There are some things you won't understand.'

'Because I'm not one of you elite? Too working class and Black?'

'No, that's not what I'm saying. At all. I'm saying, some of the girls who disappeared or ran away, were from "my" background. They were one of us "elites", as you call us. They had mothers who went to Axton. They *still* disappeared.'

Like Mariana. MJ is scared that if she talks and someone finds out, Viola will disappear or will be disappeared. These people . . . For someone like MJ to be scared, they must be everywhere. *Everywhere.* This is why, I suppose, she came to me. For MJ, it wasn't just about the board of trustees and governors wanting to find some warm bodies to throw under the bus of salvaging any reputational damage that may occur if Noelle and Harry Kingston keep on talking about what happened to their daughter, it's about finding the killer, finding out what happened to Fredi so Viola will be safe.

MJ is scared for her daughter and is doing everything she can to keep her safe. Even asking me for help.

'Please don't ask me anything else,' she says. 'I've told you everything that I can.'

'I doubt that, but OK.'

'How are you getting on? I know we agreed I wouldn't ask, but . . . how is it going?'

'I know what you're really asking, MJ,' I say as gently as possible, 'but I can't tell you anything other than I know who Viola is and I've seen her around the school premises.'

'She told me she's seen you, had some sessions with you,' MJ explains, thankfully not pushing me to betray the confidentiality of therapy. 'She said you're funny.'

'Funny ha-ha or funny peculiar?' I reply before I can stop myself.

MJ's reply is silence.

One beat.

Two beats.

I suppose the best I can hope for is that she thinks I'm both.

'I have to go, Kez. I will speak to you soon.'

'Yeah, sure, bye.'

We hang up at the same time and for a moment or two it feels like I actually know less than when I got here.

Kez

April 2026, Axton Manor

I am one of the first in the breakfast hall this morning and the only other teacher in there is Portia Akande, Mac's ex-fiancée. She's wearing the school staff PE kit and has a whistle around her neck. Her hair is folded back into the two neat cornrows again. She beckons me over with a big smile and I nervously go over to her.

I'm not sure what the nerves are about.

'Hello,' she says with a smile. 'How are you? How did you sleep?'

'I'm good, thank you. How did you sleep?'

'I don't know. You're one of the first people to ask me that in years! Hmmm . . . how did I sleep? Good, I guess.'

'Did I hear you right the other day? You're an old girl?'

'Yes, yes I am, for my sins.'

'Did you know MJ Hudson, or Parsons as she was back then?'

'You mean Maisie?' Portia replies.

'Yes.'

'That will never not be funny to me,' she replies. 'That she changed her name to MJ. When we were in school we all agreed that anyone who wouldn't own their name, however ridiculous, was an FE.'

'An FE?'

'An iron-ist. The most available element. It was a way of calling someone common without using the words. You know, that's such FE behaviour. Changing your name was what FEs did to get ahead. And look what Maisie did first chance she got.'

Portia speaks like someone who has been personally harmed by MJ. Like someone who would be very pleased to witness her downfall. Or the downfall of her offspring? 'So you did know her?'

'We all knew Maisie. She's pure Rh, that's—'

'Rhodium,' I interject. 'I know. My husband is a scientist of sorts. He talks about precious metals a lot in relation to his work. Rhodium is one of the most expensive precious metals on the planet.'

'So you understand that Maisie was top tier?'

'I get that now. You didn't hang out at all?'

'No, I didn't. I wasn't an Rh person. Didn't want to be, to be honest. It was stressful. It's hard to get into that group without meeting certain criteria. I mean, Maisie met it before she even stepped into the building. Her mother was an old girl.'

'And her mother was an Rh-er, ist?'

'No.'

'OK, was she one of The Platinum?'

'How do you know about The Platinum?'

'It came up in conversation with another old girl.'

'I see.'

'So Maisie's mother? Was she a Platinum?'

'No. Well, sort of no. It's not that simple. The Platinum are headed by the girls with the longest family history at the school.'

'So wouldn't MJ's mother be one of them?'

'Yes, but no as well.' Portia lowers her voice and shifts closer to me across the table. 'The Platinum used to be the ones in charge. They used to run things and, yes, your heritage, bloodline or last name almost automatically earned you a spot amongst them. They were the elite of the elite, because, look around you, this is the elite. The Platinum were – are – the brightest and the best. If you don't have the breeding or the family name, you can still get in by being obscenely wealthy.'

'Right. I see. Or at least I think I see.'

'But The Platinum aren't who run things around here now.'

'They aren't? I'm guessing it is the Rhodiums? Rhodium is part of the Platinum group and, like you said, the most expensive precious metal on the planet, so stands to reason they'd be the ones in charge.' I feel rather smug that I managed to work that out so I sit back to bask in my brilliance.

'No. We just called individuals Rh-ers. The Platinum are known about. They're meant to be this secret society, but it's all about wealth and name with them.' She leans even closer, her voice dropping even lower. 'It's the Quiet Girls you needed to be worried about. They hold the real power. Inside and outside of this place. They're the proper secret society. They're the ones who everyone knew to be terrified of.'

I draw back a little and frown. I search Portia's beautiful face for micro-expressions, even the tiniest hint of mocking or having me on, but there isn't any sign of that at all.

'MJ was one of them?'

'You never know who exactly is one of them, but it seemed like she was. When she first arrived, she was bullied mercilessly, then she had her accident and, after that, the bullying stopped and her Rh status – elite of the elite – was established. A lot of us thought she became one of the QGs.'

'What was the accident?'

'She fell from one of the lower levels of the clock tower.'

'Where Pemberton died?'

She nods. 'It was curious, a few girls fell from there. After they fell, no more bullying for those who weren't left with life-changing injuries, of course.'

'You think it was an initiation ceremony? To become a QG?'

'I think I had better go and set up my classroom for this morning's sessions.' She smiles at me in a way that reminds me that secret societies, especially ones that require people to be willing to harm themselves to get into, don't generally like people to talk about them in any detail. Yes, you can whisper their name, you can be scared, you can use it as a threat to anyone who thinks about stepping out of line, but you can't just openly talk about them. Speculate. Especially not out here, where anyone can overhear. Because the thing about these sorts of societies is that they are by their nature hiding in plain sight. You never know who you're talking to and what their connection is. The only person you can ever really know isn't a part of them is yourself.

Mrs Sanford knew this, so only told me about The Platinum, not the Quiet Girls. Even with her daughter gone and Fredi in danger, possibly gone, too, she didn't give up the Quiet Girls. What they do to gain the girls' loyalty must be brutal.

'Can I just ask, before you go? If MJ did become one of *them*, then would her daughter be expected to join them as well?'

'You take care of yourself Dr Lanyon,' she says and stands up.

Mac enters the dining room just as she is leaving and they pause, smile at each other with deep, familiar affection. She places her hand on his chest for a moment and he nods at her. I'm pretty sure she isn't the woman he said he was seeing, but the connection between Mac and Portia is deep and powerful. It's blatantly obvious they're back together or on the road to getting back together and while I'm truly pleased for them, it's probably not going to be so great for the woman he said he was seeing. Not that any of that is my business.

Especially when my mind is currently whirring with thoughts of the other huge element of this that MJ didn't tell me about. If she was a part of the Quiet Girls, that means her daughter is likely to be a member, too. Does that mean she did something to Fredi? Have their initiation rituals evolved into hurting other people?

Maybe even murder?

Part 7

Part 2

Fredi

● **Record Voice Note** ▶ **Recorded: January 2026**

One of our compulsory co-curriculars are deportment lessons. I am not even joking.

We have to learn how to carry ourselves in polite society and generally through the world. They don't tell you any of that on the website or in the brochure, but it is something all the girls have to do.

We have to learn how to walk tall, speak carefully, which cutlery to use, how to set a dinner service, which wine goes with which meal, all of that. I kid you not. We also have to learn how to dance. I mean, I can drop all the latest moves without even breaking a sweat, but they mean formal dancing with a male partner.

They are kind of affiliated with Dewhurst College for Boys, which is quite near Little Buxley. It is an elite private school with partial boarding, but most of the boys come from the rich families within an hour or so drive to the school.

Although, they don't like people using the word 'rich'. It's like a swear word or a slur or something. The way the girls from rich families look offended if you mention that word or suggest they are rich . . . it could get you cancelled around here. Even the girls who come from ordinary backgrounds like mine, the ones who have to clear plates on Sunday evenings like me, don't use it.

People don't like the words 'rich' or 'wealthy' or 'privileged'. It's impolite and rude to talk about it, so they just use words like 'well-connected' or 'from a good family' or stuff like that. They *never* talk about money. Or like to suggest they have money. But they do like to make it clear that they are in charge. It's really hard to explain. My family is 'good'. I come from a good – great, actually – family, but we don't qualify in the way that they mean it.

This term we are taking formal dance lessons. Most of the other girls have been doing it for years, so they know what they're doing. I do not. I watch *Strictly* with Mum and Dad, but I've never thought of actually doing those dances. Because of my inexperience, the boys from Dewhurst were not interested in dancing with me.

All right, it was one of the reasons why they weren't interested in dancing with me. Most of them could tell I wasn't one of them, and quite a few of them had girls in their sights who they were obviously already hooking up with. When I say all these people know each other because they're from the same 'good' families, I am not joking, bro.

When we were told to pick our partners, I just knew I was going to be Fredi all alone, left on the side and then forced on someone who was late to class. But one of the boys headed straight for me. He stuck his hand out for me to shake.

'I'm Silas,' he said. He was confident like the other boys, but he was the only Black boy in this class.

'Fredi,' I replied. 'Short for Winifred.' Bro, what? Why did I even say that? I never say things like that.

'Silas is long and short for Silas,' he said and smiled. 'Would you care to dance with me?'

'If you want,' I said.

He took my hand like the other boys did to the other girls and led me onto the dance floor. He put his hand on my waist and I flinched because no boy had ever done that to me before. I don't think anyone except my mum and maybe a doctor or two has done that to me before.

'It's OK,' he whispered, 'I'm not going to hurt you.' He placed his hand more firmly on my waist and then whispered, 'Put your hand on my shoulder.' I did as I was told. And then he kept moving my hand in his until the hold was correct. It's quite fiddly this formal dancing stuff. 'Just relax,' he said once we were in position. 'Just go along with the music, I'll guide you. Move your feet in time with mine.'

He made it sound so simple and easy, so when the music started and the teacher's voice started barking instructions, I tried. I looked at the other girls, the other couples, and tried to follow them as well. 'Glide,' the teacher kept saying. 'Glide.'

I am not born to glide.

'Are you new?' Silas asked. He was talking to me like normal, even though I had stepped on his feet like a hundred times in the past five minutes. 'I haven't seen you here before.'

'Yes, just started. I'm from London.'

'Cool. London is fantastic. One of my favourite places to visit.'

'Visit? Where are you from, then?'

'Right here in Axton Vale, the village. My mother owns one of the shops in the village. Dr Jewel's Herbal Emporium. Don't know if you've seen it?'

'Oh, yes, I think I saw it when I went to the village. But we didn't go in.'

'It's quite popular, but people always act like they're ashamed of going in to get their herbal remedies. And of course, being a Black woman, everyone thinks she's selling drugs.' He couldn't stop himself smiling. 'She isn't, by the way. Ask her about it and she'll give you all these reasons why you shouldn't take drugs. She's a qualified herbalist, but before that she was a GP. So she's kind of the best of both worlds, but also a total pain about anything like drugs or drinking. Don't know why I'm telling you about my mother. Like that's cool or something. Total loss of aura.'

I was about to say it wasn't a loss of aura to me when Miss Perlich's face appeared beside mine. 'This isn't a social club, Miss Kingston. You have a lot of ground to make up. I suggest you stop the chatter and concentrate.' Then she turned to Silas. 'I expected better of you, Mr Mallossi.'

'Apologies, Miss Perlich,' Silas said smoothly, the biggest grin on his face. 'I am trying to get to know my beautiful companion so I can understand how to help her grasp the tenets of dance that you're trying to impart to us. I will refrain from chatter from now on.'

The stern, angry look on Miss Perlich's face melted clean away and she looked absolutely flattered, as though he'd just told her that she was the most amazing teacher in the world. I'd never seen anything like it. Not from someone my age. The guy had mad rizz.

When Miss Perlich walked away, Silas raised an eyebrow and smiled a little smile at me. 'Talk afterwards,' he whispered.

Outside the dance studio, Silas was waiting for me. And it made my stomach go all funny. 'You need to practise to catch up to everyone else,' he said.

'Do I?' I replied, offended that my efforts in the class were clearly fooling no one. I didn't like to be behind everyone else. I tried really hard all the time. I hated that my best wasn't good enough right now.

'Yes, you do, Miss Winifredi. I and my badly bruised feet are offering to assist you in this matter.'

'Are you now? How are you going to do that?'

'Very simple, actually. I will ask my mother to email my school and your school to allow me to come to your school so we can practise.'

'What? They would allow that?'

'Yes. Maybe. And if they don't, you can ask to come to my house and we can practise there.'

'Why would you do that?'

He shrugged. 'Why not?'

He got his phone out of his pocket, and asked for my number. I hesitated. This was the first time I would be giving a boy I didn't know my number. It felt like the sort of thing I should totally be talking to Bev and Carina about. I mean . . . he is really good-looking and he has so much rizz. And he seems really nice.

It's not the same talking to Viola and the others about it. I don't think they'd get what a big deal this is. Astrid, Haniya and Issy have boyfriends who go to Dewhurst. I don't know if Viola likes boys, and Paris wouldn't tell us anything anyway. And I'm sure she's still seeing Headmaster Rhodes's son.

This is the first boy I've noticed, I think. I don't really tend to like boys that much. Not in that way. I never really understood Bev's obsession with Marvin or why Carina was so willing to go through all that stuff with Jeanette over Dexter. It just didn't make any sense to me. The things that girls seem to be willing to do because of a boy or to get a boy to notice them or to get with a boy just seem so unnecessary. But do I think that because I haven't met the right boy?

This one, Silas, is he the right boy?

Is this it, now? Am I going to lose focus and start doing silly things because I like him? Oh, OK, I like him. I guess that came out of nowhere, admitting that. I hope I don't start losing my mind and behaving weirdly because I like him.

How will I know if I do? Bev and Carina aren't here to tell me. The girls here don't know me. And, anyway, what am I even talking about? I met the guy for an hour today and I gave him my number – that is literally all. It doesn't mean anything.

Except I low-key feel like it does.

■ **End Voice Note** ↓ **Save Recording** ↗ **Send To Private Cloud**

Kez

April 2026, Axton Manor

For some reason, the knock at the office door makes me jump.

'Come in,' I call, trying to calm my speeding heart. I don't have any appointments for another half an hour, so I'm not sure who it is. The door opens and in walks the headmaster's assistant, Miss Barkway. My heart calms down. Talking to the girls is stressing me out more than I realise, I think. It has been bringing up feelings of my times at school. Worries about Zoey and Jonah. I feel sick thinking about what they go through at school. What they don't tell me. What could be happening to them that I don't know about.

You trust your children with the people you send them to, to be educated. You don't expect them to have to deal with ongoing sources of trauma. Your teen years are fraught, but I had forgotten how deep a vein of angst, trauma, emotional and mental instability it is possible for young people to experience.

One of my constant issues with being a therapist is the toll it can take on me. How I feel, sometimes, like I am being dragged under with the weight of other people's problems. Admittedly, since I started to confront the reality of Brian's death with Mac's help last year, things have improved. I don't feel the lacerations of other people's pain as much. I still feel their shared burden, but it doesn't incapacitate me.

And, whenever I've had to speak to someone as a therapist at Insight, their experiences are so far removed from most people's reality that it doesn't feel real. It doesn't encroach on my everyday thoughts. I have empathy for them, I can counsel them, I can even go as far as to understand them. But it is not the same as listening to a girl describe how the words get stuck in her throat, literally, and how speaking out in class, in public makes her choke. It is not the same as hearing someone talk matter-of-factly about knowing her teacher is purposefully downgrading her because the teacher is racist, but there is nothing she can do to prove it. It is not the same as watching the effects of someone telling you that their parent told them they were a mistake and they've been trying to correct that mistake by making themselves as perfect as they can be ever since.

Insight has shielded me from the reality of people's lives and I hate Dennis for that. Actually hate him. I had forgotten what I was meant to be doing with my life. How I was meant to be out there helping people in any way that I can. How I was meant to change the world one mind at a time, one patient at a time. I hate Dennis for taking me away from what I am meant to be doing. Because, much as I might want to, the devil's bargain I made with him means that I can't. This is what Jeb meant, what Mac meant.

I had stopped seeing what Insight was. Why I was there in the first place. I'd started to blend in, which meant I had started to think like Dennis and the others. Something I was never meant to do.

'Mr Rhodes asked me to invite you to dinner,' Miss Barkway says.

I eye up the computer in front of me before I suspiciously eye up Miss Barkway. 'And you couldn't email me? Message me?'

'He requires an immediate response.'

It's the telephone's turn to be eyed up under suspicion. 'Couldn't have called?'

She smiles and she looks a million years younger than I thought her to be. All right, hyperbole. I assumed she was older than me, but now I'm thinking she may be my age or younger. She dresses in the way you would stereotypically expect someone who would have the position of assistant to a headteacher of a private school: floral, fussy dresses, low beige court shoes, brown hair rolled back into a forties, wartime style. 'Mr Rhodes . . . likes to watch,' she says.

That's a very deliberate turn of phrase. I stare at her, slightly alarmed. She is telling me something and I'm not sure I like what it is. I profile her again. Her dress says one thing, her words say another. She is someone who is constantly overlooked, dismissed. She is someone who knows a lot more than she's ever really asked about. She blends into the background so people are very often open and indiscreet around her.

'Can I ask you what you mean by that?'

'Mr Rhodes . . . he . . . likes to watch . . . people's reactions to his requests. If he cannot observe the reaction to something himself, he likes me to do it for him and to report back.'

This, I was not expecting. 'Do you have a moment?' I ask. 'Could you please come in, shut the door, sit down and give me a moment of your time?'

Miss Barkway – Daphne – does as I have asked. She sits in the chair opposite me as though waiting to take dictation.

I stay on my side of the desk because I think she would be more comfortable with furniture separating us. 'I know there was a history of sharing what was discussed in this room, but that doesn't happen any longer, so whatever you say to what I'm about to ask you will stay between us. You don't have to answer, but if you do want to answer, it will stay confidential.'

'That sounds rather ominous, Mrs Lanyon,' she says. 'Sorry, Dr Lanyon.'

'It's not ominous . . . I just . . . Has Mr Rhodes been inappropriate with you?' I ask.

Her whole expression jerks into surprise before she fixes her face. I'm not sure why when she has just opened the door to that line of thought. Is it because no one has picked up on it before?

'Why are you asking me that?' she replies.

'Again, I want to reiterate that you don't have to answer and, if you do, anything you say will be kept between us. I ask because I sense some ambivalence towards him?' I am treading as gently as possible, trying not to scare her. 'I am wondering if he sometimes asks you to do things that go beyond the remit of the position?'

She relaxes, her whole body unclenching. She thinks I think she just doesn't like him because he gets her to do things that aren't part of her job description. Her secret, as far as she's concerned, is safe. Far from it. It's just confirmed that he has put hands on her and/or has said things that are unwelcome and unwanted. She hates him. It's clear on her face.

'I do know too much about him,' she replies diplomatically. 'He treats me like his housekeeper and nanny sometimes. I often have to rewrite the missives he sends out to stop them sounding like the deranged ravings of a dictator. He does acknowledge that he would be lost without me.'

'Do you like your job?'

'Well . . . yes. I love it. I . . . When I left school, I didn't think I would be able to do much. But I managed to get into secretarial college and after two years I had so many qualifications. I worked for many different companies at a very high level, but when Mr Rhodes became headmaster he contacted me and asked me to be his assistant.'

'You knew him before?'

'Yes, I'm an old girl. He was a junior master here.'

'Right, I see.' He has been grooming her since she was a girl. *He likes to watch.* A very specific turn of phrase. I feel sick all of a sudden. I know he likes to test boundaries. I know it's very hard to keep your boundaries in place when you're young, especially from adults you come into contact with every day. Hell, it's difficult to keep your boundaries in place as an adult. I know Dennis and I go at it, that I stand up to him and fight him, but he has from the moment I met him tested my boundaries. Eroded them, too. So much so that I didn't even notice it had happened. *He likes to watch.* Jeez, what has this man done? What is this man still doing?

'I know how it is to work for a difficult and demanding man,' I say. 'If you ever want to let off steam or talk to me about anything, anything at all, my door is always open. Not literally, usually because this building is draughty, but metaphorically.'

'The same,' she replies.

'I'm sorry?'

'If you ever want to talk to me about anything, anything at all, my door is always metaphorically open, too.'

That takes me aback. Why would she say that? For the same reason that I'm saying it? Is this foreshadowing? Does she know that Mr Rhodes is planning on doing something to me and she is warning me in the only way she can? Is she playing with me? Are her and Rhodes in on it together?

'Do you think something is going to happen to me?' I ask her. 'Do you think I'm going to meet the same end as Dr Pemberton?'

'No, no!' she replies. 'You don't smoke. And you don't strike me as someone who regularly goes up to high places when you have upset and annoyed a lot of people.'

Is this woman telling me that Dr Pemberton was definitely murdered as MJ suspected? That he got people's backs up and there was a queue of people waiting to push him off the building?

'No, no, I'm not.'

'Then you should be fine, Dr Lanyon.' She stands up. 'What shall I tell Mr Rhodes about dinner at his residence with his family?'

'Ummm . . . yes? I guess? When would that be, exactly?'

'Tomorrow night, he suggested. All of his family will be there and he would very much like you to meet them.'

'Sounds lovely. Can't wait. Do I need to bring anything?'

'I wouldn't have thought so. You're the first person to have ever asked me that.'

'I feel weirdly proud of myself. Thank you for coming over to ask me. Will you be at the dinner?'

'I will not. You couldn't pay me to sit through one of those dinners.' She grins at me. 'I have to go and see Dr Mackenzie now, ask him to dinner, too.'

'Well, I will see you soon.'

He likes to watch. That keeps echoing through my head. *He likes to watch. He likes to watch. He likes to watch.*

Fredi

● **Record Voice Note** ▶ **Recorded: February 2026**

'Well, I am very pleased to meet you, Fredi,' Silas's mum said to me. 'Or would you prefer Winifredi, like my son calls you?'

Silas has been teaching me to dance. The school allowed him to come over on the weekend to help me and he did actually want to help me with dance. We would talk for five minutes beforehand and then we would dance and dance. He's taught me all the moves, all the little cues you're supposed to pick up from your partner, how you're supposed to move your body to match or contrast or complement his. How to know where to put your feet at any given time. He's such a good teacher and because of him, Miss Perlich now ignores me rather than constantly being on my case. In one class she even used Silas and me as an example of how to do something.

'Teacher's pet,' Paris had joked after that class. And she *was* joking. She wasn't doing that thing where she made a joke and her eyes would be shooting daggers and threatening all sorts. She seemed genuinely OK with it. Which was a relief cos it means things have settled down since she threatened me.

Viola asked me the other day if I was going out with Silas and I said I didn't know. And she asked if I wanted to go out with him and I said

I didn't know again. And then she asked if he kissed me, what would I do, and I said I didn't know. And then we both laughed because for someone who thinks as much as I do, I didn't know much at all.

Anyway, now that he doesn't have to come and help me with the dancing any more, Silas invited me to his house for dinner. And so I can meet his mum. He never talks about a dad or another mum or another parent, so I assume it's just the two of them. After a note from his mum, the school gave me permission to go down and see him, so he came to pick me up.

He asked if I wanted to go the long way or through the woods. I chose the long way because those woods are too creepy to be going in there unannounced.

'My mother can be a bit overwhelming when you first meet her,' he warned as we walked up from the school towards their house. They have a small flat above his mum's shop that they rent out as a holiday let, and they have a large cottage at the edge of the village where the village meets the woods. 'I mean that in a good way,' he added quickly. 'She's a bit like me, but full on.'

I think what he meant, too, is that his mother is very tall and statuesque. I've heard tall women called that before and it seems fitting. She is tall and curvy and strong. She has dreadlocks down to her waist and the biggest smile. Silas looks exactly like her.

'Silas talks about you all the time,' she said to me. 'It's nice that he's met a girl he can bring home. He meets those girls all the time at the various functions and events, but he never brings any of them home. But now you're here.'

'You see what I mean?' Silas said to me. 'Mum, enough of the aura killing. Do you want to see my room and listen to music before dinner?'

'Yes, sure,' I said.

'Door open at all times, OK?' his mother said.

And I smirked because what did she think was going to happen with her right there? Did she think we'd do it or something? We haven't even kissed or held hands.

'Oh my God, you're just determined to make sure the game is gone, aren't you?' Silas complained before leading us upstairs to his bedroom.

He has a nice bedroom. It's big, double the size of my bedroom at home. It has a desk, a bed, loads of shelves and two huge windows. I went to the bookshelves closest to the door and started reading the spines, trying to work out who he is from his collection of books. There were so many academic textbooks and non-fiction ones on business and decolonisation. Some of them were in French and Xhosa, one of the South African languages. This guy is super smart, I'm not kidding you.

'Have you read all of these?' I asked him.

'No, not really. Well, some of them.'

'You're a big old nerd, aren't you?' I teased.

'And what of it? My mother taught me to never be ashamed of being clever. She always says the world is going to try to convince me that I'm not good enough, that I'm not smart enough, and I need to know from now that I am.' He shrugged. 'Besides, I have enough rizz to make up for the nerdiness.'

'I thought I was the only one with a mother who says things like that,' I said. 'My mum's always trying to convince me that I am good enough, that no one is superior to me.'

'Funny, isn't it, that the people at our schools never seem to need to be convinced of that, do they?'

'Yeah!' I said. 'The confidence and the audacity! I'm sure they have moments of doubt . . .'

'But they rarely show it.' He finished my thought for me.

I turned to look at him and he kissed me. Just like that. He put his full, soft lips on mine and kissed me. I froze. Didn't know what to do, because no one had ever kissed me before. I mean, of course no one has ever kissed me before. It's only meeting Silas that made me realise that I actually am interested in boys at all. I've got boys who are friends, but not boyfriends. And look at me, with a really good-looking, clever boy who likes me. Who kissed me.

I'm not thinking I'm his girlfriend or anything, but that kiss was nice. I pulled back and he looked at me. And I looked at back at him. And then, at the exact same time, we both burst out laughing.

'That's the first time I've done that,' he said. 'I mean, I've been kissed by girls and by a couple of women, but that's the first time I've actually made the first move. First time I've wanted to.'

'What, grown women have kissed you?' I asked, ignoring the bit about me being the first person he's wanted to kiss.

'Yes. They think because I'm tall and I'm Black that I must be all about getting into bed at the first opportunity. It's all those stereotypes. It can be scary sometimes. They don't even care when I tell them I'm fifteen. Adultification, innit.'

'Innit,' I said. I put my hand on his chest. And he covered it with his hand. 'I'm glad that I'm the first person you wanted to kiss,' I said. 'And you're the first person I've ever kissed.'

'Really?!' he asked. 'A pretty girl like you? I would have thought . . .' He stopped talking when he realised what he'd been about to say. 'Adultification, innit,' he said instead.

'Innit.'

Over vegan, gluten-free lasagne with tempeh, Silas's mum had us laughing with her tales about the people who were ashamed to come in but needed her potions and remedies. 'If they could come in the back door, they would,' she said.

Pretty soon it was time to go home and I so didn't want to leave. As I got up from the table, she said, 'Your face was a picture when I told you what we were eating for dinner!'

I admit, I was not a believer when she said what we were having. I didn't think she could get any more cliché, but it was actually one of the nicest things I've ever eaten. I laughed and said thank you again to her, and she hugged me and said she hoped to see me again.

Silas walked me back to school. Outside the bottom gates we both stopped and he said: 'So, do you want to come back again sometime?'

'Yeah!' I replied.

'And do you want me to kiss you again?'

I nodded.

And he did.

■ **End Voice Note** ↓ **Save Recording** ↗ **Send To Private Cloud**

Jeb

April 2026, Brighton

He's being followed.

He'd noticed it not long after Kez went to stay at the school, and had brushed it off. But now he feels the weight of scrutiny wherever he goes – to work, to the supermarket, to the post office, even sometimes to put out the bins. There is someone there. Watching him. Watching them. He is sure they are watching Zoey and Jonah, too, so he has taken to driving them to and from school. Even though Zoey protested, wanted to come home on the bus or to walk with her friends, he insisted she come home with him. It feels safer when they are all together.

He hasn't really noticed anyone different in his neighbourhood. But there are a myriad faces in the supermarket, and outside work there were always different faces, he can't keep track of them all.

More people speak to him now at the school, when he is waiting for his children to emerge. Ironically, what Kez had done standing up to Penny, what he had said to Penny in the playground, has made him more popular, not shunned like he thought they would be.

Despite that, despite recognising most of them, he is always on edge at the school gates. He still hopes it's paranoia, the worry about Kez not being here that is doing this to him, but he suspects it isn't. He suspects ... Who would be following him, though? Watching his family? All the stuff with L-King was finished with a lifetime ago. He is the only person Jeb could think of who would do that. The only criminal who would have the resources or motivation to do it.

Or is it what Kez is doing now? Has that spilt over into their life here? She is two hours away – why would they think to come here?

He has taken to double- then triple-checking all of the locks on the doors and windows, setting the alarm for downstairs at night. He does everything he can, but he still can't shake the feeling that they are in danger.

Earlier, talking to Kez, before they had phone sex, he almost told her. Almost brought it up in a casual way to see what she thought, but then he had seen the tiredness in her eyes. He saw the effort she was putting in to sound normal for him. So he left it. Told her he loved her, cut the call and made himself go to bed.

But they're being followed. Watched. And he's still not sure who is doing it and what to do about it.

Kez

April 2026, Axton Manor

The headmaster's house is a building on its own on the grounds of the school. While his office overlooks the entrance to the school, his house is well away from the school buildings near where the high, high fence backs onto the woods. I'm sure one of the girls said it wasn't a wood but a forest, but I don't care enough to find out if she's right or not. I'm sure Mac will know because it seems like the sort of information he would likely be interested in retaining. I may ask him one day. But I'm sure it'll be like when Jonah explains something with football or Zoey outlines something with maths or Jeb expounds upon catalyst theory – my brain shuts down. It develops this hard glass dome around it and no information can enter and any information inside that might piece together what is being said to me shrinks away and is unable to connect because of the dome. When I fail to retain new information imparted to me by others, people think it's because I'm not able to learn new things when it's actually my brain protecting me from stuff that is completely unnecessary for me to know.

So, yeah, I'll call it a wood in my head and that way no one will ever correct me and I won't have to learn the difference. Or ever hear about the difference.

This house has been built in the image of the school; it looks from the outside at least like a smaller version of the main school manor-house-type building. It is large, substantial and made of the same red brick as the school. The front door is an arch with old wood and dark iron rivets in the wood. It looks like something that has been there centuries, but I'm sure it's been updated since then. At the centre is a large iron ring knocker. It feels like standing in front of a castle, waiting to be admitted for my audience with the king or to have hot oil poured on me from above.

'This is going to be fun,' Mac says, arriving at the door just as I'm about to push the doorbell. The façade of the place is very old, but there is a modern video doorbell as well as a small discreet CCTV camera to the top right of the doorway.

'I think it will be,' I reply without looking at him. It's still difficult, navigating the effect this man has on me when he isn't actively trying to charm or flirt with me.

'Can I advise you to not be yourself,' he says, immediately catching on with what I meant.

'I have to be. Just like you have to be yourself. Otherwise, we won't get him to reveal what he is hiding. Because for someone to die in suspicious circumstances and a pupil to go missing and for him to just carry on, business as usual, that is not normal. Nor the actions of a man who doesn't have something to hide.'

Mac puts his head to one side, seeming to size me up. 'Do you know how much I hate you being right?'

'Not that much, because you knew it. That's why you're here.'

Mac grins at me, the kind of grin that is dangerous. *Dangerous*. 'We both know that's not why I'm here.'

'Yes, you're right, we both know you're here to live out your James Bond fantasies.'

Before he can reply, the front door opens and Mr Rhodes is standing there in what Zoey and Jonah would call a 'dad jumper'. They of course *do not* mean their dad. He would never wear anything that heinous. It is a round-neck creation in mustard yellow with two white stripes across the middle. It is form-fitting and, while it sounds not too bad on paper, in real life it is disgusting. Under it he has a white shirt with the top button open in what I just know he thinks of as a risqué move. He also wears slightly stonewashed jeans. I'm actually scared standing in front of him but I don't know why. His clothes aren't that awful, but they are at the same time. I take a look at Mac and from his face I guess he is thinking pretty much the same things as me.

'I thought I heard you,' Mr Rhodes says, all smiles and welcome and genuine bonhomie. Which scares me even more. And how did he hear us through this extra-thick door, unless he was standing behind said door, waiting for us? Which would be creepy as all hell. But then he does have a video door camera. But then it didn't ring out here. Does it only ring inside the house?

He sweeps his arm wide to show that we should enter his lair. I can't stop myself thinking that this guy is a bad guy and he has a lair and Mac and I may never leave. Like I always say, it's a good thing I'm not an over-dramatic, completely ridiculous person.

The house is warm, the lighting is low and orangey, making it feel very much like we have stepped back in time to an old-fashioned castle or manor and I am, indeed, about to be granted an audience with the king or the lord who owns the manor. Rhodes walks us through the large hallway into the sitting room where his family are standing and sitting as though posing for a casual 'family-at-home' portrait, with two of the biggest German shepherds I've ever seen curled up on the fireplace hearth. His wife sits in a chair by the fire, what looks like a glass of sherry in her hand, dressed in a long-sleeve, red-brown silk dress that reminds me of the colour of the foxes that run through our garden. Her grey-streaked long blonde-brown hair is rolled away from her face into a chignon at the nape of her neck like the first time I met her. On the other side of the fireplace stands a tall young man in his twenties. He looks like a younger version of Mr Rhodes but with wavy blond-brown hair, big brown eyes, a slightly hooked nose and a chin that seems to stay lifted so he can seem more than slightly arrogant. Sitting on the sofa opposite Mrs Rhodes is the standing Rhodes boy's twin. He is exactly like his standing brother, right down to the grey suit trousers and white shirt with the open top two buttons.

They all paint on smiles when we enter the room and it feels very much like they have been furiously arguing before we arrived and now have to pretend everything is just tickety-boo between them for their guests.

Rhodes's sons are called Garwin and Duncan and I suspect they both live at home still. Victoria Rhodes treats us to a beaming smile and she seems genuinely happy that we're here. I'm guessing she likes entertaining.

'Humphrey will see to your drinks,' she says on her way out of the door. 'I am going to oversee dinner.' She grins again before leaving. Mr Rhodes makes small talk while he fixes a whiskey sour for Mac and a small sherry for me. Neither of us requested these drinks – he didn't ask what we wanted, he just introduced us to his children, went to the well-stocked drinks cabinet and bar and started mixing drinks.

I accept the drink with good grace and I can tell by the way Mac receives his drink that he doesn't drink whiskey sours, just like I don't drink sherry. Rhodes really likes to be in control. He, apparently, likes to watch and he also likes to be in control. Two big signs that this man is dangerous.

Fredi

● **Record Voice Note** ▶ **Recorded: February 2026**

I've been sneaking into the basement luggage rooms of the different house dorms to have a look around. Franklin house dorm is the last one I've visited. [*Sighs.*]

Even though I've been spending a lot of time with Silas, I am still investigating what happened to Mariana. Which is why I've been looking around the house dorm basements.

Mariana was here at Axton Manor. And then she wasn't and nobody seems that bothered about it. Not even Viola, when I know she was friends with her. That's really weird. But what's weirder, though, is that this keeps happening. Girls keep disappearing.

They're not usually like Mariana, who is the daughter of an old girl. They're usually like me – girls who come from working-class families or who are on bursaries. Poor kids, girls who don't come from privileged backgrounds, basically.

I've been doing some digging and reading and the more I look, the more I find about the amount of girls who disappear. If it's mentioned at all in the local papers or online, the story is always the same: the girl comes to the school, they can't handle the pressure and the expectations that are on them beyond the academic stuff. They start to crash out – acting up or sneaking down to the village, smuggling in booze and drugs, hanging out with the boys from the village. Then they totally crash out and run away. They take some things, leave a note, and then are never heard from again.

It just doesn't make sense that all these girls do the same thing. And no one here thinks it's odd. They all say the same thing if it makes it onto the internet at all: Axton Manor has such high standards that girls from working-class backgrounds, and girls from ethnic-minority backgrounds, can't take it.

I just don't believe it. Mum and Dad have always told me that people from the working classes do the exact opposite of that. We always know that we need to work harder than anything to get anything. And if you're Black or a person of colour? You have to work even harder to get half the returns. I just don't believe that collectively, girls who've had to work hard to get into the school in the first place, who didn't know the exam system to get in here so will have worked so, *so* hard to excel in the exams, would just crash out at the first opportunity.

I don't buy it. I think something happened to them. That they didn't fit in, that they didn't know all the little ways that you're just supposed to know here and then they were . . . Well, that's when my head starts to hurt. Because if what I'm thinking is true and correct, the only logical next step is that they've been murdered. And I can't think like that. Because that's too scary and it would mean that Mariana is actually dead and that's something I don't want to think about, either. I'd rather the girls were just chased away.

That's why I've been looking in the luggage rooms at night. It's a bit stupid to think that might be where they keep the stuff of girls who have supposedly run away, rather than return it to their families, but they might. They might have slipped up or something. Whoever 'they' are. I'm guessing The Platinum and/or the Quiet Girls.

Mariana doesn't fit the usual archetype of girl who runs away from Axton, though. She was brought up rich and in privilege. Her mother is an old girl, her father went to Eton or Harrow or one of them. We only met at all because her parents moved to a huge f-off house near where my parents lived when Auntie Jacinta was pregnant. She needed to make friends since all her other friends lived far away, so she joined the expectant mothers' club and met Mum.

Mariana and I could not have had two more different backgrounds, but we were friends right from the beginning of our time on Earth. That's why I agreed to do this. I loved Mariana like she was my sister. Even when she went away to Axton Manor she rang me, messaged me, left me voice notes and wrote me letters. She didn't say that she was having trouble. She didn't say she was going to run away. And she would have told me if she was. I know she would.

Which is why I don't believe she ran away. I think someone took her. But would they keep her alive this long? That's another thought that makes my head hurt. If she didn't run away, does that mean someone harmed her? If she didn't run away, does that mean someone took her? If she didn't run away, and someone took her, does that mean that she might possibly be alive?

If she is alive, where is she?

I'm always aware of the woods at the back of the school. How vast they seem. They're not that big, only three acres, but if you wanted to bury a body out there, you would have a lot of space and time to do it. And, let's not forget, Mariana and all those girls are meant to have run away. That means the police won't be out looking for them. They won't be checking the woods for freshly dug graves.

They – the girls who 'ran away' – could be out there right now in the woods and no one would ever know.

But I'm trying not to think about that. If I find something, something that isn't meant to be here, then maybe I can convince the police to take sniffer dogs out into the woods to see if there is something there. Those dogs have a really strong sense of smell and can hunt things down. They might find the other girls' remains. I'm not going to think they might find Mariana's remains because I don't believe she's gone.

It's just something I know. It's something to do with us being so close from birth. If she was gone, I would know. And if there's one thing I know it's that she's not gone. She's still alive. Out there, somewhere. I'm sure of it.

I didn't find anything in the basement/luggage room of Franklin house dorm. I didn't think I would. I keep doing it because it makes me feel like I'm doing something to find Mariana. Find out what happened to all those other girls.

I think I'm going to have to focus on the Quiet Girls. If I find out who they are, one of them may crack and tell me something. Possibly confess everything. Paris practically did the other day. I don't think she meant to tell me that she did something to Mariana, and that may have been a complete big bollocks lie, but I don't think so. I'm sure Paris is a Quiet Girl. I need to work out who else is.

And then I need to get them to talk.

■ **End Voice Note** ⬇ **Save Recording** ↗ **Send To Private Cloud**

Kez

April 2026, Axton Manor

Their dining room is luscious. It is designed like the Great Dining Hall and it is lavish. The napkins have an extremely high thread count, I'm sure the napkin rings are made from real silver, as is the very heavy cutlery. The plates look like fine-bone china.

We move into there when Victoria Rhodes tells us that dinner is served, the dogs coming with us, and, unnervingly, they both settle at my feet when I sit down. I've always been a little scared of dogs – and people tell me all the time that's why they usually make a beeline for me. The theory is that dogs can sense fear so they come to me to reassure me that there's nothing to be scared of. These two seem to have taken to me beyond reassuring me that they aren't scary beasts. Carefully, I pat them on their heads and they growl happily before settling their heads on their front paws and staring into the distance.

Neither of the sons has spoken since we arrived, adding more weight to my theory that an argument had been going on prior to our arrival.

'Where did you school, Dr Mackenzie?' Rhodes asks as his wife sets our starter – alternating slices of tomato and discs of mozzarella, topped with three leaves of basil, drizzled neatly with balsamic vinegar – out in front of us.

Mac looks pained. 'I would answer that question, but I fear I will sound like one of those, "I went to a top university and I never shut up telling anyone who'll listen about it" people. And I promise you, I am not one of those people. So, on reflection, I have decided I am going to demur on answering that question.'

Dr Guy Mackenzie is an unserious person. It's that which endears him to me. But his unseriousness has not impressed our host. At all.

'Where did you school?' I ask Rhodes before he can turn that question on me.

He looks at me and smiles – the smile of displeasure from someone beneath him trying to take control in his domain. We are all drinking red wine, even though I really don't like red wine. I mean it's good in a way because he is unintentionally making sure I stay sober.

'I have an interesting story, actually,' Mr Rhodes says, wresting control of the conversation out of my hands and back into his own by not answering my question. 'My wife and I actually met in this very school.'

'Humphrey, darling, nobody is interested in that,' Victoria says, and his sons look like they agree. They are not at all interested in that, and I suspect we won't be, either.

'Of course they're interested. It's not often that two people meet at nine years old and then are still together nearly fifty years later. Victoria's father was headmaster of Axton Manor, his mother was the headmistress before him, and her father the head before her. Victoria has a long pedigree and a deep connection to the school.' I glance at his wife and I'm taken aback to find her not looking proud at her heritage and its connection to this school, but seeming almost embarrassed and weary that she has to hear this story again.

'I,' Rhodes says, pressing his hands onto his chest, 'grew up in the village. We used to watch the girls arrive at this place, being driven here in big cars, all the parents looking important, some so important they sent nannies in their stead. I put a stop to that for the most part. If parents want their children to be schooled here, they need to visit at least once. I tend to make an exception for royalty, however, most of them are highly engaged and involved parents despite their punishing workload, which means we do often have to prepare for royal visitations.'

I nod thoughtfully. His use of the word 'punishing' there is certainly a . . . *choice* when you think of the types of occupations where your body, mind and sometimes soul are truly tested, painfully punished. I don't think he'd tolerate me questioning his use of that word. Especially not when there are so many other things that I can ask that will get his dander up.

'How did a village boy meet the headmaster's daughter from the big house?' I open my mouth to ask to find that Mac has said the words instead of me.

Rhodes's eyes flash and for a moment, just a moment, everything feels dangerous, like it is about to kick off. The other three around the table, who know him, all stiffen, brace themselves, I presume, for the explosion. Rhodes obviously reconsiders blowing up and instead forces his mouth into a shape approximating a smile. A very strained, restrained smile. 'Did you mean to sound so dismissive and rude about something that is important to my wife, my family and I?' he asks casually, the anger broiling just below his surface.

That is an old psychological technique in dealing with people who are unpleasant and rude – you skewer them to their words by asking them if they meant it that way. It often elicits an apology or embarrassment, at the very least, it gets the person to shut up. This guy is very skilful; he has done a lot of reading and/or courses in psychological methods. He is a clever, dangerous man. The thought that he has dominion over so many young people – *girls* – concerns me greatly.'

'Not at all,' Mac replies, unfazed at being called out by Rhodes. 'I was rather captivated by the way you began your story and I was hoping to find out how it developed. I wasn't dismissing your story at all, in fact, I was trying to find out more of it.'

Rhodes is stuck now. He can't very well accuse Mac of not being interested when Mac has spelt out how interested he is. And he can't demand an apology when Mac has practically begged him to speak. And he can't get all huffy and not speak because he will look pathetic since he was the one who insisted we would all be interested in his story.

Checkmate to Mac, I think.

'I should defer to my wife on this and change the subject. As always, she is right about these matters and people probably do not want to hear chapter and verse about my life.'

We eat in silence. Each time cutlery hits porcelain, the sound is amplified and reverberates around the room; each time someone puts something in their mouth, the sound of chewing is like a mechanical macerater.

I bet it's like this all the time, I think. *I bet every meal is determined by his moods, and if his mood is like this then no one is happy.* Once everyone's plate is clear of the starter, Victoria takes the dishes into the kitchen. I'm about to offer to help when I decide not to – I'm not falling into a 'female' role around Rhodes. The atmosphere is extremely tense and it's definitely gone a bit wrong quicker than I expected. Mac is actually worse than me for getting people's backs up. I'm impressed.

After a few minutes of continued, tense silence, Victoria brings out the main course on a huge silver tray: the biggest leg of lamb I have ever seen. It is as thick as an ancient oak tree trunk and probably about two foot long. Surrounded by small roast potatoes, and encrusted with herbs, it is glossy and dark brown, lying on a bed of huge sprigs of rosemary.

'That looks delicious, my darling,' Rhodes says, getting to his feet. She places the meat in front of him and I don't think I've ever seen a man look so happy. She hands him a large carving fork and a large carving knife. The way he sticks the fork into the top of the joint actually causes my stomach to lurch. Slowly, precisely, he pushes the knife down into the flesh of the meat, and my stomach turns all the way over. I have watched people carve meat many times and none of them have enjoyed it as much as this man. He is almost salivating as he moves metal through meat, as he slices one piece of flesh away from the other.

He is enjoying this way too much, way too much. Even if this is a well-done piece of meat – instead of red in the middle – I am going to feel creeped out eating it. It feels very much like we're being forced to take part in an intimate ritual, bear witness to his particular fetish that he likes to perform in front of other people. He likes to watch, but he also likes to be watched. Mrs Rhodes dishes out roast potatoes, broccoli, carrots and peas. The meat, the dividing of the spoils, seems to bring Rhodes out of his sulk, and he starts to chat as he places slices of bright red meat on the proffered plates.

'I hear that you and Miss Akande have a relationship. An intimate relationship,' Rhodes says to Mac. He clearly sees Mac as an alpha male that he needs to either dominate or get on side or both. He is surrounded by women and girls all day, and with someone like him who sees himself as superior to all, but especially females, he will have created a world that does not challenge but merely serves him. And on those rare occasions when he does encounter another male on an equal footing, he has to very quickly prove his absolute authority. He has clearly made sure everyone in his life is cowed: his sons look barely able to cope with being around their father (but they are here, so it must work on some level), while his wife puts on a brave face, makes the food and entertains.

Victoria Rhodes profiles as someone who finds enjoyment in creating a home, socialising, being around other people. *Her* kind of people, though. Strangers with other experiences, who might expand her world or change her views or make her notice her unhappiness at her circumstances are not welcome. They would cause too much trouble and upset and *mess*. This house, this room, makes her happy. Even when her husband is playing up, Victoria enjoys cooking for people, watching them devour her food, sitting and talking. Her husband on the other hand . . . he likes to watch people battle his intelligence, to fail at meeting his standards. He needs to 'alpha male' his way in every situation.

Rhodes sits down, takes his time returning his napkin to his lap and raising his knife and fork, he then looks directly at me before focusing on Mac again. 'You and Miss Akande were together for quite some time, I gather?'

He is desperate to put Mac down, to prove there is only one alpha at this table. How does he know about Portia and Mac, though? I can't imagine she mentioned it. So I can only guess that, like he did with me and Mac, he has watched their interactions and seen there is something there. Because there is definitely something there between them still. That is obvious. And this man likes to watch, so he has probably seen it, too.

'Yes,' Mac says proudly, making it clear he has no shame in the matter. 'We were engaged. Our story is not remarkable: I met her at the university that I didn't mention, we were together for several years and then sadly we went our separate ways. For lots of reasons that I would share if she was here and I had her permission. But we're still close. I think we always will be. Life gets in the way, though, which is why I didn't know she worked here again. We were together during the time you first recruited her to work here.'

Kudos to Mac for not sounding defensive in any way. That would have given Rhodes the indication that it was a pressure point to be exploited at any given moment.

'And yet we never met?' Rhodes says. 'Miss Akande was always accompanied by other men at our casual and formal social functions from what I remember?'

'Yes, she was. My job at the time meant I wasn't able to attend those functions,' Mac replies without one hint of upset or jealousy. 'Portia, as I'm sure you know, is a friendly, open person. She has no shortage of friends – male friends – who would accompany her to pretty much anything. She is spectacular in so many ways. I was punching well above my weight, I always knew that.'

He lights up when he talks about her and I am aware that Rhodes and Victoria are both watching me while Mac talks about his ex. Weirdly, I suppose, given my complicated, confused and confusing 'feelings' for him, this doesn't make me in any way jealous. I think it's nice that he has a good relationship with his ex. I also think it's none of my business. I have a husband who I love and a life that will not involve Mac once I leave here. But these two think I am jealous and uncomfortable because of Mac's affection for his ex. When, really, it's because I cannot eat pinkish-tinged meat let alone the red, bloody-looking pieces of meat on my plate. When, really, I have been secreting pieces of that inedible meat and feeding it to the very grateful dogs at my feet.

'What was your job?' Victoria asks, openly fascinated.

Mac smiles at her, in that way he does when he's charming someone. 'I'm not allowed to tell you that,' he says teasingly, 'but I can assure you, it was very, *very* boring.'

Victoria grins at Mac and he grins back, raising a flirtatious eyebrow, and, just like that, he makes a true, lifelong enemy of Mr Humphrey Rhodes.

Fredi

● **Record Voice Note** ▶ **Recorded: February 2026**

The Quiet Girls did get rid of Mariana. I heard them admit it.

I followed Paris. I've been hiding outside the Franklin house dorm most nights for the last couple weeks. It's not been easy, and it's really cold, but I had to do it so I could follow Paris.

Earlier, she came out of Franklin house dorm dressed in black with her hood up. She went towards the back of the school. I had to stick to the shadows thrown by the buildings and keep out of sight. She walked with purpose, as though she knew where she was heading.

It was the middle of the night, 1 a.m., and the school was still. At rest. Asleep. As we got closer to the back of the school, I noticed more people coming out of the different buildings, heading in the same direction as Paris. They all had their hoods up so I couldn't see who they were.

Right at the back of the school, beyond the outbuildings where I'd seen Miss Akande and Dr Pemberton, beyond the equipment shed, there is a stone building. It looks very old and run-down, but the door is solid and it has several locks on it. The windows have been bricked over and the roof is in good repair. It just *looks* run-down and like it's abandoned.

I waited until they were all inside, then I crept up to the door. I gently pushed at it, but it was locked. I wasn't sure what to do. In the end, I moved as close to where one of the windows was and stood very quietly, listening to them speak.

I couldn't hear much. But some of the voices were familiar. It was also hard to hear because I was breathing so loudly. I was convinced they would hear me so I kept holding my breath. Then I heard, 'Mariana.'

And someone raised their voice and said, 'We agreed we were never going to talk about that again.'

The first voice said, 'We have to. That girl has been snooping around. She's asked about her. If her mother ever finds out what we did to her . . .'

'Well, we'll have to do whatever it takes to make sure she doesn't.'

'I'm not doing that again. It was bad enough with Mariana.'

'That's only because she was one of us. If she was one of the others, then it wouldn't be a problem.'

'How can it not be a problem? We don't do it for fun. We do it to protect ourselves. And I'm not doing it again. Not so soon. Who's going to believe another one has run away?'

'Nothing is going to happen. There's no problem here.'

Their voices were all talking over each other, louder than before because they were all agitated. But I had heard enough – I'd heard that they *had* done something to Mariana and that they were planning on doing something to me if they thought I was getting too close to the truth. They'd done something to Mariana. And to others, it sounded like.

I was in an awkward position, my legs were bent at an angle that was painful, and when I shifted a couple of the stones moved underfoot. It made a sound too loud in the darkness and they all stopped talking.

They started whispering and I realised I needed to be somewhere else.

I crept away from the side of the house, moved around the back and then dashed to the furthest corner of the equipment shed. I pushed myself flat against the back of it, holding myself still so they wouldn't know I was there. The door opened and I heard a few of them spill out. Several different footsteps moved around, obviously searching for the source of the noise.

'Must have been a fox or something,' one of them said.

And they went back inside. Or, at least, most of them did. I heard one of them stay outside, waiting, just in case it wasn't a fox. Just in case it was someone like me. It was freezing out there, and I could feel my heart beating really rapidly in my chest. I was shaky all over, but I had to keep quiet. So quiet.

I think they were all spooked so they wrapped it up after that. I heard them chant a few things, say a few things in unison and then they left, the last one to leave locking the door behind them. Still I waited. I didn't know if all the footsteps had gone away, so I stayed and stayed, still and silent until I couldn't take the cold any longer.

I came gingerly out of my hiding place and decided to walk around the back fence in a big circle to approach the house dorm from the front of the building. I put my headphones on and started jogging when I got to the front of the school, to make it look like I was out running in the middle of the night.

And it's a good thing I did, because as I came out of the darkness towards my house dorm, I could sense someone in the shadows. Watching. Waiting for me come back.

I didn't see who it was, but I know they clocked me. Hopefully they bought my out-jogging-late act.

Hopefully.

I'm really worried, though. I heard them admit that they hurt people. What do I do? Is this the moment to tell my mum what I've been doing?

Shall I send her all these voice notes? Or should I just try to lay a bit lower and not give them any reason to think they should come after me?

I can't tell Auntie Jacinta, not after what they said about her and Mariana. And I don't trust her, not after she didn't tell me about The Platinum and the Quiet Girls. But I need to talk to someone. Maybe I'll try Dr Pemberton?

Miss Akande went here, she's an old girl, so she might actually be a Quiet Girl. She might have been one of them who was out there tonight, because I'm sure some of them were disguising their voices.

I know that Dr Pemberton has a thing with Miss Akande, but I think I can trust him? I don't think he'd be allowed to tell her anything if I talk to him as a counsellor. I'll talk to Dr Pemberton. He'll keep my secret and he'll know what to do.

■ **End Voice Note** ↓ **Save Recording** ↗ **Send To Private Cloud**

Kez

April 2026, Axton Manor

'Miss Lanyon—' Rhodes begins while holding a particularly red piece of lamb on his fork.

'Dr Lanyon,' Mac corrects.

'Of course . . . forgive me, Dr Lanyon. As you might have seen, it is the annual spring ball next weekend.' I had seen various notices about it and had heard some of the girls talking about what dresses they would wear, how they would get their hair done, what make-up look was in at the moment, but it hadn't occurred to me that I might be expected to attend, participate. But of course I would. I need to see group dynamics, work out how the group of girls I'm focused on relates to Fredi's disappearance, Dr Pemberton's murder.

'Do you know the history of the ball?'

I shake my head while his sons both wilt a little in their seats and Victoria Rhodes looks uncomfortable. It's exhausting witnessing these moments with his family, what must it be like to live it? 'I do not know the history of the ball,' I confirm.

He smiles in satisfaction, places his knife and fork on the table and settles back into his seat, ready to enlighten me. And scare me. I can see that his eyes are twinkling with the delight of someone who is about to upset someone he doesn't like. I have to pause in feeding the dogs because all eyes are on me.

'It was originally called the Hunters' Rest Ball, held to signify the end of the hunting season. There is a long tradition of fox hunting connected to Axton Manor. The whole village was reliant on the hunt. We came alive during hunting season and many of the villagers had jobs that were in service of the hunt. Taking care of the horses, kennelling dogs. Farmers would take in and train young fox hounds on their land so they became used to general livestock and animals and would learn how to identify foxes and ignore other creatures.

'Hunt days were always so special.' Rhodes closes his eyes, as though in perfect, blissful rapture. 'The whole village would turn out to watch. The excitement, the atmosphere, it was electric. *Festive*. I was blooded at nine years old by Victoria's father.' He opens his eyes and smiles warmly at his wife. She manages a smile back, but with far less enthusiasm. 'Do you know what being blooded means?'

'It means the huntsman or the master of the hunt, the men in the red coats, dip their fingers into the blood of the fox that has been killed and mark your face. Forehead and cheeks,' I reply tightly.

'No, you misunderstand me, do you know what it *means* to be blooded? It means you are being blessed. You are being initiated into the glory of the hunt. You don't wash those marks off; you leave them to wear off. You look in the mirror every day and see that you are a chosen one. From that moment on I was devoted to the hunt. To that way of life. I worked hard, I moved from the village school to Dewhurst School for Boys, the boys' boarding school that is connected to Axton Manor. I was accepted into Oxford, I achieved a first-class degree, I returned to the village and secured a position as a kennelman.

'My contemporaries were securing positions in industry, in

business and government; I was taking care of hounds. Some might say I was idiotic, but I knew that I was born for great things. I was born for the hunt. When Victoria and I were betrothed, her father offered me a position as a junior master in the school. And I advanced in the hunt. I became the huntsman and eventually the master of the hunt.'

I'm glad nepotism came through for him in the end. It would have been tragic if after all of that he'd remained a kennelman when he so clearly thought it was beneath him. Ethics of fox hunting aside, if you love dogs, what's not to love about looking after them day in, day out. But I sense he didn't do it for the love of the dogs.

'And then, slowly, public opinion began to change, people didn't understand the need for the hunt, so they decided we were not allowed to do something they didn't understand.'

'They did understand it – they just didn't like it,' Mac says. 'They didn't like how foxes were killed, how the dogs were damaged, how the horses were hurt. They did understand it and they didn't like it.'

'They did *not* understand it,' Rhodes snarls, his eyes flashing. '*Reynard* needs to be kept at bay. Away from livestock, away from young children. *Reynard* needs to know his place.'

Reynard is what some of them called the foxes they killed. It was a name, a set of stories that made foxes demonic and worthy of slaughter. His use of the term suggests to me he has *serious* problems. He didn't just enjoy the chase; he didn't simply enjoy the adrenalin-high that came from tracking an animal that is deemed clever and sly. No, he loved to watch the hounds being whipped up, ready for the chase; he adored observing as the fox ran from place to place, scared, terrified, knowing it was about to die. I bet he got the biggest sexual highs from snatching up that poor doomed creature, tossing it in the air and watching the hounds rip it apart. I bet he leapt on Victoria the moment he got home from the hunt, and was insatiable.

'With the change in the law,' Rhodes says, 'we had to stop the hunt. It killed the village. We are only allowed to trail hunt and even that is frowned upon. Axton Manor dropped a lot of the connections it had to the hunt, but when I took over as headmaster I reinstated the connections, especially the Hunters' Rest Ball when we celebrate and give thanks for the end of another bountiful season. We also toast the coming Hunters' Moon in October, which will mark the start of the season, but the Hunters' Rest is our main event. We used to parade the final spoils of the hunt through the school and would blood those who were willing.' Rhodes picks up his knife and fork. 'It's possibly one of my favourite nights of the year.'

Everyone is silent for long seconds and I fear we're all going to allow him to get away with saying this stuff, and, even if we don't agree, we will defer to him and allow his version of what fox hunting is about to be the dominant narrative. I fear that if someone else doesn't speak soon I will have to say . . .

'You know, my first boyfriend . . . actually, "boyfriend" might be overstating the nature of our relationship. We held hands once or twice and while I was completely enamoured with him, he wasn't that bothered about me. Although having said that, he did marry someone who looked exactly like me so maybe he wasn't as uninterested in me as I thought.' Everyone looks at me, confused. And I remember what Zoey and Jonah told me before I left them. *'Anyway,* let's call him my friend. When I was about sixteen-seventeen, my friend was a hunt saboteur.' That causes everyone in the Rhodes family to stiffen. 'Every weekend he was out there, sabotaging hunts, and getting his head kicked or arrested for his trouble. But it never deterred him because the things he saw haunted him.

Pregnant vixens being ripped apart so that huntsmen could stamp on their unborn babies, months-old cubs being thrown to dogs, terrified foxes being deliberately hobbled to make catching them easier. And then there were times hounds were trampled by horses, or were shot because they'd disobeyed their master. Or horses were destroyed because they'd become lame from barbed wire. He told me so many stories, so many horror stories, I knew I would never hear anything that justified fox hunting. *Ever.*'

Rhodes and I lock eyes and any chance that we might salvage some kind of reasonable working relationship from the horror of our previous encounters melts away. We will never find anything like a middle ground. His soul-bearing about his love of the hunt was also another boundary push, a chance for him to remind me of my place in his world. This is his little empire and I am supposed to accept its structures and traditions without question.

'I find fox hunting abhorrent,' Victoria Rhodes says. She speaks in a low tone, but her voice is absolutely resolute and certain. 'I have always found it abhorrent. I cried the first time my father blooded me. My mother would go to the hunt for the social aspect, but, after a while, I couldn't bring myself to even do that. To watch those beautiful, innocent creatures baited and then murdered. I couldn't do it. I hated it then and I hate it now.'

'Me, too,' her son Garwin says.

'And me,' her other son, Duncan, adds.

'As you can see, Miss Lanyon, my family are very much out of step with me and one of the tenets of Axton Manor, which is to observe and maintain the traditions of our ancestors.' He lays down his knife and fork, dabs at the corners of his mouth with his napkin and then grins at us all. 'Victoria, I do hope you've made my favourite, spotted dick, for dessert,' he says, and that, we all know, is the end of that matter.

Fredi

● Record Voice Note ▶ Recorded: February 2026

Someone was in my room earlier. I came back from visiting Issy, Haniya and Astrid in their house dorm, and I knew from the moment I stepped in that someone else had been in there.

The door was locked, and nothing looked like it had been disturbed, but I just felt like someone had been in there. There was a slight scent in the air – aftershave or perfume, I couldn't tell, but it was definitely there in the atmosphere. I stood looking around for ages, trying to work out what was different.

I'm sure they took something – I'm just not sure exactly what. But, even if they didn't take anything, the fact that they were there and went through my things is terrifying. Someone must have a key. Is it one of Headmaster Rhodes's boys?

Were they there to make me a 'girlfriend' or to find something? Or both?

All of this makes me so scared. But I can't back out now. No way. I have to stay and find out the truth. No matter what it takes.

■ End Voice Note ↓ Save Recording ↗ Send To Private Cloud

Kez

April 2026, Axton Manor

Victoria Rhodes sees us out. Her husband grinned and toasted us with a goblet of whiskey and his sons continued their virtual silence by nodding at us as we left.

We thank her for a lovely meal – not evening – and then start to walk back. A few seconds later, Victoria comes out after us in her stockinged feet, having kicked off her slippers.

'Dr Lanyon, Dr Mackenzie, please allow me to apologise for my husband,' she says quietly.

'You've nothing to—' we both begin, and she interrupts us by taking one of our hands in each of hers.

'Tonight was not ideal,' she says kindly. 'All this business has upset him so much. But, stiff upper lip and all, he can't show it. Please do not judge him too harshly. Once things settle down, you'll find he is a most generous and effusive host.'

'Thank you for saying all of that,' I respond. 'We really appreciate it.'

'We really do,' Mac says.

She squeezes our hands and then returns to her house.

Mac and I restart our walk back towards our dorms in silence. I'm a little shellshocked, and Mrs Rhodes hasn't really changed that by asking us to excuse her husband.

I've worked with all sorts of 'challenging' people. I still do work with all sorts of 'challenging' people – my current boss is an outright psychopath – but to have someone behave in such an openly aggressive way is disorientating. And, heartening, I suppose that I still have the capacity to be shocked. It means I still have hope for humanity.

'I'm just going to say it,' Mac states quietly as we round the corner that will take us to the old stables, 'I think he killed Pemberton.'

I stop walking and frown at Mac in the dark. 'You think?'

'Yes, why, don't you?'

'Not really. Not enough drama, not enough alpha male show of strength in the way Pemberton died.'

'True. But I just get the impression that Pemberton was on to him. He'd worked out what Rhodes was up to – and there's no doubt that he is up to something bad – and that's why Pemberton was killed.'

'I agree with that. Maybe he ordered one of his silent sons to do it? They won't need the drama?' I suggest.

'Maybe. Could be his wife? She's another one who seems to do his bidding, even if she doesn't agree with it. Did you see that ceremony with the meat? That man has everyone in that house in a chokehold. Which is why, I think, no matter who actually did the deed, he is definitely involved. And—'

'And, yeah, he is involved in Fredi's disappearance. And Mariana's, I'd wager.'

'Abuse?' Mac says cautiously.

'Yes, probably. But I feel like there's more that we're missing. The way he talks about the hunt, the blatantly sexual pleasure he gets from it . . .'

'Yeah. It's not great that he's in such a position with young people under his watch when he so obviously gets off on control.'

We come to the first of the house dorms and Mac stops. My eyes flick up towards the doorway. There, the outline of a woman stands, clearly waiting for Mac.

'Portia and I are going to have a catch-up,' he explains.

'Enjoy yourselves,' I say. 'We'll pick this up tomorrow. Although I'm meeting up with the teacher who everyone said bullied Fredi tomorrow at seven. Maybe drop by after that?'

'See you then,' he says.

'See you then.'

I continue back to my room with the swirl of thoughts about the dysfunction in the Rhodes household with me every step of the way.

Part 8

Fredi

● Record Voice Note ▶ Recorded: March 2026

Dr Pemberton welcomed me into his office earlier with a smile. I haven't really had cause to come and see him recently. When I was first here and feeling homesick, Viola suggested I go and talk to him. She said he was really helpful. And he was.

He mostly listened and gave me techniques to not feel so alone and not beat myself up for missing my mum and dad and friends. He said it was normal to feel like that. And he said it was normal to sometimes forget to miss my family and friends back home, to have a good time here and not think about them. He said it's normal for that to happen and not to feel guilty about it. He was so helpful that I didn't really need to see him much.

'Can I trust you, Dr Pemberton?' I asked. *Yeah, all right, it was a stupid question since he wasn't going to say no, was he?* But I felt I had to check.

'Of course,' he said. 'Although I probably would say that even if you couldn't trust me. But I hope that you have seen me and confided in me enough times to feel that anything you say to me will stay confidential.'

'It's about the Quiet Girls.'

'The Quiet Girls?' If he knew about them, he didn't give away anything.

'They're the secret society who run the school. No one knows who's in it. There's The Platinum, who are kind of enforcers, and then there are the Quiet Girls, who run everything.'

'And you belong to this group?'

'No, but I found out where they meet and I overheard them. And I think . . . I think they made Mariana disappear.'

'What do you mean?'

'They made her disappear. I heard them talking. They made Mariana disappear and made it look like she ran away.'

'How do you know Mariana?' he asked suspiciously.

So I had to tell him. I told him everything. About how I knew Mariana, how her disappearance devasted Auntie Jacinta and probably contributed to Uncle Jacob's death. And how Auntie Jacinta begged me to come here, so I could try to find out what happened to Mariana because none of us believed that she ran away. And how I've loved it here and how I've hated it here and how I've been trying to find out what happened to Mariana. That it looked like the Quiet Girls got rid of her, but I didn't know *why* they got rid of her. And how it was scary because they said they would get rid of me too if I carried on snooping.

He listened and listened and didn't interrupt at all.

At the end of it, he looked visibly shaken. Like he couldn't believe what he had just heard. Then he looked like he was about to be sick.

'This is very serious, Fredi,' he said eventually. 'Very serious.'

'I know. I think I should tell my mum, but if I do she'll make me leave and I need to stay to find out what happened.'

'No, no, Fredi. You need to call your mother straight away. You need to get her to take you far away from here. Far, far away. If even a fraction of what you have just told me is true, then you are in real danger. As your therapist and trusted adult, I need to do everything I can to keep you safe.'

'But what about Mariana and the other girls?'

'I will find a way to talk to the police and keep your name out of it.'

'But we can't trust the police. If we could, they would have investigated all those disappearances. But they didn't. I mean, even if the girls had run away, you would think that they would investigate why so many of them needed to do that. But they didn't. Which means they can't be trusted. You can't go to the police. At least not yet. If we have proof, then we can go to the police and they can't dismiss us.'

'Fredi, it is not your job to investigate this. Your mother's friend should never have asked you to do this. This is very dangerous and I need to make sure you're safe.'

'But I need to find out what happened to Mariana.'

'We will. Look, if you trust me, please drop this for now. I think there's someone I can trust in the police who will tell us what the best course of action is.'

'Do you mean that?' I asked him. 'Do you really know someone who can help?'

'I think so. But, in the meantime, I think you should tell your mother and I will talk to this police contact.'

'I honestly can't tell my mum. She will pull me out before I find out what happened. And I haven't been through all of this to not find out.'

He sat thinking for a long time. He looked really unhappy about the fact I wouldn't tell Mum straight away. 'All right,' he said. 'I will talk to my police contact. Once I have called them, you have to promise me you will tell your mother. Straight away. And if she pulls you out, she pulls you out.'

'But—'

'This is the only way I can allow you to stay here. You have to promise to tell your mother as soon as I've spoken to the police. If you don't agree to that, I will call your mother right now and this will all be over today.'

'OK, sir,' I said.

I have to trust him. I have to believe that he is going to help me and that it will all work out. I have to believe him.

■ **End Voice Note** ↓ **Save Recording** ↗ **Send To Private Cloud**

Jeb

April 2026, Brighton

Knock, knock, knock, knock, knock, knock, knock began in the middle of the night. Jeb wakes up, checks the clock. It's 4 a.m. He thinks he was imagining it, but then, *knock, knock, knock, knock, knock, knock, knock* again.

Jeb dashes downstairs to the front door, but there is no one there. The knocking begins again. It is coming from the back door. Confused, he enters the kitchen, turns on the light. His soul nearly leaves his body when he sees the outline of a man at the back door.

The older white man, dressed in blue chino trousers, white shirt, red tie and beige rain mac, starts to urgently beckon to Jeb through the glass. He is holding up something for Jeb to look at. Cautiously, Jeb approaches the back door. He recognises the man from last year when Kez was shot. He had seen him leaving her hospital room and Kez had told him he was the man responsible for all that had happened to them in the last eighteen months.

Dennis Chambers.

Jeb's heart turns over in his chest.

Kez. Dennis Chambers is here because something has happened to Kez.

He unlocks the back door, lets him in. 'What's happened? How hurt is she?'

'Kezuma is fine. Forgive the intrusion, Mr Quarshie, my name is Dennis Chambers.'

'I know who you are. What do you want if Kez is fine?'

'As you know, I work with your wife. But right now, I need you to go upstairs, wake up your children, pack some bags and come with me.'

'What?' Jeb replies. 'What are you talking about?'

'Your lives are in danger. I need you to come with me right now.'

Kez

April 2026, Axton Manor

'Thank you for taking the time to come to see me,' I say to Mrs Lazloe.

She is one of the teachers who always wears the thick black academic robes because she wants everyone to know how seriously she takes her job.

Right now, she sits so upright in the chair opposite me that I feel obliged to do the same. My back is now ramrod straight and I feel a little underdressed in my suit jacket over my white T-shirt and dark jeans. In fact, I feel like I'm about to be subjected to a telling-off because I'm not in uniform. Why are people like Lazloe and Rhodes so able to make me feel like a child? A disobedient one at that.

'I wasn't given much choice in the matter,' she replies sourly to my opening gambit.

Her and Astrid . . . very good at pointing out when they're forced to do something they don't want to do, such as talking to me. I mean, they aren't wrong that they were told to do it, but the open hostility is a bit unnecessary.

'I asked to see you because a few of the girls I've spoken to mentioned that you and Fredi clashed on a few occasions. I thought you might have some feelings, given her disappearance, that you want to explore with a professional.'

The way this woman's right eyebrow arches at the word 'professional' makes me wonder, momentarily, if I did actually go to college, complete a masters, complete my qualifications via working for the government and then gain my doctorate while working in private practice. That eyebrow is so lethal it makes me momentarily question all of my abilities. How am I feeling like this when I've been in this woman's company for less than thirty seconds?

'Which girls have been saying these things?' she demands.

'Does it matter?'

'Of course it matters. I need to speak to these girls about the privacy and sanctity of the classroom.'

Sanctity? OK.

'My concern, Mrs Lazloe, is that if you did have a difficult relationship with Fredi, you may have feelings of guilt and regret that can lead to anxiety and stress.'

'Why would I feel guilty?'

'If she did, in fact, run away as has been suggested, that might have been because of something that was going on at school. And if you had a difficult relationship with her . . .'

Mrs Lazloe sits up even taller, which shouldn't be possible. 'I. Did. Not. Have. A. Difficult. Relationship. With. Her,' she replies, frost edging every word. Her eyes fix on me with such violence that I'm thrown into that space of having to work out if I can take someone in a fight.

Sometimes, there are people I meet who I wonder if I could take them in a fight. Not that I'm aggro, not that I necessarily think I can fight, but sometimes I see someone or I have an interaction with someone and they get my back up. And I idly wonder if I can take them.

Because that fight is never going to happen, I often think I can do it. I'm not good at fighting at all, but I often think I can take a person who's got on my nerves.

Unfortunately, I don't think I can take this woman, even though it's looking increasingly likely I might actually find out if I can or can't take her.

'I think we've got off on the wrong foot,' I say, trying to calm things down, seeing as I am trained in calming techniques.

'We most certainly did not,' she says. 'We got off on exactly the right foot for this type of conversation.'

I'm sure my neutral therapist expression drops and my eyes widen in surprise.

'Mrs Lazloe—'

'You believe that bursary children like Winifred Kingston belong in these spaces when they are, by nature, not cut out for this environment.'

'From what I understand, Fredi wasn't a bursary pupil.' *Not that it should matter.*

Mrs Lazloe makes a sound so nasty it makes my hackles rise. 'Believe me, Winifred Kingston *was* a bursary student. Children like her will always be bursary, no matter how much money they pay to be here.'

'Bursary isn't a dirty word, you do know that, don't you?'

'There are certain girls who do not belong here. We are very clear about what we do. We are raising the future wives of the men who run the world. They need more than just the ability to pay the fees. Anyone can pay fees. Being a part of Axton Manor is about having the breeding, the decorum and the resilience to go on to help run the world.

'When you are not born into our world, you struggle. You slow everyone down. That is why I have no reason to feel guilty about how

I schooled Winifred Kingston. If she belonged here, if she was one of us, there would have been no problems.'

The way this woman talks about children, other humans . . . I have changed my original assessment: I could take her. I could so take her.

'Can I just pick up on something you said? You said you are raising girls who will go on to be the wives of the men who run the world. They are going to go on to *help* run the world? Don't you want more for them? For them to run the world themselves?'

She smiles at me as though I am stupid. As though I have no clue about anything. That's happening to me a lot around these parts. 'Your question is exactly what I mean about those who belong and those who don't. No one who is one of us would ask such a question. No one who is one of us would not know the importance of supporting the leaders of our world.'

I don't want to be one of you, I feel like saying while sticking my tongue out at her, ner-ner-ner-ner style. But I suspect that may just prove exactly what she's saying. 'Are you an old girl, by any chance?'

'Of course,' she replies. 'This is my world. I have been through everything these girls go through, which is why I know who does belong and who doesn't.'

'It must really get to you when working-class children rock up and want to mix with your "well-born" children,' I state.

'Get to me?' she replies, as though she doesn't understand what I and my commoner mouth is saying.

'Yes, it must really get to you. That they don't stay where they're meant to. They don't "make do" with a state school education and getting what you think of as a menial job. That they might want what "your" girls get as standard. You must *hate* it.'

She looks at me askance, as though I haven't literally just parroted back to her what she has been spouting for the past ten minutes. Maybe it's because it's me saying it. Maybe it's because I have removed all the pretty, fancy terminology and words and it sounds horrible when vocalised. Although, I'm sure if it was one of her cohort saying it, she'd be fine with it.

'I do not hate anything,' she spits.

'What I can't help but wonder is, how far would you go to make sure someone knows they don't belong?'

'What are you saying?'

'I mean, you said it yourself that you had to make people believe they don't belong, would you go as far as harming them? Just so it's absolutely crystal clear that they should leave.'

'How dare you! I would never . . .'

'I know, you would *never* make sure that young girls who are far away from home and friends and family feel terrible every day because they aren't born with privilege? They aren't one of your kind?'

I have just heard how those words sound and I internally cringe. This is truly the worst therapy session I have ever been a part of. To be fair to me, Lazloe wasn't at all interested in talking to me. To be not at all fair to me, I am a professional and I should not have allowed myself to be dragged into this mess. It's a good thing my supervisor in this matter is Mac, because, well, I have messed up on a grand scale.

'I apologise, Mrs Lazloe,' I say. 'I genuinely wanted to have a conversation to make sure that you were OK. I didn't mean for things to take the turn they did.'

'I expect nothing less from someone like you.' She stands and glares down on me.

'Someone like me being?' I reply.

'I'm sure you know,' she states and sweeps out of the room.

Yup, yup I do, I think.

I stare at the space Mrs Lazloe has left in the room. She was prickly and unpleasant for that entire conversation. But when I suggested she might have harmed Fredi, she became defensive. She derailed the conversation, something guilty people do all the time.

She profiles as a woman who believes – genuinely, passionately – believes she is part of the ruling classes. She knows she is better than most people, those masses 'out there'. And she does not like to let those masses into her world. In fact, she will fight very hard to stop that happening. Lazloe profiles very much as someone who would stop at nothing to remove interlopers from her world. She profiles as someone who would resort to murder to get what she wants. And with someone like Rhodes as her boss I think it's actually a miracle more girls haven't 'run away'.

Jeb

April 2026, Motorway Outside Brighton

'I would advise you against telling Kezuma about this at the moment,' Dennis Chambers says to Jeb.

They have been driving for hours, so long that the world around them is brightening as the sun comes up. 'I'm sure you would,' Jeb replies, staring straight out of the windscreen, watching the road being eaten up in giant chunks by the speed at which Chambers is driving.

Jeb hates being so out of control. Right now, he has no idea where they are going, they had to leave almost everything behind and he doesn't know how long they're going to be away in hiding, but he has no choice. When it comes to keeping his children safe, he has to do anything, let anyone help him. Even this snake, this man who has consistently tried to ruin his wife's life.

'I am not sure what you mean by that, Mr Quarshie, but if Kezuma finds out about this, she will come home and that is the last thing anyone needs right now. She needs to finish what she is doing otherwise this will never go away. You will all always be looking over your shoulder.'

Jeb aggressively clears his throat then side-eyes Dennis, a snarl on his face that he hopes neither of the children can see in the dark of the car.

Zoey and Jonah may have seemed to be asleep in the back, but Jeb knows them. He knows they will be awake, listening.

The man next to him obviously hasn't thought about what saying something like that in front of young teenagers would do to them. How it will scare them, creep into every moment of their lives. This is already more terror than either of them should have been subjected to. As it is, this is going to unsettle and scare them, the thought that this will never go away is not something either of them should be considering.

This is why Kez doesn't tell him anything, Jeb realises. He's not stupid – he's always known that she doesn't share as much with him as she used to since taking this job at Insight because she doesn't want to bring the outside into their home; she wants to compartmentalise as much as she can. When she walks through the door, he knows that she wants to be 'Mum'; she needs to be the woman who doesn't shut cupboard doors, who doesn't really know where anything but Ghana is on the world map, who he teases and screws because she's the love of his life.

He hasn't realised until this moment that Kez also keeps things from him because she wants to protect his peace of mind.

He worries about her. He's scared all the time that she won't come home, that this job will wind up getting her killed, but he's never been scared that the children will be hurt, that them knowing something connected to Kez's work could result in one of them dying. He understands now, too, that it is the thought of that, the fear of that, which she has been trying to protect them from.

'Whether I tell Kez about this now or not, this is all going to be sorted very soon,' Jeb says with certainty and conviction, his tone telling Dennis not to argue with him. 'In a few days we'll be able to go back to living our normal lives. All of this is just a precaution.'

Dennis says nothing for a while, then: 'Yes, yes, you're right, of course. I'm just being paranoid. All of this will be resolved in a couple of days.'

Jeb is grateful that Dennis understood what he was saying. Because he really didn't want to fight him. But he would have. To give his children back some semblance of peace of mind, he would fight absolutely anyone.

Fredi

● Record Voice Note ▶ Recorded: March 2026

I had a note under my door last night.

> KEEP YOUR MOUTH SHUT.
> IF YOU TALK TO THE POLICE OR ANYONE,
> WE WILL COME FOR YOU.
> WE WILL END YOU.
> T Q G

I don't want to be, but I'm scared. I'm really scared. Dr Pemberton said to meet him later today by the clock tower. He said it wasn't safe to talk in his office.

I don't know how, but it sounds like they know. I don't think he told them. Which means they know that I know, even though I was really careful. They know everything. They are everywhere.

I'm going to call Mum as soon as I've spoken to Dr Pemberton. Even if the police officer says there's nothing they can do, I have to talk to Mum. I have to tell her. I have to let her come and get me before the Quiet Girls take me out.

■ End Voice Note ↓ Save Recording ↗ Send To Private Cloud

Part 9

Kez

April 2026, Axton Manor

It is the Spring Ball, previously called the Hunters' Rest Ball, tonight. I have settled into a routine of seeing pupils and a couple of staff members during the day and then writing my notes at night. I call Jeb and the children, I go for dinner in the canteen and Mac joins me, but we only talk about the case. It's been helpful, actually, him seeing Portia again. It's stopped us from, well, whatever it was that we were doing. I have a routine that works and is becoming a part of my life. But I don't feel any closer to solving the mystery. I can't work out the connection between Rhodes and what happened to Pemberton and Fredi. Unless he just ordered the Quiet Girls to deal with them. Like I said, though, not enough drama for someone like him. He needs ceremony and ritual to get off.

I do not have a dress for tonight and I've been told in many ways, including several times by email from Miss Barkway, that I *have* to wear a dress. And it has to be smart if not a ball gown. So, I have pushed away my innate fear and loathing for clothes shops and come down to the village to a small boutique a few doors down from Dr Jewel's shop that has floaty dresses and tops in the window. Not my type of clothing, but I'm hoping there will be something I can wear.

The dress I choose to try on is on the sale rail, but it still costs three figures. THREE FIGURES IN THE SALE. I ignore that, though. It doesn't matter. All that matters is that I do not stand out tonight. It is cream, ruched up over the chest area, cinched in at the top of the waist, flows down to my ankles. I would have to have my arms out, but I can wear a normal bra without the straps showing, and it fits all over. I look at myself a bit longer in the mirror, pleased that I will look all right tonight, and take it off.

I step out of the changing room, ready to pay for the dress, which is back on its hanger, and at the same time Portia pulls back the curtain to the second changing room and exits. She is wearing the same dress that I've just tried on and was about to buy. She is far more slender than me, so it looks completely different on her. Not better, just different. But still the same dress. She grins when she sees me, then her face falls when she notices what I'm holding in my arms.

'Can't believe it!' she says with a laugh. 'If I had got here three minutes earlier, I could have bagged this beauty.'

'You can still have it, I'll find something else,' I reply. 'It looks gorgeous on you.'

'I bet it looks just as gorgeous on you. I'll just have to look again.'

'I would have thought you'd have dresses suitable for this?' I say to Portia. 'You've worked at Axton for years.'

'Yes, well, every time I leave, I promise myself I'm not coming back. The school is like that boyfriend who you know is really bad for you so you leave them, then you get lured back with pretty words and shiny trinkets. There is so much wrong with the place, things that need changing. I keep telling them what they need to do, how they need to change, and they keep promising me that they'll look over what I've said and then . . . nothing. But I love those girls. Especially the ones that no one notices, the ones who are always in the background or who get bullied.'

This is not the place for this conversation. 'Do you fancy walking back to school together?' I ask. 'I'll wait for you to find something.'

'Oh no, don't worry, I've got lots of clothes back at home. I just wanted something special, because . . . Ah, never mind. Let's go.'

I pay for the dress and take the bag before we head out of the shop. The village is full of pupils from the school, going in and out of shops, making last-minute purchases for tonight, I guess.

'Did you know the girl who disappeared? Fredi?' I ask Portia as we start down the cobbled street.

Portia suddenly looks distraught, she keeps her eyes fixed on the horizon and struggles to stop her face collapsing. 'Yes. She was a new girl, meaning she started slightly later in the school year, so I tried to take her under my wing. I thought . . . I would have thought that if she was going to run away she would have spoken to me first. I feel like I failed her. I thought . . . I just failed her.' Her eyes mist over as she continues to stare into the distance. 'I had no idea that she was that unhappy. I mean, yes, recently she seemed troubled, but I thought she would talk to me before she did anything.'

'What about Dr Pemberton? How well did you know him?'

'Not at all if those messages he was exchanging with Fredi are anything to go by.'

'You know about the text messages?'

'Everyone on staff knows about those messages. People gossip. And I'm still completely floored that he could be such a wrong 'un and I didn't know.'

'Almost everyone says they had no idea. But what they usually mean is they ignored small things that indicated who that person was.

We all do it, we don't see the things that are sometimes right in front of our faces.'

'Exactly that,' she replies. 'That's why I'm floored. He was polite, friendly, but not overly so. He sometimes baked cakes because he said it helped him decompress. He would listen to you, even outside of office hours. He was respectful of people's space, especially women and girls. Guy used to talk to me about what narcissists are like, the difference between psychopaths and sociopaths . . . things like that. And I swear, Angus – Dr Pemberton – didn't come across like that at all.' She shakes her head. 'It just doesn't make sense. None of it makes sense. So that's two things that don't make sense – Fredi running away, Angus being a pervert. Things just don't add up. And I'm not sure why I'm the only person who can see that.'

'You think the police gave up too easily?'

Portia looks around, double-checking who can overhear us on the street. When she's sure no one is eavesdropping, she confides: 'I think . . . I think the investigation would be on-going if those messages on his phone had been to another girl. And there would be a huge media story about a missing girl if she was someone else's daughter. You can't convince me that everyone would have just shrugged their shoulders if the pretty *white* daughter of the CEO of the biggest corporation in the UK went missing. They'd be tearing apart every single stone in this country to find her.'

I know she's not wrong about that. I'm only here because a powerful white woman's daughter has been implicated in the disappearance and death of a man. We walk past Dr Jewel's shop and I look in. At that exact moment, she looks out and spots me. Our eyes snag on each other and stay there. I want to tell her that I went to see Fredi's mum, that I'm looking for Fredi, but of course I can't. And of course she'll still see me as the person up at 'the compound' where someone she knew disappeared. I rip my gaze away, go back to talking to Portia.

'I'm keeping everything crossed that they find her alive,' I say because I can't let Portia know that I am desperately trying to find Fredi. I can't let anyone know, because at this time, everyone is a suspect in this. And, nice as she seems, she could be the criminal mastermind behind all of this.

'Me too, Kez, me too.' She sighs sadly and I watch another emotion skitter across her face before she pushes on a bright smile.

'Hey, wait a minute, where are we going? This isn't the way back to the school.'

'Yes, it is. We're going through the woods.'

'Yeah, no thank you.'

'Oh come on, it's fine. The girls aren't allowed to take a shortcut through there, but we are. And I'm right here with you, so you'll be absolutely fine.'

We reach the entrance to the woods, an uncovered stony path that leads into the heart of the dark green and bright green forest, wood, whatever.

'How am I not encountering a serial killer in there?' I ask.

'You'll be fine. I'm right with you. And I've never encountered a serial killer in there. You will be fine.'

'That also makes sense if you're the serial killer, by the way.'

'Come on, Kez. Guy told me how you stood up to Headmaster Rhodes the other night. This is a cake walk compared to that.' Portia crosses the road and marches up to the wooden gate at the centre of the fence and unhooks it. 'Come on.'

I notice how she didn't respond to my 'you could be the serial killer' comment. Maybe it should have been a question.

We walk slowly into the green and the other world behind us disappears as the thicket of trees and large plants becomes our backdrop. It's hard to see the sky, so many tree branches and other greenery overhang and touch that we are essentially walking in the dark. Every so often, sun spots break through, but it is dark and close in here. There is so much foliage, so many pine needles and leaves underfoot. This path is wide and well worn, but it still feels as if we've stepped out of our normal reality into this fairy realm.

'What's the story of you and MJ?' I ask Portia. 'Whenever I mention her, you get a funny look on your face. Like she wronged you years ago or something. But I've seen you with her daughter and you don't seem to have any animosity towards her so I can't help but wonder what the story is?'

'What's the story of *you* and Maisie. Urgh, sorry, can't get used to calling her MJ. How do you know her? I wouldn't have thought you'd run in the same circles.'

'We don't. I used to work with her. Well, trained with her, really. After my masters, I got on a training programme and she was one of the other people on it.'

'Wasn't that training programme with the intelligence services?' she asks quietly, looking around even though we are alone.

'Was it?' I reply. *How does Portia know this? Would Mac really have told her? I got the distinct impression that he didn't talk to her about anything and that was one of the reasons why they split up.*

'I might not have been friends with Maisie, but other people I know kept up with her. I know she joined the intelligence services at one point. I also know that she's a bigwig in a government-ish job. What's your job?'

'Therapist.'

'And you just so happen to end up here, where Maisie once went to school? And her daughter still goes to school?'

'Well, no. MJ got me the position. I was looking for more work because, well, my husband's job has been a bit up and down of late. And nothing's getting any cheaper. I ran into MJ and she mentioned what had happened and suggested I speak to the school board to see if I could come in as a temp therapist. She didn't think the headmaster would take to me. She was spot on there. But I'm here, so it's kind of nepo-ish but not. More who-you-know-ish. That's all there is to that. What about you and MJ?'

'We weren't friends, we had some crossover friends, though. As I told you, her fortunes changed after her accident. We didn't really speak. I reckon if I had aspirations to be one of them, we might have been a bit closer.'

'One of them?'

'Yes, one of them.' She looks around again. 'A Quiet Girl.'

'What's so special about the Quiet Girls.'

'They run the world, Kez. They are the sisters of privilege and they run the world. They are everywhere. I was not one of them. And I didn't want to be one of them.'

'You speak about them with such disdain. And yet by your own admission you can't keep away from Axton. You keep leaving and coming back.'

'You mean, I was an Axtonite so why am I not spouting the party line? I don't know. There are levels of privilege. Some of us were never going to reach the higher levels, no matter how much money our families had. How successful we are. There's always this . . . glass ceiling, I suppose, on what you're allowed to be, what you're allowed to be a part of. It didn't bother me. I mean, I was technically from a single-parent family, which limited my ability to join the ranks of the Maisies of this world. My father, the one who paid the school fees, he's super successful at what he does. But him not being married to my mother and him giving my mother the money to pay the fees rather than paying direct meant I was always limited. Not that it bothered me. I was who I was; I am who I am. But when you're on the inside, and also a little bit on the outside, you can see things very clearly.

'You have a perspective on this world that is quite unique. You're not quite one of them, but you're enough of one of them to be privileged and to be absolutely hated outside of these hallowed walls.' She grins at my shocked face. 'Oh, we know everyone out there hates us. We know they think we have it easy and that we look down on them. And do you know what? They're not wrong. *I* don't look down on anyone, but most of these girls, they do. Not on purpose – they just come from a world where they can't conceive of doing without luxury foreign holidays and not expecting to walk into any job they fancy.

'I come back because it's what I know. I've talked it over enough times with Guy to realise that. I know this place. It's in my blood. It's in the blood of every single girl who goes here. She may not like to admit it once she leaves, but it's true. So they will help Axton out whenever they can. Sometimes indirectly, sometimes directly. For me and why I keep coming back? I'm very unlikely to have children, so I often think of these girls as my own. Especially the ones who don't come from privilege. I am here for them, to look out for them. To try to protect them from the people who don't believe they belong here.'

'Like Fredi?'

Portia swallows hard, and then sighs heavily. She moves like I have hit a raw nerve and the reverberations of that verbal blow are still making their way through her. 'Like Fredi, yes. Like Mariana before her. Although Mariana's mother was an old girl and she came from serious money, she was still biracial like me, so that still put her in a different category. But I tried to help her. And, of course, there was Audrey before Mariana.'

'Audrey?'

'Another girl who ran away. She was white, from a middle-class family, but she wasn't "one of us", if you understand me?'

'She was never heard from again?'

'They found her. Months later. She'd been living rough in the countryside on the other side of the village. She was so traumatised that she was put into an institution long-term. From what they could make out, she'd been chased through these very woods and had to hide for hours, possibly days. Who chased her? No one knows. How she got to the countryside where she was found? No one knows.

'But I felt responsible. I had put her in my sorority to keep an eye on her. To protect her as much as I could. And I failed. Just like I failed with Rachel before her.'

'Another girl who went missing?'

'No, she was American, from a very old, very wealthy, established family. Engaged to an actual member of the royal family up at Dewhurst, the boys' school. She was biracial. But she was rejected by his family. She was bullied mercilessly. Something happened to her in the woods, which was the height of the bullying. Then it stopped, just like it did with Maisie after she had her accident. Rachel had one of *those* accidents where she fell from the tower.

'I thought she would be OK after that. Most girls are. But she never recovered. She was physically fine, but emotionally fragile. She ended up returning to the States and her fiancé went with her. I took that personally. I take all of it personally, to be honest.

'When the thing happened with Audrey the following year, I resigned. I was obviously not good enough. I spent a lot of time on the phone to Guy, and he did his best to counsel me through it. I came back. Mariana happened. I left again. Then I come back and look – Fredi, another of my protectees, runs away. But I'm not leaving this time. I am going to find a way to make the board listen to me. They need to shut down some of the groups that are doing this.'

'You sound as though you believe that they target specific types of girls, do all they can to make sure they know they don't belong.'

'Do I?'

'Yes. Do you think there's a teacher behind all of this? Someone wanting to drive the message home?'

Portia stops in the middle of the glen to face me. 'If you're asking if I think Mrs Lazloe is capable of creating her own personal hit squad, and asking them to hunt down and terrorise the girls she doesn't believe deserve to be here, then yes. I think she is more than capable of doing that. She makes no secret of her contempt for those she doesn't think belong.

'She's said all sorts of messed-up things to me in my time here. And don't forget I'm older than her, have been a part of the school for longer than her. I eventually confronted her one time in front of everyone and she backed off. Stopped doing it. So, whilst I know she's capable, I don't know if she'd have the guts to actually go through with it. But is it possible? Yes. Absolutely. Is it likely? I'm not sure.'

Kez

April 2026, Axton Manor

I answer the door to Mac who said he would accompany me to the Spring Ball. I would have thought he would take Portia, but nope. I didn't get the impression earlier that they were sleeping together, but it's obvious every time you see them they are definitely close again. And I'm sure she was trying to buy a nice dress to impress him. So I was surprised when he messaged to ask if he could take me to the dance. Well, go to the dance at the same time as me. This is most definitely not a date.

When I see him . . . I think my mouth drops open a little, because he is breathtakingly handsome in his black dinner suit, white shirt and black silk bow tie. His hair is freshly washed and still damp, his face has a just-shaved freshness to it. And he is, I presume, wearing contact lenses. Handsome. He looks so handsome and we all know how completely well-behaved I am around handsome men.

'Hi,' I say, telling myself to stop it. I didn't go through all I went through to be with Jeb to throw it away on a man who is so good-looking, so good-smelling I want to lick him— *Stop it, Kez!* I tell myself. *Just stop it.*

Rather than reply, Mac looks up into the air above his head, his face wincing as though he is in agony. He takes a deep breath in and then lets it out slowly like he is releasing pressure from a valve. Eventually, he returns to looking at me. 'It's like someone is trying really hard to torture me,' he says.

'What do you mean?' I reply.

'Never mind. Hi. How are you?'

'I'm good, thank you. How are you?'

'In a bit of pain, actually. It'll pass.' His gaze sweeps over me again. 'Or maybe it won't. But let's not dwell. You look incredible.'

'What, this old thing? I've had it, what, five, six hours.'

He laughs out loud and treacherous sparkles of joy dance in my stomach and chest. Instead of laughing, too, I clear my throat, and sling my wrap around my shoulders, pick up my smallest bag, a black leather thing the size of a hardback book that Jeb bought me for our first anniversary. He'd wrapped it in a large piece of paper (the symbol for your first year of marriage) upon which he had written everything he loved about me. I had been bowled over by the bag and its wrapping. Jeb. I have to focus on Jeb. My husband. Who I love. Who is looking after our children so I can do this. Who doesn't deserve for me to do the dirty on him.

I step out of the room and shut the door behind me. Mac offers me his elbow and I look at it like the gateway to hell that it is. I am not going to do this. Any of it. I am not going to pretend taking his arm won't be the start of something I can't – or won't want to – stop. I smile at him closed-mouthed and instead take my bag in both hands so I'm not tempted to slip my arm into his.

The large courtyard is like a magical realm, decorated with fairy lights and pink cherry blossoms. A string quartet is positioned in the back right corner playing chamber music and wait staff in white shirts, black trousers and black bow ties circulate among the guests, offering glasses of sparkling wine. Champagne, I think. Other wait staff offer canapés.

'They know how to throw a party,' Mac says, sounding as awestruck as I am. The Axton pupils are all dressed up in ball gowns, the boys from Dewhurst College for Boys, the nearby boys' school, are dressed like Mac in dinner jackets. Everyone looks so elegant and polished. I imagine they have spent hours getting ready. They do indeed know how to party. This is what money looks like, I realise. This is what it's like to live among those who are always in the room where it happens. These are the children of the people who run our world. None of them look unsure, like they are worrying about whether they should be there or not. They move around each other, stopping to speak to each other, hugging each other like old friends, preening and posing to capture the attention of the ones on whom they are focused.

This is so not my world. These people move and behave like they are used to this. That this is nothing too out of the ordinary in their lives. Yes, it's special, but not out of the ordinary, they have been to these types of things before; they have attended and have been surrounded by people like them.

One of the things I discovered since being here is that they all know each other. Even the boys. Their families spend time together outside of school: they go on holiday together, they meet up for events, they support each others' pet projects, they have lunch with each other, they get internships at each other's businesses. The room where it happens is around them twenty-four–seven. They don't need to write letters to introduce themselves, they don't need to tart up CVs or wonder who to send an email to because it's very likely that their parents had drinks with that person just last night and they call that person Uncle or Auntie. These children belong together.

Which is why I worry about Fredi. Would she have fitted in here? Would she have come here and felt out of her depth?

I don't believe she ran away.

The more I learn about her from listening to her parents' appeals on social media, from what Portia said, she definitely doesn't profile as a runaway. She profiles as someone who something happened to. However, I do have to keep in mind that I may be wrong. That while there is no evidence of it, that Fredi might have been involved in some shady stuff. That she did maybe have a thing with one of the boys from the boys' school and that she might have had a breakdown when things went wrong. It is something I have to consider. However, my gut feeling is that she *wasn't* having an inappropriate relationship with Dr Pemberton and she ran before they were found out. It just doesn't feel right.

And the fact that her phone, email, cards and bank account haven't been used in all the time she has been missing, suggests she's not in any position to use them. Which further suggests someone has taken her. Taken her, *and* killed Pemberton?

Maybe it was a member of staff? Maybe it was some random person?

Or maybe it was the Quiet Girls.

They run this place from what I gleaned from Portia. Maybe Fredi broke their rules and they had to silence her?

'If you think any harder or faster, your head is going to catch fire,' Mac says, pushing a glass of fizz into my hands.

'Yeah, sorry, just trying to work out what happened to—'

'Where did you get that dress?' Mac interrupts. I'm used to his mid-conversation hijacks, to him completely changing direction in a conversation and expecting me to keep up, but not like this. And why would it interest him where I got the dress?

'I'm sorry to say, they didn't have anything in your colour,' I reply.

'How do you know what my colour is?' he teases, his eyes dancing.

'Miss, miss,' one of Fredi's 'friend' group says, coming to stand in front of us. Astrid. The one who acts like she is the leader of the group, like the alpha girl, when it's the other one, Paris, who stands beside Viola who is really in control of this group.

'How can I help you, Astrid?' I ask.

She is very drunk and, by the look in her eyes, she has taken something else. I scan the group and they all have. They have all had a drink or five and taken something. Except for Paris. She would never allow herself to lose control in an environment such as this.

'We've been talking and we want to know if you're bench pressing with Dr M?'

Bench pressing? Is that what they're calling it these days? Or is that what *she's* calling it? They all crack up, smirking and giggling and hushing each other, even Paris joins in, without ever taking her cold, sober eyes off me. I notice, despite her calm demeanour, she is playing with her gold bullion keyring, a sign of stress.

'I'm not sure that's an appropriate question to ask a member of staff,' I say.

'You're not really a member of staff,' Astrid giggles.

'No? What am I?'

'You're a . . . you know,' Astrid continues.

'I don't know, actually,' I say sternly. Although I do know. This conversation reminds me of one I had with Brian and MJ years ago, when we were all trainees at Dennis's T. H. I. U. (The Human Insight Unit). Brian and MJ had told me to my face that I was an unworthy, unqualified diversity hire. Then they both did shocked faces when I told them that I'd had to jump several more hoops than them, I'd had to show far more evidence than them, get more references than them to end up at the same position as them. It didn't stop them thinking and believing it, but they had been shocked at how much more rigorously I had been vetted before I could become a trainee like them.

'You're a—'

'You're a temporary member of staff,' Viola says over Astrid. Even though she is drunk and drugged up, she still has the good sense and diplomacy to step in. I remember in the group therapy session Viola had said Astrid said racist stuff all the time. 'At least that's how we understood it. You've been brought in to cover until they find Dr Pemberton's replacement.'

'Something like that,' I reply.

Issy, who is standing beside Astrid, nudges her and glares at her, silently telling her to shut up. Haniya does the same. Astrid is suddenly aware that the group is unhappy with her. She turns her head to look at Paris, who is glaring at her with those cold eyes.

'Sorry, miss,' Astrid says, looking both scared and embarrassed. More scared than embarrassed, though.

'Don't worry about it,' I say, suddenly worried for her. Fredi was one of this group. Did she step out of line? Did she have occasion for Issy and Haniya to nudge her, Viola to speak over her, Paris to glare at her? Did Fredi's disappearance start like this? 'It is not a problem. Let's put it behind us. Forget it ever happened.'

'That's very magnanimous of you, Dr Lanyon,' Paris says. 'Isn't that right, girls?' I've known international villains sound less scary than this fifteen-year-old. When I get home, I am going to hug my daughter so tight she will think I have lost my mind because she is nothing like this girl. These girls, in fact. She is nothing like them and I am so grateful.

Paris's group all rush to agree that it is very magnanimous of me, and the chill of her control over these girls freezes my spine. 'We'll leave you to enjoy the rest of your evening,' Paris states before turning and walking away. The rest of the girls turn, almost in unison, and follow her into the crowd.

'I don't know about you, but I am so scared right now my tongue has gone numb,' Mac says.

'Same,' I reply. 'Same.'

Kez

April 2026, Axton Manor

Tink, tink, tink. A teaspoon against a champagne flute.

'May I have your attention, please?' Mr Rhodes says, standing at the front of the courtyard, framed by the archway. Victoria Rhodes stands beside him, glowing with pride. 'Thank you for gathering here today for our annual Hunters' Rest Spring Ball. You are all looking radiant and I appreciate not only your attendance but your strength at what is a difficult time for our little family here at Axton. We have lost a much-valued, much-loved colleague, and one of our flock has flown the nest. Too soon, I fear. We miss Winifred. Terribly. We pledge not to rest until Winifred is safely home with us. And we will keep a light shining for little Winifred, to guide her home to us. We will hold her in our hearts and keep her in our prayers. Come home safely, Winifred. Come home.'

I turn to Mac, about to say something, and he shakes his head a little, telling me not to speak. Not to say a single word.

'Please, continue to enjoy the spoils of the hunt. The spoils of the season. And to begin the festivities, as is the custom, I will ask our two newest members of staff to lead us in the dancing.'

Say what now? I think as all eyes turn in our direction.

'I feel like I'm being punished,' Mac murmurs. 'Being punished with one of my biggest nightmares.'

I look at him. 'Dancing with me or dancing in public with hundreds of people watching?'

'Both,' he replies, not even glancing in my direction. I am looking at him so I do not look at the expectant faces of the surrounding crowd. I know Rhodes hates me, but this? *This? Tradition, my shiny right shoe!*

'Please, clear the way for Dr Mackenzie to lead his partner in the first dance,' Rhodes says.

How exactly did I get here? I ask myself as Mac holds out his hand and I take it. *Oh yes, that's right: twenty-five years ago I decided it would be a good idea to take a job working for the government. There is a direct line from that decision to this moment where I am going to be humiliated in public.*

Mac and I make our way to the middle of the dance floor, and he slips his arm around my waist, I put my hand on his shoulder and we link our hands together.

The music starts and neither of us moves, not sure what to do. The music continues, everyone is watching us, but still we do not move. Cannot move. We're both avoiding looking at each other, too. Over Mac's shoulder, I spot Portia, looking immaculate in a royal-blue ball gown. Her hair is in a high bun on top of her head and she wears perfectly applied make-up. She mouths, 'Move. Just move.'

'Just move,' I murmur to Mac. The scrutiny of everyone in the courtyard burns holes into my skin. 'Just move and I'll go with you. I mean, it can't get much worse, can it?'

'I hate it when people say that,' he replies in a low tone. 'It's never a statement of fact. It is always like a challenge to the universe to prove things can, in fact, get worse.' Despite this, he moves backwards and I step with him, probably with the wrong foot, but I don't care. I never learnt to dance like this. I've watched a few episodes of *Strictly* like everyone else and I have never pretended that this is something I can do. So I don't care if people smirk.

We give it a good go, Mac moving around the dance floor and me fighting tooth and nail my natural aversion to allowing anyone to lead me anywhere. We carry on for a few more minutes, then the music changes and that is everyone's cue to fill the dance floor. Young men with white gloves go to young women, bow, and then offer their hands before the young lady is led onto the dance floor. Soon, the dance floor is packed and everyone has forgotten us. Or have put us out of their minds until later when they'll mock us. And, honestly, the fact that we didn't fall over or injure each other means I literally couldn't care what they say next.

Under the cover of other bodies moving in time to the music around us, Mac pulls me closer to him, ignoring the rule that says for this type of dancing there needs to be a gap, a distance between us.

Rhodes is suddenly beside us, with Victoria, who is wearing a gold strapless ball gown. He has tails on, a gold bow tie to match his wife's dress and the obligatory white gloves. I unfortunately catch his eye and his long face, with its scooped-in cheeks and flat forehead, creases up when he smiles with the satisfaction of a man who has managed to put someone in their place. It's impressive what he will do because I thwarted his efforts to find out what his pupils talk to me about.

'Very . . . *good* effort with your dance,' he says. 'Very . . . *interesting*, shall we say?'

'Thank you,' I reply with a wide grin. 'It's our speciality. We're always so pleased that people are so entertained by us. Tell your friends, we're almost always available for parties and formal dances. Aren't we, Dr Mackenzie?'

'We certainly are,' Mac replies, grinning at Rhodes. 'Obviously we'll give a discount to repeat customers and friends of previous customers.'

Rhodes's face loses its smugness – it's no fun when the people you tried to humiliate aren't cringing or desperate to hide away.

'Excellent party,' I say.

'Really rather excellent,' Mac echoes.

'Top notch.'

'Top drawer.'

We both grin at him and Victoria Rhodes mouths, 'I'm so sorry,' then fixes her face before her husband sees. So it *was* a deliberate way to humiliate us.

When I tear my gaze away from the Rhodes couple, it unexpectedly collides with Mac's dark-blue eyes. And stays there. I haven't looked at him like this – unguarded – in over a year. Probably eighteen months, when my crush-but-not-quite-a-crush feelings were at their height. As my therapist, he didn't look at me like this. He would, week after week, look at me like a professional. He would talk to me like a professional. He took my hand, and guided me through the maze of horrors my mind had built to allow me to exist after I killed my friend.

All of that professionalism was dropped when he told me he couldn't be my therapist any longer. He explained that his supervising therapist had told him that it wasn't good for his mental health to keep seeing me in any capacity, but especially not as my therapist.

I hadn't argued because he was obviously right. I'd thanked him for all he'd done to help me and we both silently agreed not to contact each other again. It was for the best. Now, we're staring directly into each other's eyes. Mac's grip on my waist increases and he brings us closer together, until our bodies are touching. My heartbeat quickens; my breathing becomes shallow. I'm sure he can feel my heart against his chest. I can certainly feel his growing interest.

This can't happen, I tell myself. *I can't do this.* I'm about to step away, to go get a drink, some food, anything to abruptly stop this when he increases his hold on me. He knows I want to end this interlude and he doesn't want to let me go.

'Come back to my room,' he says quietly, staring directly into my soul.

I shake my head. That really can't happen.

'Please, Kez. Come back to my room with me.'

'No,' I reply. I'm aware that other people's eyes are on us. Rhodes, definitely. Portia, too. Maybe others. I can feel the intensity of their gaze as I try to navigate this situation I have never been in before. I've been propositioned before, sure, but not by someone I would actually have sex with.

'Do you trust me?' he asks.

It's me I don't trust. Me who Jeb doesn't really trust. And with good reason. I am too flawed for this. 'Yes.'

'Then please come to my room. Please.'

When I first met Mac, when I suspected him of being a Svengali-type lecturer who was controlling a vulnerable young woman, he had told me with a look on his face that he wanted to talk to me away from the person I was paired with to work on that case. I remember seeing that expression and knowing that I had to speak to him alone. He has the same look on his face now.

At least, I think he has? I could be fooling myself so I can be alone with him. I guess I'll never know until I do it, will I?

'OK,' I murmur. 'OK.'

Jeb

April 2026, Secret Location

Jeb has been playing with the cigarette for a while now. Sitting on this covered patio, staring out into the darkness, he threads the white stick with its beige-brown top back and forth through the fingers of his right hand.

The children – miraculously – went to sleep on arrival. In the same room. There was space enough for them to have their own rooms, but Zoey had given him a look that said Jonah needed to be with her in the room with twin beds. Within an hour, they'd both fallen asleep, sparking out as if they regularly left their house in the middle of the night to rock up at a place in a secret location hours away from everyone and everything they know.

They'd been given new mobile phones and tablets, spoofed with their own numbers so if Kez called it would connect to the new number and she wouldn't know anything was amiss. They all understood that they couldn't tell anyone – least of all their wife and mother – what was going on. Now, after dinner, the children are in their room playing computer games and reading. And Jeb is sitting out here, staring into the dark, thinking about the picture Kez sent him of the outfit she is wearing to the party at the school. He hasn't seen her looking like that in an age. And she was going to the party with that man.

Jeb puts the cigarette between his lips, closes his eyes. He hasn't smoked since the night he met Kez, well over twenty-seven years ago. *And look how* that *turned out*, he says to himself in his head. He'd been at that party, partially thrown in his honour because he was meant to be getting married the following week and he'd seen Kez. He'd noticed her straight away and had been captivated. It was something so unexpected. He'd never felt like that about anyone. He'd known Hella forever – she was his friend from school and he loved her. He was going to do right by her. He was going to get married, they were going to move out of their flat, buy a house, have children, the whole thing. And then Kez was there. Walking around the party, lost. She seemed untethered, as though she was drifting and wanted someone to anchor her. He had wanted desperately to be that anchor.

He rummages in his pocket for his lighter until his fingers close around the smooth, cold case of the Zippo lighter he's had since he was sixteen. It was the lighter that everyone had back then. The coolest of the cool lighters.

The night he met Kez, he hadn't smoked in over three years. But after the shock of her letting him kiss her, her coming upstairs with him, them doing what they did, he'd needed calming down. Afterwards, sitting in the garden, he'd smoked that cigarette he'd been carrying around since he'd quit and had tried to work out how to end things with Hella, his wife-to-be. He wasn't a cheat. What he'd just done was so not him and it made him feel a little bit sick that this was who he was. He was a cheat. He was a liar. He hadn't seen himself that way, had always thought he was a fundamentally honest person, but here he was, sitting beside a woman he had already fallen for. He smoked the cigarette, the realisation dawning on him that he didn't even know this woman's name. He'd made love to her, but didn't know her name. And that didn't matter because he couldn't see her again. He had to forget her. He had to put her out of his mind and move on with his life. And then he'd looked at her, saw how she was looking at him, and he'd been lost all over again.

There was something about her that made it impossible to think about not seeing her again and stay sane. He wanted her in his life. *Needed* her in his world. And he couldn't have her. He was pretty sure she would freak out if she knew he was meant to be getting married the following week. He would just have to finish with Hella, he'd decided. He would take this woman's number, end his relationship with Hella, wait a bit and then call her.

When he'd walked her back to where she was staying, he'd been desperate for her to ask him in. Yes, so he could take her clothes off and make love to her again, slower this time, less frantic and craven, but he also wanted to talk to her. She was so funny, she got his sense of humour and she had a unique way of saying things that fascinated him. He wanted to spend the night with her in his arms, both of them naked, talking. But he'd restrained himself . . . And, as a result, he didn't see her again for another eight years. He didn't get to make love to her again until nine years after meeting her. *After* he'd lived a life, made a home and child with Hella. Well after he'd thought he would see her again.

And now look at him.

Sitting in the middle of nowhere, his life in danger. His children's lives in danger. Kez off somewhere, probably in danger. Possibly screwing someone else. It bugs him that this thought keeps coming into his head. After she told him the identity of the man she had developed feelings for, Jeb had looked him up. He was very different to Jeb, but there was something about him – his pictures and his work – that Jeb knew would appeal to Kez. He probably needed her and didn't need her at the same time. That would attract Kez to him, more so than his admittedly good looks. This man obviously had feelings for Kez, otherwise she would never have mentioned it. And, now they're in that place together, he can't help imagining . . . Jeb lights the cigarette.

'You should try to get some rest, Mr Quarshie,' Dennis says, coming out onto the patio. Without being invited to, Dennis takes the seat one over from where Jeb is. Jeb doesn't reply. Why would he speak to this man? Everything bad that has happened in his life since he met Kez again can be directly traced back to this man. Everything.

After Jeb doesn't respond to Dennis, he says: 'I'm not sure what Kezuma has told you about me?'

Jeb knows that this is not just to get him to engage in conversation – it's so Dennis can work out how he should approach Jeb. How patronising he can get away with being, how much he has to reveal to try to get Jeb onside.

'She told me that you sexually assaulted her,' Jeb replies, looking directly at him. 'You spent months sexually harassing her and then you assaulted her.'

Dennis doesn't flinch, doesn't even seem to react. This man is every bit the demon Kez has indirectly said he is. 'It wasn't quite that simple.'

'She told me that you would have raped her if she hadn't decided to quit. That you would have done so and said it was part of her training. A pressure point, she said you called it.'

Again, Dennis doesn't flinch, he simply stares back at Jeb.

'She told me you've always said that she is your favourite. Of all your recruits over all the years, she's your favourite. Which is why I have never been able to work out why you hate her so much. I mean, she's told me multiple times that you hate everyone, but it seems particular with her.'

'I do not hate Kezuma,' Dennis replies. That's all. That's all he says.

'So why are you always trying to break up her marriage? You created a narrative to try to split us up two years ago. Must have stung when we got back together, right? And you're doing it again now. Sending Dr Mackenzie down to where she is, hoping she'll, what, sleep with him and then leave me?'

Dennis momentarily registers his shock that Jeb knows this.

'Yes, Kez told me about him. She told me about her feelings for him when she met him and that you've sent him down there now. She, like me, knows that you're trying to activate a pressure point. But I can't work out why you're trying to split us up again. Unless –' Jeb makes sure that Dennis is still focused on him when he says '– unless you want her for yourself? You're into her and you want to be with her?'

Dennis's face registers instant revulsion at the very thought of it. 'Don't be disgusting,' he spits.

'Then why are you constantly trying to destroy her relationship? Stop her from living full-time with her children? Because that seems the most logical conclusion.'

Dennis takes a deep breath, then exhales. 'Kezuma is exceptional at what she does. From her first interview, she stood out. Even back then I knew she was going to be my replacement. Unlike most people, I don't fear the thought of a successor. Kezuma is it. But – this is the part I haven't told Kezuma – this job is hardest on the people you're closest to.' He waves his hand. 'Look around you. Look where you are. I only just found out in time that you were being watched. And that they were coming in the next couple of days to pick you up and take you who knows where because someone – I don't even properly know who yet – wanted more information about your wife.

'This could be your life in perpetuity. You could become a target, your children could become targets. You won't be able to live in your house as it is without extra security. Possibly permanent security guards. You won't be able to live without always looking over your shoulder. The reason why Kezuma is where she is now is for that very reason. Someone is threatening the family of someone powerful, connected. Your marriage and the solidity of your family needs to be able to withstand more than your wife finding a mutual attraction with a good-looking therapist who has a background like hers.'

Jeb smiles at him. Grins. 'You had me in the first half, not gonna lie. You almost had me convinced that what you were doing was for the greater good and that I needed to think about how Kez and I would survive going on. I was starting to wonder if I should maybe think about us splitting up permanently. But you couldn't help yourself, could you? You had to slip in the "good-looking" and the "background like hers" bits. That made me realise you're an unserious person.' Jeb turns to watch the dark horizon again, lifts his almost burnt-out cigarette to his lips. 'Thanks, Dennis. You've made me feel a whole lot better. You've just told me that you want Kez all to yourself. You need her lonely and sad because you think it makes her easier to control. It hasn't occurred to you that what makes Kez, Kez, what allows her to do what she does, is her family. Having us is what keeps her on an even keel. And that keeps her safe. Without us, Kez wouldn't be able to function. Thanks for the reminder.'

Jeb keeps looking out at the horizon until he hears Dennis get up and leave. His stomach is in knots. Not about having to leave their home. He knows that if Dennis is here with them, then they are safe.

What's driving him crazy is the fact that he isn't as OK with Kez being around Dr Mackenzie as he just made out. He knows that for Kez to have told him about someone for whom she'd developed feelings, it must have meant something. It must have meant a lot. It must have been all she could think about so she had to externalise it by telling him. And, while she may think she would never cheat, he knows that it's not something you actually think you'll do. Not until you're in a situation where someone is so incandescent, so heart-stopping, that you can't help yourself. And then your fundamentally honest self will find you in a kitchen, asking this someone why they ran away when you flirted with them, and then you'll be kissing them, and then you'll be upstairs ordering them to take off their knickers so you can screw them against a wall in a way you've never had sex before, all the while wondering what this person has done to you. Jeb guesses that no one thinks they'll cheat until they do.

Until they do.

He pats his pockets down in the vain hope that he has put an extra 'last ever' cigarette in there somewhere. He really could do with one right now. He really could.

Kez

April 2026, Axton Manor

Mac's room is exactly like mine: a bed, desk, bookcase, door to the en suite, area near the window with a toaster, plates, cutlery, kettle, mini fridge.

Bed.

Bed.

Bed.

I stand in the middle of the room, trying to ignore the bed. Trying to ignore how handsome Mac looks, especially when he looks so troubled and vulnerable with it. He comes to stand in front of me.

'Kez,' he begins, then stops talking. He reaches out and hooks his fingers into mine. We both stare down at our intertwined fingers, our breathing heavy and shallow at the same time. 'Come here,' he says, and pulls me into a hug. He nestles his face against mine, his lips brushing my cheek.

Slowly, I raise my hands and rest them lightly on his back. 'This isn't a good idea,' I whisper.

'I know,' he replies, even quieter than me. 'I'm going to tell you something. Don't react. Just keep hugging me, OK?'

'Yes,' I murmur.

'There are cameras everywhere, recording everything. Including in this room.'

What? WHAT? My eyes widen, but I don't otherwise physically react.

Mac moves his face closer, acting as though he is kissing me but instead he says, 'I think it's only cameras in the bedrooms. But I know there are microphones in your office.'

Again, I try not to stiffen, try not to let my horror show in my body language.

'I'll disconnect them tomorrow, but, for now, we have to act like we don't know.'

'OK,' I reply.

'I'm going to do something out of order. React however you want so you can leave.'

I don't have a chance to process what he just said before he runs a hand down my back, over my bum and then squeezes. In shock, I push him away. 'What the hell are you doing?' I ask him.

'We both know what you came here for,' Mac says, an edge to his voice. If I didn't know better, I would think he actually was a creep. He points to the bed. 'Ready when you are.' He sheds his jacket.

'Get lost.' I march out of the room, slamming the door behind me.

I stand outside his door, trying to process what I've just heard. Of course, that is what Miss Barkway meant. *He likes to watch.* She was telling me why she couldn't say anything. Couldn't tell me if he did do something to her because he would know. *He likes to watch.* If my office is also bugged with audio, I'll bet that was how he got the info about the pupils. Pemberton didn't pass the info over – Rhodes was listening in.

I wonder if Pemberton found out and then confronted him? I wonder if that's how Pemberton met his end? He found out and the old pervert killed him. Mac was right. Rhodes did kill him.

I feel sick thinking about that man sitting there, perving over young girls getting changed, and more, probably. And what's Miss Barkway doing, not going straight to the police with this information? Fredi may not have disappeared if Barkway had gone to the police when she'd found out what he was doing. Other girls might not have gone missing. Barkway clearly hates Rhodes so why wouldn't she put an end to his behaviour? Because he gave her a job? Because she knew him when she was a pupil? Or because he has something incriminating on her? Whatever the reason, she should have gone to the police.

This is so messed up. *So* messed up. We need to put an end to this. I'm not sure I can stand the thought of him getting off to young girls. We have to do something.

Kez

May 2026, Axton Manor

Of course I haven't slept very much.

I went back to my room, pulled on a jumper and joggers, then took my dress off under my clothes. The thought that Rhodes could be watching me made me feel physically ill. That he had watched me have phone sex with Jeb was disgusting. That he'd been potentially watching me all this time, listening in on my therapy sessions with children while they were being vulnerable . . . I want to get him arrested. But I can't until we have some idea where Fredi is. As I lay in bed, I'd heard the girls head off to their rooms and common rooms for breakout parties around 3 o'clock. I wasn't sure what time the staff retired, but the children didn't seem to know when to stop partying. Which was gratifying and life affirming to hear.

'How are we going to disable the cameras?' I say to Mac in the car park after we get into my car. He had texted me after I returned to my room last night to meet here this morning at seven.

Mac says, 'I already have.'

'What? How?'

'I hacked the system, took it offline and planted a virus in the system so even if they get it back online it'll keep cutting out.'

'You did that?' I ask.

'Yes.'

'You?'

'Yes.'

'All right, what's going on, because you did not hack the system. If you could do that, you would have done it straight away and told me. You wouldn't have been as panicked as you were. You might as well tell me, because the longer it takes for you to tell me, the angrier I'll be.'

'All right, OK, I had help.'

I hitch up an eyebrow at him while my stomach is clenching and a wave of heat is sweeping over me. My body knows where this is going, but my mind is still playing catch-up at this point. 'Help from who?'

'Dennis.'

'Dennis talked you through what to do?'

'Not exactly.'

Mac hasn't been able to properly face me since we got in the car, but now he looks at me. And when he looks at me, my brain finally picks up what the rest of my body knew. There is only one reason why Mac is acting so jittery. Why he can't look me in the face. Dennis. This is all about Dennis. And him crossing the line with my family – again.

This is what Jeb meant. This is what Mac meant. I have got way too comfortable with Insight. With Dennis. I have forgotten that when you start hanging out with snakes and scorpions they will eventually bite you, sting you. No matter how much they like you, need you, no matter how much of a favourite you are, they will still turn on you.

'The next time you speak to Dennis, tell him to stay the fuck away from my son. Tell him, if he goes near him again, for whatever reason, I will fucking kill him.'

The reason I am here, living in a boarding school and trying to find out why a man was killed and where a girl has disappeared to, is because of Dennis. Because I made a deal with the snake, the *devil* that is Dennis. I am here and he thinks it's OK to encroach on my family again. *Again.* This is what happens when you let your guard down around someone like Dennis. Once he sees you don't think of him as a threat any longer, he thinks he can start to push at your boundaries, take advantage of you in ways you'll find hard to argue against.

When my stepson Moe got into trouble a while ago, the only way to save him, to stop him going to prison, was to make a deal with Dennis. It was an unspoken deal: once I had gone back to work at Insight, once Dennis had kept Moe out of prison, Dennis would leave my family alone. Maybe it should have been a spoken deal, because to sort this out Dennis has gone to Moe. My eldest child, Jeb's son from his first marriage, is a tech whiz, always has been. The things he can do with computers have always been completely beyond my understanding. But to him it's like being able to speak another language. He would absolutely have been able to do what was needed to dismantle the network through which the cameras and microphones in this place run, he would also be able to plant a virus that would stop them being rebooted easily. It would have taken him no time. He could probably set up something that would alert us if they tried to reboot the system. But there are people employed in Insight, in the intelligence services, who are just as capable, just as quick and natural at doing this stuff. And, more importantly, *it's their job.* It's what they signed up to do. Even if it was 2 a.m. and they were on holiday in the Bahamas, a call from Dennis would have had them dropping everything to fix it.

Dennis using my son, my already damaged boy, would be a way to not only get at me, but also to remind Moe the reason he isn't in prison and/or doesn't have a criminal record is thanks to Dennis's intervention. He doesn't want Moe to ever forget that. Like Moe could, like Moe could ever forget why all of this is happening. Dennis also wants to damage my marriage. When Jeb finds out that Dennis has gone to Moe, he will lose the plot. He will absolutely lose it. For Jeb, it's bad enough that I work with Dennis, but when he finds out that Dennis has been creeping around his firstborn, making him feel guilty and *working for him* . . . I'll be lucky to stay married. Which is Dennis's goal, of course. Trying to separate me from any realistic support.

'Sorry,' Mac mumbles. 'I didn't realise he would do that. I know you said things are still a bit difficult with your son, but I didn't realise Dennis would exploit that in this way.'

I swing my gaze to look out of the window; I fear I will cause Mac to burst into flames or eviscerate him if I keep staring at him. 'I haven't fucked you yet, so Dennis needs to get his kicks another way.'

That isn't fair to Mac, but I don't feel like being fair. And he is the closest thing I can have a go at.

'Erm . . . I noticed the use of the word "yet" in that sentence. So am I right in thinking there is still a chance I may get lucky? Because if there is a chance, I need to finish up with my girlfriend, get a playlist together, find a few candles—'

I whip round to look at him and he waggles his eyebrows. He knows exactly how to bring me back from the boiling anger that is a hair's breadth away from making me storm out of here and down to Insight to deliver my message to Dennis in person.

'You,' I say with a laugh.

'I'm sorry. I honestly didn't realise he would do that. I just wanted it sorted as soon as possible. I thought he had people who would do it. Not use it as another way to get at you.'

'It's not your fault. How did you find out about the cameras?'

'It was the "he likes to watch" comment from Miss Barkway that you told me about. It kept coming back to me. And then when I was talking to Rhodes the other day he told me that when he dislocated his knee a few years ago, he would rub in magnesium oil. And I thought, "how does he know about that?" since I only mentioned it to you. In your office. I knew for sure you hadn't told him. I haven't told anyone else, not even Portia. Which meant he had heard. I went around the school, looking for anything that could conceivably be a listening device. And I found cameras everywhere.' Mac shudders. 'There are signs up saying CCTV is in operation, but it's more than that. You'd expect them in the corridors, but not everywhere.'

'Do you really think he has them in the girls' bedrooms?' I reply.

'It might not be him,' Mac offers. 'But, yes, I think there are cameras in the girls' rooms. Which adds a whole new level of disgustingness to this. That's why I panicked last night and called Dennis. The thought that Rhodes can just dip in and watch any girl he wants makes me physically sick. And it makes me wonder again about what happened to Fredi. And Mariana as well. Did she find out something? Did he realise they knew and put an end to them?'

'I keep thinking that, too. But how long have those cameras been there? And if he was listening to the therapy sessions then he knows everything I've been talking to the girls about. He most likely knows why we're really here.'

'No, no, I don't think he does,' Mac says. 'I don't think he'd be treating us like he is if he did. We only speculate about the death and disappearance – we don't talk about anything else. He doesn't come across as someone who can keep his powder dry if he thinks he is about to get caught. Hence the disappearance of Fredi. The death of Pemberton.'

'This makes me think all the emails, and other stuff found on Pemberton's phone and computer were fake. If something *was* going on, Rhodes would have seen. He would have put an end to it straight away. The last thing this lot want is any type of scandal. So if all that evidence was fake, who put it there? Clearly, they wanted to put an end to any investigations by smearing Pemberton and Fredi. But I don't believe he was working alone. If it was him at all.'

'I really don't know which way to go from here,' Mac admits.

'Don't worry,' I reply, 'I suspect something will come up that will show us what we need to focus on. And of course, if we've disabled the cameras and got rid of the microphones, that will make him desperate. This will force his hand. Which is basically what we want.'

Part 10

Kez

May 2026, Axton Manor

'I find it curious that you haven't once asked about Guy and me,' Portia says as we lift weights in the gym. It's Sunday morning and I have been unsettled ever since finding out Rhodes has likely been getting off watching teenage girls. Several times an hour I have to talk myself down from marching over to his office/house to confront him, to punch him out. Then calling the police and punching him out again before the police arrive. The need to find out what happened to Fredi and Mariana, what really happened to Pemberton, has to come first. But it is a close-run thing. And I'm still not sure I'm doing the right thing. Consequently, I am lifting weights to try to tire myself out.

I actually came to the gym to be alone, but had found Portia in here, wearing her pink tracksuit with white edging. I'd thought, for a moment, of walking straight out because I didn't really want conversation, but she saw me so I had to stay.

'What would I ask?' I reply.

Portia Akande profiles as someone who is, on the surface of things, open. She will answer all your questions, she will give you information, but she has secrets like the rest of us. She has a hidden side that drives the things she does, that decides who she allows in her life, what conversations she has. Portia is bringing this up at this moment for a reason. It seems like a straightforward question, but there is much loaded into it, so much that she wants to know that she has dressed up as vague, innocuous questioning.

'I don't know,' she replies. She is watching me in the mirror while I am avoiding looking at my reflection. 'I just . . . I just find it odd that you haven't asked about our relationship at all. I mean, you strike me as the curious type and you've asked me all sorts of things, yet you're not at all curious about what happened between us.'

'It's not that I'm not curious, it's more that if you or Dr Mackenzie wanted to tell me, you would.'

A frown corrugates her face. 'Dr Mackenzie? Why are you calling him that?'

'Because that's his name?'

'Why are you acting as though you and him aren't sleeping together?' she asks.

'We're not sleeping together. We never have. He's my colleague at most. Not even a friend, really. And we are not sleeping together. I am married. Happily.'

'Really?'

'Really.'

'Really, really?'

'Really, really.'

'It's just that I thought . . . the way you are with each other, the way you were looking at each other last night, and how he was holding you, the heat between you two is palpable. He used to look at me like that. Add to that the fact that you've never asked about our relationship, it seemed obvious that you two are sleeping together. I asked why you didn't ask because it might be a way to get you to open up about your affair.'

'Sorry, no affair.'

'Are you really not curious about our relationship?'

'You seem very keen on talking about it. So I'll ask: what happened with you and Dr Mackenzie?'

'We broke up!'

I burst out laughing and Portia laughs with me. She's actually very funny. I can see why she and Mac worked, they must have been quite formidable together.

'In all seriousness, I haven't really talked about what happened with us,' she says quietly.

OK, she wants a therapist. She wants to explore what happened with the most significant romantic/sexual relationship she has had. She has clearly never had the space or opportunity to open up about it, to be vulnerable. She has had to be stiff upper lip about it and now is reaching out. 'You can talk about it with me, if you want,' I say. That's what I'm here for, to help people. When I left The Human Insight Unit (Dennis's original organisation), I became a therapist and started to see people, treat people, and it felt good. It felt amazing knowing I was doing something that could help people navigate the difficulties they were going through. I was desperate to make up for what I'd done, giving therapy was a way to do that.

I am still desperate to redress the balance.

'I've made such a big thing about it, I feel a bit foolish now,' Portia says.

'Nothing to feel foolish about, if you want to explain what happened and how that affected you, honestly, do talk to me. That's literally what I'm here for.'

'We didn't really break up – that's the worst part of it,' she says. 'We just kind of stopped. We were going to get married. We weren't just engaged and the marriage was never going to happen, we had a plan. I was working here so I had to travel home at weekends and I could honestly see our life all mapped out. He could, too. I mean, he'd get wedding magazines and call up about reception venues. We were going to be husband and wife.

'And then something happened with his work. He wouldn't really tell me what, but it devastated him. He became insular, wouldn't talk, wouldn't do anything. It was like someone had dimmed his light and there was no way to turn it back up.

'I lost him by degrees. He just stopped showing up in our relationship. He said he still loved me, but he couldn't show it. Do you have any idea what it's like to have someone slip away from you and not be able to help them?'

I shake my head. I know it. Of course I know it. Now that Brian has stopped haunting me, I can look back at our friendship and I can remember how I lost him. How he slipped away in stages and no matter how hard I tried to reach him by ringing, texting, emailing, he kept slipping. He was in a downward spiral and there's nothing I could do because he would not let me in. And then . . . and then he died. No. And then I was forced to shoot him. Brian didn't want my help at any stage of his decline. And I was there to witness its terrible conclusion. So I do know what she means, but not in the way she means, which is why I say no to her.

'I started staying at school for the weekends so we barely saw each other. When I was home, he was often out working. It was like he was trying to burn himself out. Something was consuming him and there was nothing I could do to help him. I tried so hard to reach him, but nothing worked.'

If Jeb and I had been together when I . . . when I . . . killed Brian, I don't know if we would have stayed together. What I did fundamentally changed me and my relationship with the world. I couldn't function for years afterwards. I don't know if Jeb would have been able to handle it. We have been together years and what I did still rocks our relationship, I doubt we would have survived going through it in real time.

'When I said to Guy we should break up, he just stared at me. He seemed so defeated, like he wanted to object but couldn't get the energy together to say anything.'

'Was it a quick end or did it drag on?'

'Bit of both. I decided to move permanently to the school, became a housemistress. Whenever I went back to London to collect my belongings, we would end up in bed. And then I'd be devastated all over again because he didn't beg me to come back to him.'

'How do you feel about it now?'

Portia inhales deeply and suddenly reveals the soft, vulnerable part of herself to me. She shows me that she is not over Guy Mackenzie at all. 'I still love him. It must be obvious to someone like you. You can read people. And it's not as if we're subtle.'

'You still care for him, he clearly still has a lot of affection for you – what's holding you back?'

'He said he has a girlfriend, but it's casual. I thought he was sleeping with you, as well. But the main thing is, he hasn't actually made a move or said that he wants to get back together. We spend all this time together now, but nothing. And I am never going to be second best. My mother spent years in love with the same married man. He was never going to leave his wife. I used to watch her and think that could never be me. So, that's what is holding me back. I have far too much self-respect to let him just Vaguebook us back into a relationship. If we get back together, he's got to want it. More than anything else that's going on in his life. I learnt that lesson the hard way from my mother.'

'Do you think that's a reasonable expectation or something you've put in place to stop yourself being hurt?' I ask.

'You think I'm being unreasonable to expect someone to want me more than anything else going on in his life?'

'No. I think you were very hurt by Ma— Dr Mackenzie and you're now – rather sensibly and understandably – cautious. And one way of keeping people at a distance is to have unreasonable expectations. Expecting someone you love and who loves you to put you first is not unreasonable. Expecting to come first over everything all the time *is* unreasonable. It sounds like you are wanting the latter. And the latter always means you are alone because no one will ever put one particular person first all the time.'

'You might be right. You might also be a bit wrong, too.'

'You mean because you got married a year after you properly split up with Dr Mackenzie, you feel you can have reasonable expectations of a relationship?' I say.

Her gorgeous face, glowing with the efforts of weight-lifting, changes into wide-eyed shock. 'Did Guy tell you?'

'No.' To be honest, she profiles as someone who needs comfort, who needs to do something that reminds her that she is loveable. After the big hurt of Mac, she will have needed someone to put her first. She is so beautiful that I bet there was a whole host of men who wanted to take care of her. And I bet there was one who cared just that bit more for her and that would have been intoxicating after the way things ended with Mac. She would have married him and they would both have discovered not long afterwards that they were in infatuation, not in love. The split would have been less damaging than the one with

Mac, far more definitive. It won't have devastated her as much as the Mac break-up did. 'Lucky guess,' I reply.

'What do you think I should do?' she asks, which surprises me. She is that brand of confident that rarely asks what they should do, and if she does need advice she asks someone who she has known for years, possibly a family member.

'If you were my patient, I would advise you to talk to him. See if you can now finally have the conversations you wanted to have back then, try to soothe some of those wounds and then work out what to do next.'

'And what would you say if I wasn't your patient but your friend?'

I shrug. 'Go jump his bones, see what happens.'

She laughs and while she laughs I add, 'And that is why I'm talking to you as a ther—'

The door of the gym slams open and Viola runs in, out of breath and frantic. Her usually neat auburn-blonde hair is wild and her face is deathly pale even though she has clearly been running. 'Miss, miss,' she says urgently, trembling and on the verge of tears. I'm not sure if she's talking to me or Portia. 'Please, miss, come quick. It's Paris. She's going to jump.'

Kez

May 2026, Axton Manor

Portia and I come running out of the gym and onto the green area on the other side of the building to the courtyard. I follow Portia, who obviously knows the quickest way to the clock tower.

We run through a covered outside walkway around to the front of the property, out through the main entrance and then left towards the clock tower. A group of girls in their pyjamas cling to each other at the base of the tower, looking up. One of them is Astrid, who is distraught and is being comforted by two other pupils.

The dark wooden door of the clock tower is now open when it has been closed the whole time I've been here. I would have thought they would make it impossible for people to get in there at all, seeing as someone died there. With all that's going on, making this place inaccessible to stop anyone else getting hurt would be extremely low effort. But no, these people don't seem to be able to do that.

By the time we reach the base of the tower, my memory has gone to my past, to those moments when I walked across the road to Obsidi-blue, the place where Brian died.

He had reached breakdown and wanted MJ, Dennis and me to watch while he hit the self-destruct button. The fear of that memory grips my chest. That situation ended in the worst way possible. This can't turn out that way. It just can't.

Portia bolts up the stairs and I hesitate for a moment, the fear of going into another situation where someone might die almost submerging me. Only a moment, then I follow her up. It is tall, the staircase steep and narrow. My chest burns the higher up we go, but I ignore it because this cannot turn out badly.

Issy and Haniya stand on the top steps of the clock tower, the door open, staring at Paris. They are both stricken. The top of the tower is a large stone square with turret shapes rising quite high around it. An iron safety bar has been erected, but it will not deter even the most vaguely interested person who wants to go over the side – it certainly won't stop someone being pushed over the edge.

I am not good with heights. I remember that as Portia and I step outside. I am actively bad with heights, actually.

Paris, dressed in shorty pyjamas, has her back to us, facing the view. Portia is in front of me and is about to say something, but I put my hand on her arm, tell her to hold back. She is openly frantic, totally terrified, and she can't talk to Paris in that state.

Gently, I push her behind me.

'Paris?' I say quietly, careful not to scare her. 'Paris, what's going on, eh?'

'She made me do it,' Paris sobs without looking round. 'I didn't want to do it, she made me. She made me.'

'That doesn't matter right now,' I say. 'All that matters is making sure you're OK.'

'It does matter. I can't stop thinking about it. I think about it all the time. All the time.'

'Tell me. I'll listen to you, just tell me.'

'That's what he said. That's what he said and then he fell . . .'

'That sounds like it was an accident,' I reassure.

She violently shakes her head. 'He . . . No,' her sobs become louder. 'He was so nice. He said he would help me. And then she found out and she said she would tell if I didn't do it. And he was so nice.'

As she's been talking, I've been edging closer. She hasn't looked round, but I suppose she recognises my voice. 'Talk to me, Paris. Just tell me one bit. You don't have to tell me everything all at once. Just tell me a little part of it. Who is she?'

She violently shakes her head again. 'I can't. I can't tell you.'

'OK, OK, not a problem. If you close your eyes now, tell me the first thing you see.'

'His face. His face.'

'And what is he doing?'

'He's saying it's OK. He's saying he understands and he wants to help me.'

'Do you believe him?'

'Yes.'

'What's the main thing he understands?'

'That I'm not stupid. I just need help sometimes. I'm not stupid. I'm not stupid.'

'I know you're not. I knew you were very intelligent from the moment I met you.'

She turns, then. Faces me. She is watching me warily. And I am trying really hard not to let the memory of Brian enter this. He has been quiet for so long, but now he is trying to break through; he is trying to come back and shout at me. And I will not be able to function, to help Paris, if he succeeds.

'How did he say he was going to help you?'

'He . . . he spoke to Duncan. He got Duncan to help me. Duncan would come to my room in secret and help me with my homework. He would help me study.'

'And did it help?'

'Yes. Yes. Duncan told me my brain just works in a different way. He taught me how to see things in the way my brain works. He taught me to be OK with not getting things the first time. He helped me.'

'So he was right. He understood. He knew you weren't stupid and he got you the help you needed.'

Paris's glazed-over eyes melt slightly, the tears ease off a little. She scrubs at her face with the heels of her hands, causing red welts to come up.

'What happened next, Paris?'

'She found out. She found out that Duncan was helping. First she thought we were together, then she realised we weren't. And what was really going on and she . . . and she . . . she said I had to do whatever she said or she would tell everyone that I was stupid.'

'They wouldn't believe her.'

'They would. Everyone thinks she's amazing. I tried to give her money, but she wouldn't take it. She just kept saying that I had to obey her. She took my place. She was in charge. I had to do whatever she wanted. I had to hurt people.'

'It's OK, Paris. You didn't want to do it. It's not your fault. It's all her fault. Hers.'

'I can't stop seeing his face. I can't get it out of my head. His face. He looked so shocked. So hurt. She made me do it. And he looked so shocked as he fell. I can't stop seeing his face. She made me tell him that I wanted to meet him here. She made me—' She covers her face with her hands. If she's saying what I think she's saying . . .

I hold out my hand. 'Take my hand, Paris. I can help you. I promise I can help you.'

She doesn't take my hand, but I do edge closer to her. 'Take my hand, Paris. Please, just take my hand. I know how you feel and I know how to make you feel better.'

Paris stands rock still, and I edge closer, close enough for her to take my hand if she does what I tell her to do.

'Come on, Paris. Let me help you.' I edge closer still.

She nods, reaches out her hand. And then she looks behind me, and her face changes. She looks like she has just seen the demon that is tormenting her, and she turns, runs and jumps into the air to throw herself off the clock tower.

Kez

May 2026, Axton Manor

I caught her.

When her face changed, when I saw her terror, I knew she was going to jump so I threw myself at her. Grabbed the back of her pyjama top and yanked her backwards to counteract the trajectory of her leap. I pulled us both off our feet and all the air was knocked out of me as I landed with Paris on top of me. Even though I was winded and physically shaken, I wrapped my arms and legs around her, holding her tight as she cried and begged me to let her go. Other teachers had arrived on the scene by then, and someone had called an ambulance, but I didn't let go until two ambulance crew arrived and gently took her from me. They sedated her and carefully escorted her downstairs.

After they had gone, I sat with elbows on my knees, my face in my hands, trying to deep breathe as adrenalin raced around my body. Portia went with Paris to the hospital and eventually Mac came up. Touched my shoulder, tried to get me to move.

'Leave me, please,' I managed to whisper.

I didn't want to do anything. Or be with anyone.

This was all out of control.

The Quiet Girls were killers. One of them made Paris kill Dr

Pemberton. She probably killed or got someone to kill Fredi and Mariana. They almost drove Paris to end her life. But is it one person acting alone? I doubt it. No one person could get away with all of that on their own. They had to have had help. It sounded as though Paris was one of the heads of the Quiet Girls, but this one exploited a weakness to take her place. But does it work like that in secret societies? Will they allow just anyone to step into someone else's shoes if they are still alive? And how does that all tie in with Rhodes? Because he is involved in all of this. He controls all of this. With the number of cameras he had around the place, he had to have known what was going on. And if his son was tutoring Paris, he will have seen that on the cameras. I don't know what the connections are, but he has to be in charge of this. With the cameras, there is no way he wouldn't know about the Quiet Girls. And what was it he said? Something about observing and maintaining the traditions. The last two headteachers have been men, and the Quiet Girls have still existed. He *must* control them.

I wonder if this Quiet Girl, whoever it is that Paris was scared of, has overstepped the bounds? What if they weren't meant to kill Dr Pemberton, weren't meant to terrify Paris? Or, maybe, this is exactly how things operate around here: they will do anything to get ahead, they will hurt anyone who gets in their way, they will cover up anything that brings attention. I mean, how will they deal with this? How will they spin it? *'Paris was under too much stress,'* I'd imagine. *'Paris is taking some time out to recover. Paris is a much-valued member of our Axton Manor family and we look forward to welcoming her back soon.'*

I'm sitting here, as well, because I do not want to think about who the person Paris was so scared of could be. When she looked behind me, she decided to jump. Behind me were Issy, Haniya and Viola. And

Portia. Things make a lot more sense if it is Portia. I know that the Quiet Girls will do anything to keep who they are a secret from outsiders. Including lying to someone who is the very definition of outsider, who has been asking all sorts of questions.

And the way she called Pemberton 'Angus'. No other teacher has done that. She doesn't do that with other members of staff – she calls them by their surnames. She called him 'Angus', twice. I use my fingertips to massage my temples, trying to rub away the headache that is forming. I'm getting a headache because I do not want it to be Portia. I like her. And I know Mac loves her. I do not want her to be the mastermind behind this, or even just involved.

I fold my arms across my chest and lower my head. On the ground is a small, gold-bar keyring and key. I've seen Paris with this. She's constantly playing with it, using it as a stress reliever. I pick it up to return it to her and find that it's quite heavy. I turn it over in my hands, and spot that around the middle of the fob, when you look very closely, you can see a join. I pull and the fob comes apart to reveal that it isn't simply a keyring. It is, in fact, a USB stick.

Kez

May 2026, Axton Manor

Ring, ring, ring!

My mobile interrupts my pacing of my room. It's been forty-eight hours since I came into possession of the USB drive and I still haven't worked out what to do with it. I suspect it might give me some of the answers to the questions I have. I suspect that because even though Paris was up on the roof in her pyjamas she had that keyring with her. Not her mobile or anything else, just that. It's not even the key to her room. She would only be carrying it if it was super important. I don't want to invade Paris's privacy, but I do want to find out what has her so terrified. My ethics and my detection duties have been battling it out ever since.

My heart turns over when I pick up my phone and see the name on the caller ID display. I answer it and put it to my ear. 'Hello, Moe? Is everything OK?' I ask urgently.

'Erm, hi, Kez, yeah, I'm all good. Why?'

'Because you rarely call me,' I reply. Ever since the trouble two years ago, he calls me even less than he used to. He barely speaks to me unless he has to even if we're sitting in the same room. 'But if you're OK, then that's fine. What's up?'

'I'm just checking in with you about the stuff from the other day. The cameras and that. Did it work?'

'Yes, I think it did. There was a repair van out here earlier today and it's still here so I think the whole thing is still down. Thank you for that. Although I'm sorry Dennis tapped you up like that.'

'I didn't even mind.'

'I mind.'

'Kez . . . No cap, I don't mind. I wanted to ask you, actually, can you talk to him for me? See if he can get me a job?'

'Talk to Dennis?'

'Yeah.'

I'm shocked silent. I was not expecting this. My first instinct is to say: *'You want your father to leave me? Is that it?'* but after what happened that would be inappropriate. My second instinct is to say: *'I told Dennis via Mac that if he comes near you again, I'll kill him. And I actually mean that.'* My third instinct, the one I go with, is: 'Why would you want to work with him?'

'Not necessarily him. I just want a job doing the sort of thing I did the other day. I can do good, Kez. I want to start making up for what I did.'

'You have nothing to make up for.'

'I have. You know I have. I feel guilty all the time. I ain't told anyone that, not even Matt.' Matt is his therapist who helped bring him back from the brink. 'I feel guilty about what I did and I want to make up for it. If I can get a job doing that sort of thing, helping to put things right, then maybe I'll stop feeling as guilty.'

I could tell him that trying to assuage your guilt by doing good feels like a fool's errand sometimes. That you very often end up hurt or damaged as well as still dealing with lingering feelings of guilt. But then, when you *do* help someone, when you set someone free mentally or emotionally, it does feel like you've tipped the balance in your favour. It does feel like the world isn't a terrible place filled with all your awful deeds. 'Look, Moe, it's not that simple. There isn't a straight line between doing good and feeling less guilty, trust me. However, that doesn't mean you shouldn't try.' I hear him smile down the phone, excited for what I'm about to say next. 'The however to that however is that Dennis Chambers is a poisonous snake. And if you make a deal with a snake, it will eventually bite you.'

'I can handle that.'

You really can't, I reply in my head. 'How about I say I'll think about it?'

'Come on, Kez, I'm not nine.'

'All right, but I will have to think about it. And how to bring it up with your father. If you think I've got a problem with this, he'll have an asteroid-size problem with it.'

'You leave Dad to me. But you'll talk to Dennis for me, yeah?'

'I didn't say that.'

'You pretty much did.'

'No, I said—'

'Kez, listen, you know me. You know that I can do this. I can do good, like you're doing good. I know you didn't want to go back there, and I know you only did it for me, so help me out with this, yeah? Please?'

'All right, Moe. If this is really what you want, I will think seriously about the best thing to do. It might not be Dennis I need to speak to – it might be someone else.'

'Dennis is the man, though. He has insane rizz.'

'What did you just say to me?'

'Dennis has enough rizz. Charisma? He's got a lot of charisma?'

'Right.' *Yeah, most psychopaths do.* 'Before you go, Moe, I need to ask you something. Can you tell me how to get into a USB drive if it's password protected?'

'What sort of password?'

'I don't know. I haven't put it into a computer yet.'

'All right. Get your computer up and I'll log in to it and we can see if I can get into the USB.'

'Are you sure?'

'Yeah, it's nimps.'

'Thanks, Moe. But this doesn't mean I'm going to talk to Dennis or whoever for you, OK?'

I hear him shrug over the line. 'OK.'

'I mean it, Moe.'

'I know you do, Kez. I know you do.'

Two hours later, after many false starts, we finally manage to get into Paris's keyring USB drive. Well, Moe does. It isn't Paris's USB drive, though. It's actually Dr Pemberton's. I'm guessing she picked it up when he was murdered. I guess she has been carrying it around ever since, and it's been adding to her worsening mental state.

But once we are in, once all his files are available to read, I finally understand what is going on. I've been able to work out why he was killed. I've worked out what probably happened to Fredi. And I've finally been able to work out who the Quiet Girls really are.

Angus

March 2026, Axton Manor

My name is Dr Angus Pemberton and if you are listening to this, then I am most likely dead.

I am not as OK with that as I could be. But I don't have time to deal with it in this arena.

As you will see from the other files on this data disk, I have amassed information that suggests Mr Humphrey Rhodes, headmaster of Axton Manor School for Girls, is a predator, abuser and murderer. There are two historic elite groups at Axton Manor, and during the time of his appointment as headteacher he has overseen and directed the pupils in these groups to bully, terrorise and subjugate their peers in this school.

The girls who are chosen to join the lower elite group, called The Platinum, are selected from across the different year groups and, once initiated, are Platinum for life. Above them, there is a smaller elite group of girls, again across the different year groups, who make decisions about who is allowed to be installed into certain school positions, such as head girl, and who will be frozen out or, in some instances, forced to leave the school.

Once initiated into this group called the Quiet Girls, they are members for life. They go on, like The Platinum, to hold influence in wider society. If anyone requires help, for example, if they need a driving offence to go away, any Platinum or Quiet Girl who is in a position to help will do so. It is my belief that the local police force has more than one Quiet Girl and/or Platinum amongst their number.

This is my belief because historic crimes committed at the school, as well as incidents where pupils have disappeared, have been either covered up or dismissed. It is my belief that two incidents where teachers died by accident or by taking their own lives (detailed in other files) were, in fact, murders. When Rhodes discovered that these teachers knew what he had done (more on that to come) he either ordered or carried out their executions, making their deaths look like accidents. I do not have concrete proof of this; however, I have spoken to several other teachers who were here as pupils or staff at the time of the teachers' deaths and none of them think those deaths to be misadventure nor suicide.

It is this that has made me believe my life is in danger.

I am planning on speaking to a police-officer friend who I used to share a house with years ago. They work in another county and I know them, so I am hopeful I can trust them and that I will be able to find out the best course of action. If, however, you are listening to this, it's clear that my attempts to bring Rhodes to justice have failed.

Over the course of the last few months, I have had meetings with several girls who have detailed abuse – both sexual and emotional – at the hands of a figure of authority. Each girl has refused to name the perpetrator, however, they have all given enough information for me to know that the man who has abused and assaulted them is Humphrey Rhodes. I am not going to name the children involved to protect their identities, should this fall into the wrong hands.

One girl – Girl A – has said that she believed Rhodes was watching her from a spy camera because he knew things that she had not told anyone, including the times she had been intimate with herself. She explained that he used this knowledge and images of her pleasuring herself to force himself on her. She also explained that he had shown her images of him forcing himself on other pupils.

Girl A explained that she went to the police after the first time she was raped by Rhodes and returned to find him waiting for her in her room. He proceeded to threaten her and explain that he knew everyone in the local police force and he would be protected no matter what he did. He also explained that if she told anyone again he would harm her family. He told her that he knew enough people everywhere to make sure her parents would die if she told. He said that he would decide when she left.

Girl A came to me because she was having thoughts of self-harm. She was too scared to tell her parents what had happened and ask to leave, so she felt stuck. I wanted to help her, but she would not reveal the name of her abuser. And, because of her previous experience with the police, she made it clear she would lie and say nothing happened if I tried to report it to the police myself.

I made it my mission to get something on Rhodes. But he is protected. At every turn people seem to want to protect him, not say anything against him. None of the girls will go against him.

Another girl – Girl B – came forward recently to tell me all she knew about the Quiet Girls and The Platinum. She filled in some of the holes in my knowledge. I have a complicated history with her. I initially saw her because she was homesick and had some trouble adjusting to living away from home with people so different from herself. She seemed to quickly settle down and I was confident that she would flourish.

However, Girl B did catch me and another member of staff in an intimate moment. It was a moment of weakness with someone I care about deeply. We were both concerned how witnessing us in flagrante delicto would disturb her, but she seemed to forget about it and we all moved on.

Girl B explained to me what she had found out, especially about her friend who had disappeared last year. From everything she said, I worked out who the current ruling Quiet Girls are.

One of the Quiet Girls – Girl C – has been coming to see me. She was having problems and I arranged for her to secretly go for some tests, which revealed she is dyslexic. Girl C didn't want anyone to know, especially not her mother. I found her a tutor. I'm not sure it was the wisest, but I know the Rhodes boys tutor some of the girls on the quiet. All of the girls who have been tutored by them report them to be respectful and considerate. They say the boys help them to understand that their brains process information in a particular way and they give them ways of studying that helps them. They seem so different from Rhodes that I sometimes forget how abusive and criminally deviant he is.

Girl C, who I suggested was tutored by Duncan Rhodes, told me that two different people – Girl B and Girl D – saw him going into her room. While Girl B didn't really react to the news, Girl D become extremely upset. It came out that Girl D thought she was dating Duncan so thought he was cheating on her with Girl C. Girl C then revealed that she had worked out that Duncan hadn't been dating her friend – someone had catfished Girl D using his identity.

The only person I could think of who would do that was Humphrey Rhodes. Girl C, who Duncan was tutoring, was distraught because Girl D threatened to tell everyone that she is stupid. More than anything, she did not want to be called stupid. Through our conversations, I realised that Girl C is, in fact, the current leader of the Quiet Girls.

And that Girl D is also a Quiet Girl. Girl B is not. It seems Girl C wants out of the Quiet Girls, while Girl D is keen to take over the role.

She has asked me to meet her tomorrow to discuss what she can do.

I have told Girl B, who filled in the missing gaps about the Quiet Girls, that I will talk to my friend in the police and find out what we can do. I do not like that she knows so much. It is dangerous. I tried to convince her to call her mother but she refused. The only way I could get her to agree to tell her mother and immediately leave the school was by saying she has to once I have spoken to my friend.

I have amassed this evidence and I am still not sure what to do with it. But once I have spoken to the head of the Quiet Girls, I will speak to my friend and hopefully will be able to have Rhodes arrested by people who he does not have a connection to and control over. Once he is out of the way, the girls will be free. And I won't feel this constant, gut-wrenching dread and anger and guilt all the time.

I should have known what was going on. I should have found a way to stop Rhodes by now. It is so unnerving to not know who I can trust. Which is why I haven't done anything yet.

I feel impotent.

But I will turn this around. I feel a deep guilt. And an unfathomable responsibility to make this right. Protect those girls. Put that evil man away for good. He is evil. I do not say that lightly. As a therapist, I try to avoid using that kind of language. Ascribing something otherworldly to an ordinary man is easy and lazy. It is removing culpability from him, allowing there to be some reason other than plain ordinary human intent. But he *is* evil. What he does is evil. And I am going to put an end to it.

I hope I am not dead, but, if I am, I hope this helps to nail Rhodes once and for all.

Kez

May 2026, Axton Manor

Mac and I have been arguing for the last two days about when to bring Humphrey Rhodes's reign of terror to an end.

Mac wants to do it now, I want to wait a few more days until the upcoming exeat weekend. During exeat weekends, all the pupils leave the premises on the Friday night and don't return until Monday morning or very late Sunday evening. That is the best-case scenario, because most of the girls will be gone and they won't be caught in the line of fire.

It's an issue that there are a few pupils who need to be arrested, and it will be harder to pin them down when off school grounds – however, we can have back-up waiting at their location when they arrive there.

Mac has finally agreed that we'll call Dennis on Friday evening. They can then send people late Friday night, early Saturday morning, when we will confront Rhodes. If we call Dennis, we can be as sure as we can be that he will send people that we can trust. Well, as much as we can trust anyone. If there is one thing I have discovered, it is that Rhodes has people everywhere. Every. Where. That was why Portia kept saying The Platinum and the Quiet Girls are the ones who run things. From what his files on his USB stick show, it's clear Pemberton discovered that at a high level in every institution you can think of there is an Axton old girl.

They literally run the world.

That was why Pemberton's death wasn't properly investigated. The police officer who wrote the report on Pemberton's death is the aunt of an Axton pupil, so likely a former Axton pupil herself. Axton old girls are loyal to the school. Axton first. Axton always.

If we tell Dennis on the Friday night, it won't get back to any Axton alumni in time to give them a chance to sanitise everything before The Platinum and Quiet Girls are arrested. It's a big risk, letting there be even a small amount of notice, but we can't confront him with no notice when there are only two of us and an untold number of former Platinum and Quiet Girls on these grounds alone.

One good thing is there is no evidence that Portia is involved in anything. Despite being an old girl, Pemberton didn't mention her as being involved at all. Thankfully, she has chosen this weekend to go and visit her ex-husband in Scotland.

This is almost over. I'll soon be back home with my family. Mac and I just need to keep a low profile until the weekend.

By 9 a.m. on Friday, all the pupils have gone. Cars and taxis, limos and luxury cars have all pulled up to the building this morning, taking the girls away. By the time they are ready to come back on Sunday, everything will have changed. Whoever is left behind will have to pick up the pieces.

Part 11

Kez

May 2026, Axton Manor

Knock knock knock at the door makes both of us jump. The last of the girls have left and I was literally about to ring Dennis.

'Come in,' I call.

My heart somersaults when the door opens and in walks Humphrey Rhodes and his wife, Victoria. He is smartly dressed in his tweed suit with an Axton Manor-orange waistcoat and tie. He even has a purple flower in his buttonhole. His hair is washed and carefully styled. He has done this for the exeat weekend. A lot of UK-based parents come for this weekend and he likes to wave them off.

And now he's here, in my office, with his wife.

He knows we know. Even without his cameras and his microphones, he knows that we know. And we haven't had a chance to contact Dennis yet. I'm not sure why we didn't realise this would happen. Of course he's not stupid. Of course he'd realise that his camera network went wrong not long after we showed up. He's listened to the questions I've asked in sessions. He already knows that I know about Mariana. That I've been asking about Fredi.

Why didn't I think he would just show up the second the school was empty and bring the fight to us? I am a ridiculous person. I'm glad Mac is a ridiculous person, too. Although it will mean we're both probably going to end up dead because of it.

'Mrs Rhodes, Mr Rhodes, hello. How can I help you?' I say, getting to my feet.

'Well, Dr Lanyon,' he says in a calm but cold voice, 'you can help me by telling me exactly who you are and exactly what you are doing in my school.'

It's only then, as he moves further into the room, that I notice he's carrying a gun.

'Humphrey! What are you doing?' Victoria Rhodes screeches when her husband raises the gun and points it at us.

'Shut up, Victoria!' he snaps, the first time I've ever seen him lose his cool. From the look on her face, this is the first time she's seen his calm, aloof mask slip in front of strangers. Behind closed doors, he definitely rages all the time. But a narcissist like him would hate for his good-guy image to be publicly tarnished by such behaviour.

'Please stop this, Humphrey,' she begs, wringing her hands as her terrified eyes stare at the gun.

'I said *shut up*!' he snipes at her again. 'Just shut up! I won't tell you again.' He waves the gun, indicates I should get out of my chair and move to the other side of the desk to sit or stand near Mac. He lowers himself into my chair, looking very much like someone who has always wanted to sit there and is finally, *finally* getting his big chance.

'That's not a very nice way to speak to your wife, is it?' I state. Everyone looks at me like I have taken leave of my senses. 'Well, it's not, is it?' I reply to them. 'You lot are the ones in the wrong here, I'm one hundred per cent right about it not being a very nice way to speak to Victoria.'

'Tell me who you are, Dr Lanyon.'

Oh yeah, sure, get my name right twice now, just when you're about to kill me. 'The board of governors and the trustees sent me. Well, us. They wanted us to investigate the disappearance of Fredi Kingston. They are very worried about the school's reputation. Dr Pemberton's death was deemed an accident and everyone moved on. But not Fredi's disappearance. Her parents are determined to find out what happened to their daughter and have threatened to make as much trouble as they can, so the governors and trustees ordered a private investigation to prevent Axton Manor becoming embroiled in a public scandal.'

'And what exactly are you going to tell the school board?'

'That you most likely killed Fredi Kingston and disposed of her body. That the school is run by a narcissist who is also a sexual deviant, who preys on young girls. That he is also in control of a secret society that is probably behind what happened to Mariana Sanford as well as the death of at least one member of staff.' I look at Mac. 'I think that's about it, wouldn't you say?'

'Yeah, yeah, that's about it.'

'Obviously, it's not just the governors and trustees that we've been talking to. Especially not about the part of you being a sexual predator. That part we've been talking to the police about, too.'

'What are they talking about, Humphrey?' asks Victoria Rhodes, despite being told to shut up before.

'They're bluffing. They don't have any evidence of anything they just said.'

'But what are they talking about? Evidence or not, what are they talking about?' she asks.

'He has cameras in all the girls' bedrooms. He watches them. And, over the years, he's begun "relationships" with underage girls by catfishing them. That is, he used his sons' identities to start online or phone-text-based relationships with these girls. He groomed them, using the information he gained from watching them. By the time they found out the truth, that it was him and not Garwin or Duncan they were messaging, it was too late. He had enough blackmail information – photos and videos they'd sent him – to force himself on them without fear of being reported to the police. When Dr Pemberton found out, because he knows neither of your sons would start relationships with the girls, your husband coerced one of the girls into killing him.'

Victoria turns to her husband. 'Is this true, Humphrey?' Her voice is high, bordering on hysterical. 'Is any of it true?'

'Of course it isn't, you stupid woman. If it was, the police would be here, wouldn't they?'

'The police will be here soon. We were just waiting for all the girls to leave so there isn't a chance any of them will be harmed. They'll be picking up Issy at her home shortly.'

'Issy? Issy Grenville?' Victoria replies. 'Why are they picking her up?'

'She killed Dr Pemberton. He called her Girl D when he talked about her. She was the latest catfish victim. When she saw Duncan going into Paris's room, she thought he was cheating on her. She confronted him online. "Duncan", who was really your husband, said he had been teaching Paris because of her dyslexia. Issy used that against Paris. Pemberton called Paris Girl C. And when Paris told Dr Pemberton about Girl D and Duncan, he realised what was really going on. That "Duncan" was actually Humphrey Rhodes. Pemberton was going to go to the police, but your husband had this office bugged so he knew Pemberton was coming for him. "Duncan" told Issy they had to get rid of Pemberton. So Issy got Paris to lure Dr Pemberton to the clock tower, where she forced Paris to watch while she pushed him off. What I used to think was Paris's coldness was actually her trauma at feeling responsible for Dr Pemberton's death.'

As I've been talking, Victoria's eyes have been growing wider and more horrified. 'YOU USED OUR SONS' IDENTITIES TO ABUSE GIRLS?' Victoria says. 'HOW COULD YOU? HOW COULD YOU?'

Kez

May 2026, Axton Manor

While she screams at her husband, I examine Victoria Rhodes's body language and demeanour. And there is a disconnect. She is screaming at him, but her hands hang limply at her sides; she is shouting her surprise but her micro-expressions reveal this is not new information.

Something is not right with her.

Victoria is not a stupid woman. She is not a clueless woman, either. It's hard to believe she didn't know. How do you live with someone for so many years and not know what he is truly like? That he was a child abuser, a rapist, a terrible human being? Especially when his control and domination tendencies are so evident he can't even hide them for a few hours at an innocuous dinner party. Did she really think he was only like that with her and their children? No, of course not. She knew. Her micro-expressions. Her body language. Her existence as someone who lives with him tell me that she knew.

'Are you trying to pretend you had no idea about any of this?' I say to her. 'Because you clearly *are* pretending right now.'

She swings back to me. She clasps her hands together, brings them up to her lips. Again the movements are correct, but the micro-expressions are not. 'I knew some things weren't . . . *right*, but very early on, if I ever challenged him about something that seemed inappropriate – private meetings with pupils, or inappropriate material in the house, he would always become so angry. And, worse, he would tell my father, who would rage at me. It became easier to look the other way, to pretend that nothing was amiss.' She closes her eyes in regret. 'It became easier to pretend that everything was normal.'

Mac's whole body stiffens in utter rage beside me. 'I'm sorry, you ignored your husband catfishing, grooming, filming and doing worse to young girls because you were scared of being told off by your father?' he says through gritted teeth. 'Is that what you're seriously telling us?'

'My father was a formidable man. You have no idea what it was like to grow up with him. How he terrified me. In our house, what he said was law. When I wanted to go to college to become a schoolteacher so I could one day take over the school, he refused. He said I had to go to secretarial college, because he was grooming Humphrey to take his place. I would be allowed to be school secretary at the most.'

'Just because he said something doesn't mean you had to do it,' I point out.

She shakes her head. 'You have no idea what it's like to come from a family with heritage and breeding, do you?' She is despairing and vicious at the same time, quite a feat.

'God, this again,' Mac says. 'I am so sick of hearing it!'

I add: 'We do know what it's like to come from a family with heritage and breeding, actually. My parents have heritage that they passed on, the fact I have a family at all means we have breeding, just like your family. We don't have the money, land and contacts everywhere like you do, but we are proud of who we are. We don't care who tries to look down on us. We know we are just as important as you.'

Victoria scoffs at this. 'When you are from my background, *duty* is everything,' she spits. 'Tradition is everything. We are bound to uphold the traditions of our ancestors.'

'So your father was an abuser, too?' I say, finally catching on. 'He was an abuser and he made sure to choose his successor accordingly. You need to uphold those traditions, after all. When all of this comes out they are going to ask some very hard questions of you. And, believe me, "I let it happen because my daddy was scary" is not going to cut it. I'll be surprised if they keep Axton Manor open.'

At that thought, Victoria pales so dramatically I think she may lose consciousness. Instead of fainting away with the vapours, she snatches the gun out of her husband's hand and points it at us. This makes Rhodes grin. She isn't going to help us; we haven't wooed nor said anything to get her on our side. To be fair, we weren't trying to woo her, we were trying to shame her into doing the right thing. But, at the end of it all, her devotion and loyalty to Axton Manor will trump everything. Even child abuse and murder.

'My father was not scary,' she hisses as she aims the gun in a direction that means just a little to the left or the right and she'll hit either me or Mac. 'He was terrifying. He made sure I was scared every single day of my life. And he was determined to keep me and every other girl in this place subjugated. He was determined to keep every girl in the world subservient to men. It wasn't that bad when I was younger and I didn't know better, but the older I got, the meaner he got. And the more determined he was to keep me and my mother under his control.' She swallows hard, the emotion of what she is saying and reliving rushing to her cheeks and colouring then a high, bright red. Now she's being honest, her micro-expressions absolutely match her words and body language. 'He was horrible. *So horrible.* And that's why my mother killed him.'

What? I think.

What? I'm sure Mac thinks.

WHAT? Humphrey Rhodes clearly thinks from the way his head whips round to stare in shock at his wife.

And she calmly turns the gun on her husband, aims it at his head and without a moment's hesitation pulls the trigger.

Jeb

May 2026, Secret Location

Jeb and the children have been staving off going stir crazy by cooking elaborate meals; going for long walks, on which they are accompanied by two men who clearly have guns; playing board games; watching television and reading.

This place has everything they need and more. So much space, a huge library of books, a massive kitchen, comfortable beds, quiet. True quiet. If Jeb had brought the family here for a holiday, they would have been over the moon. They would be hard pressed to leave. But, despite how they are keeping themselves occupied, they all know why they are there. They all know that Kez could be in danger. They may rarely talk about it, but they all remember the terror they felt after hearing that she had been shot last year.

As they start to gather the ingredients to make a large pot of Ghanaian stew, Dennis enters the kitchen, looking troubled.

'May I have a word, Mr Quarshie?' Dennis asks.

Jeb's heart turns over – again. It does that a lot whenever Dennis appears. It's because he has been waiting to hear that Kez is hurt. No, not hurt. Dead. He has been bracing himself for that news and from the look on Dennis's face, this is it. This is the news he has been dreading, finally arrived at his door.

They move through the building, to the front porch, the furthest part of the house away from the kitchen. Jeb guesses this is so if he screams in grief, Zoey and Jonah may not hear.

'Have you spoken to Kezuma today?' Dennis asks.

Jeb unclenches when he doesn't hear that Kez is dead. It takes him a few seconds to understand what he's asking.

'No, I haven't. I usually speak to her at night. Why?'

'She hasn't checked in. Neither has Dr Mackenzie. He said earlier in the week that he would be contacting me early on Friday to provide an extensive update. Neither of them have been in touch. It's not like them.'

'You think something has happened to them?'

Dennis holds Jeb's gaze for several seconds. Several long, loaded seconds. Then he looks away. 'I am going to have to leave it twenty-four hours before I contact them,' Dennis says quietly. 'They may have a plan that I am not privy to.'

'But you think there's something wrong, don't you?' Jeb asks.

'I . . . I will have to leave it twenty-four hours,' Dennis replies. 'Let me know the second you hear from her. The second.'

'I will.'

'But don't call her. Don't do anything out of the ordinary,' Dennis says. 'We're just going to have to wait and see.'

Wait and see? Wait and see. Jeb's stomach and heart start to turn over and over. He should have added cigarettes to the last shopping list. He really should have.

Kez

May 2026, Axton Manor

The loud BANG from such a small gun makes Mac and I both jump and grab out for each other. Victoria doesn't jump, she simply stands, splattered with bits of red from the perfect circle in her husband's forehead, staring at his slumped body. Mac and I are both backing away, preparing to run, when she returns to pointing the gun at us.

'You have no idea how long I've wanted to do that,' she states simply. 'I hated him *so* much. Not at first, of course. When I was first with him, I loved him. I never loved anyone as much as I loved him. But he truly was the son my father never had. He behaved just like my father and treated us appallingly.' She rolls her eyes. 'And his obsession with fox hunting! He knew all the ways to get away with fox hunting even though it is illegal. I begged him and begged him not to kill them, but he thought he had that right.

'My father was exactly the same, obsessed with the hunt. My mother thought it was wholly appropriate to kill him and make it look like a hunting accident. Everyone knew he liked to go out walking in the woods with a couple of dogs and his shot gun. It was very easy to do.' Victoria grins at us, the type of grin that suggests she is several steps ahead of us in all of this and we are pretty much screwed. 'As you quite rightly pointed out, Dr Lanyon, we old girls, ex-Axtonites, Platinum, Quiet Girls, are everywhere. And we are always ready to help each other out. It was very easy to ensure that no one looked too closely into my father's death. They all knew he was a hunting man. Live by the hunting gun, die by the hunting gun.

'Just like no one questioned how Mr McCutheon died back in 1989 when your friend Maisie Parsons was a pupil here. And no one really questioned how Dr Pemberton died.'

'So *you* were behind Pemberton's death?' Mac says.

'You were right about most things. I knew what my husband got up to. But I could overlook it for the most part. In the grand picture, I had to put up with him so we could carry on our work, keep building our network. Any scandal could have put an end to that. When Issy told me about "Duncan" and that Pemberton intended to go to the police, I told her to do whatever it took to stop him. She knew what I meant. She has always been a committed Quiet Girl. I should have chosen her to be that year group's leader, but Paris had shown such promise. I was impressed that Issy took over in such a decisive fashion, and she still let everyone think Paris was in control. Just as I taught her.' She sighs dramatically. 'All of this does present me with a problem, though. You two.'

'Not sure it's going to be as easy to kill us as it was the others,' I say. 'We're part of the intelligence services, people know we're here investigating the disappearance of Fredi Kingston and the death of Dr Pemberton. It's not going to be easy to kill us and get away with it.'

'Are you sure about that?' She is not at all fazed by the revelation that we work for the intelligence services. She knows that I know MJ, which suggests she not only knew about us for quite some time, but that she already has a plan in place to deal with us. 'Do you have any idea how many girls have come through here? How many people I have in my pockets?' She points casually to what remains of her husband. 'He thought he was in charge. That his raging and his violence was keeping me in line. He had no idea who I am, what I have done, what I have created. The Quiet Girls, The Platinum, they began as sweet little groups for girls to get together. But, in my time, I shaped them all into the true Axton tradition.

'I made them into the powerful elite force they are today. Humphrey thought, like my father thought, that I was a meek little thing that needed direction from them. "Behind every great man there is a great woman." We've been taught that for centuries. And that is what people think we teach the girls here. How to be a support for the men who run the world. What we really teach is that true power is quiet. It is hidden. It rarely shows its hand. We teach these girls how to be quiet. How to watch. To wait. To be patient. To exercise power from the shadows. We run the world, those men just think they do.'

'Still not sure you have enough people out there to get away with killing us.'

'Did you know that Winifred Kingston's godmother was an old girl? But Jacinta Sanford didn't know how to keep her mouth shut. She kept talking about The Platinum and the Quiet Girls. She was a Platinum. But when we asked for help, when the time came to give back to her true family, she was "reluctant" to get involved.'

My blood runs cold. Not only because of what she has just said, but because my mind is racing ahead. Racing and racing. It is going where I do not want it to go. Where I do not want to contemplate.

'You know about Jacinta Sanford's daughter "disappearing". You know that no one has heard from her since she "ran away".' Victoria smiles a smile so evil I feel parts of my body start to numb. 'We had to show her, and all the Platinum and Quiet Girls, what happens when you say no to us. What happens when you defy us.'

I am not going to let her know that my mind is racing ahead, that I am scared because I know what she is about to say. I am just going to give her my neutral face and pray she doesn't say what she then says: 'And you, Dr Lanyon, someone who has tried to defy us, do you know where Jeb, Zoey and Jonah are?'

The kind of terror that has just ripped through me because she knows my children's names almost takes my legs out from under me. I can't show it, though. I have to keep my face neutral, my body strong.

'I suspected you weren't exactly who you said you were from when I engineered that meeting when you both first arrived. Dr Mackenzie is very straightforward: he is who he says he is. Miss Akande confirmed that. Not the case with you, Dr Lanyon. But all the searches came back saying you are just an ordinary therapist and profiler who worked with businesses, a mother of two with a loving husband who lives in a nice part of Brighton. We went back many years and each time – nothing. We talked to former clients, your neighbours, even people at your children's school and still nothing. So I decided we needed to talk to your husband, to find out exactly who you are. And, wouldn't you know it, he and your children are suddenly scooped up and disappeared into what I can only guess is some kind of witness protection. I knew then that you weren't simply a therapist.'

She was going to harm them. She was going to harm my family to get 'information'. Dennis must have stepped in. I'm not going to think about where they are. I have spoken to them and they have acted as though nothing was wrong, and they would only do that if they are safe. I have to believe that Dennis has got them and he is keeping them safe. I mean, I know he will use this as an opportunity to try to get into

Jeb's head, but I can't think about that right now. I can't think about any of that. If I do, I will fall apart. They are safe and I need to forget about them for now. Concentrate on what Jeb has always said when I am in these situations: do whatever it takes to get back home to them.

This woman, though. She is lucky that she is holding a gun on me. Because, if she wasn't, I would jump her for trying to harm my family. And, yes, I would absolutely be able to take her in a fight. I can take anyone who messes with my family in a fight.

'However, finding out who you both really are doesn't change the fact that you both have to disappear.' She smiles sadly. 'I am not a monster, though. I am going to give you a sporting chance. If you make it through the woods to the other side, I will let you go.'

Sporting chance. Those words are the big neon sign in that sentence. 'Sport' to people like the ones around these parts means one thing: *hunting*. She's going to hunt us. 'I thought you said you hated hunting,' I state, just to check that I haven't misunderstood her.

'I said I hated *fox* hunting,' she replies. 'Foxes are beautiful, innocent creatures. They should never be treated the way they are. Humans, on the other hand . . . One of the most important lessons I learnt from my father is that sometimes hunting is the best way to take care of a problem. No messy bodies to dispose of. No lengthy clean-up. When you train hounds correctly, and you have a natural burial ground close by, the clean-up is swift and quite effortless.

'Please believe me that I would not be doing this if I had any other choice. Which is why I am leaving things in the hands of fate. I always leave things in the hands of fate. If the hunted creature gets away, then that is how it's meant to be.'

So this is how I'm going to die: being hunted in the woods by an evil headmaster's homicidal wife, who quietly runs the world. Of course it is. Because I couldn't just be run over or something. No, I have to die in one of the most extreme ways possible.

'How are you going to explain our disappearance?' Mac asks.

'Murder.' She nods towards her husband. 'And then you ran off together. Everyone has seen how the pair of you are together. They know you're sleeping together. With my husband's videoing fetish, I'm sure we can find footage of you together. Just like we "found" messages between Winifred Kingston and Dr Pemberton. People will believe you ran away together, never to be heard from again.'

I would never leave my children. Jeb would know that. He knows that I would never walk away from them, not to run off with some rando, as Jonah would say. It is good, I suppose, that Victoria Rhodes doesn't know this about me. That she thinks she'll get away with it by spinning this lie, because that is what most people expect. I'm sure Dennis would never believe it, either. But what would he do about it? Probably nothing. Dennis has always put his job before anything. He likes me. I am his favourite. But I'd be an idiot to think that he would risk anything to investigate my disappearance if all his buddies, all the people of influence around him, spin a lie that I ran away with the man he put here specifically to get me to cheat on my husband. Dennis is not going to save me before I die nor save my reputation after I die.

'For there to be a hunt, we have to take part. I'm not going to take part,' I state.

'I'm not taking part, either,' Mac says.

I shrug. 'We're not going to take part. That's the long and the short of it.'

'Oh, but you will. Jeb and Zoey and Jonah may have disappeared, but not Moses. Not Brandee. Not . . . young Arie. They aren't protected, are they? And I'm not sure you know this, but Viola Hudson, your friend Maisie Parsons' daughter, is spending her exeat weekend with Issy and her family. Whether she comes back to school rather rests on your shoulders right now.'

Victoria Rhodes has me. She absolutely has me.

'At least let Dr Mackenzie go,' I say to her. She won't do that, but I need to keep her talking while I think. While I work out how to get us out of this.

'How can I let him go? What do you think the first thing he will do is?'

'If I ask him not to, he will tell no one.'

'You think I can trust him?'

'Yes. I do. And I don't trust anybody, not even myself.'

'Nice try, but I think leaving your fate to the hunt is the best course of action.'

'How many other humans have you hunted?'

She seems thoughtful for a second and also amused by my use of the word 'humans'. Standing here, I need to reprofile her, to find out if she is in any way redeemable. I suspect not. I suspect that there is nothing redeemable in a woman who has just shot her husband in the head and admits to hunting other people. Who has hunted *children*. Portia told me that at least two of the girls had been chased through the woods by persons unknown. It must have been this woman. She is not redeemable, but I still have to give it a go. It always amuses Dennis that I try to talk down terrible people, to connect with them even when they are holding a gun on me. *'You really will try to talk anyone into doing the right thing,'* he once said to me. But what choice do I have? If I get her to talk, she may rethink this.

'Can I ask you how you came to this point? I'm just curious. Because I might be wrong here, but I don't think you woke up one day and thought, *You know what? I'm going to put people in the woods by my house and hunt them down.* I think something must have pushed you to it. Especially when you hate seeing other creatures hurt and terrified before being killed. How do you go from that to chasing children to their deaths? Because I presume that's what happened to Mariana and Fredi? How did this start?'

Victoria

May 2026, Axton Manor

Miss Valorie Axton's Prep School for Girls was started by my great-great-great-great-grandmother in 1898. She began the school to make sure that the boys who went to the finest schools in the land would have well turned-out ladies to marry, to breed with.

Miss Valorie was one of the smartest women you will ever meet. She was shrewd and she was astute. A pioneer. She knew that noblemen would pay to put their daughters out of sight, out of mind, until someone came along to marry them. The girls were schooled in the arts, in embroidery, in how to run a house, horticulture, fashion. They learnt to be pretty, to sit and be quiet. While the men ran the world, the girls were told to be quiet.

Her school and her impeccable reputation were second to none. Noblemen flocked to have their daughters turned into the kind of young woman who royalty, noblemen or captains of industry would be happy to marry.

And then Miss Valorie made an error. She met and married a man who saw her as nothing more than an income source. He took everything. He took her money, her standing, her business, her school. He even changed the name of the school, only keeping the Axton part, because it had become known the world over for producing the most accomplished wives.

Miss Valorie, devastated by the loss of her independence and standing in society, decided to use her position as headmistress to start teaching the girls the important lessons that boys learnt. She wanted none of her Axton girls to feel as powerless as she felt. But she also taught them how to blend in. To become invisible. How to speak very little, how to listen a lot. How to amass information. When you are a mere woman, when you are invisible, people – *men* – speak freely in front of you.

Miss Valorie realised that quiet girls could become the powerful ones. Men need a constant stream of accolades, awards, bluster, fame; they are always desperate to show their faces. Real power is quiet. It is hidden. It guides so subtly no one notices. Miss Valorie became the most powerful woman in England. And no one knew it. She collected the daughters of the richest, the most famous, the most accomplished, most connected, the most important families in the country. *In the world.*

And when she rid herself of her husband, she committed herself to making her school the best in the world. She brought up her daughters to know they would take over the school. This school was their legacy.

For the pure, to the pure became her motto. Our motto. For the pure girls, the pure life.

Some of the girls were rebellious, thought they were more important or were bigger than Axton. Miss Valorie solved that particular problem by creating The Platinum, an elite council of girls who would speak to those who stepped out of line. They kept order, they made sure every single girl knew what was expected of them and would stick to the rules.

But there were also certain girls who are better than the others. I know, I know, we're not supposed to say that. Everyone is meant to be equal. But there is an upper class above the upper class.

These are the hands that rock the cradle, that still the tremors, that turn the world. They are the Quiet Girls. The ones born to rule.

Miss Valorie could see who they were. She knew who was meant to rule. So she taught them how to fade into the background. To become invisible, to learn by listening, to rule silently.

An Axton fist in a silk glove.

To become a Quiet Girl, you have to show bravery and commitment to Axton. You have to be willing to fall from the first-floor window of the clock tower to show you would lay down your life for Axton. You have to pledge to send your daughters to Axton to create the next generation of Axton girls. You have to commit to doing whatever is asked of you by a fellow Axtonite. And, once a Quiet Girl, always a Quiet Girl.

To the pure, for the pure.

And you must always be prepared to eliminate those who don't belong or who cause you trouble. Or who commit the biggest sin of all – not following the Quiet Girl rules.

That is how it started, Dr Lanyon, that is why you are here.

We will do whatever is necessary to continue to run the world, quietly.

Part 12

Fredi

March 2026, Axton Vale Forest

Mental voice note: They grabbed me and put a bag over my head on my way to meet Dr Pemberton. I was terrified.

I thought I had been scared before in my life, but this was like nothing else. I was panicking, my heart was beating really fast and I couldn't breathe. I couldn't keep air in my chest. I knew they were going to do to me what they'd done to Mariana. I should have called my mum. I should have told her. I should have at least sent her the voice notes.

I wasn't sure if Dr Pemberton would still be waiting for me at the clock tower, but it didn't matter. Nothing mattered. They were going to disappear me, and Mum and Dad would never know what had happened to me. The Quiet Girls would write a note, take some of my things and say that I had run away. Like the others.

I was blindfolded as I bumped around in the back of whatever vehicle I had been thrown into. They drove for so long that I was sure they were taking me to another part of the country. Eventually, they stopped and it was growing dark.

They got me out of the van and threw me onto the ground. My hands weren't tied up, so I removed the blindfold and found I was in the woods behind Axton Manor. I was always scared of the woods. I knew the whole place was bad vibes and that if I went into there I probably would not be coming out again.

I wasn't sure why they drove around so much if we were just going to come back to the woods. I looked around me and saw there were seven of them. They all had fox masks on and were wearing hunting gear. There were two big German shepherds on leads that looked really vicious.

I thought I had been scared before, but I hadn't been. *Now* I was properly, totally scared.

'You were warned,' the biggest one of them said.

'You were told,' another said.

'Now you must pay the price,' a third one said.

'The rules are, there are no rules,' the first one said. They were all adults, and although this one was disguising her voice I knew it was Mrs Lazloe. You could tell by the body shape, the height, the way she spoke.

'If you make it to the other end of the woods, you are free to go,' the second one said.

'But you must never tell anyone what has happened here,' the third one said.

'If you do, we will come for you and everyone you love,' the fourth one said.

'You know we will,' the fifth one said.

'You have a twenty-minute head start,' the sixth said.

'There are no rules,' the seventh finished.

'For the pure, to the pure,' one of them said.

'For the pure, to the pure,' they all repeated as one.

'Now, run.'

'Run, run, run, run,' they all began to chant. 'Run, run, run, run.'

The dogs growled, barked. Their lips pulled back, their bright pink gums and sharp teeth dripping and exposed.

Is this what they did to Mariana? Is this how she died? I wondered.

'Run, run, run, run. Run, run, run, run.'

I took off. I didn't know where I was. How far in the forest we were. I knew it was a forest because Silas and his mother had explained the difference. Forests often have woods as part of them, but forests are a preserve of land that was traditionally used for nobility to hunt.

Which is what these people were doing: hunting.

Me.

I ran down the path, the ground under my feet dry and crispy. I turned back, watching them standing there. The dogs barking, them holding crossbows casually by their sides as they watched me. I couldn't stay on the path. They would easily find me. But if I veered off the path I wouldn't know which direction I was going in. I wouldn't know if I was going round in circles or if I was getting close to the other end of it. I should have taken Silas up on his offer to walk through the forest every Saturday that I went over for dinner. I would have got to know it a bit better. I maybe would have seen some landmarks that could tell me I was coming close to the other side.

The path bent round and pretty soon I couldn't see them. Which meant they couldn't see me and which way off the path I went. Right. When I went to Silas's house, we went right out of the school, so I went to the right, running into the green brush. I remember Silas's mum trying to teach me about the different types of leaves you could find in the forest and I didn't really pay that much attention. She said there was a whole medicine cabinet's worth of herbs and plants in there. I ran, aware that the time was ticking down until the end of my head start. But, really, they weren't going to give me twenty minutes. Why would they? Why would they when they were obviously going to kill me?

I was trying to think as I ran. Trying to work out what to do because I couldn't outrun seven adults and two dogs. The dogs were vicious and they would be able to track me by scent. I needed to do something. The hunters would be able to see me, as well – my orange and purple trim blue uniform was so bright.

Different types of leaves and plants were pulling at me, rubbing against me, scratching at my face, hooking into my hair, catching at my clothes. I pulled off my blazer, stopped and looked around me. I balled up the blazer in my arms and then ran back a bit the way I'd come. Then I threw the blazer as far as I could to the left. It didn't go too far, but it might be good enough to make them think I had gone in that direction.

I turned back and carried on in the direction I had been heading. The ground was uneven and I couldn't be sure where I was stepping, but I pressed on. Running. I had been a good sprinter at school. My old school. Here, we hadn't got to athletics yet. But at my old school I had been in the athletics team and I had been good. I pulled off my white shirt, too, that would stand out too much against the foliage. I was down to my black vest, which was against the rules according to Mrs Lazloe, but I wondered now if she was such a stickler for uniform because it made it easier to track her prey.

That thought made me freeze and stop for a second. My horrible teacher was trying to kill me. There were people who were trying to kill me. I balled up the shirt, and lobbed it to the left again. Hopefully that would help me. I was cold. Shivery, but not really registering it because I had to keep moving.

Behind me, rustling. Rustling, movement. I couldn't tell where. It seemed to be coming from all around me. Scampering, like dogs, and larger forms moving towards me. I didn't stop but my fear levels started to max out. Very soon, I wasn't going to be able to keep going. My chest was on fire, my lungs burning with the effort and the terror.

Gaining. They were gaining on me. They didn't wait twenty minutes. They didn't even wait ten minutes. I pushed my legs, urging them to move faster, faster. I didn't know where I was going. And that made running difficult. The uneven ground, the green in my face, the buzzing around my ears, the ache in my muscles. All of it slowed me down.

The whistles, loud and intrusive, set off another type of panic. They were signalling to each other. Telling themselves and the dogs where I was. My decoy moves obviously hadn't worked that well. The rustling grew nearer. And the whistles.

Then, silence, stillness. I almost stopped, almost stopped out of instinct, but thankfully my legs kept me moving. I ran past a large silver birch, its trunk a shimmery white, striated with black, and – *THUNK!* – something smacked into the wood of the tree. I turned to look at it – an arrow. Buried deep into the wood. *An arrow.* They were shooting at me.

I had to use the trees as cover. I had to keep running in different directions so the trees could be my protection. The whistles changed, fanning out, trying to trap me in.

I wasn't sure how much longer I could keep going. Everything hurt, ached, burned. I had no idea if I was heading in the right direction, if I would soon reach the other side or if it was ages away. The tree cover made it seem dark. Late afternoon. Heading for early evening.

Another *THUNK!*, another arrow into the tree nearest me. They were trying to get me to turn. To run away from where they were shooting the arrows, which meant I was probably heading in the right direction. I ran out of the wooded area, into a clearing where a couple of fallen tree trunks lay, and again I was tempted to stop.

I jumped over one of the tree trunks and dashed across the clearing, heading for the next tree trunk, and – *THUNK!* – and then an explosion of pain in my thigh.

I screamed, but somehow kept going, somehow made it over the tree trunk, and then collapsed in the bushes on the other side of the clearing. I wanted to scream but couldn't, because they already knew where I was. If I kept quiet, I could maybe hide.

But the pain. The agony. I dragged myself into the bush, trying to find somewhere to rest. The whistles changed, they seemed to bring the dogs closer, making them sound more threatening.

But they didn't dash in after me. Why? What were they waiting for?

Were they baiting me? Did they want me to bleed a bit more before they finished me off? I wasn't going to wait for them to come to me. Silently screaming, I pushed myself up and started limping. I was going to move as far as I could. I might even be near the end of the forest, which is why they'd shot me. I might be this close to escap—

Kez

May 2026, Axton Vale Forest

Apparently, while we have been talking to Victoria Rhodes, her hunting pack has been getting ready for this afternoon's 'sport'. They are all waiting for us at the entrance to the woods at the back of Axton Manor.

The thought that they'd done this to Fredi, to Mariana, to all those other girls over the years is mind-blowing. The cruelty of subjecting those girls to this is an evil I can't contemplate. They only did it because those girls didn't belong. They weren't part of this elite for whatever reason.

At the edge of the woods, forest, whatever it is, someone in a silver fox mask hands Victoria Rhodes a black zip-up hoodie like the ones they are wearing, a silver fox mask and an automatic crossbow. Two of the others keep their crossbows aimed at us while she slips the gun into the waistband of her jeans and gets herself ready for the hunt.

'I already know that Mrs Lazloe is here, and Miss Barkway – that's obvious. But who are you others?' I ask.

The two I have named remove their masks, Mrs Lazloe grinning as though she hoped it would come to this. She clearly prayed that she would get the chance to put an arrow or two into me. Miss Barkway just looks like she is ready to take dictation or transcribe a letter. This is all in another day's work to her.

'If you're going to kill me, I think I at least have the right to look you in the eye first,' I say, goading them to come out from behind their masks if they're brave enough. I'm doing this for several reasons. One, of course, so I know who I'm going to have arrested should I survive this. But mainly because it's harder for people to do this kind of thing when you look the person in the eye first. I'm already off to a bad start because they hunt humans, so they obviously have no problems classifying certain people as animals that can be chased to their deaths. But it's likely they are being coerced into this. They know that the people they love will be harmed if they don't go along with it. So looking them in the eye will give them doubts. It may even make them pause when it comes to taking the kill shot.

They will, of course, choose people they know over me, but a few seconds' hesitation may be all that we need. I have no doubt this isn't the case with Victoria Rhodes, Bridie Lazloe and Daphne Barkway. Those three are true killers who will feel no remorse.

What about the other four? Are they true stone-cold killers, too? Looking at their faces will be able to give me a clue. One by one, they remove their masks, each one looking familiar, but the last to remove her mask sends a shockwave through me. I saw her at the hospital the other day when I went to see how Paris was getting on.

'Ffion Grenville,' Victoria Rhodes introduces. 'Nyssa Barron. Shruti Vyas. Tiffany Montgomery.' Issy's mother, Astrid's mother, Haniya's mother – these women are all the mothers of MJ's daughter's friends. And Tiffany is Paris's mother. Her daughter is still in hospital, damaged by what has been going on at that school and she is still here, ready to kill on behalf of that very same school. If they did this to

Fredi, to Mariana, then they most likely knew those girls. Or at least knew of them. And they still hunted them down. I suppose I should be grateful that MJ isn't here. But I understand her fears now. She obviously knew the others were further embedded into this lifestyle than she was. She knew that they were fixing up to throw her daughter under the bus because MJ is not properly one of them. And yet she kept her daughter there because she needed her to have the background and make the connections that being at Axton Manor provides. Staying as part of the elite is one hell of a drug.

They all replace their masks, pick up their crossbows again. They're really going to do this.

'We will give you a ten-minute head start,' Victoria Rhodes says. 'The rules are: there are no rules. You just have to make it to the other side. If you do that, we will let you go and you can use the information as you wish.' I somehow doubt that, but I don't say so. I glance at Mac, who is staring at Victoria, watching her like the deadly animal she is.

'Oh, one last thing before you go,' she says. She pulls the gun out from her waistband, aims it at me and then fires.

The bullet doesn't hit me, doesn't embed itself in my stomach, because Mac has stepped in front of me. That was why he was watching her – he suspected she was going to do something like this.

'No!' I gasp. 'No, no. Why did you do that?' I hold on to Mac, who has staggered back but not fallen over. He covers his abdomen with his hand, trying to stem the bleeding. 'WHY DID YOU DO THAT?' I scream at her.

'We have to make things fair,' she states. 'Even the odds. Two able-bodied people can easily make it across the forest in under thirty minutes, running. We can't have that. That's not what the hunt is about. One of you being injured will stop your need to hide and wait us out, because he will need medical attention soon. Plus, it will make things a bit more fair for us.'

'Are you OK?' I ask him.

He nods, but he is not OK. Of course he is not OK.

'For the pure, to the pure,' Victoria Rhodes says.

'For the pure, to the pure,' they all repeat as one.

Victoria Rhodes lifts her arm, checks her watch, grins and then says: 'Run!'

'Run, run, run, run,' they all chant. 'Run, run, run, run.' The dogs growl, obviously they know these are the words that start the hunt.

'Can you move?' I ask Mac.

'Yes. Yes, I can.'

'Then we have got to get going.'

He winces in pain, but walks with me, trying not to lean too much on me. I hook my arm around his waist, he slings his arm across my shoulder and we head off down the wide, bark-covered path, heading into the forest.

'We're going to have to come off the path in a few minutes,' I tell him. I'm desperately trying to remember which way I came with Portia, which direction. 'It would help if I had any sense of direction at all.'

He is breathing hard, and I'm aware every movement probably jolts the bullet, causing more internal damage, pumping more blood out of his wound. There's no way we can carry on like this for much longer. The path curves out of sight of where they're standing, and as soon as it does I tell Mac we need to head left.

'Being shot is shit, isn't it?' he says as we trample ferns and other greenery and grasses to get away.

'It really is,' I reply.

We keep moving, Mac keeping pace with me, despite his pain. We can't hear them, but that doesn't mean they aren't here. Or very close by.

'Why did you do that, Mac? Why did you step in front of me like that?'

'Why do you think?'

We come to a thick part of the forest. There aren't many trees, but the undergrowth seems impenetrable and very tall. I suspect we're going in the wrong direction because the height of this grass and foliage suggests no one has been here in a while. A little way ahead, there is a giant tree stump on its side that looks hollowed out. Grass has grown up all around it, making it a good temporary hiding place.

'Over there,' I direct.

Mac is leaning heavily on me. I can tell he doesn't want to or mean to, but he does. The tree *is* hollowed out and it is big enough for us crawl into it and sit upright. I rest him half propped up against the side and crawl in to sit beside him. The front of his shirt is bloody but not completely soaked through, which means he's probably bleeding internally with the bullet embedding itself into his muscle or damaging organs. He is deathly pale, his skin clammy and his eyes dulled.

'I'm just going to take a look, OK?' I warn him.

'Yup. The first time you take a peek under my clothes and it's this. I can't even suck in my stomach or fake a six-pack. Talk about bad luck.'

'I don't know why you're using all your energy to make jokes.' The wound is small, but it is bleeding. A lifetime ago, I was trained in identifying what the different-sized bullets do to different areas of the body; how to treat those wounds. 'I need to apply pressure to it. It's going to hurt.' I slip out of my long shirt, ball it up, press it to the wound. He winces and flinches, but allows me to push down hard.

Eventually, it looks like it is stopping. On the outside, at least. I don't know about internally, but I can't do anything about that now.

I still can't hear them, which makes me nervous. Quiet often means they have your location and are sneaking up on you. Noise means they don't know where you are and are still looking.

'How did you know she was going to do that?' I ask.

'She has too much to lose. They all do. She knows we have training in evasion techniques. They can't risk us escaping so she had to do something to slow us down.'

'That does suggest it's possible to escape, though. If she knew she'd get us no matter what, she would have just let us run. And that means others have escaped. Which means Fredi might still be alive.'

'Maybe,' he says faintly. His eyes slip shut . . . and stay shut.

'Mac, open your eyes. Don't go to sleep. Please. Open your eyes.'

He sighs, forces his eyelids apart. 'I'm not going to make it, Kez.' He says this quietly, but firmly.

'You are. It's just a flesh wound. You can walk it off.' I'm making jokes because I'm terrified he might be right. I can't contemplate that reality, though. I can't entertain a single thought of him dying on me.

'Don't make me laugh, it hurts.'

In the distance, I think I hear a whistle. I know those who hunt with dogs use different whistles to control and call the dogs. They must have caught our scent. They're going to be here soon. And there's no way we can move.

'OK, Mac, I'm sorry about this, but I'm going to need your shirt. You've got mine on your wound, and you need to keep it there.' I unbutton his shirt and I know he's in a bad way because he doesn't even make a joke about me undressing him. I ease him up so I can slip off the shirt, most of it covered in blood. Once I have it, I look for a loose seam or thread, but I can't find any. I pick a part of the shirt at the back that isn't covered in blood, put it in my mouth and bite a hole in the fabric. It takes a few goes, but eventually I manage to tear it. From that, I stick my finger in, waggle it about to make the hole bigger then rip the shirt apart.

'What are you doing?' he asks.

'I'm not running any more.' I tear the shirt into long strips. Once I have shredded most of the shirt, I slowly begin to wrap those strips around my knuckles and fingers.

'Kez, you can't go out there. Face down crossbows.'

'I'm not running any more, Mac. I'm not a runner. I forgot that for a second. I'm someone who stands and fights. I forgot that to deal with these people, you can't argue with them on their terms, you can't play their game by their rules. You can never win that way. That's why I don't run.'

'They're going to kill you.'

'They're going to try. But not with crossbows because I'm going to get them to fight one to one.'

'What if they set the dogs on you?'

'Then I'm dog food, but I ain't going to let them chase me down and have the satisfaction of my fear as well as killing me. They don't get that, too.'

He closes his eyes. Agony claws its way across his features, and he visibly pales. I didn't think it was possible for him to get any paler. His pallor is dove grey; his body is becoming still despite his laboured breathing.

'You just have to stay alive until I get back, OK? Promise me you'll do that. Just stay alive a little longer.'

'Kez, I'm not going to make it. We both know that.'

'You're going to be fine. Come on, Mac, you're going to be fine.' *You have to be*, I add silently. *I can't have you die on me. I can't lose you.*

'You have to make sure you survive this, Kez,' Mac says. 'You have to survive so you can tell the world how much of a hero I was.'

'You're going to be fine,' I tell him.

'Aww, mate. It could have been . . .'

I stop strapping up my hands, and slip my arms around him. 'You're going to be fine.'

'I'm about to lose consciousness, Kez.'

'Mac . . . if you can hold on for just a bit longer. I—'

'Did I ever tell you that I lo—' Mac stops.

Stops talking, stops moving.

Kez

May 2026, Axton Vale Forest

He's not gone. That's what I tell myself so I can finish winding material around my hands. *He's not gone.* That's what I tell myself so I can take off my watch and restrap it across my knuckles. *He's not gone, but he will be soon if I don't get us out of this.* That's what I tell myself so I can take the necklace off from around my neck and wrap it over my other set of knuckles.

I'm not a fighter. I never want to physically fight, and I know that a woman of my age and fitness has many physical limitations, but that doesn't mean I'm not going to fight if I have to. That doesn't mean, as I told Mac, I'm not going to stop running and take a stand. Victoria Rhodes doesn't get the satisfaction of my fear before the kill; she doesn't get to do that to me because she thinks she's somehow superior.

I crawl out of the tree trunk and listen for the movement of the hunters but can only hear distant whistles. Maybe the others went the other way? Maybe they were expecting me to head in the opposite direction? What do you know – my lack of a sense of direction has finally come good.

I head back the way we came. I'd imagine they'd leave someone at the entrance with a dog, just in case we tried to double-back. Which leaves six of them out here. Three teams of two. Each team will be headed up by one of the Axton ones who are here for the kill. They can't risk letting the mothers team up together because they may convince each other they have too much to lose and run.

To my right, I hear movement – not a dog. Two people, moving slowly through the brush. I keep going in the direction I was headed. I need a clearing. It'll be easier to make a stand if I can see who I'm fighting. I have to keep shaking my head to remove the image of Mac's still face. And Brian's. All my feelings about Brian and how he died are rushing to break free.

Ahead, I see a small clearing and I head for it. I hit the clearing just as two hunters enter it. We all stop, frozen still with surprise when we see each other. These two are Lazloe and, from the shape, if I remember correctly, Astrid Barron's mother.

They both raise and point their crossbows at me. They expect me to run.

'I'm not running,' I say loudly, in case there are any others waiting in the undergrowth. 'If you want to stop me, then you're going to have to fight me one on one. Or you can just take the coward's way and shoot me. Either way. I'm not running.'

Lazloe lifts her mask, rests it on the top of her head. 'Where's your boyfriend?' she asks, a huge grin on her face.

'Dr Mackenzie is dead.' When I say the words, a huge wave of grief and realisation washes over me, nearly knocking me off my feet. But I can't let it. I push my feelings aside. 'It's just me left. So, like I say, we can fight properly, if you're brave enough, but for me the hunt is over. I'm not running.'

The woman in the other mask lifts her face covering and rests it on the top of her head, too. It is Astrid's mother. She's alarmed. This isn't what she was expecting.

I put up my strapped fists, thumbs on the outside, ready. 'Are you going to fight me?' I ask Lazloe. 'Or are you lazy and entitled and only able to win by having an unfair advantage like we know you "elite" lot always do? Best of the best? Best of the overprivileged, over-pampered babies, more like.'

That's it. That's what gets her. Calling out her people makes her drop the crossbow, toss her mask on top of it, put up her fists, and then come towards me to defend their reputation.

I stand on the spot, moving from one foot to the other, waiting for her to get to me. She comes in fast, ready to strike me. When she's in punching distance, she swings for me and I pull back out of reach, causing her to stumble forwards slightly. As she struggles to steady herself, I lift my leg and bring my foot down hard on the side of her right knee. She has just transferred most of her weight back to that leg so she has nothing holding her up. She howls, as if this is a pain like nothing she's experienced before, and crumples. I raise my leg and bring it down hard on the other knee, smashing that, too. Another scream. This one causes a dog in the distance to bark, unsure what is going on.

Nyssa Barron is horrified. Her dark eyes are wide in her suddenly pale face. She's contemplating raising her crossbow, getting me before I get her.

'I'd run if I were you,' I tell her. 'I'd run while you still have the chance.'

Like a lot of people who are doing things because of the crowd, when the crowd isn't there, she has no real commitment to it. She drops the crossbow and mask, then runs back through the brush. Lazloe is still wailing, howling on the ground, unable to lift her knees to cradle them because I think I've actually broken the bones.

It's not even a fraction of the pain she deserves. To make sure she doesn't get up, I stamp on her shoulder, hear the satisfying crack. I didn't need to do that, but at the same time I actually did. She hunted little girls for sport, because she decided they didn't belong in her elite world. She deserves that and more.

Taking the crossbows with me, I head for a tree just beside the clearing and wait. It's not long before two more bodies are running through the brush, heading for the sound of a wounded creature. I wonder as Miss Barkway and Haniya Vyas's mother come into the clearing if they think it's me. They both stop, clearly aghast and confounded that strong Mrs Lazloe is down. Down and wailing. Miss Barkway rushes to her friend, gets down on her knees beside her.

'What happened?' she asks.

'I happened,' I say, stepping out from the cover of the tree. 'I told her and I'm telling you. I'm not running. We can fight, but I'm not running. You can shoot at me if you want. But it'll never be as satisfying as landing a punch. I mean, look what I did to your little friend there. It's going to take her weeks to recover. You can try to get revenge by causing me real pain in a proper fight or you can just accept that you'd get your arse kicked if you tried to fight me properly and use your little crossbow there.' I raise my fists again. 'It's up to you.'

Miss Barkway runs at me, crossbow still in hand. I manage to pivot out of the way, while catching her ankle with my foot so she trips. She falls face-first onto the ground on top of the crossbow. There's a sickening *thunk* and then Miss Barkway is screaming. She rolls onto her back, revealing an arrow buried deep into her shoulder. She is not going anywhere soon. Her screams mingle with Mrs Lazloe's, while Haniya's mother stares in sickened, shocked alarm.

'Astrid's mum ran for it. I'd do the same if I were you,' I tell her. She doesn't need telling twice. She drops her weapon and runs. I grab her crossbow and Miss Barkway's and am about to stand upright when an arrow whizzes past my ear.

Victoria Rhodes has arrived with Tiffany Montgomery and one of the dogs. Victoria holds it on a leash.

There's nothing I can say to Victoria Rhodes that will get her to fight me one on one. She will shoot me rather than risk losing in a fight. She has far too much to lose – Mac was right about that – and she doesn't think twice about killing.

'You've felled two and scared off two,' she says, raising her crossbow to me. 'I'm impressed. No one has come back to challenge us like this before.'

'I'm not the running type,' I say to her. She's going to shoot me very soon. 'Tiffany, did Victoria tell you that she's the reason your daughter is in hospital?' I say.

Tiffany removes her mask to get a better of view of me.

'Victoria told Issy to make Paris push Dr Pemberton off the clock tower. She couldn't do it. So Issy did it instead and Paris has been traumatised ever since.' I am appealing to a woman who hunted other people's children, but it's all that I've got right now. Victoria fires at me, but her aim is thrown off by trying to control the dog, who seems keen to come to me, and I manage to dodge the arrow – just about. The next one is probably going in me. 'That's why she's shooting at me. She doesn't want you to know that your daughter nearly took her own life because she has been so traumatised by what Victoria made Issy do.'

I move just before Victoria shoots again.

'I'm the person who stopped her jumping off the clock tower. I grabbed her pyjama top and pulled her back. She told me everything.'

'Put it down,' Tiffany says to Victoria Rhodes. She holds her crossbow centimetres from Victoria's right temple. 'I want to hear what she has to say.'

Victoria does as she's told. I run and pick up the crossbow, avoiding the dog, which is panting at me as though it remembers me as the woman who fed it lamb, but I know it could turn on me at any second.

'Tell me!' Tiffany orders.

'Only if you promise not to shoot Victoria in the head. She needs to go to prison for what she's done.'

Tiffany smirks without humour. 'People like Victoria do not go to prison, no matter what they've done. Their whole life is built to avoid consequences. But I promise not to shoot Victoria in the head.'

So I explain it to her. Tell her everything I know as it relates to her daughter. She becomes more and more incensed as I explain. But, at the end of it, she is as good as her word. She doesn't shoot Victoria in the head. She shoots her in the back, instead.

By the time I make it back to where I left Mac, his body is gone. My top is still there, blood-soaked, but he isn't. Panicked, I look around for him. But he's nowhere. He can't have moved by himself. Even if he was able to, he couldn't have got far. Tiffany, who knew her best bet was to stay and claim self-defence of herself and me, called the police and three ambulances and I can hear them arriving, navigating their way through the forest.

I stand there, looking around, searching for any sign of where he could have gone. The place is awash with green, glinting like many shades of emerald in the fast-retreating sunlight. And suddenly I know. I know exactly where Mac is.

Part 13

Kez

May 2026, Axton Vale

It takes Dr Jewel some time to open her front door.

I found her address – separate to the flat above the shop – online and have been knocking for a long time. She opens the door and is alarmed when she sees me. I have been through the wars and it shows. My hands are still bound, and my clothes are covered in bits of grass and seeds. My hair must be wild.

'Did you take him to the hospital?' I should have said hello or something, but I'm desperate to know where she took him.

'I don't know what you're talking about,' she says.

'The hunting is over at Axton Manor. The headmaster is dead. His wife is probably going to die after being shot in the back with one of her own crossbows. The ringleaders are all in the hospital. A whole load of enablers are being arrested as we speak. Everyone, including the creatures in the woods, are safe now. I just need to know if you took my friend to the hospital or if you brought him here?'

Jewel closes her eyes, takes a moment. Reluctantly, she steps aside and opens the front door. She gestures towards the back of her house. Sitting at her kitchen table is a boy of about fifteen or sixteen. He stands when I enter the room, then he peers quizzically at his mother.

'Take a seat,' she says begrudgingly.

'I just need you to tell me if you took my friend to the hospital,' I say urgently.

'Can you run what you said by me again?' Jewel asks. 'I'm not sure what you're talking about?'

I rub my hands over my face in frustration. 'Please . . . Look, some terrible things were happening at Axton Manor, but it's over now. The headmaster, Humphrey Rhodes, is dead. His wife is in hospital, probably about to die too. The people who were hurting girls have been arrested or are being arrested. The whole criminal institution is over. I just need to know if you took my friend to hospital and—'

'Is it true?' a voice asks, as someone appears from behind a door beside the pantry. 'Is it true that Headmaster Rhodes is dead and his wife might die? Is it true?'

I stare at her in wonder, amazement, joy, happiness and utter, utter shock.

She's alive.

Fredi Kingston is alive.

Fredi

March 2026, Axton Vale Forest

Mental voice note: Silently screaming, I pushed myself up and started limping. I was going to move as far as I could. I might even be near the end of the forest, which is why they'd shot me. I might be this close to escap—

A hand came up over my mouth and then I was being pulled backwards into the undergrowth again. I started to struggle, but the hand was clamped hard over my mouth and the pain in my leg made fighting almost impossible.

This was it, then. It was over. I would never see Mum again. Never see Dad again. I would never see my house again.

'Winifredi, it's me, Jewel,' the person whispered in my ear. 'Stop struggling.'

I did as I was told, not sure what she was doing there.

Once I stopped fighting, she let me go. She immediately reached into the bag she had slung across her body and got out a large spray bottle, started spraying me down. It smelt of leaves and trees and the forest. She slipped off her hooded cloak and then started pulling up the surrounding foliage and laying it on top of me. Then she sprayed me again. Sprayed and sprayed until I was absolutely drenched in it. I could hardly breathe for all the stench of it.

'I know you're in pain, but you have to stay still and quiet for me darling,' she whispered. She lay her dark-green cloak over me, covering my head, and then I felt more leaves and foliage covering the top of me.

Moments later, she was shifting away from me, grabbing another spray bottle and she started spraying around the area where I'd been standing before she pulled me here. This spray smelt rank – like onions and vinegar and chilli peppers. She moved quickly and quietly, spraying a large area. The whistles, which had changed again, were coming closer, the dogs moving through the heavy brush, edging closer and closer. I closed my eyes, held my breath. Closer and closer. Closer and—

Then the dogs were moving off. Away from where I was, away from where I had been.

The dogs darted on, desperate, it seemed, to get away from where Jewel had sprayed the chilli-pepper mixture. The whistles altered again, became frantic. Whistling and then shouts. Commands to come back. To come and check again. But the dogs had moved on, had got a scent elsewhere and weren't coming back to where they had been. Still I didn't move. I wasn't sure if one of the human hunters was going to come and check where I'd been or not. I didn't know where Jewel was, where she had gone, but I stayed as still as I could, taking deep silent breaths to try to stop myself from crying. My thigh hurt so bad. I'd never felt pain like it. It was ages later – much, much later – when rustling started up again. I braced myself. Ready to fight off dogs or whoever was coming. It wouldn't be a long fight, but I would give it all I'd got.

'Winifredi. It's me, Jewel. They've gone. They think you managed to double back. We need to go. I know a quick way out of here.' She cleared the leaves and foliage off me, took her cloak and put it on, and then bent to pick me up. 'We have to move.'

I didn't even know I was crying with relief until she led me, limping, out of the forest and into the field that backed onto their garden. She helped me down the side of their house to where there was a gate in the high, high fence.

She brought me into the house through the back door, and then to a door in the kitchen. 'We have to hide you,' she explained. 'Sometimes they come here to check. And I pretend I'm not in. But I can treat you down here. And keep you out of sight for now.'

She was still talking as she helped me down the steps into her basement, but I didn't really notice. My head was swimming with the pain from the arrow in my thigh. 'You'll be safe here,' she said to me as she helped me lie on the couch in the corner of the room. 'You'll be safe.'

Fredi

● **Record Voice Note** ▶ **Recorded: May 2026**

Jewel saved Mariana. She saved Mariana and another girl called Rachel. And, of course, she saved me.

She started when she was fifteen, disrupting the fox hunts. She got in trouble, she got beaten up, she got arrested. Being Black in a village as small as Axton Vale, they knew what she was doing and she was pressured to stop. But she didn't. Wouldn't. Couldn't. Her parents and family didn't want any trouble, but they all agreed that fox hunting was wrong.

She learnt all she could about Axton Vale Forest, she taught herself about herbs, then she went to university and trained to be a doctor. And when she came back to the village she settled down. Fox hunting was illegal, but they still did it. They called it trail hunting, where they never actually killed the fox, but somehow the foxes still ended up hurt, maimed, close to death.

Now that Jewel was a herbalist, she knew what would put off the hunter dogs, what would fool their senses, push them in the wrong direction. And then, out collecting supplies one day, she saw something that changed her life: she witnessed a girl in a school uniform running barefoot in the forest. Chased by seven people in fox masks and two big dogs. She knew immediately what was happening and she had been petrified, literally unable to move. Then when she did move, when she did run after them, it was too late – they had gone. The girl had gone. But she could never forget the terror on that girl's face, the horror at being chased to her death, probably.

No one came looking for her, there were no newspaper articles, no TV news bulletins, no radio reports. She had been disappeared. Permanently. Quietly. Jewel knew it was because the school had the resources, connections and expertise to cover things up.

She kept an eye on the forest after that. Before, she went to the forest to find plants and to forage for ingredients, but now she kept an ear out for the whistles, for unusual activity, for them driving their van around. She would head into the forest, and she would find the girls and she would help them. Take them home, keep them safe until they were ready to leave. A couple of them wanted to go back. One returned and said she couldn't remember what had happened so ended up in an institution. The other who went back stayed as long as she could, but then decided to leave for home in America. The other one Jewel saved wanted to go back but she was scared. Her mother was an old girl. She was sure that her mother had something to do with what happened to her, so Jewel helped her to leave to live with friends in Scotland. That was Mariana.

Mariana is alive.

Thanks to Jewel, she is alive.

And then there was me. Jewel saw the van drive through the village and she knew something was about to happen. She was certain of it. She ran to the forest and tracked the hunt with their whistles. Found me. Saved me.

She wanted to send me home, but we were both scared that they would come for me. Or they would hurt my parents. They knew people. We were told all the time that the girls from Axton Manor were everywhere. We were told that the Quiet Girls ran the world. We believed them. We knew they had got away with what they had done in the past and we were scared they could still get to me. So I decided, we decided, I would stay gone. We would see if they found out who had murdered Dr Pemberton and, if they did, I would come forwards. If not, then I would stay out of sight. Protect myself. Protect my parents. Out of sight would hopefully lead to me and everything connected to me being out of mind.

And now the police are here. I am going to turn over all these voice notes. I am going to see my mum and dad. I'm going home after I have given my statement. We could call them, but I don't want them to come here. I want to see them away from this place. I never want to come back here. If I see Silas, I want him to come to London.

I won't see the other girls again. Not even Viola. Apparently, she was in danger and the woman who came to Jewel and Silas's house had been trying to find me and find out who had killed Dr Pemberton.

She also told us that the Quiet Girls from the hunt were the mothers of my so-called friends. And my so-called friends had all been the Quiet Girls. She said Issy had killed Dr Pemberton. And that they had been part of the plan to hurt me. Kill me. That's what they were going to do: kill me.

Viola wasn't involved in any of that, but she is part of Axton Manor and I don't ever want to think about it again. I liked her, but I want to put her and all of this in the rear-view mirror for real.

■ **End Voice Note** ↓ **Save Recording** ↗ **Send To Private Cloud**

Kez

May 2026, Brighton

Jeb stares deep into my eyes, into my soul, as he slowly, carefully moves inside me. I gaze back at him, my hand on his face, whimpering slightly with every languid, purposeful thrust. We're taking our time, stretching this out as much as we can, because we can . . . until, silently but powerfully, we orgasm together.

'I'm guessing you missed me, then,' I joke as I cuddle up in his hold.

'Nah . . . I had Dennis to keep me company. He has mad rizz,' Jeb replies.

'You don't even know what that means.'

'Yeah, I do.'

'Prove it.'

'All right, I did miss you,' Jeb laughs. 'A little bit. OK? A little bit.'

Jeb, Zoey and Jonah had to stay in the safe house for an extra day because the police and the people working on this from the intelligence services wanted to be as sure as they can be that they had picked up everyone who had been involved in the plot to hurt my family.

I'd been worried about how Zoey and Jonah would be affected by the time away from everything and everyone they knew, fretful that they would be scared and mentally hurt by it all.

'Mum,' Jonah had said when I was hugging him to pieces when they returned, 'can't believe you're such an opp we had to go into hiding.'

'No one would even believe me if I told them that my mum is, like, a super spy,' Zoey added.

I am going to have to keep a close eye on them – the feelings of fear and danger may manifest at another point, but for now they seem completely unscathed.

'So this Jewel woman has been just going into the forest and saving people?' Jeb asks in the present.

'Yes. It started with foxes and grouse, but then when she realised they were hunting humans she tried to save as many of them as she could. She wouldn't talk very much. In fact, she wouldn't talk at all. Fredi told the police that she had lied to Jewel about her mum giving her permission to stay with Jewel and Silas after they found her. She also said that she'd told Jewel that she was going to school for lessons every day. It was an obvious lie, but I don't blame her for not telling the police everything – you literally have no idea who is one of them.'

Issy has been arrested for murdering Dr Pemberton. She swings between hysteria and cold indignation. She's horrified that neither her mother nor Victoria Rhodes can get her out of trouble. The other three mothers have all confessed to being a part of Victoria Rhodes's hunts. Humphrey Rhodes had no idea about it, apparently. They've all confessed and are making deals to avoid prison since, they have all claimed, it was Victoria Rhodes, Bridie Lazloe and Daphne Barkway who did the actual killing. As I knew she would, Tiffany Montgomery is claiming self-defence of herself and me in the attempted murder of Victoria Rhodes. It doesn't hurt her claim that Victoria had killed her husband, shot Mac and was hunting me. I'm sure the other mothers will manage to spin it. Their daughters are still being questioned about the other things that went on, but at the very least they'll all be charged with historic assault and grievous bodily harm.

The only person who seems, so far, to not have been involved with the Quiet Girls is Viola Hudson. She was, according to Dennis, completely thrown that her entire friendship group had been involved in the disappearance of two girls and the murder of Dr Pemberton. I suspect the girls all knew a lot more about what was going on than they are currently saying. But, like their mothers, I'm sure they'll be able to spin it so things don't turn out too badly for them.

Victoria Rhodes is in for a lot of pain if she recovers from her injuries. Barkway and Lazloe are facing false imprisonment, assault, attempted murder and murder charges. They've been cooperating by telling the authorities literally where the bodies are buried. I hope they never get out of prison.

The Rhodes boys have disappeared, vanished off the face of the Earth. No doubt, they tapped into the vast network of contacts their parents had and have gone. There is no evidence of wrongdoing on their part. They actually were tutoring girls in secret, as recommended by Dr Pemberton.

'Can't believe I finally get to do this again,' Jeb says, bringing me back to the present by teasing gentle strokes over my hip, kissing the top of my head. 'It hasn't felt right not having you in easy touching distance.'

'I'm so sorry that I put you all in danger. So sorry. I didn't think that would happ—'

'Stop saying sorry, Kez. It's not your fault.'

'It is. Me and that stupid job. I've been thinking about what I can do so this never happens again.'

'Kez, it wasn't good. In fact, it was really bad, but at least I now understand why you can't tell me stuff. I mean, I knew it, I knew you wanted to keep us safe, but I didn't realise, until I couldn't tell you what had happened or where we were, how terrifying it must be for you to be in that situation and not be able to share the burden of what is happening. It's a huge undertaking. I had no idea.'

'I wish you still had no idea. And I'm sorry Dennis tried to mess with your head.'

'I didn't say he did that.'

'You don't have to. It's what he does.'

While Jeb and Zoey and Jonah were still in witness protection, I had gone to the hospital where Mac was being treated. I couldn't see him because he had back-to-back surgeries, but while I was waiting, Dennis had shown up there, too.

'I'm sure he'll be all right, Kezuma,' he said. 'They say that a woman brought him in just in time. I'm sure he'll be fine.'

'You know the world really is upside down if you're trying to comfort me,' I replied. 'Thank you for looking after my family, Dennis. For keeping them safe.' I turned to him and held his gaze so he was very sure about what I said next. 'But don't try to mess with my husband's head again, please. I'm saying please so you know I'm serious. Do not try to split up Jeb and me. I can only do this job because of them. If they aren't here, or me and Jeb aren't together, there is no Kez at Insight. Are we clear?'

Dennis smiled in return, 'this is why you're my favourite' dancing on his lips. 'Crystal.'

I could tell he was already formulating a way to punish me for that, but I didn't really care. He needed to be told.

'I'm going to find a way to get out of Insight,' I reassure my husband. 'I might see if I can transfer away from him and that unit.'

'I don't think you should, actually, Kez,' Jeb states.

'What are you saying? You hate me going there.'

'I know I do. But Dennis clearly sees you as his successor. And maybe you should think about accepting that.'

'Who are you and what have you done with my husband?'

'I'm serious, Kez. You've just seen up close and personal what happens when only one type of person is in control of these institutions. You've seen what they do to people who are outside of their little world, who don't have their connections and money. You don't have to worry about how to get in. You're already there. And that means you can do some good. You can help change things. Make it a better place. You can bring other people like you through. I'm not happy about you being there, no. But if you are then maybe you can make sure that you do good in other ways, too.'

'It's not that easy, you know. Changing institutions like Insight. And others.'

'Yeah, but when have you ever taken the easy way for anything. Anything at all?'

'This is true.'

'Just think about it, Kez. You know you can't leave there, at least not in the short or medium term, so how about you start the fight to try to change things while you can?'

'I will think about it. I will.' I'm not sure how much of this Jeb will be saying when he finds out that Moe wants to enter this world. Actually, I'm sure he'll be less than enthusiastic that his child become a part of the change process. Because change is not easy and it can be brutal on the changemakers.

Jeb lies flat on his back and pulls me up to sit astride him. He runs his hands over my breasts and then rests them on my waist, while I look down into those huge brown eyes of his.

'So tell me again about you wrapping up your hands and challenging people to a fight? I just want to get a really clear picture in my head of you in your vest channelling your inner Bruce Willis and trying to take on the world.'

'Don't say it, don't you dare say it . . .'

'It's giving, Kez Lanyon is *Try Hard*!'

'I said don't say it,' I laugh, and dig him in the ribs, tickling him until he squirms away and pulls me down onto the bed.

'Or was it Kez Lanyon is *Try Hard 2 – Try Harder*? . . . or Kez Lanyon is *Try Hard with a Vengeance*.'

Hours later, something wakes me up. I go to the window and spot the car across the street. Occupied, but with the internal lights off.

I pull on a dressing gown, head downstairs and open the front door. Barefoot, I gingerly make my way to the end of my path. MJ pops open her car door and steps out.

We stare at each other in the dark for long, silent seconds.

She nods at me. Mouths 'Thank you,' before getting in her car, starting her engine and driving away.

Kez

May 2026, Salisbury Hospital

'Have you had your visit from Dennis where he tells you he's grateful that you almost died, yet?' I ask Mac. He is in a private hospital room, the least that Dennis could do for him when Mac has spent days in intensive care because he was so close to not making it. If Dr Jewel hadn't found him and taken him to hospital when she did, he would not have lived.

'Oh, so it wasn't a special visit to me where he updates me on everything and then claims that the outcome was the reason why he wanted me to come back to the intelligence services? That the way I do things means this outcome was the best for all concerned?' Mac's voice is very croaky, loaded with pain.

'Not even close to being special . . . I've had that speech twice now, and only one time when I was in a hospital bed, after I, too, was shot.'

Mac lies back, closes his eyes while his whole face becomes grey again, looking how he did just before he fell into the near-fatal coma. I reach out to touch him, to stroke his face, to make sure he isn't going to die imminently, and then remember myself. I can't be touching him like that. Even though he has his eyes closed, he smiles as though he knows what I almost did. He opens his dark-blue eyes, stares up at me with the smile still on his face.

'I'm glad you're not dead,' I say.

'Not as glad as I am, I can tell you,' he replies. I check the various tubes and wires going into him, wondering which one is the painkiller pump and if he needs to use it, because his voice is full of agony. 'Thank you for looking after me, Dr Kez.'

'Thank you for taking a bullet for me, Dr Guy.'

'Call me Guy. You can call me Dr Mac, if you really want to, but I'm fine if you want to call me Guy. In fact, I'd prefer it. Guy. Dr Guy doesn't really work. Or Mac, if you so choose. Although I hate that, people find it the most comfortable.'

I grin because he said that to me the second time we met. And I remember thinking he was an unserious person. I also remember telling him that whenever he flirted with me like that it made me trust him even less.

'But, Kez, I like it when *you* call me Mac. Not that you do it out loud very often.'

'Thank you for taking a bullet for me, *Mac*.'

'Any time.' Moving as though everything he does takes a huge amount of effort, he holds up his hand. I stare at it, think once, think twice, then press my palm against his. The touch of him is incredible, makes all of my insides melt. Our eyes fixed on each other, I slowly, carefully ease my fingers in between his until we're linked. Together. In unison, both of us relax, sigh into being connected. *Dangerous.* I know it's dangerous. But I thought he was dead. I thought . . .

'Please don't do that again, yeah?' I tell him as we both break eye contact and focus instead on our fingers, how they fit together. 'I don't know if I'll be able to cope with you almost dying in my arms again.'

'I'll do my very best not to do that again,' he says. 'Did I . . . Did I tell you . . .'

'You did not,' I interrupt. 'You started to, but slipped into a coma before you could say the actual words.'

'How gallant of me.'

'I thought so.'

'I do, you know?' he says, looking up from our linked hands to face me. To hold my gaze in that way I find impossible to look away from. 'I do lo—'

'Please don't,' I interrupt again. 'Please don't say it. Once you say it, you can't unsay it. And it'll mean I can't be around you. At least this way I can pretend that we're just colleagues or sort of friends or whatever. And I can still be around you. I'm not ready to never be around you. And, yes, I know, I'm fucking selfish. But there it is.'

'My kind of selfish,' he says. 'Is this going to become an annual thing? We go right up to the boundary of talking about our feelings for each other and then decide not to actually address it and then the next year do it all over again?'

'If it ain't broke, why fix it?'

Mac laughs, and then decides against it because it sparks pain. The handle to his door turns, so we quickly rip apart our connection and I move back from the bed just before Portia steps into the room.

'Oh my God, Guy!' she says, dashing to his side, grabbing the hand I was just holding. 'I've been calling and calling to find out how you are. They said you were finally awake so I ran down here. I can't believe you almost died. Are you OK?'

'Yes, I'm fine. *Now*. I'm fine now. Dr Kez helped save me.'

She turns to me, seeming to notice me for the first time. 'Thank you so much. I don't know what I would have done if I'd lost him.'

Me, either, I think. 'Not a problem,' I reply. 'Well, now you have company, I shall be heading off. I might see you at some point, Dr Guy,' I say. 'It was *interesting* working with you again.'

'You, too, Dr Kez. You too.'

Fredi

● Record Voice Note ▶ Recorded: May 2026

My last voice note. Mum stared at me when she opened the door.

She stared and stared like she was imagining seeing me. And then her face started to quiver and wobble and she jumped on me, engulfed me in the biggest hug while crying and saying, 'My baby, my baby, my baby.'

I lost it then. Started crying on her. I couldn't stop. It was like everything I've felt these past few months, since I got in the car to go to Axton Manor, came out in my crying. My whole body was crying and I couldn't hold myself up without Mum's arms round me.

We cried and cried. Dad came home straight away and we all cried again. We spent all of yesterday crying.

And today I have spent all day with them. Mostly eating popcorn, mostly watching movies and mainlining TV.

Mum has said I need to go back to school, a completely different one, but not quite yet.

Bev and Carina wanted to come over, but I said no and I'd see them soon.

Right now, I just want to be here, with Mum and Dad and the real life we have within these four walls.

And that's it. That's my story. That's how I survived a walk onto the other (privileged) side of the tracks. It's been wild. But I survived. I survived.

Bye now.

Bye.

■ **End Voice Note** ↓ **Save Recording** ↗ **Send To Private Cloud**

Epilogue

Kez

May 2026, Salisbury Hospital

'Kez, Kez, wait a second,' Portia says urgently, racing after me into the hospital corridor.

Jeb is waiting at the end of the corridor by the exit. He has made it clear that he is not letting me out of his sight for a while, so drove me over here to see Mac. I told him about the night of the Spring Ball, explained there was probably video of me and Mac in his room that could look bad. I also explained that nothing had happened. That I still found Mac attractive in an abstract way, but nothing had come even close to happening. He didn't say anything, just listened. When I said I was going to see Mac, Jeb said he would drive me, but he declined to meet him.

I stop walking to look at her. I'm so weary of Axton Manor and everything connected to it, including the people who technically didn't do anything wrong. They may not have been part of the killing or the disappearing, but they all knew messed-up stuff was going on and looked the other way. Or, like Portia, they pretended they were protecting the girls by their presence, when all they were doing was upholding the whole rotten institution. If she is coming to berate me for what has happened to Axton Manor in the wake of me being there, I can do without it.

'I know who you are,' she says in a tone that suggests she wants to fight me. Good luck to her if she does because I've just shown I can and will fight if I need to.

'Well, yes, we've just spent the better part of six weeks together, I'd be concerned if you didn't know who I was,' I reply. I'm being flippant, but I have a creeping feeling that something is about to be revealed that will make me feel sick.

'I know who you are to Guy, I mean.' The hostile tone is understandable now.

'Who am I to Guy?' I reply.

'You're the one . . . Last year, he rang me, distraught. Absolutely inconsolable. He didn't know who else to call, who else he could talk to. He was devastated because he said he'd met someone he'd fallen in love with. He said he hadn't realised that this is what love felt like, that he had finally found the missing piece of himself and that he'd never felt that way before.'

Ouch. Ouch, ouch, ouch.

'Obviously not what you want to hear from the man you thought you were going to marry,' she says.

'I'm sure he didn't mean it like that. I'm sure he didn't mean it at all, actually. People get themselves into a spiral, a frame of mind, and they can't see their way out of it. Once they step out of it, they can see that things weren't as extreme or binary as they originally thought.'

She grins at me. 'That's pretty much word for word what he said in the next breath, when he realised who he'd said that to. I can see why he loves you.'

I point down the corridor. 'That's my husband. As I told you before, I am married. And it may seem like I'm protesting too much, but I am happily married. I plan on staying married. I can't do that if I allow feelings for someone else to infect my thoughts.'

Portia grins even wider. 'He said that, too. Almost word for word. You two really are just the other half of each other, aren't you? But it's OK, because Guy has a big heart. Just like he says you have. And I plan on sticking around him. Not pining for him or anything like that, but with my new job I won't have much time for more than a part-time relationship anyway. So it's going to work out fine. I'm going to make sure he gets over you and back on track with me.'

'I hope he does,' I reply. The words 'new job' set off that tingling that something is about to be revealed again. 'What's your new job?'

'Oh, didn't you hear? I'm going to be the new head of Axton Manor. This is why I haven't been around these past few days. I've been talking to the board of governors and the trustees, and they have agreed to install me as the interim headteacher. I've been wanting that job for decades. There are so many changes I want to make. Starting with that ridiculous uniform policy. But, yes, I am going to be the headteacher. Only temporary at first, but once they see how I transform the place they will make it permanent.'

It was her, wasn't it? All of it. It was her.

'Axton Manor needs to be brought into the twenty-first century. I'm the woman to do it. Literally nothing has changed since I was there as a girl, and I remember what I wanted to be different back then, so I now have the chance to change it.'

'Why are you telling me this?' I ask, feeling sick. I went through all that. All those people went through all that only for this woman to have been behind it all. So she could get the job as headteacher.

'Because, while I know who you are, you don't know who I am.'

'I don't?' I reply.

'No, and I need to tell you.'

I hold up a weary hand. Mac's blood was all over this hand a few days ago. I thought he was going to die – as far as I was concerned, he did die – and now I find out it was because of this woman? 'If you're about to tell me how you manipulated this whole situation so you could become headteacher, I'd rather not know. I'd rather just walk away, and pretend every bad person got caught and the good people lived to fight another day.'

'I'm not going to tell you that!' she says, slightly confused. 'You think I planned all that? Just to get a job? Who has the energy! Not me, certainly.'

'So what do you have to tell me, then?'

'I'm Maisie's sister. MJ's half-sister. On her father's side.'

I freeze. Time freezes. *Because what?*

'What?' I say. 'But you're . . .'

'Yes, I'm the same age as her. I'm only a few weeks older than her, actually.'

'A few weeks?'

'Yes. My mum and I are my father's second family. Maisie doesn't know. *MJ* doesn't know. I was sworn to secrecy my whole life. I've always known who she was; she doesn't know I exist. My father was always in my life. He put me in the same boarding school as her because it made it easier to see us both. And he wanted the same opportunities for us both. It was so weird, being in the same place as her, watching her, seeing her, knowing who she was, but not being able to say anything. We were never friends, never hung around with the same people. Everyone just assumed because I'm Black and from what they believed was a single-parent family that I was from working-class stock. No one knew how rich and well-connected my father actually is. That we lived in luxury, funded by him.

'He was actually a good father. Wasn't around as much, but I spent a lot of time at boarding school, so it didn't make that much difference.

'We'd have him Boxing Day, they had him Christmas Day. We'd have him for two weeks over the summer holidays when he went "away for business". He helped with my schooling. I went to Cambridge because Maisie chose Oxford. After that, when I could see how messed up everything was, I stopped taking his money. Refused to let him help me in any way. And he would have, you know. He would have got me jobs and opportunities, like he did MJ, but I decided that once you take someone's money they have dominion over you. They'll never say it outright, but they will always use it.

'But even after I refused his money and help, I *still* couldn't tell anyone because my mother begged me to keep his secret. And it is his secret, not mine. I still hate myself for agreeing.

'And, you know, I still hate my mum a tiny little bit for being so reliant on him, so willing to give up her whole life waiting for him to make her number one. I mean, it's obvious that's not going to happen. Not even if his first wife passes or divorces him. He is never making Mother number one. I do understand what it was like for her when she first met him – in the sea of white faces and privilege where she was working, when someone is nice to you, takes care of you, tells you they love you, you're going to fall for it. You're going to cling on to it. I mean, it couldn't be me, but we're all different, aren't we?'

My heart sinks as I realise what this conversation is really about. What has actually happened here. I sigh as I say: 'You're telling me all this because of the promise you made to your mother. You promised her you wouldn't tell Maisie or her mother. But she didn't say you couldn't tell someone else who might tell her. You're telling me so I will do your dirty work and tell MJ for you.'

'Or not, you don't have to tell her. I'm fine whatever you decide.'

'And either way I lose, right? Either I keep it to myself and can never look MJ in the face again, which means I can't go to her for help if I need it. Or I tell her and ruin her life and family.'

Portia grins at me because now I truly understand.

'Because of what Mac said, you really hate me, don't you?'

'Like you wouldn't believe.' She smiles even wider if possible. 'To be fair, a little bit is because of you. You're so full of yourself.'

'Right you are. Well, thank you for that. Good to know that Axton Manor is going to be run by another type of psychopath. Upholding traditions and all that.'

I leave before she can say anything else. I know she's watching me walk away and watching when I slip my hand into Jeb's. But I don't care, not really. I've been in worse situations. Have had to keep worse secrets for the greater good.

'All OK?' Jeb asks as we leave the hospital.

'Yes,' I reply. 'So where are we meeting everyone?'

'Portslade,' he replies.

'Portslade? Why? Why not Brighton or, radical thought here, Hove?'

'Because, my darling wife,' he says, dropping a kiss on my head, 'Portslade means we can meet them there instead of at home. And Portslade also means stopping off at home, where we'll be all alone for at least an hour. That's just you, me and the en suite.'

'You, my dear husband, have all the best ideas,' I reply to him. 'All the best ideas.'

THE END

Acknowledgements

To...

my wonderful family

my agent, Ant

my publishers

my fabulous friends

my beloved MK2

my girls F & J

you, yes, YOU for buying my book

thank you for everything.

And, to G & E all my love forever and always.

Credits

These are the people who helped me make
The Quiet Girls:

Amazing Editing
Jennifer Doyle

Other Fantastic Editorial
Hannah Bowstead

Copy-editing
Sam Stanton Stewart

Proofreading
Jill Cole

Audio
Carrie Hutchison

Cover Design
Becky Glibbery

Production
Tina Paul

Marketing
Katrina Smedley

Top-Notch Publicity
Emma Draude
Katey Pugh

Sales
Becky Bader
Sinead White
Jess Harvey

Amazing Agenting
Antony Harwood

Expert Advice
Graham Bartlett
Althea Wolfe
The boarding school pupils who generously
gave me their time and stories

'No one is better than you'

If you've read *The Quiet Girls* (and I hope you have before you get to here) you should know that those are words that Fredi's mother encourages her to say out loud to remind her that no matter what she is told, she does belong in spaces where the elite exist such as her posh new boarding school.

I loved reading boarding school stories when I was younger. I was completely fascinated by the thought of living where you went to school. And not seeing your family. That spun my brain a bit, the thought of not seeing your family for weeks or months. And solving mysteries as well.

But, as I hope you know by now with my books, *The Quiet Girls* is about so much more than what it seems to be on the surface. It is about the world we're currently living in, it is about those with money and/or influence and/or privilege believing they are somehow better than those without those things.

It is about remembering that no one is better than you.

Things seem out of control right now, and many of us are feeling powerless. The people who have been entrusted with the power to run our lives, as well as those who have seized the power to run our lives, are treating us like nothing; they are behaving like we should just accept whatever they decide to do with our lives and money.

We aren't powerless. That is what *The Quiet Girls* is about. It is

AUTHOR NOTE

about reminding us that, despite what we're told and how those in charge behave, we are not powerless.

Back in 2024, the University of Brighton gave me an honorary doctorate for services to literature and my attempts to open up the world of literature to everyone. At the ceremony I had to give a speech. Here is an abridged version of that speech that talks about how we can fight back against the terrifying things going on in our world.

When someone tries to tell you that an equally powerless person is the reason for your dire situation, I hope you look at who is saying it, why they're saying it and if it's really true. I hope you realise that you don't have to fall for the narratives you're being fed, even if they sound vaguely plausible. I hope you question why the people who are feeding you these messages never seem to suffer as much as you are.

Lovelies, I hope you enjoyed *The Quiet Girls*, and I hope you never forget how powerful you really are, more.

Please, always remember: no one is better than you.

Dorothy Koomson, 2025

From my speech at the University of Brighton Graduation Ceremony, 2024

For the next stage of your life, you're going to have to be brave. I know being brave can be more than a little terrifying, but you are going to have to be brave because the world needs you.

It needs your uniqueness, your humanity, your story, your youness. The world needs everything that makes you who you are, to ensure our societies are a rich, vital, varied tapestry of human endeavour.

As wiser people than me have said, 'There is more that unites us

AUTHOR NOTE

than divides us.' And we need to celebrate those points of unity and connection and togetherness, while understanding that we deserve to revel in and honour everything that make us distinctive and irreplaceable, too. There is room for us all on this planet and we must remember that, we must strive for that.

We're seeing in horrific real time what happens when only one type of voice is listened to; when only one narrative – one story – is allowed to be heard. We are on the front row, watching and hearing what happens when some humans are considered more important than others, when some histories and stories are twisted and hidden because the realities of them are too horrendous and shameful to face.

Even as governments across the world refuse to listen to us or follow our wishes, we still need to raise our voices, we still need to stand up and be counted in any way we can. You . . . you are the ones who can do this.

You are the ones who can prove that there is space for *everyone* in this world of ours. You are the ones with the abilities and tools, the voices and the creative means to remind every single human that the current gaslighting doesn't work because we know everyone is created equal; we care about everybody no matter who they are.

And it is you, every one of you in this room, who can make sure that message gets out there in many different ways. You can overtly or subtly subvert the dominating, unequal narrative by, for example, writing political essays, producing ground-breaking research, or bumping off truly objectionable public figures in your latest murder mystery novel.

Say it however you want to say it, but just keep saying it and keep showing up for other people in our global community – keep speaking out about what is going on in Congo, Sudan, the Yemen, Palestine, Bangladesh, Tigray, the US, as well as speaking out about the poverty and inequality that we see and experience closer to home.

AUTHOR NOTE

As civil rights activist and politician John Lewis once said, 'If not us, then who? If not now, then when?'

Despite how it may sound, I am *not* saying you have to leave this place and then spend all your life fighting. I *am* saying we should all do what we can to make the world a better place; everyone deserves the chance to rejoice in the connections we can create in our local and global communities.

This brings me to my next bit of advice: surround yourself with people you trust. People who will always support you, who'll be your cheerleader, who'll have your back but will also respect you enough to lovingly tell you when you're being out of order. I have several people like that in my life, they keep me going and they keep me safe – I hope you find those people for you. Don't forget to be that type of friend for others, too.

In my husband's favourite book, *The Woman He Loved Before*, it says: 'Happiness shouldn't be the destination in your life. It should be part of the journey of your life . . .' Let me paraphrase that to say: Enjoyment shouldn't just come from completing a piece of work, reaching the end of a particular milestone, it should be part of the journey of your work and your life.

A very wise person said to me the other day: 'You know your job is basically using dead trees to make other people hallucinate?' After I picked my jaw off the floor, I felt quite smug that I have a job that is pretty darn cool when you boil it down to its basics like that. A job that has brought me here to you, today.

I hope you find a job, a way of being, a way of living that is equally as cool.

Enjoy your work, enjoy your journey, enjoy your life.

Dorothy Koomson, 2024